THE OLYMPUS TRIALS

BOOK 1

THE STORY OF
THE
UNTOLD TALE

BY

C. G. LEEDER

Cover design by: msgdragon
Cover image: © Mr. Annapol Kla-asa/Shutterstock.com (Zodiac wheel)
© Arcaion/Pixabay.com (Forest)

The Olympus Trials Logo
Designed by: Dane Rogers

Illustrations by:
Suzanne Anthony Marchant
Sacred Rose Tattoo Pty. Ltd.

First Published 2019 by
Austin Macauley Publishers

Second (Revised) Edition Published by
Tried and Trusted Indie Publishing

For permission requests, address the request to the author c/o
C. G. Leeder
leederchauntelle@gmail.com
www.theolympustrials.com
Facebook: www.facebook.com/theolympustrials/
Instagram: @theolympustrials

Tried and Trusted Indie Publishing
Rowville, Australia
Web: www.tatindiepublishing.com.au
Email: triedandtrustedindie@gmail.com

DEDICATION

To my soul mate and best friend,
Les Clarke,
whose light nurtured this seeded project into maturity.

And to my children,
Saxon, Rogan and *Mia.*

ACKNOWLEDGEMENTS

Thank you to my dear friend, *Michael King*. If it wasn't for you, this book wouldn't have reached its full potential. You gave me the path I had yet to discover - considering you drew the bridge that introduced me to my editor - *Margaret Gregory*.

Thank you, Margaret, for putting up with my creative grammar and bringing my outrageous ideas into the reader's true experience. You will forever be my team mate, bringing 'The Olympus Trials' into reality. I can't thank you enough for with my constant chopping and changing of concepts, you have shown true patience and tenacity.

To *Yasmin Mahic* and *Charles Fernandez*, thank you for seeing my vision of 'The Olympus Trials' before even reading it, and understanding what I was trying to achieve and having the 'know how' to market it to the world. Alongside *Sherwin Vangunster* who had to put up with editing and listening to my voice for hours on end, bringing forth the captivating videos and 'The Olympus Trials' audio book. I really do appreciate how much time that took, it couldn't have been easy listening to my voice for that duration of time.

To my smelly flower *Grace Watson* - thank you for taking on the role of becoming the social media director. Your charisma and creative spark really bring forth the little empowering snippets to those who are yet to experience TOT. Thank you *Suzanne Marchant*, my mythical woman of colour and altruism. Thank you, for taking the little spare time you had in creating the elaborate and captivating illustrations displayed in this book. You are a true and inspiring artist and I hope I can show the world how talented you really are.

To my Mum (*Cheryl Leeder*) – thank you for allowing and encouraging my curiosity into the unknown realms as a child, considering all I did was day dream majority of my time. Thank you for reading and making up the stories that are subconsciously sprinkled throughout this series. I will forever love you.

Adele Tissot - thank you for being the strong woman I needed during my many hard-battling times, without you I wonder where I might have ended up.

Big Les and Jules – thank you for unwavering love and support, without you both I wouldn't have had the time to write these tales. You have taught me so much through our time together. I love you both dearly.

And to my *Proof and Test Readers*, I thank you so much for taking the time to read and give feedback during the original creation of this series, without you the book wouldn't have been at the standard it is today and for that I cannot thank you enough.

TABLE OF CONTENTS

FLAG OF THE TAURUS CONSTELLATION

PROLOGUE

NIRVANA

Within a land we do not call our own, lies a place where all languages are spoken and all the stories told. You might find yourself peering up to this place, questioning life's purpose or blissfully wondering what lies above. It twinkles as it tells the story you wish to know, in a language you no longer remember – the story untold. It is the place that knew you before you knew yourself, this place we know of as Nirvana. The place where the first indigenous were born; this place is your birthright: it is your zodiac home.

Within this land lie twelve Constellations, ones you may have read about, and ones you may not know. Now all their secrets, from the day they were born, are going to be revealed to you. Travelling through the harshest lands of the Scorpio's Solitudiem Desert, through the Libra's harmonious village known as Arbor Domus, hidden within the tallest trees of Pacem's Forest, you are about to witness the dawn of time.

THE TWELVE CONSTELLATIONS

Capricorn Constellation
Elders: Aldous & Amelia
Darcy
Region colours:
Black and Indigo
Region stone: Garnet

Aquarius Constellation
Elders: Cassidy & Brigantia
Dion
Region colours:
Gray and Ultramarine Blue
Region stone: Amethyst

Pisces Constellation
Elders: Galen & Calypso Murdoch
Region colours: Sea green and Aqua
Region stone: Aquamarine

Aries Constellation
Elders: Ardon & Athena Cadman
Region colours: Red and Scarlet
Region stone: Diamond

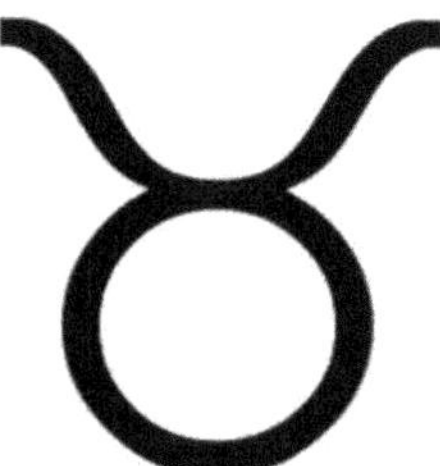

Taurus Constellation
Elders: Iden & Constance Terran
Region colours: Green and White
Region stone: Emerald

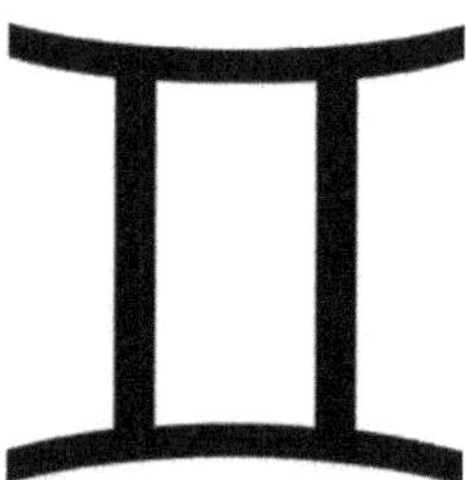

Gemini Constellation
Elders: Eldryd & Amora Findal
Region colours: Green, Yellow, and Orange
Region stone: Pearl

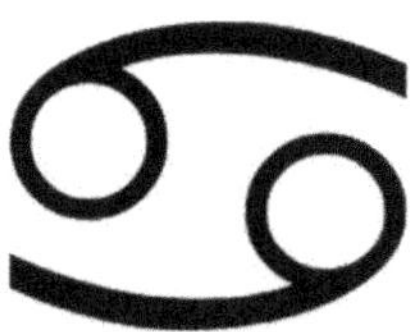

Cancer Constellation
Elders: Dimitri & Selena Griswold
Region colours: Sea Green and Silver
Region stone: Ruby

Leo Constellation
Elders: Leander & Albertina Maximillion
Region colours: Gold, Orange, and Yellow
Region stone: Peridot

Virgo Constellation
Elders: Theophilus & Adora
Malis
Region colours:
Green, White, and Yellow
Region stone: Sapphire

Libra Constellation
Elders: Adlai & Isadora
Dempster
Region colours:
Blue, Jade, and Green
Region stone: Opal

Scorpio Constellation
Elders: Archibald & Ambrosina
Erhard
Region colours:
Red and Violet
Region stone: Citrine

Sagittarius Constellation
Elders: Emanuel & Abigail
Galloway
Region colours:
Light Blue and White
Region stone: Blue Topaz

INTRODUCTION

Time is an illusion within this realm, but it was during a fragmented moment in Nirvana history, the land became stuck within turmoil. Nirvana was confronted by a dark hand, Apophis, the snake, a trusted and respected friend who held great power. He was the only one who could read the creator's language known as Unum and who did not embody a physical form: he was everything and one with all. The zodiacs relied heavily on Apophis to see unknown forces and predict futures others could not foresee.

No one knows why Apophis turned on them but the zodiacs' grief at his betrayal became his gain, creating a dark spell, intertwined within a lullaby which enchanted them, placed them under his control, and captured the weak who had lost faith. Those who became enchanted would leave their homes and family to live within the darkness of the Uncharted Forest, the thick woodland beyond each Constellation where no zodiac would now dare venture. Once lost, they held extreme power, an extension of Apophis himself, but became shells of their former selves. Apophis is now believed to live deep in the Uncharted Forest amongst those zodiacs who follow his every command and sing the same lullaby to which they succumbed, to others who step into the forest. These zodiacs are now known by the name 'Infernum.'

During this time, chaos and ruin began to riddle the land. The Constellations did not know how to fight such evil and were unable to work together due to different ideologies. As tension and hatred grew between them, the lullaby became stronger. More zodiacs lost faith and the Infernum increased in numbers. Of those first born to this world, Apophis was one of the oldest. Created by Unum's hand, he was gifted with great power and his intuition was aided by his third eye. Zodiacs were terrified as they knew the power he controlled. So, they tried everything to protect themselves. They built large walls around their Constellations, stopped leaving their homes, boarded up doors and windows, never went anywhere alone.

Over time, the male and female paired elders of the twelve regions chose the Virgo pair as Patriarch and Matriarch over all Constellations. They led Nirvana back to a strong working unity by banding all Constellations together to fight back. The Olympus Trials were designed to bring Zodiacs from every region closer together. Base studies, both theoretical and physical, comprising knowledge from each region, gave the young adults a broad understanding of the culture of each Constellation and trained them to be reputable zodiacs capable of working together. This in turn, gave them defences against the once impenetrable spell as their faith started to rebuild. As they grew stronger, the enchanted lullaby was only heard by those who had not yet entered the Uncharted Forest, now thought to target the innocent who still suffer with self-doubt and lack of faith. The sturdy walls built around the Constellations were retained to protect the zodiacs from the now dangerous and infested Uncharted Forest. They wanted to diminish every aspect that factored into a possession, like the visual of the enchantment which caused the initial fear within the shadows of the dark woodland.

The Olympus Trials, were established for each new generation. Before a zodiac sits the trials, they have been secluded within their Constellations since birth, brought up and groomed by their family and peers to endure the most mentally and physically challenging tasks that are deemed acceptable by their paired elders. When they come to age 21, they have learnt all about the traditions and way of life within their Constellations in the hope that when they make the journey through the Uncharted Forest to the Doh to participate within the Olympus Trials, they will be strong enough to resist possession. But unfortunately, every year zodiacs are still taken from each Constellation when they embark upon the journey. But it's the cost they must pay; a few weak lost while the strong survive to keep the land united.

The Children's Tale

There once was a snake called Apophis, one of the very first creatures born to this world able to understand our creator's messages and calls. In the beginning, Apophis was known as the wisest creature of them all. Zodiacs came often to converse with him, for him to foretell the future, counsel them about what to avoid and what to build to prevent harm from ever coming upon them. But one day, for no apparent reason at all, he disappeared with not a whisper, not a story told. Zodiacs banded together looking high and low, travelling to places they should not venture, hoping they had not been left alone. It was on this unfortunate day, Apophis was witnessed slithering into the Uncharted Forest.

Zodiacs called his name, but he did not answer.

Our creator, whose name is Unum, gave us everything you see before you. On that dark day, Unum's voice ceased to be heard even by the most sensitive ears. Did Apophis kill Unum in a way we do not know? He was the wisest of the wise, how were we supposed to know? Taken by greed, he now wants to consume us all; eaten by gluttony, we hear him call. Be wary, do not let him in; do not shed a tear. Sadness is the key. It is what allows you to hear the enchanted song of the ones that make the call from the darkest place, the ones that have no soul. We call them Infernum, the embodiment of hell.

Now another lullaby was made to keep the Infernum at bay, one you may hear within each sturdy wall, the one children sing as they play:

Deep within the forest, Infernum would creep
If you would hear one, beware the end of sleep
If blackness consumes you, beware your family too
That's why we stay away from Infernum view.

Now you've heard the woeful tale that places fear upon this land. Let me take you to the girl who will continue this story, one who lays within the Taurus land. She is not like any other nor does she embody that of what is known to be a bull. Constantly faced with adversity, some which you may know too well.

Now let us begin the story of the untold tale.

CHAPTER ONE

THE GIRL

Conformity, the mask that drowns individuality and desire.

Hidden amongst bushes and trees, I can see the moonlight glimmer upon an open field, but I am constricted within a tight warm blanket. I peer up at a woman who holds me, feeling deep security and comfort. Her face is unfamiliar but I feel an unconditional attachment to her. I press my head into her chest, hearing her heart beat, and the pulsating rhythm lays a blanket of comfort. Now, it begins to pick up pace; I feel anxious as moisture forms on her face and her eyes dilate. Her breathing becomes irregular and heavy. I feel hot, claustrophobic. I try to speak but only a curdling cry escapes through my mouth. She cradles me close.

"Shhh amica mea shhh."

Suddenly a deep rustic voice is clearly audible.

"Did you hear that? She's over there!"

Galloping hooves now trot hard and fast towards us, stopping right next to us. The abrupt silence is only broken by the horse's deliberate snorts. The woman places her sweaty hand gently over my mouth. I feel her tremble. I hear the horse's hooves break twigs and branches as it moves slowly around our position, which is poorly concealed by bushes and hidden mainly by the darkness. All sounds cease. A glimmer of moonlight reveals a distorted figure of a horse, frighteningly close. Then, a high-pitched squeal and the giant horse rears above us and comes down hard, its hooves narrowly missing us. The woman holds me tight and I squeeze my eyes shut.

She whispers in my ear, "*Tu es via, veritas et vita. Nemo venit ad Patrem, nisi per te.*" I don't understand the language she speaks, but I can sense the deep sorrow within her. This is goodbye. I start tearing up. She looks at me, and now, with all the concealing bushes smashed away, the moonlight gives her blue eyes a visible gleam, and I can see the single tear travelling down her cheek. She attempts to smile as she says her last words to me, *"Te amo"*.

She drops me as she is yanked up and dragged to the horse. I fall to the ground with a thud. My small body trembles as I struggle to breathe. I take a few deep, quivering breaths. I start to scream, a bewildering cry after my lungs gasp in air once more.

My body trembles uncontrollably as I hear the woman pleading for her life and mine. A sickening crunch and her voice is silenced. The woman's body hits the ground beside me, startling me. I look at her, but her gleaming blue eyes have become an empty grey.

Tears fall down my face and I wriggle from the tight blanket, extending my tiny hand as a strange illuminating blue aura expands from my fingertips. Then blackness consumes me.

I wake up in my own room with a heart-wrenching feeling of guilt as though the woman's death, is somehow my fault, but how can I feel guilty when the woman is only a figment of my imagination? I look towards the table beside me, at the framed picture of my father, Adonis, thinking how many times he's told me this reoccurring nightmare never happened. He always tells me it's a reflection of my deep yearning for my mother. An old picture, of her holding me when I was a baby, sits beside mine and his. I always wondered if the woman in the dream was her, but they look nothing alike. My eyes linger on the pictures of a time when my father appeared to be truly happy. Then I place my hand on my sheets and realise they're soaked through. Breathing heavily, I shut my eyes and bring myself back to reality.

My heart skips a beat as I hear two big thumps on my door.
"Taura, get up! You got registration today!"

I rub my face and sit up. It's the year of my 21st birthday, and I have to register for 'The Olympus Trials'. These are studies every 21-year-old must endure while living within the Doh's walls, residing with other zodiacs they have never yet encountered. I pick up my introductory scroll that has unravelled on the floor, begin reading it for the second time since yesterday when my classmates and I received it at the end of our last lesson.

Skimming through, I begin reading through bits and pieces:

"The trials can take a few years or decades depending if you show little or great promise, then you are classed, assigned the career you're best suited to, which is carefully chosen by the elders."

But I fear I won't even make it to the trials, as we have to pass through the Uncharted Forest, the place where the Infernum infest the shadows of the woodland. I continue reading on.

"Every zodiac takes years to master their abilities and power before reaching their full potential. Young zodiacs especially, lack the maturity and wisdom to control their abilities properly. How much time is spent on learning to control and master the abilities depends on the assigned classification. Extensive training might not be necessary for the associated field of work. This structure provides protection, order, balance, and purpose which must be kept for the zodiacs faith within the Nirvana unity, reducing the risk of another Infernum infestation."

The next part I knew by heart, having been taught this from our first lesson.

Strong-headed, independently determined, generous, and patient at times, although Taureans are stubborn and ignorant of others' emotions when expressing their truth.
In the Taurus Constellation, as descendants of the bull, the males have large horns and the females have small stumpy horns, both

have a bull tail, and are incredibly muscular and lean. The females being smaller in stature. Their power is that of incredible strength, making them natural great warriors. Their ability enables them to pick up any weapon and wield it with great accuracy, agility, and strength. Although this talent comes at a price with an upbringing of toughness and rigid routines. If a Taurus wants to make it to adulthood, they must be fastidious in their approach, otherwise they'll perish as the elders are incredibly regimented, constantly testing their physical capabilities. They're generally seen as great officers/second-in-command within the Nirvana Army as they are great at following orders, rarely failing to deliver.

I drop the scroll on the ground again, feeling a gagging feeling in my throat. I pick up my *Zodiacs Appearance, Ability and Power* book from my bedside table and flick through the information about the zodiacs from the other 11 regions. I may meet many of them for the first time today, at registration, if I can make it through the Uncharted Forest.

I open the first page, reading over a particular part that always caught my eye before reading on:

All zodiacs have some form of human appearance with aspects of their ancestors. Although a human is only myth and the only human connection known is that of Adam and Eve, but even that is only legend. It is still unknown as to how we came to evolve in this way.

I continue on, hoping to memorize the traits and features of the different zodiacs so I am ready to meet them.

After closing the book, I get out of bed to go and put on my tattered constellation clothes. They are plain brown leather, made from the hide of one of the cows or bulls that lived in our region. These don't fit me very well as they are hand downs from other families, and are now wearing thin and developing holes from constant wear. My father, uses the clothes I have grown out of to mend the holes. I don't mind, because I feel comfortable in them, which makes me feel safe. We are not wealthy but we have a roof over our heads and enough food to keep us nourished.

Rubbing my hands through my hair, I walk over to my small mirror. It's lost its youth and was supposedly my mother's. I look at my plain green eyes, small features, and the long mousey brown hair sprawled out over my shoulders. I don't believe I'm a stunning Taurus, more average, but I was never meant to be special.

Walking out into the small but homey living room, I breathe in the scent of the smoky fireplace, touch my hand against the cold brick wall, walk under pots, pans, and the herbs from the garden that hang from our low ceiling.

My father is standing in his usual big bear coat, thick brown leather pants, and black leather shoes tied with an old rope above each ankle. He has a thick brown beard with Taurus tribal tattoos on his neck, dark brown eyes, noble nose, and thick long brown hair that's half tied up at the back. His huge horns threaten to take out the cottage door every time he steps through and he has a thick bull tail that insists on whacking me in the face whenever we're in close proximity. He also has the number '1' imprinted on the back of his neck. That is his 'purpose number' which he obtained on his registration day. The numbers identify your traits and purpose for this lifetime along with the characteristics inherited from your zodiac ancestors. His number is a representation of leadership, hard work, determination, self-motivation, ambition, independency, and innovation.

The numbers also give you your individuality within your community and enable you to teleport to and from the Doh.

There are nine known purpose numbers and 3 known but rare master numbers which help us relate to one another and which aid the Elders in allocating our classification.

My father is an old-school, tough Taurean, having overcome many difficult times in his life, like the Infernum dark era. He became one of the biggest heroes throughout the land as he fought hard and strong against the Infernum when many wouldn't and couldn't and he helped to keep the last surviving zodiacs' faith strong. His biggest hardship was my birth. But he has always been an incredibly noble, supportive, and loving father. He is not only my dad but also my best friend.

In his hand, he holds the same repulsive medicine I've had to take every day since I can remember. It's a potion to keep my immune system strong. When I was born, I was incredibly weak and fragile, and within Herba, such children are meant to be carried to uncharted territory and left to die.

When a baby is born, the Elders determine if it is strong enough to represent the Taurus Constellation. Like it was written on my scroll, being a natural great warrior comes at a price; you are carefully selected. Adonis told me when I was born: he knew I wouldn't be accepted by the Elders. My parents had trouble conceiving and endured many heart-breaking miscarriages. I was his first surviving offspring. His only child. So, the thought of leaving me to die without a chance to live was unbearable.

He told the Elders, when they came to inspect me, that I was a stillborn and they had already buried me. My parents kept me a well-hidden secret until someone saw and reported my existence, knowing that Adonis and Penelope had no acknowledged children. Before they could hide me, soldiers came and took my mother and me away. Adonis was stripped of all his rankings, which left him with nothing but an old abandoned cottage at the end of the Constellation. Now he hunts within the Uncharted Forest, braving its dangers to put food on our table.

Adonis, being one of the most respected Taureans, was told they'd make an exception in his case for his heroic acts in the dark times. But one of us had to be made an example of so this occurrence would never be repeated. Otherwise the Taurus Constellation would become weak and the Taurus way of life would perish. They tried to convince him to take my life, warning him that I'd never be accepted by the other Taurean children. My whole life would be a struggle and once I'd come of age, I'd certainly be taken by the Infernum as a lifetime of bullying would weaken my resilience and make me susceptible. My father was torn, but my mother chose for him. In order to save my life, she told the Elders to do as they wished to her.

They murdered her in front of all of Herba. Adonis had to watch so the community would see a great warrior broken. Then, the simple Nebula Classified (NC) folk would know that they could not endure the same heartache and their fear would prevent future repetitions of the unsanctioned act.

Adonis never told me the details of her public execution, obviously wanting to protect me but not wanting to lie either. I try to remember my mother, Penelope, but there isn't a single memory that comes to mind. It's as though she never existed within my reality.

Adonis hands me the cup. "Here you go, same as usual."

I gulp it down as fast as I can. It's revolting, like itchy grass mixed with dust, doused down with water and the backside hair of a bull. But no matter how bad I despise this potion, it keeps me alive. Without it, I'll most likely die from illness due to my under developed immune system. That's why Adonis never lets me do much; he blames the condition for my lack of aptitude for everything. Although he still believes I'm incredibly special somehow, I don't have the natural gift of strength and as a consequence, I can't lift much. I still have small horns on my head and a bull tail. I'm lean like everyone else, but I lack muscle. All my life I have been physically bullied and judged by the community due to the life I've been allowed to exhibit. A big part of me understands and takes on the guilt of their pain from children they lost, but there's a part of me that wishes to disappear. So, I spend most of my time engrossed in my books, reading about all the zodiac powers, history, and astrology. I don't feel like I belong anywhere but in the pages of times past.

Adonis sits down and his expression becomes serious. "Now Taura, remember what we have spoken about; you must not let fear seep into your heart when you enter the Uncharted Forest. I want you to think about your achievements; you're very intelligent, smarter than any other Taurean in Herba. You must have courage and remember you have an inner strength."

My expression must have betrayed my doubts. I agree with

Adonis but I shouldn't even be doing the trials. He continues, "Taura, the Elders are well aware of your condition, but unfortunately, they must treat you like everyone else. It was part of the agreement when you were a baby. I don't want you to go either, but I cannot fight this, Taura, and I don't want to lose you too."

I peer at the ground as his words stab me. I can't stand the thought of him going through any more heartache. I reply with a positive undertone, "It's okay, Dad, you won't. I promise I'll stay strong. You'll see me straight after registration today."

Adonis gives a big sigh of relief, shuts his eyes, wanting to be convinced by my words. He opens them and says, "I know."

We embrace one another for a long moment. I step back, smiling with confidence and say, "I'll see you tonight and tell you all about it."

He smiles with a strong affirming nod and we walk to the front door. After pulling the broken door open, Adonis hands me my backpack that was sitting on the small stool next to the front door.

Outside, the light now shines through the morning haze, and we hear the searing cries of crickets. Adonis stares at the broken door. "Should fix that today," he says expressionlessly.

I nod. "Good idea."

He grabs my shoulder and squeezes it, gently pushing me through the door. I turn, and he kisses me on the forehead and shuts the door in front of me.

I linger at the door for a moment, glancing from our somewhat dilapidated clay and white cottage with its small crooked windows on each side of the door, to the huge old tree that grows in the back corner. It casts a giant shadow over our home which keeps it cool when hot days occur. I turn around, breathing in the smell of plants and the crisp fresh air of the morning. Then I grab the straps of my backpack, pull it higher on my shoulders and begin walking towards the Halls of Ivy.

I follow a narrow gravelled path, one created by my father. He'd dug it out and laid the gravel so that we did not have to force our way through the tough grass that grows thickly in this area. Adonis was given no help since every Taurean would rather have us isolated in our home. It was a prodigious achievement, considering its length and the incredible amount of time it would have taken him. I feel grateful every time I travel on it.

It's a nice warm day and the sun warms my back as I listen to the birds chirping as they swoop down amongst the grass, grabbing bugs for breakfast. I eventually come to the small village where most Taureans live. Within the centre, are large brown clay cottages that aren't much nicer in appearance than our small home, but are structurally more sound and creative as well as having decent waste removal arrangements.

The people who live there sell and provide many different kinds of services and goods, although they would never trade with the likes of me or my father. There's also an arena not far from here and I can hear the sound of swords colliding and the grunting, groans and panting of early training.

Although the culture is selective and rigid, the Taurean community live off the land, never taking more than they need, although they're paradoxically materialistic. When they can, they trade foods that are commonplace in our Constellation for expensive indulgences from the Doh. Popular ones are 'Herba Pulmenti' a rich root broth created from the roots of rare nutritious plants and 'Poppy Papaver' a cookie made mostly from poppy seeds and bounded together by Agave Syrup. They also trade the enormous hides from our cows and bulls for exotic furs from other regions.

Cows and bulls from our Constellation are mooing loudly as the village begins to wake; they're ginormous in size, easily three times the size of my father and he's a large Taurus male by anyone's standards. The cows weigh up to four thousand pounds and the bulls weigh up to seven thousand pounds.

Luckily the Constellation's grass evolved to nourish such immense creatures. Our grass is immensely thick and fast growing and it takes the cows and bulls a long time to chew and digest it. Even so, with the number of animals that need a lot of nourishment, they keep the ever-growing grass neatly cropped.

These animals are highly respected and honoured within the community as they are a representation of our ancestral bull. Using their hides to create the leather clothes we wear, means that we embody their strength while honouring the long lives they have lived.

The NC Taurus villagers that live within the Constellation are outside already, smacking mats over fencing or carefully washing their leather clothes in tubs of warm, soapy water, rinsing them or wiping them carefully with a cloth. Some of them are using a vile smelling solution known as 'Vocatus' to treat the material this helps give it a long life.

As usual, their penetrating eyes follow me as I walk by. I know their resentment stems from the children who were deemed unworthy of life and I'm a reminder of that pain they try so hard to forget.

I continue on my route to the Halls of Ivy, but I find myself appreciating the smell of fresh food from the market, finer than anything my father and I have ever consumed. Briefly closing my eyes, I imagine myself indulging in such exotic nourishments. Then unexpectedly, I find myself falling and my hands hit something hard, but my face was cushioned somewhat by a pile of slimy warm dung.

As I pull myself on to my feet, wiping the muck from my face, I hear a deep penetrating, "Mmmooooo!" A large cow stares at me as her jaw moves from side to side chewing her cud. I sigh with annoyance, cleaning myself up as best I can. Then I feel sharp pains coming from the palms of my hands. Wiping away the slimy residue on some nearby grass, I notice they're scraped and bleeding and have bits of who-knows-what stuck in the wounds. I try not to think of how delicate I am. Then I notice I'm missing a shoe. Looking around, I see it under the cow's large hoof and I know there is no saving it now. I take off my remaining shoe and decide to go bare foot today.

I leave the village behind and take a short cut through a large grassy field to make up time. This brings me to another footpath that leads towards the Halls of Ivy. I stop unexpectedly to watch a school of duckas, cross the path from the meadow on one side to that on the other. Duckas are a small bird with an abnormally large spiky shell attached to their back to deter larger birds from picking them off. They waddle past me and I smile in awe of their cuteness, until their mother hisses in warning. She watches me carefully as her babies disappear into the tall grass. I put my hands up in submission and she follows after her babies.

I finally come to where I can look up at the school which is built on top of a high hill. I keep one hand on a strap of my backpack and I extend the other, reaching down to touch the tips of the grass. I see some poppies and decide to pick some to take in with me. Then, breathing deeply, I try to alleviate the anxiety I'm abruptly beset with. The Halls of Ivy make up a large wooden structure with a high ceiling and small windows. At the front, colourfully engraved on the wood, is the Taurus flag with its background of green and white - the Constellation colours. Above the two large entrance doors and beneath the flag is written our Constellation's poem which I know by heart:

Taurus, a bull we see,
Oh so generous is he.
Dependable and patient,
Loyalty nor absent.
One as Independent,
Persistent intendant.
Tunnel like vision,
Move for revolution.
With good there is bad,
Possessive gone mad.
Stubbornness breeds,
Like self-indulgent needs.
Beware colour red,
Fixed arrow makes his bed.

CHAPTER TWO

THE UNCHARTED FOREST

Our dreams sometimes take us through the darkest of places.

As I walk up to the steep hill to the school, I think about our teacher, Constance Terran, the female Taurean Elder from the Doh. I decided to give the poppies to her to say thank you, as she has been a great mentor to me and a close friend of my father, supporting him after my mother's death. Her once frequent visits became few and far between once I started school. However, she continued to look out for me when she could.

The Elders have many duties within their Constellation community to make sure all is well and secure within the working unity. I have never met Constance's partner, the male Taurean Elder Iden Terran. He spends most of his time within the Doh, and rarely visits the community. I heard his purpose number is eight – authority, efficiency, organization, visionary, ambition, toughness, and materialism. He is concerned with overseeing the bigger picture of the community's welfare and as such, he was the one who ordered that either I or my mother be executed as she was, to make a strong visual impact on everybody.

Constance has a purpose number of seven, so she is mystical, intuitive, sensitive, a dreamer, playful, introspective, and a perfectionist. She stays within the community, implementing what is ordered. I guess that's why she's so involved, feeling obligated to balance Iden's less forgiving nature.

Approaching the Hall, I take my backpack off one shoulder and pull it around to bring out the bunch of poppies. When I look ahead again I see Isa Edlyn, who is noticeably more muscular than the average Taurean female and someone I try to avoid at all costs, standing near the doors. Her face has its usual hard and unsmiling countenance, as if she is ready to beat up more of the toughest Taurean males in combat practice. She keeps her blonde, frizzy hair tied into a long braid which I doubt she ever washes. It is probably her best feature, but quickly forgotten once anyone sees the intimidating tattoos that cover the majority of her body. In my opinion, she's one angry, hot-headed bull.

I keep my head down. Isa leans against the wall beside the two big entrance doors. When I attempt to push one door open, she places a hand on my shoulder.

"You think you can just walk past me without saying hello?"

Without changing my stance, I look at her thick strong hand and the large forearm connected to it. She could crush my shoulder in an instant. But I hate it when she patronizes me.

"No, I just want to head inside is all."

Isa tightens the grip on my shoulder, making it painful. "Don't play coy with me, runt."

Irritated, I retaliate, "Look, I don't want to do this today, Isa."

She gives a twisted smile and releases her grip on my shoulder. "Okay," she says.

I know she isn't intending to be nice, and that makes me both anxious and annoyed. I step inside and suddenly, the front of my collar pulls tight around my neck and I hear my clothes tear as I'm propelled backwards. The poppies fly from my hands as I react to break my fall. I land straight on a garden bed, the poppies beneath me.

Isa's expression becomes fierce. "That'll teach you for being rude and stupid."

I don't say anything, just roll to try to save the poppies before they disintegrate into the soil that is still saturated by the overnight rain. Isa strides closer so she can tower over me. She holds her foot up for a moment then slowly, deliberately squishes the poppies into the mud. I look up at her, my eyes welling tears of anger. She smiles maliciously then spits on the ground beside me. Knowing that I am defeated, I feel the tears travelling down my face.

I hear strong, deliberate steps approaching along the gravel path behind me, then a deep familiar voice, "Isa! Get inside."

I feel two large hands lift me up as Isa keeps glaring at me.

"Why? Someone needs to teach her she doesn't belong in here. A Taurean as pathetic as her won't even make it past the Uncharted Forest anyway."

Even though the words pain me, I know she only speaks the thoughts of everyone else in the village. I'm the exception no one else was allowed to be. It probably is my fate to be taken by the Infernum.

Isa looks me up and down then storms into the Hall in a huff. I roughly wipe the tears from my face before turning to face Demetrius Ambrosia.

He looks like a younger version of my father - huge and muscular with strong features, a noble nose, kind grey eyes and long sandy hair showing dark brown at the roots. The Taurus symbol is tattooed on the shaved sides of his head with the hair on top falling back into a ponytail. He is wearing armoured plates in our Constellation colours of green and white.

Demetrius is our Supernova Classified (SNC) Taurean overseer. There is only one SNC in each region and they're in charge of overseeing the development of every generation of zodiacs. Assigned as a mentor to the new-blooded zodiacs, they play an important role during the transition period at the start of The Olympus Trials. While in the Constellation, he is Constance's right-hand man.

Demetrius is another Taurean of few words. His purpose number, like that of my father is a '1'. He teaches the students how to harness their power of strength within various fighting techniques and combat skills. I've never participated in those classes as Adonis has forbidden it due to my relatively petite stature, what he refers to as my 'condition'. If it wasn't for Demetrius, Isa might have killed me on several occasions, although it's also considered unseemly to let someone else fight your battles.

"Are you okay?" he asks and I nod. Feeling ashamed, I wipe

away the still trickling tears as he bends down to pick up the single poppy that hadn't been crushed.

"Thanks," I manage to say as he hands it to me.

"Don't mention it," he says without judgment.

I try to rub the dirt from my clothes. Unexpectedly Demetrius takes my arm, uses his other hand to hold my face and turn it towards him. I stiffen as he wipes away a tear I'd missed with his rough thumb. I feel it scraping against my soft skin.

"Tears are a delicacy...keep them hidden," he says softly but with a serious undertone. He lets my face go and I stare at him, feeling my face flush. Then in a moment of near panic, as my heart races frantically, I pick up my backpack and gather myself together. I look at Demetrius, not knowing what to say, then turn hurriedly to head inside.

The large door creaks as I struggle to pull it open enough for me to enter. I let it shut behind me then lean against the sun-warmed panels and sigh with relief. I feel as though I'd survived a dangerous encounter. Is that what they call attraction? I disregard such a foolish notion as I know he only meant to advise me to keep my pain masked, as Infernum prey on the weak-hearted. I have to have strength to survive. Besides, Demetrius would never court me, he's only following orders set out by Constance.

Calming myself down, I walk along the old wooden hallway, smelling the musky heaviness of a room so full of history. Tiny bits of light shoot through the cracked timbers of the wall. Portraits along the inner wall, depict Taureans who have made history within Herba. There is a picture of Adonis, once captioned 'The most heroic of our time,' but someone has scratched out 'heroic' and replaced it with 'traitorous'.

When I've walked with my father through our village, I always noticed the obvious distress of those around him. I've never asked its cause, just presumed it had something to do with me. Whether they feared that my existence would corrupt them, or the average NC Taurean is scared of someone as heroic as my father, doesn't explain why they would call him a traitor.

Still, the caption has been changed since before I started at The Halls, I just ignore it. In my eyes, my father will always be my hero. I rub the dust away from his engraved name with the end of my sleeve, thinking again, 'If only I had come out right.'

As the deep burdening thoughts begin to drift away, I become aware of the chatter coming from the end of the hall. Realizing I'm already late, I hurry down to the green door that opens into to my usual classroom. Already waiting, are the other seven Taureans who, like me, turn 21 this year.

I see Isa leaning against the far wall, arms crossed, giving me an arrogant look of superiority. Flanking her are her two disciples, the twins, Dalton and Henrietta Hamlyn. They're not built like Isa, but they're both athletic with large ears poking out from below their horns, unproportioned features, missing adult teeth, greasy light brown hair and identical tattoos on both their faces and arms. Their idea of hygiene is non-existent – flies even stay clear. Although they're undesirable and physically repulsive, they are also two of the most innovative young Taureans. It has always amused me as to how they keep building new contraptions to help out the community whilst almost constantly bickering with each other. For now, they just stare at me.

"Taur!"

I turn, relieved to see my best friend, Europa Castellanos. I admire her beauty as she is one of the prettiest Taureans I know. She has small blue eyes with wavy, long blonde hair and although small in stature, has a strong physique. This is demonstrated by her elegance when she fights, relying more on agility than brawn, but still being immensely strong. She doesn't have many tattoos like the majority of new bloods; just a few on her hands and feet and the Taurus emblem on the back of her neck.

I smile as she beams. "Am I glad to see you," I say. She looks at me up and down inquisitively. "Don't ask," I state.

Glancing over at Isa, who now stares out the small window as the twins bicker, Europa walks around me for a further look at my current state. "Your shoes too?"

I manage to smile awkwardly, "Oh no, that was my own doing. Clumsy effort."

Europa smiles.

Looking down, she notices the wilting poppy I still hold within my hand. "And what's with that?"

I bring the poppy up to eye level. From all the ill-treatment, it looks sad now. I can't give it to Constance, it would be insulting.

"Oh, I picked it before. But looks like it won't survive the trip." I place the dying poppy in my bag and she looks at me solemnly.

"Wanted to take something to remind you of home?"

I nod, not wanting to elaborate. Then she gives me a big hug and I stiffen again, not used to affection from others. Taureans are generally only affectionate to their children and their romantic partners when they procreate, or so I've read. In public, they are passionate about their individual purpose, and see displays of affection as a sign of weakness. I think this must be a trait passed down from harder times, when Taureans had to show a stoic façade, to seem to be able to take care of themselves, and came to distrust everyone lest someone tries to take what little they had. But Europa doesn't consider showing affection as being weak, and I admire her for that. She is confident in displaying who she is.

The atmosphere of the room changes when Constance walks in. Her calming aura seems to mellow all moods and arguments. Looking at her, she has the youthful appearance of a 21-year-old, but as an Elder, she is surely much older. It's an unspoken truth that has never been explained, and to question an Elder is forbidden. I just figure this youthfulness is a compensation for the duties of her position. She has full lips, big blue eyes, tattoos covering her whole right arm up to her neck, long brown hair that's tied into a neat high plait and a necklace that has a peculiar tooth tied at the end. She stands at the front of the class, wearing a tight green and white dress with long black tights. She tucks the necklace under her garments and begins.

"Alright everyone, let me remind you that this is the most important day of your life. Before you can register for the

Olympus Trials, you must first survive the Uncharted Forest. This is your first test. If you are not strong at heart, you will be taken by the Infernum. There is no easy way to say it. You must stay strong or the forest will try and play tricks on you, and I don't mean children's mind games. Pulling on your heart, it'll target the most psychologically vulnerable and deepest parts of your subconscious. You won't hear the lullaby right away, it will try and enchant you first. So don't indulge in its nonsense, because once you hear that lullaby, there is no coming back. You will become possessed, forever a part of the Infernum.

"Once you have made it through the forest, you may never have to travel through it again, but that will depend on the classification and title you receive. However an Elder such as myself, or Demetrius who is your overseer, have travelled the forest path many times. Those positions, though, are incredibly hard to attain.

"Gaining the purpose number, which will define you as individuals, will also allow you to obtain teleportation. Now, let's get this over with, there is no point holding back now. Every new-blooded zodiac in Nirvana will be embarking on the same venture this morning... Stay strong and good luck."

The atmosphere within the room became tense and uneasy. No one felt like speaking as reality set in. This might be our last day alive! Europa grabs my hand and gives me a strong affirmative look and we both nod with determination.

"It is time," Constance announces, and gestures everyone to follow.

She turns, walking over to the small door at the back of the classroom. When it opens, I instantly hear the soaring cries of crickets, louder today than normal. We form a double line and follow closely behind Constance, taking weathered wooden stairs down the slope at the back of the hall. The bright sun now radiates enough heat for the flies to be attracted to us. I notice Demetrius, who walked down the steep grassy hill, catching up to walk beside Constance.

We follow a gravelled path, flanked by recently cow and

bull-cropped grass, which weaves around sparsely spaced trees. No one talks. The only sounds other than our footsteps are the rustle of tree leaves as they move with the breeze and the distant mooing of cattle. Cresting a low hill, I have my first look at the high wooden barrier surrounding our village and the big gates that will open onto the footpath leading to the Uncharted Forest, and eventually to the Doh.

I think how my whole reality so far has been created within the safety of these walls and the outside has only existed in stories. The idea that we are now willingly venturing into the Uncharted Forest feels like a total illusion. Fear of that place has been instilled within each of us through stories we've been told. Everyone knows someone will be picked off today by the Infernum. It happens every year and I know everyone believes it will be me, and that it should have happened when I was born. If that idea supplies the others with comfort, I don't mind, considering the pain I have unintentionally caused many families.

Europa stares defiantly ahead, still gripping my hand and I think of the nightmares I had as a child about the Uncharted Forest and the Infernum. Now the day has come when I'm supposedly ready to face this nightmare. *Am I?*

I realize old fears are starting to get to me. So, I take deep even breaths, trying to control my nerves. To clear my mind, I move off the path to feel the grass beneath my feet and listen to the birds singing and the branches of the nearest tree rubbing against one other as though warning us of the nightmare hidden amongst their forest kindred.

We approach the large wooden gates where six Taurean soldiers, armoured from head to toe, await our arrival. They move around our group, two in the front, two in the back, and one on each side. As I watch them, I notice that a crowd of NCs from the village are nearby; standing still and quiet. They have come to show us their respect and demonstrate their united mental support, knowing that not all of the eight new-blooded Taureans will return.

I look around for my father, but I cannot see him and allow myself to be distracted by Europa, who squeezes my hand, and gives me a 'here we go' expression.

Constance calls up to the two guards that watch from high platforms on either side of the gates, "Let the new generation commence!"

Slowly, the silence from the onlookers is replaced by a murmuring of foot stamping. The sound becomes louder and louder as more NCs join in. The stamping feet take on a rhythmic beat. The vibration through the ground is almost comforting and I squeeze Europa's hand. Constance throws her hands in the air, the giant doors begin to open.

An unexpectedly cold gust of wind comes blasting through the gap. The doors sway, creak loudly and are slammed open. Dirt and dust are blown hard into our faces, causing me to close my eyes. I shiver as the day's heat vanishes and the chirping birds are startled into flight.

Constance places her forearm over her eyes, turning to face us as she speaks with a loud and confident voice, "Everyone who witnesses now is honouring the transition you'll be making from boys to men and girls to women. Although it will be your choice to make that transition as no one else can be strong for you. Now, do not leave the group. You all know what lurks deep within the Uncharted Forest. We have done all that we can as a community to help you grow into strong men and women. Now the rest is up to you. Good luck, Taureans."

She makes eye contact with every one of us and gives us a strong, confident nod. Then, turning around again, she gestures for us to follow. Demetrius stays close to her and gives the guards a decisive signal to move. They hit their chested armour once, and give an affirmative grunt. We begin to walk again and ahead of us, through the gates, I see the long tree branches hanging down on either side of the deep, dark forest path and I feel as if time has slowed. The Herba community begin stamping their feet even harder to give us strength. But now I cannot hear them as fear unwillingly begins to take control of my heart and the blood pounds in my ears. The children's nursery rhyme enters my head, playing over and over again as though whispering specifically into my ear to drown other noises out.

Deep within the forest, Infernum would creep. If you would hear one, beware the end of sleep.
If blackness consumes you, beware your family too. That's why we stay away from Infernum view.

The thick sturdy wall is left behind us and we have no protection from the blustering wind. It plucks at us as if trying to drag us forward, and its icy fingers chill us to the core and blanket us with an eerie sensation of terror. Even the sun, radiating so warmly inside the wall, loses its intensity and disappears above the thick, tall trees.

As we slowly move forward, we hear the gates creak as they begin to close. The wind gusts, and as if it had reached in and grabbed them, the gates slam shut. I turn briefly. Now there is not even a glimmer of the natural sunlight we had left inside the wall.

The stamping feet become a distant memory as we realise that we are completely susceptible to the Uncharted Forest. With unexpected abruptness, the wind ceases and the cloud of dust settles. Everything is eerily quiet as we enter the forest. Instinctively, we look and listen for some sign of an animal or creature - a footprint, scampering, chattering, but not even a bird dares to sing. There are no normal sounds of nature to reassure our unsettled minds.

The dirt path isn't very clear as the forest has almost overgrown it. The forest is lushly verdant. The trees are ginormous – their girth so big they could fit the trunks of four of the familiar trees of our region inside them. If you weren't aware of the danger that lurks within, ignorance could possibly save your life. Demetrius breaks the silence, sliding his long thick sword from its sheath with a definite swish. He signals to the soldiers and they copy the action. The susurration of six more blades being drawn in unison, is equally audible. Our attention goes to Constance when she turns to look at us. She presses her index finger to her lips, before gesturing for us to keep coming. She turns and begins walking deeper into the forest with Demetrius close by her side. He and the soldiers ahead of and beside us begin hacking at the thick undergrowth to clear the path. Cold branches and damp leaves scrape against me, bringing a chill to the surface of my skin.

Europa squeezes my hand so tight I begin to lose circulation. But I know it brings her ease, so I don't complain. Sweat begins to dampen my clothing, making me feel colder still.

As I listened to the blades slice through the foliage, and branches falling to the ground, I seemed to lose track of time and place. Nor did I realise that my focus had gone from the shirtless back in front of me, to staring deep into the forest. The reverie was broken when I walked into Latham Hampton's back. I knew it was him, from the huge, ferocious looking Taurus emblem tattooed on his back. He is a strong male, who always complains of being too hot and rarely wears a shirt. I apologise for bumping him and while I wait for him to move on, I idly wonder if he regrets his lack of shirt today.

Moments pass and he is standing immobile in his tracks. Europa nudges him in the side, and he unexpectedly stumbles back into me and I fall straight on my arse. Europa pulls me up, now letting go of my hand, which tingles as blood rushes back into it, and I rub my hands together as the uncomfortable prickling sensation kicks in.

Latham's head hangs, his long hair falling over his face, his big horns tipped forward. His tail, usually never still, dangles lifelessly. Europa slowly reaches out to touch his shoulder, to see if he is okay, but she is stopped by Constance. Grasping the outstretched hand, she shakes her head in a stern but sorrowful manner and pushes Europa's hand back down by her side. Constance then gestures for the rest of us to give Latham room. Everyone moves accordingly, making a wide circle around him.

We go still, our eyes are drawn to watch as we all sense the turmoil within him. Then he abruptly gives a horrifying and penetrating scream, one that echoes in our ears long after it has been swallowed by the eerie, silent forest. It wakes an echo of his pain as a tremor deep within my core.

He claps his hands over his ears as he falls to his knees. We all jump back further as the soldiers widen the space around him, and bring their swords into a ready position.

I place my hands over my ears, as he screams again, long and penetrating. It's not enough. I squeeze my eyes shut, and press fingers into my ears when I feel the capacity of my eardrums about to reach their limit. A part of me wants to run back from where we came but our Constellation is no longer in sight. I look back at Latham when his screaming subsides and see him cradling himself on the ground. His stare is no longer his own. Is this the Infernum? I look around anxiously, waiting for something to appear. Europa must feel the same way. She holds a clenched fist on her heart and the other over her mouth as she watches in wretchedness. I open my mouth to speak, but a large hand presses against my face, firmly and softly at the same time. Peering around, I see Demetrius' stone-cold face looking down at Latham. He presses me into his chest but leaves my nose free to breathe. I see his large dagger at a ready by my side.

Latham now kneels in an upright position, head hanging as he presses his knuckles deep into the earth. Suddenly, all tension goes from his body. He stands up without struggle or resistance. I feel the difference in his aura as he turns slowly around, eyeing the circle in an unsettling manner. The Latham we knew has disappeared.

Constance indicates for everybody to move quickly behind her, but Latham has stopped moving and is looking directly at where Demetrius has me pressed against his side. Demetrius intensifies his hold of me and I can feel his breathing change and the solid muscle of his body contract, ready for combat.

I wait for Latham to lunge forward in an attack, but nothing happens. He makes eye contact with me and I notice his eyes are now a bright, glowing, shade of purple. Demetrius roughly and quickly turns me away, raising his sword so it points at Latham's throat.

I manage to keep watching using my peripheral vision. Latham begins to speak, expressionlessly, in a voice that is not his own, "This is an unstoppable force... Soon, all will be restored." After every word spoken, a vibration of repeated words echo as though many voices speak at once.

Demetrius gives no response. Latham begins to approach, leisurely, undaunted by the swords sharp point. He sees me trying to look and circles slowly to make eye contact again. Even though the sword follows his movement, he comes even closer until the sword tip presses into his throat, drawing blood. His purple eyes hold me captive, and it seems he is searching for something inside of me. It feels like there are invisible fingers touching me on the inside. I hear the tune of a lullaby, as if from far away, feel relaxed, delirious.

Breaking eye contact with me, Latham glances at Demetrius's face, giving him a questioning look. Demetrius, perhaps sensing an attack, eases his hold on me. I fall, waking back to myself. Latham, with terrible deliberation, presses closer to me. The sword pierces his throat and blood spurts from his neck, onto my face, and I feel the warmth of it drip over my mouth. I don't dare move.

Latham stands there, seemingly unaware of the blood saturating the front of his body and dripping to the ground. He steps back, so the blade slowly withdraws. He turns away then, and silently, emotionlessly, walks amongst the trees, disappearing deeper into the Uncharted Forest.

Demetrius sheathes his sword and then leans down to help me up. He turns me to face him and holds my gaze for a moment, looking over me with analysing eyes. He wipes the blood off my face with his hand, and nods as though confirming that I'm in good health. I hear him let out a big breath, as if in relief, as he urges me forward and pushes me into the centre of the group behind Constance.

He stops next to her to have a conversation which no one else can hear. I stop abruptly, noticing that everyone is staring at me with expressions of bewilderment. They were probably thinking that I cheated death again, which is how I felt, because no one would argue that Latham hadn't been the stronger one out of the two of us.

Europa moved to my side and took my hand again in reassurance. Clenching her other fist, she pounded it twice into my chest and nodded. I was relieved further when everyone else's attention went to Constance as she counted heads, but the anxious look on her face unsettled me. She looked at Demetrius then and he peered around at the group several times before shaking his head in dismay. Constance placed one hand over her face in a gesture of sorrow and I felt the chill of the forest become more prominent than ever before. Europa squeezes my hand to get my attention. She displays six fingers, switching from eight to six, pointing to the rest of the group. I look around; we started with eight Taurean students and now there are only six. Only Latham had become consumed by the Infernum, surely? Then I realized who else was missing. Beverley Fleur had genuinely kept to herself, I guess that's why no one noticed she was gone. I may stick out like a sore thumb, but Beverley just blended into the background, never making a fuss, always doing well. She was great with a glaive too.

The others were looking around frantically now, but before chaos broke loose, Demetrius banged his fist against his armoured plates to get everyone's attention. He points two fingers forward to insist we get moving and grunts to the soldiers, making a hand gesture circling around us, then clenches his fist and punches it into the palm of his other hand.

The soldiers push the rest of us together, until we are tightly constricted in terms of personal space. Europa and I are together at the back of the group with two large soldiers stepping closely behind, their armour clinking loudly with each step. I feel claustrophobic as I'm used to my own space. I begin taking deep breaths and focusing on a focal point in front of me which happens to be Kendall Warren's full head of black dreadlocks, half tied up at the back. He's an unusually tall Taurean, so he makes a great focal point.

As I try to keep my head full of simple thoughts, ones that won't make me drift towards negative emotions. I start to shiver, as if an icy wind had found a way to chill the sweat on my skin. Then I hear movement coming from within the forest, a slithering sound. My heart nearly stops and as my eyes widen in fear, I try to stay focused on Kendall. Then I hear a 'hiss' as though some huge creature was slithering right beside me. I glance to Europa and the others, but either they're ignoring it or this is the Infernum trying to use fear to enchant me. Maybe it thinks snakes scare me, but they don't. On hot summer days, snakes would often slither out of the grass around the cottage and bask in the sun. I used to get Adonis to kill them. They were good eating. The hiss intensifies and gets louder, perpetrating deep into my ear. Paralysing fear begins spread within me. My heart pounds hard beneath my chest. I do not look towards the sound. I refuse to let my father down. I will not let the Infernum take me!

Then it speaks words in that high-pitched hissing tone, "*Tu es via, veritas et vita. Nemo venit ad Patrem, nisi per te.*" I feel as though everything falls silent within my mind and around me as those same words repeat in my head, an echo from the woman in my dream. Then the nursery rhyme, sung in a daunting whisper by unseen children, repeats over and over.

Deep within the forest, Infernum would creep.
If you would hear one, beware the end of sleep.
If blackness consumes you, beware your family too.
That's why we stay away from Infernum view.

I turn towards the source of the sound. I would not listen to its treacherous voice. I would not! Would I?

My eyes are suddenly dazzled by a brilliant ray of light penetrating between two tall, robust trees. I place my forearm over my eyes, squinting as they adjust from the dark forest. There is no snake to be seen, only the forest. I turn back to the path and, in the distance, beyond the people ahead, I see an open field. The trees have begun to thin out as we approach the edge of the forest and the sun now pierces through. Moving to get a better look ahead, I have my first glimpse of the Doh.

Approaching the edge of the forest, I feel relief knowing we are nearly out of it. The soldiers seem to have found a surge of energy for the work of removing the remaining vegetation.

The sun becomes more radiant with each progressive step. I begin to hear gongs chiming in the distance soon deciding they are acknowledging our arrival, and welcoming us.

Europa pulls on my arm and I turn to look at her – beaming with enthusiasm. I look ahead to see the last bit of shrubbery removed as birds fly high at the edge of the Uncharted Forest. I don't dare look behind me as I stare at the undefinable line that separates the good and evil of our world.

The lingering disorientation of the trek through the Uncharted Forest begins to fade as the distant bells become gradually louder. I step fully into the sun's beaming light. Its warmth is like a cloak that wraps around us after our victorious arrival. It relieves me of the damp, cold sensation from the dark Uncharted Forest. My eyes adjust to the bright rays, and I look out over the vast open prairie that circles the Doh's pristine white defence walls.

Closer to us is the start of a wide white footpath, one of many that radiate from the Doh to the forest. Looking from here, the distinctive paths draw all eyes to the ostentatiousness structure standing in the middle of this immense area, piercing up into the clouds. It's the most enigmatic structure I've ever seen.

When we step onto the path, our Taurus emblem appears, glowing brightly above us in our constellation colours – green and white – rotating as we stand idle. The colours also swirl in the white of the path. I've seen a little magic, not much and never this close, as our sector is one of brawn not magic.

We are still just out of the forest as the other zodiacs begin to appear as groups, evenly spaced around the large circular meadow, at the closest point to their sector. As each one emerges, their zodiac emblems light up above them too, rotating with their Constellation colours. First, Aries: red and scarlet; then Gemini: green, yellow, and orange; Cancer: sea green and silver; Leo: gold, orange, and yellow; Virgo: green, white, and yellow; Libra: blue, jade, and green; Scorpio: red and violet; Sagittarius: light blue and white; Capricorn: black and indigo; Aquarius: ultramarine blue and grey; Pisces: sea green and aqua.

Constance calls for our attention, but I notice Kendall's withdrawn expression. I knew he and Latham had been best friends.

"Alright, everyone, I can't allow you to stay this close to the border, you saw what happened to..." she pauses for a moment, swallowing and looking away momentarily.

She continues, "Beverley and Latham. I warned you, it is a common occurrence. But we will not remember them in sadness. When we get back to the Constellation, we shall remember them for the strong Taureans they were even though they are no longer the Taureans we once knew. Everyone grunts loudly in agreement and bangs their fists on their chests in honour of their memory.

We begin walking along our path and in the distance, I see the other new-blooded zodiacs heading towards the Doh. Each group is surrounded by guards from their Constellation and have an overseer SNC in front. And I notice not all the Constellations have an Elder teacher, like Constance, which makes me have even more profound respect for her.

The paths draw closer together as we approach the Doh, the groups still distinguished by the constellation emblems hovering above. I can see now that each Constellation's path leads towards a separate entrance.

The Gemini are to our left, from afar, looking like identical copies of each other. When they walk together, their white and black hair, split down the middle, muddles the eyes as though you are looking at an optical illusion. From what I've read though, their personalities are incredibly diverse.

To our right are Aries, who stand tall on their strong goat legs, chests pushed out, looking as courageous as they are reputed to be. They are covered in tattoos much like ourselves but their horns curl around unlike ours.

With our destination in sight, our pace picks up, but even so, it seems like no time at all has passed when the white walls rise up in front of us and a gate opens. I take a final look at the swirling green and white colour of the path and wonder if there had been more magic at work. I forget that question upon seeing the next marvel. As we approach the open gate, a shadow is cast over us from a large sculpture placed above the entrance. Nirvana's emblem – 'The Wisdom Tree' – with a thick base and enormous branches expanding outwards that fall elegantly down far from its trunk. It stands tall and sturdy, painted in a brassy gold colour. We walk under it and golden leaves begin to fall all around us. Looking up, I notice the tree now moves in the wind as though it becomes alive in our presence. We place our hands out and the leaves delicately land on our palms, disintegrating as they touch our skin then blow away in the wind. From what I can see there is one above every entrance.

Constance gathers us around in a circle and says, "This is a representation of the real Wisdom Tree. Every leaf is meant to be a representation of a single essence lost and reborn. As you know when we pass away in this life, our essence is drawn from our bodies and is guided back to the Wisdom Tree and given back to Unum, as he is everything and one with all.

"Although Apophis was our direct interpreter of Unum, it doesn't mean Unum still doesn't exist within our world. Because if we lost our connection to Unum and he did perish, we would cease to exist as he uses our essences to restore what is lost and without that natural cycle, Nirvana would fall. Now, pay your respects."

Constance, blows away the golden leaves she's accumulated in her hand. We stand under the tree in awe and I watch a singular leaf fall on to the tip of my finger and wonder how something so delicate can be so powerful. No one has ever seen the Wisdom Tree as it is forbidden and sacred. It is only in your last passing minutes will you be able to undergo the most beautiful experience of our time – death.

CHAPTER THREE

THE DOH

Prodigious is only great if those roots grow deep.

The big bells begin to reverberate again, causing the air to vibrate, and a tingling in the tips of my toes. As their sound dies away, a deep, resounding voice proclaims, "Welcome!"

Turning to try to locate the source of that voice, my sight is drawn up the pristine white tower that seems to be touching the brim of the universe. High up, strange winged creatures circle it, dipping and soaring on currents of air.

Constance gathers our attention as she indicates a point above us the Doh's structure, where a Virgo stands on a wide platform, guarded by a railing, which circles around the tower.

Constance says, "That's the Patriarch Theophilus Malis."

He now steps forward and I notice his unusually large wings in comparison to his actual size. I look down from the platform to a hologram that has appeared on the wall just above us. It gives us an enlarged and easier to look at view of the Patriarch. In a quick glance at the groups I can just see to either side, they seem to be facing the wall too and I wonder if the Virgo we see higher up is also a hologram, or if we have been graced with a direct view of Theophilus Malis.

"Good morning, my new-blooded zodiacs!" Malis's voice seems to be coming from the hologram. "Let me start out by giving you my condolences. The journey through the uncharted lands is for the strong hearted, those of you who stand here now. Even so, you have lost some who were close to you. Let us remember them for who they were and not what they are now. Look to the future. We shall reclaim our lands by staying strong and working together as one. The lives of those now lost will not have been in vain. Apophis will not be our undoing, because we will take down his Infernum army! Now cheer, so he can hear you! Let him know his tactics to take our friends and loved ones will not crush us! We are strong together!"

We cheer loudly, and thump our chests. Further around the tower in one direction, I notice the Aries cheering and smashing their heads together as if practicing victory against the enemy. In the other direction, the Gemini dance with expressive gestures, moving at a fast pace that corresponds with their incredible speed. No doubt, the other Constellations are also expressing themselves as ingrained by their culture, because a cacophony of other sounds now emanates from the hologram.

A large spiral carapace horn, almost three times his size, sits next to Theophilus. Its low bass tone accentuates the cheering of the zodiacs from all the Constellations. I squint up at where I believe the real Theophilus to be, and need to shade my eyes with my hand. The horn there shimmers, reflecting the bright sunlight. When its sound diminished, I look back at the hologram and see a stumpy, hairy creature step down from behind it, where the mouthpiece must be. Everyone falls silent as Theophilus raises his hand.

"Thank you, new-bloods. Now is the year of your 21st birthdays and the beginning of your Olympus Trial studies aimed at giving you a better understanding of our world, all the creatures who live within Nirvana, and the way of life of zodiacs in all the Constellations. When you register today by presenting yourself to your Constellation simulacrum, you will be receiving your purpose numbers which will dignify you as individuals. As you've probably been informed, when you leave today you will not be going back through the uncharted forest because your purpose numbers will allow you to teleport back and forth from the Doh. When you all return here tomorrow, you will spend the next chapter of your lives here, participating in the Olympus Trials. Here, we can come to understand you better as individuals, which enables us to set you up for your future life within the specific classification you are best suited to and allocate you to a particular career path. This process takes a long time. We need to watch you grow, monitor your behaviour and individual patterns, so we know precisely how you work. Your Constellation overseers will guide you through the beginning of this process until you learn your way around, and understand your devices. But now I'll let you get registered. Good luck. And let strength run beside you."

In the hologram, Theophilus's wings ripple and begin to expand. When fully expanded, he stands for a moment and then leaps off the balcony. I look up, seeing the Virgo figure flying off, as if intending to circle the tower. While we are still absorbing the words of welcome and advice, I see a distant flyer, who might be Theophilus, circling between the tower and the Uncharted Forest boundary.

Back where we entered through the wall, the Wisdom Tree representation is still shedding holographic leaves, and these seem to be being blown around by the warm zephyr breeze before disintegrating on the ground.

Europa nudges me and whispers, "I knew you would make it here."

I smile back at her. "I'm glad one of us did."

Constance calls for our attention. "Alright new-bloods, follow me to the Taurus statue that is ahead. There you'll be given your purpose numbers and then you can enter the Doh. Once we are all inside, we will go to the dining room where you'll sit and eat with the other new-blooded zodiacs. After eating, you will be placed within your Constellation dormitories."

We follow Constance and approach another taller, white wall. There is no obvious entrance, only the statue of the Taurus bull standing large and overwhelmingly grand. As we get near, it slowly starts to break free from its solid, rigid composure, muscles rippling as it, transforms into a live image of our ancestral bull. My mouth drops open. Green and white sparkling droplets spray off as it bursts into life, amazingly animated. Out of the corner of my eye I catch green, yellow, and orange sparkles fly off the Gemini's statue of their ancestral twins as they peel apart and transform into life. In the other direction, the Aries' statue of a ram, bucks and kicks as red and scarlet sparkles emanate from him.

Constance smiles at our amazement. "Europa, you can be first."

When Europa hesitated to step forward and present herself, Constance took her hand and said to all of us, "Now don't be afraid. He's just going to imprint you with your purpose numbers. Then you'll be able to enter the Doh."

Constance guided Europa over, letting go of her hand when she stood in front of the animated statue. Europa stared at the giant beast whose horns could easily destroy a large group of strong soldiers in one thrust. Constance nudges her forward and Europa slowly walks closer to the giant bull which now stands calmly by the wall.

Demetrius now stands beside me and we watch intently as she bows respectfully to the bull. He looks at her for a while as if analysing her. He blows through his nostrils and leans down as an emerald necklace slips off the top of his horn and gently falls over her head. Then a green aura emanates from her, displaying the number '5'.

And in a profound and earthy voice, he speaks, "Europa Castellanos, you bear the purpose number '5'. Magnetic, fun-loving, adventurous, curious, flexible, restless, and a free spirit. You have the ability to adapt to any new situation, unafraid of the unknown, captivating and persuasive with words. Though you are easily distracted, have a tendency to have a lack focus, terrible with routine, and you can be too self-indulgent - these are the things of which you must be most wary." He turns his head and gestures to the wall with his horns. She moves uncertainly towards it, then reaches out with her hand to touch it. Her hand doesn't stop at wall. She snaps her head back in shock and the bull figure says, "Out of all the senses. It is the eye that is the most easily fooled." There is a smile on her face as she steps confidently through the wall.

Isa shoves past me in an attempt to show her superiority over me. I manage to keep my balance until Dalton and Henrietta, following closely behind her, finish the job and I find my face meeting a hard surface again. Though my already scraped hands took the brunt of my weight, they did not stop my nose impacting on the hard path and my breath being forced out of me. After pushing up and gasping for breath, I lifted my head and caught Demetrius looking down at me. I know he can't defend me in this scenario as it would be seen as favouritism, and I should be able to defend myself at this age. Getting to my knees, I wipe blood from under my nose onto my shabby clothes. Once I am standing again, I squeeze my nose to try to control the bleeding.

Demetrius having silently assured himself that I was alright, casually walked the short distance to join Constance. She was surprised by the eagerness with which Isa came over and gestured her to go on. Isa did so, but before taking more than two steps, tripped unexpectedly, and couldn't stop her face hitting the hard pavement. All eyes were on her as she rolled to get up. I saw Demetrius's leg swing back to its normal standing position. Dalton and Henrietta burst into laughter and I find my mouth slowly curling into a huge grin. I covered it with my hand. Isa's hair has come undone and frizzes out into a giant hairball. Her head snaps around so she can glare at Dalton and Henrietta. They try to smother their amusement by coughing and elbowing each other. Isa hurriedly stands, pulling her hair back into a rough knot. She looks at Demetrius with an expressionless countenance then glances back at me. Wincing, she continues forward, hiding her anger behind a mask of pride.

The bull looks down upon her and says, "Be careful of the concoction you choose to drink as thy will only cause cancer within one's self."

Isa says nothing, standing as though he did not speak, most likely blinded by rage and unable to see or hear anything else but the furious noise in her mind. The creature bends his head down and once again an emerald necklace slides off the end of his horn to land softly on to Isa's shoulders.

Breathing deeply and exhaling through his nostrils, a green

aura emanates from Isa too, this time displaying the number 4. The bull spoke again. "Isa Edlyn, you bear the purpose number '4'. You are strong, honest, determined, practical, hardworking, down-to-earth, and organized. You have the ability to accomplish large projects due to your organizational skills and perseverance, due to your honesty and integrity, others know they can trust you. And you are comfortable expanding small projects into large ones, though you have a tendency to be bossy and a bit of a know-it-all. You can be rigid at times and are quick to place judgment on others. You can be overly cautious, which can lead to missed opportunities. This is where you must be most wary."

Isa nods determinedly and walks through the wall into the Doh as though she had done it many times before. Dalton and Henrietta now wait impatiently before Constance, and she nods for one of them to proceed forward as the creature now swivels its jaw from side to side in a bull-like manner, patiently waiting as the twins quarrel about who will go first. Then he speaks. "Both Hamlyns, come forward."

They look at one another, grin widely and walk in perfect synchronization. He looks down upon them and says, "Both, one of the same." Continuing to chew, he leans down and breathes upon them. They chuckle, finding it ticklish. An emerald necklace appears on each horn and after a gentle head shake, they slide neatly over the twins' heads in a synchronized motion. The illuminating green auras displaying the number '3'. He says, "Dalton and Henrietta Hamlyn, you bear the purpose number '3'. You are creative, generous, charismatic, playful, joyful, optimistic, and witty. You are amazingly creative and innovative, communication comes easy to you, others are drawn to your charming, magnetic personalities, and your energy and happiness uplifts those around you, though you have a tendency to hold grudges when hurt by those you trust, have a tough time with managing finances, you also have a tendency to procrastinate, have a lack of focus when something does not interest you, and you constantly need praise and affirmation from your peers to keep your spirits high. This is where you must be most wary."

Dalton and Henrietta look at each other and nod with big grins, satisfied with the bull's reading of them; they turn to the wall and leap through.

Demetrius and Constance both turn and simultaneously look at me. Then I look at Kendall who stands patiently beside me, not appearing to be in any rush. I glance either side, at both Gemini and Aries Constellations, who are nearly finished with their purpose number evaluations. Then Constance remarks, "Come on, Taura. Aren't you excited to find your purpose number?"

She places her hand out and I walk forward. Demetrius gives me an encouraging nod and I walk slowly towards the ginormous bull. Standing in front of him, he glances at me as he did the others and leans down. I feel the power within his presence. He breathes in and just stares at me as if in shock. His eyes widen, he shuffles back, and unexpectedly snorts mucus over and around me. Then his front hoof begins to scrape the ground as if he is preparing to charge.

I freeze.

Still eyeing me, the bull gradually relaxes as he comes to some realisation. He says accusingly, "You only see things as they appear to be, not what they truly are. How did you end up here?"

I'm completely stiff with not only fear and confusion but a sudden eerie sagacity. He can see I am different.

Constance walks up from behind me and looks directly at Taurus. They stare at one another for a long moment before he goes back to his original composure and says, "This is the child?" I look at Constance who now nods slowly and her expression betrays nothing. He holds eye contact with her then glances away, as though he is ashamed in some way. His action intensifies my already sick, insecure feeling of not belonging. He looks back at me, now with an expressionless composure and merely shakes his horn. A necklace drops clumsily in front of me with the number ten imprinted on it. No illuminating green aura appears around me. I pick the necklace up, hands shaking as a blush of shame infuses my face. I wish I could just disappear.

Constance whispers in my ear, "It's okay, my Taura. You can walk through the wall now, into the Doh."

Her voice is composed but she is clearly unsettled by the disgruntled Taurus who has resumed the subconscious scraping with his front hoof.

As she guides me to the wall, with one gentle hand on my back and the other on my shoulder, I feel I am being rushed inside. She glances at the bull, before walking me through the wall and saying confidentially, "Don't think too much on this. You're perfect just as you are."

Those words do not supply comfort; how could I not think on it. Adonis and Penelope should have left me in the woods where I belonged.

As I walk through the illusion of the sturdy white wall, I feel a warm sensation slowly crawl over my body from front to back as though walking through a veil of warm water. I shut my eyes until I feel my feet touch solid ground. The warm sensation rolls off my body and fresh air makes my skin tingle. After all my earlier mishaps today, I feel properly washed and delightfully clean. I feel the necklace melt into my chest and look down and see it absorbed into my skin, glowing bright green until it slowly fades. Then there is a burning sensation at the back of my neck.

I check myself over. Then look up to see the inside of the Doh for the very first time, my mouth drops slightly open. Europa, Isa, Dalton, and Henrietta all stand ahead of me as I walk slowly towards them, unnoticed. The room is large and circular, brightly decorated with golden outlines around historic art. Other zodiacs are appearing from their Constellation sections, coming through the wall as I did, with their region emblem displayed above them, glowing brightly. I look up to see ours too, slowly fading as I step further into the Doh. Snippets of significant events told to us as children appear and disappear as images on the tall walls. As I look up into the tower, there seems to be thousands of floors separated by a large twirling staircase made of stone. It appears to go up forever, a spinning hole of the unknown, making you dizzier the longer you stare.

"Taur!" Europa is now standing in front of me. I notice her necklace, too, is gone. "Isn't this amazing!" she continues, noticing me staring at her chest. "Oh yeah, it happened to me too. Burnt for a bit. But it transfers to the back of your neck. See," she turns around, moving her thick blonde hair, displaying the number five, distinctly seen through her tattoo. I rub the back of my neck, realizing the cause of the burning sensation. "What was your purpose number?" she asks.

I feel ashamed, even though I don't know the purpose behind a number '10'. But from the bull's expression, it did not seem good. I hear Isa murmur beside us, "Bet she didn't even get one."

Dalton and Henrietta both chuckle. Europa spits them a livid glare.

"10," I say with slight malice.

She gives me an inquisitive look and says, "10? What purpose number is that? I thought there were only nine and the master numbers?"

I shrug, not wanting to elaborate on the disappointing event. "So did I, but he didn't give me an explanation."

Europa realizing this, changes the topic, "So have you checked out the other zodiacs? I can't believe we're so close to one another. It feels so surreal."

I smile slightly and nod, "It's incredible, this whole place."

We both look around further, taking in the moment and saying nothing. Kendall Warren now approaches our group as the last Taurus. His purpose number '9', is still visually burning into his chest, but his facial expression registers little discomfort. He appears to embrace the pain, representing a true resilient Taurus.

All the zodiacs are now gathered, aligned in sectors within Nirvana's circular layout. From a bird's eye view, standing next to one another.

The Geminis are close on our right, their black and white, yin and yang distinctions now noticeably different. Every individual has a youthful slender build and their own unique appearance. They are all glancing around incessantly, unable to miss a thing, making humorous witty comments as they point and chuckle to one another.

Beyond them are Cancers, their black piercing eyes, perfect porcelain skin and impassive faces are an innocent contrast to the deadly sharp skeleton armament that pierces the flesh of their forearms. They keep together in a protective cluster.

Further around again, are the Leos. Their lean athletic builds are a better representation of my own, but they have golden eyes that glimmer in the light and sharp nails retracted into hands and feet, ready to be flicked out to attack or defend. Their lion-like ears are twitching around attentively and their tails flick with a dynamic life of their own as though they wait in eager anticipation.

Continuing around the circle, are the Virgos, tall and slender, with bright green eyes that pierce through you and large wings pinned behind their backs. Dressed neatly, they stand inflexible and as if judging everyone, taking in every detail and analysing every feature. Their intelligence is well known.

Next to them are the Libras, radiant and beautiful zodiacs with pointed ears and delicate features. They move gracefully within their group, judging no one, just looking around. Their clothes seem mystical, being created from forest leaves and tree bark. But these must surely be incorporated into some flexible fabric, to move with them, so they seem like living plants. A few have one green eye and the other blue, representing an unbalanced emotion or turmoil. It probably reflects their nervousness within this unfamiliar place, which is so different to their forest home.

Opposite our position are the Scorpios. These are strong featured and hard-looking zodiacs with thorns extending from all jointed parts of their body and fierce long, black, stinging tails standing high above heads of jet-black hair. Their whole aura is one of bravery and focus. While they watch silently, barely moving, they are incredibly hard to read.

Next to them are the Sagittarius, standing tall and noble as their horse hooves clop on the floor as they move to look around. They have a strong, no-nonsense presence about them. The men look rugged and the women fierce, as they study the other zodiacs. Their impressions of each, sometimes approval, sometimes disappointment, clearly betrayed by their facial expressions.

Around from them, the Capricorns have a shy presence: they stand huddled closely together, watching everyone in a cautious, but inquisitive, manner. Some have a distinctive long fish tail trailing on the ground, others have a small goat tail. Their mysterious beauty is apparent from across the room.

The Aquarius are the largest of the zodiacs, being in stature at least head and shoulders above any other zodiac. Although they may be large with an incredibly strong and powerful physical presence, they have a calming, safe, and protective aura in contrast. They look at everyone in a friendly and welcoming manner.

Beyond them are the Pisces, the sporadic orange colour of their water resistant skin shimmers when they move and the light hits it at the right angle. They have a soft and gentle presence about them, watching everyone and smiling as though excited to get to know us. And I notice, unlike in pictures I've seen, their fins are tucked away when outside the water.

Separating us from them are the Aries. The confident, arrogant smiles on each face hints at their impatience to get started and while waiting, their dynamic movements betray a restless energy that draws many eyes to them.

We all stay close together, each within the safety and familiarities of our Constellations, now waiting for our overseer to guide us away from this surreal confrontation.

Everyone gradually becomes still, and the murmurs of conversation diminish into silence, as tiny, sparkling blue diamonds begin to fall from above, disappearing when they reach the stone floor. Everyone looks up in delight; the diamonds appear to be manifesting from out of nowhere. A profound and memorable voice begins to speak, and the blue diamonds flicker brighter in time with every word.

The deep voice says, "Welcome to the Olympus Trials. This system of study was devised to bring unity back between all zodiacs after the evil force you know of as the Infernum shattered the land and divided it into the twelve Constellations.

"The Olympus Trials have been made to give you a clear understanding of every Constellation's inhabitants and way of life, coming together as one working unity as opposed to the provincial perception placed upon you at birth. Here you will get to mingle with the zodiacs of all Constellations.

"The theoretical and physical base studies you're now registered for are designed to enhance your power, ability, and skill to become the strongest version of yourselves. You'll be classed within one of three classifications once you complete the trials. Your class depends on what promise you show within the whole of your studies. This will be established over time, after much rigorous testing.

"The first classification you know of is the 'Nebula Classification', also known as NC. This class is for those who are set in their ways, unable to change, staying within their Constellation and never leaving. During the trials, they'll generally display continuous and predictable traits from their upbringing, unable to innovate and adapt to the unfamiliar environments or task given at hand.

"Second is 'Planetary Nebula Classification', also known as PNC. This class is for the zodiacs who work and live within the Doh and those who show quick initiative, innovative solutions, and broad intelligence within stressful environments and within the Doh's working environment.

"Third is the 'Supernova Classification,' also known as SNC. This class is for the ones who give service to the Nirvana Army. Not every zodiac has the ability and mentality to take on such an evil and powerful force as that of our prehistoric enemy, the 'Infernum'. To be considered for this class, you must show great courage, intelligence, and profound skill. During the trials, those deemed worthy, will be drafted into the army to learn the skills to enhance their unique talents, making them the strongest zodiacs within Nirvana.

"Your classification will be decided by the paired elders from each Constellation. You will be introduced to the Elders today. The two who oversee all major decisions are the Patriarch and Matriarch. They speak for all the Elders and have the greatest power and knowledge. They designed the Olympus Trials."

When the voice ceased, the last of the blue diamonds drift to the floor. The ensuing silence is broken by a loud creaking noise as two large doors begin to open. All the zodiacs turn towards the sound. A light illuminates detailed depictions of all the Constellations' emblems on the panels of the doors, along with the wisdom tree which is centred in the middle. Its leaves appear to be falling.

The doors heave open, straight down the middle of the animated tree, to reveal a room which has a real tree adorned by small multi-coloured orbs that are moving within it. The living tree resembles those above the entrances leading into the Doh, except it is enormous.

Positioned on a podium before it, is a long horizontal table with twelve paired seats. Leaves falling from the tree, disappear as they land on its surface. Twelve other tables are spread below the podium, each individual table displaying the Constellation colours of one of twelve regions, obviously delegating where we must sit.

The Leos take the initiative, one saying, "Well, come on, what are you all waiting for?"

The Aries, grabbing any given opportunity to express their courage, immediately rise to the occasion and follow them, as do the Sagittarius who are the most enthralled about investigating the unknown. It makes sense that all the fire signs are quick to light the flame of enthusiasm.

We enter the room slowly, taking in the magnificent display. I stay close to Europa as we enter, but she is completely captivated by the elaborate room, unaware of my movements. The temperature increases to a warm and comfortable level, making me relax. The glowing coloured orbs are now dancing around the room, scooting in and out of the tree as though excited about our arrival. Before we could sit down at our tables, they come flying over. The various colours are drawn towards different zodiacs. The Capricorns gather orbs of white, Aquarius collect orbs of grey, Pisces blue-green, Aries yellow-green, Gemini orange, Cancer rose, Leo red, Virgo brown, Libra blue, Scorpio violet, and Sagittarius gold. Yellow orbs hover above us. Before we get the chance to look closer, they all fly straight back amongst the large branches of the huge tree. Then the Elders appear from behind the tree, ascending to the podium and approaching their seats behind the long table positioned there.

We all rush to sit down at a table decorated with our Constellation colours. My belly was already telling me it had been a long time since breakfast. Exactly six seats await Europa, Kendall, Isa, Dalton, Henrietta, and me. Every other table also has the exact number of chairs to seat the Constellation's new-bloods.

At our table, a long skinny satin cloth, centred lengthwise, drapes over either end with Taurus emblems beautifully embroidered into the material in green and white. A smaller replica hangs over the back of our wooden chairs. Similar decorations, with Constellation colour schemes and emblems, adorn the seats at the other tables. At all tables, large golden cups, plates and cutlery are on display and they glitter in the light of beautiful candles.

"With this kind of display, I expect the food to be just as good!" Europa whispers to me with eagerness as we pull our chairs in. Then the table begins to tremble. I hold on to my seat wondering what is happening. I look at Europa who is beaming with controlled excitement, then turn quickly to see a sparkling, green hologram emerging through the table. It's our Taurus bull.

Glancing around the room, I notice the symbols of the other zodiac's lineal ancestors appearing through their tables too. I nearly jump out of my seat as our hologram goes "Mooooooooooooooooo!"

and shoots into the high ceiling, followed by the other holographic symbols. Sharp explosions draw our attention upwards as each of the holograms burst into sparkles of colour, that swirls and mix before floating down over us. I have never seen anything so marvellous and my heart begins to race in a rush of excitement and pleasure. I let some fall onto my open right palm, and then blow them back in the air.

My delight is interrupted as the twins begin to nudge each other.

"Those explosions are much like Father's farts," says Dalton.

Henrietta chuckles at his comment. "I bet he could give them a run for their money." Both laughing hysterically at their unamusing humour.

Isa rolls her eyes, "Don't you two ever have anything worthwhile to contribute to a conversation."

Both look at Isa who sits dour faced, unimpressed by the display that continues to fall delicately upon us.

"Those farts are pretty worthwhile if you ask me!" says Dalton and they both continue laughing uncontrollably. Isa sinks deeper into her seat, arms crossed, rolling her eyes, unimpressed by their sarcasm.

Europa whispers to me, "They should never reproduce."

I lean towards her, "Well, they wouldn't exactly have many suitors."

Europa sniffs. "Yeah, but they're stupid enough to settle for one another and then we'd really have problematic offspring." We both chuckle and now the show is over.

The Patriarch and Matriarch, Theophilus and Adora Malis, stand proudly at the centre of the raised table as all the other Elders take a seat. They are both draped in long elegant robes made in the Virgo constellation colours: green, white, and yellow. Both are tall and slender with piercing green eyes. The beautiful Adora takes a seat and Theophilus begins to clap in a slow, steady rhythm until he has everyone's attention.

Stopping, he clasps his hands together elegantly and says, "Well, it's nice to meet you all up close, my new-blooded zodiacs. I hope that enthralling display made you feel more at ease within the Doh's premises." He raises his hands high and the coloured orbs begin to liven up, flying in and out amongst the tree branches with their usual mannerisms.

"Being able to finally meet your totems is an exciting experience, particularly as you have only ever read about them. Once you obtain your purpose numbers they are born into this space." Theophilus refers to the tree the totems move amongst it, then brings his hands back in front of him before continuing, "You will learn more about them during your classes. First though, we must eat and rejuvenate ourselves as it has been a testing time for you all. Then dormitory placement will commence and you can start to get settled before going home for one last night. But before we begin anything, I will introduce you to the residing Elders."

He clears his throat and announces, "Capricorn Elders Aldous and Amelia Darcy!"

Everyone praises them as they stand and an enlarged hologram of the pair hovers in the air above them. Aldous has a goat tail and Amelia a fish tail. Aldous has long dark brown hair tied back with two thick bits draping down either side of his ears. He seems wise and noble, with a wealth of experience concealed within. Amelia has long, salty-looking, indigo-coloured hair as though it's dried that way from salt water. She looks guarded and strong-willed. They both wear comfortable clothing in their Constellation colours, black and indigo. Amelia begins speaking in a strong and delegating voice, "We are the ambitious of the zodiac: practical, wise, disciplined, persistent, and cautious."

Amelia steps back and Theophilus adds, "If you want guidance or advice, they are the best mentors and teachers as their philosophical connection to life comes exceedingly natural in regards to the balance of the universe." The ovation resumes and they both bow in acknowledgment.

Theophilus gestures towards the Aquarians. "Aquarius Elders Cassidy and Brigantia Dion!" They stand eagerly but nearly take out the table in the process due to their large size. Pulling it back, they smile welcomingly, making you feel drawn to them. Their hologram image is more composed, but like to life. Cassidy has long blue hair tightly plaited into multiple braids with flowers and leaves captured by the plaits. He has a large smile and jolly appearance. Brigantia has two long blue plaits draping down her front; she too has flowers and leave plaited or pinned within her hair. She seems loving and caring. They both wear clothing with a floral design, coloured with grey and ultramarine blue as their Constellation colours.

Brigantia raises her large arm and says in a welcoming kind voice, "We are the humanitarian of the zodiac: friendly, intelligent, creative, independent, and loyal."

Theophilus adds, "If you or the creature you know have a life-threatening injury, they are the ones to see as they are the greatest healers in Nirvana and advanced in any language." Everyone claps. They both wave and sit down carefully, laughing at themselves for their awkwardness.

Theophilus continues the introductions, "Pisces Elders Galen and Calypso Murdoch."

They both stand delicately; their luminous eyes look over everyone in the room, observing carefully. Galen has bright orange eyes, soft features with his rope-like hair tied into a large bun at the top of his head; he looks kind. Calypso has a small delicate frame and tiny facial features. Her gentle eyes are dark, and her rope hair falls freely down her back. She seems fragile, but I get the impression not to underestimate her. Neither wears clothes as tough, flexible scales cover their body. These have been adorned with their Constellation colours of sea green and aqua. Galen speaks in a soft but confident voice, "We are the intuitive of the zodiac: imaginative, kind, compassionate, sensitive, and selfless."

Theophilus explains, "There's not an enchantment or potion they cannot conjure and not a curse they cannot cure. They are the greatest sorcerers and alchemists of our time."

Once again, everyone applauds and they nod in gratitude and sit down.

Next, "Aries Elders Ardon and Athena Cadman!"

They both stand up straight, demonstrating a strong, proud demeanour. With heads high, chests pushed out and hands on their hips they exude absolute confidence. Their floating hologram image is almost identical to their real selves, so they obviously keep themselves in top shape. Ardon is a muscular Aries with hard features, short beard, sharp eyes; tattoos cover the majority of his body including a large Aries emblem on his chest. Athena is a tough and striking female Aries. Her hair is tied back into a short ponytail and she looks incredibly fit. Next to Ardon, she appears to compete with him for the attention of the crowd. They both wear minimal brown leather clothing, and use face paint to show their Constellation colours, red and scarlet.

Ardon takes the stand and speaks boldly, "We are the courageous of the zodiac: confident, lively, ardent, bold, and daring."

Theophilus adds, "They have the strength to destroy mountains and clear any area with their large strong horns, having the courage and determination to step up to any challenge that overcomes most others."

The Aries Constellation out does everyone else's applause as they egg each other on.

Theophilus raises his hand and everyone instantly falls silent. "Taurus Elders Iden and Constance Terran!"

We all thud our chests hard at the same moment. The air from our lungs makes short grunting noise. This is the first time I have actually seen Iden. I glance from him to the hologram. He is hard and tough looking; his facial expression suggests a determined work ethic, and an expectation of efficiency. He has muscular features a thick, well-groomed beard and dark brown eyes. Standing with his arms crossed, he clearly dominates Constance, who stands slightly behind him. They both wear conservative clothing in our Constellation colours of green and white.

Iden speaks in a strong and resolute tone. "We are the determined of the zodiac: independent, generous, down-to-earth, patient, and persistent."

Theophilus elaborates, "The zodiacs most skilled in diverse weaponry. If you want to learn how to fight, they are the only zodiacs who have the patience and skill to teach and produce great warriors."

Everyone claps and we hit our chests twice in unison and sit down, like the good soldiers we were trained to be, although I'm aware I look out of place. Iden and Constance both nod their heads and sit down.

Theophilus gestures next towards Gemini. "Gemini Elders Eldryd and Amora Findal!" They both rise quickly, revealing an intense energy. They look eagerly around the room. Eldryd's black side looks solemn and watchful, hard in its appearance with a pierced eyebrow, and his white is playful and calming with two piercings in that ear. Amora's white side is incredibly pretty with a delicate appearance, her eyes are big with long eyelashes and her black side is observant and expressionless. Their clothing is intricately and brightly decorated in their Constellation colours of green, yellow, and orange. Very ostentatious attire.

Eldryd smiles with enthusiasm, rubbing his hands together vigorously and says, "We are the charismatic of the zodiac: compelling, witty, intelligent, versatile, and enthusiastic."

Theophilus adds, "They are able to create the most beautiful pieces of architecture, like the Doh you see before you. Their attention to detail and diverse intelligence can manage many tasks at once. Along with having the initiative and persistence to complete these masterpieces, their speed, carries the ability to out run time."

The Gemini Constellation enthusiastically cheer for their Elders and everyone claps in acknowledgment. They both wave incredibly fast.

Then Theophilus points to Cancer. "Cancer Elders Dimitri and Selena Griswold!"

They both stand nonchalantly, not giving much away with their piercing black eyes although I feel they deliberately give that impression for their own self-protection. Dimitri stands with his arm protectively around Selena's back. His stern features give his face mysterious look, which is complemented by the scar that goes on an angle from one side of his face to the other. Selena stands confidently by Dimitri's side, appearing faithful and strong despite her feminine features and the decorative pattern shaved into her short hair. Their clothes are tight fitting and coloured sea green and silver. Selena speaks with a soft captivating voice, "We are the protectors of the zodiac: passionate, loving, faithful, caring, and unassuming."

Theophilus includes, "The most nimble, agile, and unassuming zodiacs, initiating a murder before anyone is aware of their passing and produce a force field so vast it could cover the Doh's grounds." After that comment, they both bow and everyone follows up with applause.

Theophilus clears his throat then signals the Leo partners. "Leo Elders Leander and Albertina Maximillion!"

The Leo Constellation gave a loud, energetic ovation as the couple stood proudly, drawing all eyes to them. Leander is strong, athletic, and handsome with rugged golden hair half tied into a bun and bright golden eyes. He has tattoos everywhere visible, even on his face. Albertina is feminine and sensual; she moves seductively and has beautiful golden hair tied into a long draping ponytail with beads entangled. They both wear an armoured uniform in their Constellation colours of gold, orange, and yellow. Leander speaks with a proud voice. His whole manner is charismatic and sensual. "We are the leaders of the zodiac: optimistic, magnetic, captivating, self-assured, and fiery."

Theophilus adds to that, "The fiercest animalistic hunters of our time, to see their transformation into their lion ancestors and to watch them hunt or kill is something you should hope to see in your lifetime."

Everyone applauds and they confidently sit down in their seats as Theophilus gestures to Libra. "Libra Elders Adlai and Isadora Dempster!"

The Libras clap in a very pleasing musical rhythm as their Elders stand casually; their energy is harmonious and calm. Adlai's striking porcelain white skin appears unblemished and his eyes a crystal clear blue. His long, light brown hair is immaculately groomed. His presence is reassuring and alluring. Isadora is incredibly beautiful with the same porcelain skin and crystal blue eyes. She has bright, strawberry blonde hair that glows in the light. Her presence draws you in a sensual, calming, and comforting way. Their blue and jade green attire, fits them perfectly, and shows their magnificent physiques.

Adlai speaks compellingly and without false modesty. "We are the diplomatic zodiacs: charming, romantic, honest, respectful, and harmonious."

Theophilus continues, "Their skill in mind control goes beyond that in any other Constellation. They could control everyone in this room, all at once, if they wished. You'd be surprised to know their beautiful appearance is part of their allure, which lowers the barriers to mind control. Their beauty even grows with age, it's hypnotizing."

The musical applause is taken up by the other Constellations as the pair sit down. Theophilus then looks to Scorpio. "Scorpio elders Archibald and Ambrosina Erhard!"

Their Constellation stands as they do, focusing on the Elders as they examine the whole crowd below them. They are expressionless, giving nothing away - the only zodiacs I can't sense anything from. Some instinct tells me that I wouldn't want to anger them. From descriptions of their sting, it is something I never want to experience.

Archibald is rigid and intimidating. His features are coarse, his hair cropped short and his stinger, at the end of his rigid tail, hangs high above his head in a most threatening manner. Ambrosina is fierce and deadly too; in an enigmatic way, her threatening appearance is also very attractive. Half her head is shaved to show the Scorpio emblem, and her bright orange eyes are unlike any I have ever seen. They both stand freakishly still as though a part of the furniture. Their tails are painted red and violet representing their Constellation colours. Ambrosina speaks with a harsh toneless voice. "We are the mysterious of the zodiac: fierce, focused, brave, faithful, and instinctive."

Theophilus continues, "These two zodiacs implement the death penalty. Their skin is impenetrable and their two poisons are the most lethal of any Scorpio. Do not upset or cross these elders – they do not show mercy."

The claps more hesitant this time, as no one knows if the Scorpio Elders would be happy with acknowledgment or not.

Then Theophilus moves on to Sagittarius. "Sagittarius Elders, Emanuel and Abigail Galloway!"

The two Sagittarius were already standing as their horse bodies cannot be seated. They are sturdy and robust, having an earthy philosophical aura about them. Just looking at them evokes a deep sense of connection to the wild.

Emanuel is ruggedly good-looking with a down-to-earth appearance. His hair is rough, unkempt, and his hands calloused from living and working in a harsh forest. He is covered in tribal tattoos and has dark, limpid eyes. Abigail exudes a sensual femininity and an earthy aura, complementary to her dark skin and bright blue eyes. Her hair reflects an inner wildness.

They both have their Constellation colours, light blue and white, painted on their arms and chest. Archibald speaks with a robust voice, "We are the adventurous of the zodiac: straightforward, intelligent, philosophical, generous, and inquisitive."

Theophilus adds, "They are the greatest trackers of all time, being able to find zodiacs weeks and even months after they disappear. Their ability to converse with the forest exceeds any that of any other Sagittarius."

The Sagittarius applaud their Elders by pounding their chests and stamping their hooves, much like our approach. Everyone claps as they acknowledge the ovation.

Theophilus claps slowly then raises his hand for silence, "And last but not least, Virgo. We are the perfectionists of the zodiac: analytical, reliable, humble, altruistic, and strong-minded.

I myself, Theophilus, and my wife, Adora Malis. We are the Patriarch and Matriarch of Nirvana, and as such, we oversee the lives of everyone who lives within this land.

"Today it is our pleasure to welcome all of you to the Olympus Trials!"

I found myself cheering along with everyone else. The room seemed full of excited energy as glittering representations of the Constellation emblems appeared again and exploded into sparkles in the various colours.

Theophilus lowers himself gracefully and we look down to find our table crowded with platters of food. Large and juicy grass patties piled up on one platter, grass sweet cakes, fried grass chips, hay curries and hay salads – all the types of grass and hay delicacies, filled others.

I have only ever dreamt about eating anything like what was spread in front of me. I used to watch the NC farmer Taureans make them in the market stalls, but they wouldn't ever sell me a portion. Even if I had the price of their wares, they would ignore me. It was their way of expressing their abhorrence of my existence, which in their eyes was an insult to their own dead children.

Henrietta and Dalton announced perfect unison, "My favourite part of the day!"

Isa quickly began piling her selections onto her plate but Kendall seemed to be murmuring some sort of prayer.

Europa turned to me, "It's the meal of a lifetime!"

I nod in agreement, saliva was already accumulating in my mouth. Never had I seen such an abundance of delicious food. In the dark winter of each year, one of these platters would have fed my father and me for a month. Even in view of this bounty, I can still taste the rubbery rabbit jerky he used to make and store, so we could maintain our much-needed portion of protein. I hated it, but I pretended it wasn't too bad for my father's sake because I could see the distress in his eyes at being unable to provide anything better for his daughter.

Once our bellies were full, all the food consumed, and everything on the table removed, Theophilus stood once again.

"I hope you enjoyed your meals. We know how important it is that you stay healthy and strong during your studies. We want you to be strong, and continue to grow stronger so you can reach and demonstrate your full potential. Now your overseer will guide you to your dormitory to get settled. Then you'll be shown how to teleport to your Constellations and back so we can see you bright and early tomorrow to officially start the Olympus Trials.

"I'll leave you with this advice: spend this time with your families wisely as it will be the last time you will see them for a while. To each of you - congratulations on making it through the Uncharted Forest. Always remember to let strength run beside you."

Twelve figures march out from behind the tree and I immediately spot Demetrius. He has his eyes on us as he walks to stand at our table. I wondered if he had eaten as well as we had.

"Alright, follow me and I'll show you to your rooms."

We all jump up to obey as the large doors leading to the arrival hall begin to creak open. The other Constellation groups are also moving and it seems our Taurean group are more relaxed now. Others zodiacs are too. The friendly Aquarians, famous for their ability to make a lot of friends are already starting to mingle.

I keep my attention on Demetrius, making sure not to lose sight of him. Our bunched group spreads out. Europa, I notice, seems intrigued by a Cancerian. Her ability to speak to new individuals astounds me.

We stand at the bottom of the large twisting stairwell, the steps worn in the middle from the constant impact of feet. Some of the zodiacs are eager to see more of the tower, especially the Gemini, who are constantly on the move, easily bored. The stairs are made from ancient stone and were once highly polished. Statues of different creatures are displayed in wall niches around the ascending stairs.

The Sagittarians had reached the stairs first and stand ready and impatient to take on the unknown. They begin clopping up the stairs, following their overseer. I am amazed that their four hooves manage them so well.

When it was our turn to start, I placed my hand on the stone railing for the stairs were large and not built for my small frame. Every step feels like a big stretch and I have to pull myself up. Soon, other zodiacs are passing me and it seems my backpack becomes ever heavier.

After passing a couple of doors and weirdly arranged entrances, I come by a terrifying statue standing on a large platform. Written below is 'The Wendigo' from the Libra region. It is a frightening creature with abnormally long muscular arms extending from its shoulders with two minor arms curling around from underneath its armpits. Both sets have incredibly sharp long claws. It has large hind legs, long rigid horns grow from its malevolent skull, and its mouth has big sharp teeth. Its eyes are hollow and sticking out on top of its skull are long pointy ears. From what I've read, it lives within the shadows of the Pacem Forest, below the Libras' village, Arbor Domus. They gain longevity by eating those who get lost within Pacem.

Other zodiacs have also stopped to stare at the creature as you can only read about these monsters. As I looked up at it, I swear its eyes moved. It's hard to tell though, as they are hidden within the dark recesses of its skull. I look down and I see granite fall from its body as it begins to move. My body is suddenly rigid. The monster stretches up on its hind legs and releases a horrific, screeching cry, which penetrates the ears and echoes up and down the Doh's narrow internal spine. I fall backwards on to another, who catches me. A Gemini who passes by begins to laugh at himself as he too got quite the fright and the Wendigo goes back to its original stone-like state. Everyone pays attention as the Pisces overseer remarks in a soft voice, "Everything has a life of its own within this place...along with watchful eyes." His words have an undertone of caution and everyone heeds him before continues up the stairwell.

The zodiac who caught me remarks, "Well, I guess you've learnt, it's rude to stare." I turn around quickly to find a rugged Leo staring at me with bright golden eyes, and an amusing smile.

The hair on the left side of his head is cropped short, except for part, in the shape of the Leo emblem, where no hair grows. The rest has thick, shoulder length hair flowing everywhere. He has intense eyes, sunken in with an alluring shadow around them, a flat nose with a strong prominent jaw. Tattoos, all Leo representations, cover his right arm except for where the name Cedric Sol is written on his forearm. I become annoyed by his insensitive comment, so I pull on the straps of my old backpack and continue up the stairs.

He follows closely behind, "I've heard Taureans can't take much of a joke. Take things too personally. But surely we can come to some sort of a silver lining? I mean I did just save your life."

I become instantly angered by his confident arrogance and didn't respond.

"Ah your stubbornness exceeds you. What's your name?"

I flick him a livid stare. "None of your business."

He smiles, almost enthralled by the perceived challenge, "That's not nice to say to your saviour."

I roll my eyes, keeping them fixed on the upward stairs and ignore him. Then Europa comes pounding down, "Taura! There you are! I was wondering where you got to."

She looks at the Leo loitering beside me. "Who's your friend?" she asks, curiously, as it's unusual for me to be conversing with anyone I don't know.

"He's not my—"

The Leo rudely interrupts, "Leon Sol is my name, your friend," he pauses for a moment and looks at me with triumph, "Taura... was just introducing herself."

I roll my eyes and Europa looks at me with an odd expression. I was glad to be interrupted by Demetrius.

"Taura! Europa! What are you doing? Dormitory placement has already begun," he says sternly.

Then his eyes shift towards Leon and his expression immediately changes, his eyebrows crease together, and I sense he is angered by the Leo's presence. I realize we three are the last stragglers and a few steps further up, big wooden doors are wide open, awaiting our arrival.

Demetrius looks intently at Leon, "Why aren't you with your Constellation group, Leo?"

Leon ever so slightly smirks and replies, "Taura fell willingly into my arms. I couldn't help but introduce myself."

I feel the blood rush to my face, knowing it's turning an obvious red and betraying my embarrassment. Demetrius, unable to mask the emotion the Leo's comment aroused, abruptly snaps, "Well, don't."

Leon, now expressionless, replies, "I guess that's up to her."

Being of a fire sign, he naturally wants to challenge the situation. Now we are at the Doh, we are encouraged to mingle with other zodiacs, but in my case, Demetrius seems to be blocking that. I can tell at once that Leon has ignited the fire of anger within him. His fists clench as he fights an internal battle. Only by the deliberate way he presses down on each of the separating steps, does he give a visual promise of Leon's potential demise, "Know your place, feline."

Leon doesn't say another word but he doesn't back down from Demetrius' threatening scowl either. Suddenly, a Virgo overseer appears from in the doorway. "Demetrius, what's taking so long?" Demetrius holds Leon's stare for a moment longer. The Virgo repeating, "Demetrius?"

Still not taking his eyes off Leon, Demetrius says firmly, "I'm coming."

Turning his back to the wall, he gestures for us to go up the stairs, still eyeing Leon as he closely follows Europa and myself.

The three of us walk into a brick-walled chamber with a high ceiling and six rooms leading off to the left and six more to the right. Each has been allocated to a Constellation and is designated by the emblem and poem on the door and birth stone depicted above. These rooms are where we will live for however long the Olympus Trials takes each of us to complete independently.

Down the end of the hall is a magnificent, rotating mobile sculpture, dedicated to the ten major residing celestial bodies revolving around our precious Nirvana world. Each Constellation's god is represented there by a moving golden planet.

Everyone else is huddled around the rotating sculpture, admiring its aesthetic beauty. The other overseers stand idle on the perimeter, presumably awaiting our arrival. Demetrius and the Virgo, both annoyed for different reasons, begin walking towards the large group, firmly signalling us to follow.

At the first door, the Capricorn poem caught my attention.

CAPRICORN
Birth Stone: Garnet
A goat fish we see
oh so ambitious is he,
patience embedded,
caution dreaded.
Practical thoughts
wise as thy never sought.

Change of mind
don't react kind.
Stubborn creature
shy nature.

Don't be blind
by this frontier state of mind.

Demetrius noticed I had dropped behind. "Taura! Keep up."
I hurried after the others, but I slowed again as my eyes are drawn to the mobile sculpture.

Leon leisurely walks back to his small group of Leos, keeping me within his gaze. I am still aware that Demetrius is watching him with hawk eyes, and I wonder why he does not like Leon and if he had known of him before today? And if he had, where and how?

The golden planets are moving almost lazily at the moment, circling around some central point in an undulating motion. I notice that the ceiling rises high above the platform where the planets revolve. As each one passes close to the watchers, revealing its radiant size, there is a powerful murmuring sound, before it moves away and seems to decrease in size.

Fascinated by the moving golden planets, I mentally name them with their residing gods as they move majestically around.

"Uranus, god of the sky, represents Aquarius;

Neptune, god of the sea, represents Pisces;

Mars, god of war, represents Aries;

Venus, goddess of love, sex, beauty, and fertility, represents Taurus and Libra;

Mercury, god of trade and profit, represents Gemini and Virgo;

Moon, god of emotion, represents Cancer;

Sun, god of light and energy (self), represents Leo;

Pluto, god of the underworld, represents Scorpio;

Jupiter, god of heroic actions, represents Sagittarius;

Saturn, god of cause and effect (karma), represents Capricorn."

But I count eleven planets, not the residing ten that I know to move amongst the stars. One here I have not seen before. It's not like the others – ordinary in its appearance and comparatively small in size. I watch it particularly, trying to figure it out as all the golden planets move around, held together by some unseen force of attraction that still enables the parts to move independently.

Demetrius gets our attention. "We'll be coming back here, after you put your packs in the dormitory. Come on, this way!"

He leads us to our dormitory door, half way back along the hall. It was the one with the Taurus emblem and poem on it and the Taurus stone glowing above. There's a stone doorknocker, shaped as a Taurus head but noticeably eroded by centuries of knocking. We wait expectantly as Demetrius, who is standing in front of our small group, stares at the knocker as though he was waiting for something.

Then suddenly its eyes open, followed by an irritated yawn, "What is it?" it spits in a high creaky voice.

Demetrius stands rigid and repeats the poem from the door. The doorknocker looks up, rolls its eyes, and grunts, "I guess you guys really did get lazy, huh? Can't even remember your own poem without it plastered in front of your eyes...tsk tsk tsk."

"Another doorknocker would be an easier option," Demetrius says unrepentant. The handle looks up through his thick sunken eyebrows and grunts a sneer. It begins to levitate from the door, followed by a repeated pounding knock that's delivered with its sturdy golden head, followed by a click and a groan as the aged pine door begins to open.

Inside the large room, thick tree roots form our beds. Each has green and white sheets, a white pillow. The roots expand from our beds and attach to the walls, crawling up the ceiling into a great tree that grows upside down, flourishing dense old branches with dark green leaves and red poppies that grow from the end. Some have even fallen in the centre of the room, still glowing with life. And the same yellow orbs we saw from the dining room now move around within these branches.

Names are etched into old dark wooden planks above each bed. Europa's and mine are next to each other which brings comfort to me, knowing I'll have a friendly presence nearby during this chapter of my life.

I press on the mattress. It is so soft I might sink right into it. The idea of lying on such mattress, brings a feeling of uncertainty. I am used to lying on one made from two sewn together sheets stuffed with ferns and grasses on a wooden frame, in a room by myself. And the sheets, they are so smooth, unlike any fabric I have ever felt. But those I do look forward to sleeping between.

Demetrius stands at the door and interrupts the investigation of our individual sleeping places. "Leave your belongings on your bed and come with me."

I take off my backpack, which relieves my tired, sore shoulders, and glance at Isa whose bed is on the other side of mine. She snorts with disapproval, but this time not at me. The twins Henrietta and Dalton have bunk beds, fighting over who gets the top, shoving at each other's faces as they both try to climb.

"You have the top at home!" says Dalton.

Henrietta pushes her hand down against his head to get leverage, "And that's why I should have it here. I am three minutes older, so it only makes sense."

He grabs her leg. "How does three minutes older make any sense?"

Henrietta jabs her knee into his face and he falls to the ground with a big thud. She chortles,   claiming victory in the confrontation. She pokes her tongue out and Dalton, who glares at her as he stands up. Muttering under his breath, he slams his pack on the bottom bunk.

Isa rolls her eyes in disgust as though she has no better options for friends, but when Isa and I were young, we were good friends. To this day, I still wonder what happened to make her hate me so much.

Kendall has been sitting on his bed with his possessions lying next to him; he hasn't spoken a word since the disappearance of Latham.

"Come on, you lot! Time to get a move on. We need to get back out into the hall so you can learn to transport home."

That got everyone's interest. I felt my own excitement rising. How do we do that? Where?

Europa and I were the first to follow Demetrius, out into the hall, in the direction of the revolving golden planets. We were not the first group to emerge, but early enough to see the planets moving much faster than they had been when I saw them before.

We gathered on the outskirts of the rotating golden planets. The twelve overseers standing closest to the perimeter when all groups had emerged. When the first group had drawn near, the pace of the planets had noticeably slowed.

The Capricorn overseer gestured to her Capricorns to follow her as she stepped on the platform. The planets slowed further so she could step between two of them. The rest of the Capricorns follow warily. When they are standing in the middle of the platform, looking around uncertainly; their residing planet Saturn moves quite high above their heads and begins to press down as though it were going to crush them.

The Capricorn overseer states calmly, "It's okay, everyone. This is how you teleport home. Now visualize your homes, close your eyes and chant our creator's name, Unum, together. Unum, Unum, Unum, Unum."

They all begin chanting as Saturn cast a bright light over them. So bright, the rest of us glance away. When the light diminished and we could look again, they were gone.

Aquarius are next, their residing planet Uranus casting them home, followed by Pisces residing planet Neptune, Aries residing planet Mars and then it was our turn.

Standing on the platform, with the rest of the Taureans, I watch our planet Venus move down toward us. The number ten on the back of my neck begins to burn and spread as it crawls over the rest of my skin, tingling the top of my head. I shut my eyes, visualizing my cottage, Adonis and the grasslands and then chant Unum's name. The oppressive pressure of the golden planet representing Venus becomes more pronounced as I picture it coming closer, but a warm sensation takes over as the bright white light bathes us. Even with eyes closed, I am aware of it, then I feel myself expand with the heat.

CHAPTER FOUR

THE UNBEKNOWN

Identity is the story we have foretold.

As the day draws to a close, I watch the orange-tinged sky fading beyond my home. The tall trees silhouetted against the sky that shadow the background bring me a feeling of comfort as I arrive back from my long and unusual day. All the way, I thought of how worried Adonis must be and how thrilled he'll be to see me whole and intact.

After the teleportation brought us back to the classroom, Demetrius told us we have to be back at the Halls of Ivy by dawn tomorrow morning. I won't have a lot of time to spend with my father.

When I left the village, it was already a scene of frenetic celebration. A giant bonfire, lit in the central square, provided bright flickering light. The younger children were running around with small wood torches, and the sounds of many musical instruments provided the energetic tempo for the older ones to dance, and relieve themselves of the day's tension. Many adults were drinking beer or ale, in relief that their children had survived, or to forget the sadness and sorrow, of losing Latham and Beverly to the Infernum. The parents of those two were drinking 'Bulla', a bubble infused water that's supposedly sweet and has a distinctive odour. I've never tried it as it's mixed with potions that create hallucinations. I've heard that it enables people to see and speak to their loved ones who were taken and is a way to get closure.

Children and adults alike knew that nothing will bring back the lost loved ones. That's why I knew I couldn't be there, even when Europa had begged me to go home and bring my father.

"No one will care at a time like this," she had said. But I knew I'd just be like a knife, stabbing an already open wound and they don't need that. Right now, they don't need a constant reminder of their loss but to forget that I exist. Because everyone knows it should have been me... I know it should have been me.

Selfishly though, I'm glad it wasn't me because my survival will bring my father such happiness. He's rarely allowed himself pleasure, being ever poisoned by the guilt of my mother's death.

I can just see several dead rabbits skinned and hanging from a line beside the cottage, and from somewhere behind it, I hear wood being chopped. Adonis has obviously kept himself busy today. I walk around the back lightly running my hand on the old pinewood of the cottage wall, being careful not to get splinters. Skipping around some old shovels and a rusty axe, I see my father, who has not yet noticed me. For the first time I notice how worn out he looks. A deep line creases between his eyebrows, dark bags drop heavy under his eyes as he wipes sweat, dripping down his forehead with his forearm.

"Dad," I murmur in a moment between chops. Adonis stops, slamming the axe into the big log of wood. He wipes his face and pulls back his hair with both hands.

Unconvinced and maybe thinking it's the enchanting voice that preys on vulnerable hearts, he asks, "Taura, is that you?"

"Yes, Dad, it's me." I made my voice strong and reassuring. He turns and emits a huge sigh of relief.

He throws his arms out wide as he runs towards me, and I can hear the big smile in his return greeting, "Taura!" He picks me up, and embraces me tight. I can smell pinewood and the dark honing oil that stains his clothes. Finally putting me down, he kneels to my level and engulfs my shoulders with his large hands.

I glance down and slowly look up to meet his eyes. "I can't believe I made it, Dad, I really can't, especially because Beverly Fleur and Latham Hampton were both taken. It was sad, really sad, Dad, especially for Kendall, he didn't mutter a word all day after that."

He creases his brows together, making the line between his eyes grow deeper, suggesting his advancing age. "I do feel for their parents, but we all know the risk. I'm just grateful you're okay."

I nod in agreement but decline to tell him how we were invited to the celebration of their lives; he would know it wouldn't be the time or place. I tell him about the Doh and all that happened today and he nods his head, his expression never changing, only watching me as though he may still be dreaming.

After I finish, he waits for a moment and says, "Yes, the Doh is an extraordinary place. I doubt anyone has uncovered all its secrets. We know so little about it." He distracts me from that odd statement by standing up, awkwardly, as if his muscles ached.

I nod and touch the back of my neck where the purpose number '10' is imprinted and ask, "Dad, today the Taurus gave me the purpose number '10'. But I didn't know such a number existed? He was even dissatisfied by my presence. It's because of what I am, isn't it? What I represent? How my existence lets the Constellation down?"

Adonis stands there for a moment, as he does when I know he is thinking carefully. My whole life he's had these moments, thinking of the best way to explain things, because I am so different. He looks intently into my eyes and says, "Sometimes, we have to look beyond what we see in front of us. Be patient, my dear. I'm sure all will be explained to you in good time."

He kisses me gently on the head, holding on to me just a little longer than normal. "Now, I've made you supper, go inside. I'll be there in a moment. I just have to finish chopping this fire wood before the cold night comes."

I can't help feeling there's a subliminal message behind his earlier remark, but I still find myself perplexed by my unexpected purpose number. And I become disgruntled by the way my father never fully explains anything to me. "Dad, do you regret it?" I ask.

Adonis turns around carefully. He waits a moment once again

thinking upon his words. He sighs and says, "Taura, you are the apple of my eye. I don't regret a damn thing. I'd do it all again if I had to, just to have you. Keep such thoughts away, because they will destroy you. Such thoughts are conjured up by our own insecurities. And so many die from such poison drunk too often. No matter what happens, always know I love you... No matter what you hear..." he lets the words linger in the air for a time and adds, "So come on, let's get you inside. The sun has nearly ended the day and the cold will make you sick. Your supper is sitting on the stove, keeping warm."

I look up at him with sincerity. "So you did think I'd make it?"

His eyes squint as a warm smile spreads across his face, showing his hidden wrinkles. "I never doubted you."

I open the creaky back door, getting a whiff of my favorite supper, rabbit and pea corn soup. Taureans don't normally eat meat but rabbits are a common pest and they keep our bellies full. So, I am grateful for their infestation. I've gotten used to eating meat as the NC farmers won't trade with us because of my existence and they're the ones who own all the farmland. So Dad makes do with the little he can grow or forage, and luckily he's a good hunter. I shut the door, securing the wooden handle as it has a tendency to swing open, especially during windy cold nights. I take my jacket off and place it on the old wooden hanger.

My supper draws me to the stove, and I use some old cloth to lift the bowl across to the table. Taking a deep breath in, I inhale the deliciousness aroma and appreciate the love Dad put into making my favourite supper. As I mix the soup around in the bowl, scooping some up with my well-used wooden spoon and letting the chunky bits plop back into the savoury liquid, I think about how much I love being home. In some ways, I wished I didn't have to participate in the Olympus Trials. If only I could stay here with my dad and help him. He will have no one once I've gone, for who knows how long.

"You only see things as they appear to be, not what they truly are. How did you end up here?"

I recollect what the large Taurus statue had said to me and it irritates me. It wasn't as if it was my choice. I think about the snake-like voice that spoke to me within the Uncharted Forest. The enchantment calling to my subconscious as they said would happen. I have never told anyone about those words spoken to me by the woman in my dream, not even my father who is the only one aware of the nightmare that haunts me to this day. And I wonder why Apophis did not take me. Probably the same reason why no one else wanted me. *"Tu es via, veritas et vita. Nemo venit ad Patrem, nisi per te."* What do those words mean?

I had just begun to sip my soup, and enjoy feeling the fire warm against my back when, I hear an unexpected noise coming from my bedroom. It sounded as though something got knocked over. I jerk my head up, listening carefully but I hear no other sound. The hair on the back of my neck prickles and every one of my senses intensifies as a balmy sweat begins to drip down my neck. I stand up and turn around slowly, apprehensively peering through my slightly opened door where I can only see darkness. When I move, I step on floorboards carefully so they won't creak, until I can look through the dark gap between the door and the frame, but I see only moonlight shining upon my ragged bed cover. Slowly, I push the door open and it squeaks more loudly than I would have liked.

"Who's there?" I demand sharply, feigning confidence.

A large hairy figure steps into the moonlight and I reach in beside the door to grab the container that contains my fireflies and shake them to life. My room gradually lights up enough for me to see a large creature covered in hair from head to toe. It has a long beard, a round stumpy body with long limbs and large hands and feet. I have a strange feeling I have seen him before. His bloodshot eyes look out from an age-worn face.

"Who are you? And what are you doing in my bedroom?" I demand, staying near the door. The shock of the unexpected visitor, with his ghastly appearance, started me shaking. I squeeze the door handle so I don't look so afraid when in fact, I don't dare move out of fear of what he might do. The odd looking creature fidgets, and is extremely agitated.

"I have come here to warn you, Taura Andreas," he croaks. His eyes dart around, as if, in spite of his large appearance he is insecure. I inch along the wall to grab the metal poker from the fireplace near my door. With that in my hand and not taking my eyes off the creature, I listen to see if Adonis has come in before carefully shutting the door behind me.

"How do you know my name? Who are you? And where did you come from?"

It jiggles in place and then takes a quick glance out my bedroom window. He shuts his eyes and shakes his head. "No, no, no! None of that matters right now. You must heed my warning...you have a secret power, even if you are not aware of it yet. When you do begin to recognize its growing presence, you must remember what I say. Its evil and you must never use it or tell anyone about it. Suppress it if you must, just do what you have to so that no one ever learns of its existence. Do you understand me?"

"Huh?" I didn't understand. "What do you mean? Is it a side effect from my medicine?"

He shakes his head. "No it's not. It is a power you must never unleash for if you do, there will be tragic repercussions. Many zodiacs will die, even the ones you love. Do you understand me, Taura? Your life depends on it. You're in great danger."

I began to shiver. "Tell me why! Tell me about this power you say I have?"

His large hands thump on my bed with all the power of his frustration. "Just promise me you will not use it! Tell no one!" he demands.

I say nothing.

"Promise me!"

"Why? What will happen if I don't?"

He looks away and says, "You will die, Taura. Murdered, annihilated or torn apart by those who seek that power. Such supremacy causes those with blinded eyes to become greedy, want to control it and use it for themselves."

The creature becomes still and I feel my hair stand on end.

He looks me right in the eye and says, "Many will die... And you will be to blame. Now promise me!"

I hear Adonis come into the cottage, banging his dirty shoes on the floor and securing the rickety door. The creature looks at me intently.

I whisper, "Okay, I promise, but you must leave now."

He sighs with relief, nods and leaps to the windowsill. Holding the edge of the frame, he looks back at me, staring intensely and murmurs, "You cannot tell anyone about me or what I have told you, especially your father."

With a second leap, from his crouched position, he is out the window. I hear his footsteps, crunching grass and tree detritus, disappearing into the distance as the window shutters bang open against the wall.

Adonis strides into my room. "Taura, what are you doing? It's freezing outside." He storms past me and up to the window. I scamper after him, wanting to be sure the creature is out of sight. I grab his large arm but he rips it away and scowls at me. I jump on my bed and peer out the window, the creature is gone. I sigh with relief and sit back on my bed.

"For goodness sake, Taura, what's gotten into you? You haven't touched your supper. It's very important you maintain the little sustenance you have and are you trying to catch pneumonia?" He closes and secures the shutters and rubs his shoulders, chilled by the cold. He picks up the old thick blanket folded at the end of my bed that my mother Penelope had knitted when she was with child and wraps it around me. "You must stay warm, it's going to be a cold night."

Adonis leaves, but I remain on my bed, reaching up to open the shutters a crack to peer out the window for a short time, but there was nothing to be seen and only fading reminisce of footsteps. What was that creature on about, a secret power?

"You have a secret power you do not know of as yet...you must know its evil and never use it and tell know one...many will die... And you will be to blame...you cannot tell anyone about this, especially your father..."

My swirling thoughts slow; why didn't I tell my father? And why did I have this churning feeling in my gut? Maybe it is a side effect from my potion? The word illusion lingers in my head. I take a deep breath, not able to make any sense of it all. How did it know my name? Was the encounter all just a dream? And why did I feel as though I recognized him?

Looking from my bed, through my door, I see Adonis bring in a load of freshly cut firewood. He never says much, using words only when needed. He reveals a lot more by his actions.

I remember a time when I was younger; it was late and I had had a terrible day at the Halls of Ivy. Isa had been especially cruel to me that day, after she had caught me staring at a large bruise on her eye that appeared to be infected. I knew she trains hard but it appeared whoever had beaten her up was just as angry, judging by that eye. I sat in this exact spot, sobbing. Adonis came in without saying a word, wrapped the same blanket around me, and took my hand, indicating we were going for a walk. I had asked him where we were going but he just said, "You'll see."

We walked to the farthest part of the Constellation on the highest mound. He picked me up, then laid me down on my back. He lay next to me, submerging my small hand within his and staring up into the stars. He didn't mention the events of the day, but began to point out the Taurus zodiac alignment in the sky, then the others we could see, telling me how each Constellation resides beneath their glowing astral stars. He pointed with his index finger and said, "Each astral star was one of the first of our kind and now they watch over us."

"They must not watch over me," I'd replied.

He didn't say anything to counter my comment. Instead he picked up my tiny hand with his index finger and thumb and lifted it to the sky directing it at the Taurus alignment.

"How could they not," he'd remarked.

I sighed, feeling my father did not understand. Why would the gods watch over those who were never deemed worthy?

"Why am I not like everyone else?" I asked.

Adonis didn't answer my question. "You don't want to be like everyone else, my dear."

This comment made me mad. I rolled over, glaring at him and snapping back, "Well, that's stupid, why wouldn't I want to be a natural great warrior? I'm weak, small, and unable to defend myself. Like today, I looked pathetic. Everyone hates me."

I instantly regretted yelling at the one person who truly loved and cared for me. But once again Adonis kept his composure. I sighed, rolling back to stare once more at the stars. "I'm sorry, Dad."

Adonis glanced at me from the side, calmly rolled over and said, "One day you'll know how special you really are, but until that day, enjoy this time for what it is."

For some reason I always felt that advice had true relevance. I still did not understand, but I hadn't press further. I stay with that memory for a while as I stared at the carefully knitted patch work on my mother's blanket. Then I remembered what my father had said after I came home from the Doh today.

"Sometimes we have to look beyond what we see in front of us. Be patient, my dear. I'm sure all will be explained to you in good time."

Does my father know about this secret evil power?

I pull the blanket about my shoulders, thinking I should go spend some time with him before the trials tomorrow. I slide off my bed, which creaks as I stand. I return to the warm living room and sit down to continue eating my now cold supper. I look at Adonis who stands still in front of the fire, his back towards me, lingering its warmth.

"Dad?"

I wait for a moment. He remains still except for moving his head slightly to one side. His shadow casts upon the wall next to me, over-exaggerating his already large muscular frame.

"Yes, my girl? What is it?"

I watch him curiously as he did not turn to face me. Something seems off about him tonight. I see him rubbing something in his jacket pocket and I remember how he carries a picture of my mother around with him.

"Tell me a story about my mother, Penelope."

Adonis stops rubbing the picture and takes his hand from his pocket. He places both hands on the bench in front of him, and hunches over. I have never asked about my mother, only accepted what he has told me which wasn't much. I can tell it hurts him to speak about her, but I feel this is the right time to learn more about who I truly am and remove my uncertainties.

Adonis sighs, glancing at me, "If you eat the rest of your supper."

He waits and I begin eating my cold and now uninviting meal.

"What would you like to know?"

I continue eating my soup pondering on what question to ask as I know he won't allow me to stay on this topic for long.

"How did you fall in love?"

He thinks for a moment, then rolls his shoulders back and relaxes. "Penelope was beautiful. I first saw her in the Halls of Ivy on the first day of school and I remember admiring her beauty from a child's point of view. She was quite a few years older and she always took the time to say hello. I never said anything, I only stared back at her bewildered as to why this beautiful Taurus girl was talking to me. I was a quiet calf, never said much."

Not much has changed, I decided.

He continues, "I was always determined and focused on the task at hand. Somehow, she seemed taken by me as the years went on, not that I noticed, daft male I was. I don't know why, there were many qualified older suitors. I never showed an interest back. I was too focused on passing the trials, doing well in Orbis Bellum fights, and qualifying as an SNC. For many decades, I continued to serve Nirvana, until the duty when I was sent out to deal with another encounter with the Infernum, it was..." he paused and my mouth opened in anticipation. My father has never spoken about my mother or even mentioned his interactions with the Infernum, only stressed that I was never to venture outside the Constellation walls. He sighed again, continuing to gaze into the fire. "It was, torturous, Taura. I am still haunted by that particular incident today and now I must face it every day...reminded. But after that day, I realized there was more to life. Penelope had never married, or allowed other males to court her. For some reason, she waited for me. Knew I'd eventually come around. So, I accepted Penelope's love and wondered why it had taken me so long to see it. Soon after, you were born and she gave her life for you..."

He said no more and I stirred the soup with my spoon, taking in the story. Why had that event tortured him so? My father, the great Adonis Andreas, humble, never bragging about his achievements. I don't dare ask, as I know he would only end the conversation by sending me to bed.

This was the most information I've ever gotten from him, so instead I ask, "What was she like? My mother?"

My father lifted his right hand, swiped at what I presume to be a tear, the first tear I'd ever see him shed. "She was kind, your mother, patient, always giving. Even when she could see someone was using her. She continued to give until the end... she was perfect...she is you." He takes a big breath and sighs.

I ask no more questions; instead, I decide to sit in the blissful silence with my father. I know I'd touched a wound he'd been keeping closed for many years and I did not wish to open it further. I didn't want to see the only man I have ever loved in pain. After all, he is my hero.

I finish my supper and Adonis picks up my bowl and spoon and puts them in the basin to wash.

"Alright, time for bed, you have a big day tomorrow."

I pull the blanket up on my shoulders, yawning as I went into my bedroom. After spreading the blanket over my bed, I glance at the window, pondering on the creature who had come uninvited into my room. I decided to make sure the shutters were secure before hopping under the covers. I chose to forget about what the creature had said, feeling sure I would know if I had some hitherto secret evil power.

Adonis walks in, pulling my wooden chair over beside my

bed. "My girl, I know you have struggled with the differences between you and other zodiacs, but it is just that almost all of them just don't like different. It scares them. So, don't underestimate yourself. There is more to you than you yourself can yet imagine. I love you."

He gives me a drawn out kiss on the forehead. His eyes are shut as if he fears his thoughts will escape that way. Then turning quickly away as though already regretting the words, he leaves the room without another sound. When he pulls the door closed, he leaves a slight crack to let the light seep in as he has done since I was a baby. I am never fond of the darkness, it reminds me of the Uncharted Forest that sits beyond the tall wall we can see from our backyard.

I can sense dad lingering at the door for a moment, before his slow and heavy footsteps move away. I have never seen my father act the way he has tonight, something must be haunting his thoughts. Maybe I shouldn't have asked about my mother. He appears to be reliving the event all over again. And what is it about the memory of that last day he served as SNC for the Nirvana Army that scares him so? My father, Adonis Andreas.

I pull my hands from under the covers, analysing them. What will I create or destroy with them? What do they say about me?

"You have a secret power," the words unwillingly flooding back into my thoughts. I roll to my side, staring at my hands, eyes heavy, unaware of my exhaustion. The heaviness quickly consumes me.

I awake suddenly, screaming. My door slams open.

"Taura!"

My father is standing at my bedroom door with an axe, held at a ready. Sweat drips down my forehead, and my sheets are soaked through. It is that dream again, it's becoming more distinct every time, as though I am reliving a memory. That woman's face is so vivid, that I have to take a second look at the picture of my mother Penelope on my bedside table to make sure it is not her.

"*Tu es via, veritas et vita. Nemo venit ad Patrem, nisi per te.*" I hear again.

I take a big deep breath, closing my eyes. Adonis drops the axe on the floor, comes quickly over and kneels beside my bed to enfold me in his arms. "It was that dream again, wasn't it?"

I nod without saying a word and he rubs my head, pressing my hair against my sweaty neck. He holds my head to him with the palm of his large callused hand, so rough it scrapes against my soft skin, unconditioned for such toughness.

We stay like that for a while, and when I start to pull away, he pulls out a small green vial from his pocket and gestures me to open my mouth. Used to obeying him, I do and he slowly pours it down my throat. I nearly regurgitate it all but I know the medicine is important, although I've never seen it in a fancy vial like that before. As I control the urge to vomit, I fixate on the wooden panel at the end of my bed to keep the nausea at bay. It is visible in the amber glow from the warm fire that Adonis has already rekindled ready for the morning. I realize now, that he has done this every morning since I can remember; so, I'm not impacted by the chill of the morning's frost. Odd, it is only now that I am leaving, I appreciate the great lengths my father has gone to, to keep me safe. He must love me as much as I love him.

Adonis stands back up, appearing to be his usual self this morning.

"I purchased a hundred of these green vials yesterday," he told me, holding up the now empty vial, "I spent all night making a large batch of your medicine so you can keep your dosage up while you're away doing your studies for the Olympus Trials."

He takes a moment before he speaks again, then looks at me intently, "And Taura, while I believe immensely in your capabilities and in who you are, you must keep aware of the limitations due to your condition. Remember that. It's very important. Your life is very precious and delicate."

I don't know what to say so I only nod and let the nausea slowly subside. He seems to be waiting for an answer. I look up at him. His attitude has hardened since last night, almost as if he feels he has to make up for being too soft.

"Yes, Dad, I understand,"

He nods sternly. "Good, and one other thing, this too is incredibly important... you must never, and I mean never, tell anyone within the Doh of this medicine as it could be used against you. Do you understand?"

I nod assertively.

"Good, because I'm very serious about that detail. Now I've made your breakfast. Hurry, otherwise it'll get cold." He walks out of the room and I notice my bag is already packed and ready. Presumably it is crammed with those vials of medicine as I have already taken my necessities to the Doh yesterday.

After I've dressed in the same old clothes I wear every day and recall the events of the night before, I walk out of my bedroom with the very heavy backpack. Adonis places a bowl of hot porridge on the table, with bits of residue from the hot pan floating amongst the grains. The same old wooden spoon is placed beside it and I now empathize with the term 'ignorance is bliss'. After being exposed to yesterday's delicacies, I understand the impacting turmoil my father carries with him. The constant inability to provide for his child, what others have so much of.

I sit down feeling the weight of the day ahead and begin eating the lukewarm porridge, feeling the cold stone beneath my feet. I wonder how Adonis makes the vials not clink together. Opening the bag, I notice he's stuffed small strands of straw between them – clever. After I've finished, I place my dish in the sink and look at Adonis who stares out the window beside me.

"Dad, will I be able to see you during the trials?" There is a long quiet moment, as though he wished I hadn't spoken.

He answers without turning away from the window. "Unfortunately not, as the Elders feel it may interfere with the way you perform. But I'll see you when you need to replenish your vials of medicine, or I'll have someone who can be entrusted bring them to you."

Adonis walks over to the front door, opening it until it jams against the ground. The sunshine crawls in and the heat of the morning sun warms my cold face.

"Okay, my girl, it is time to go," he says, looking at me with unconditional love. My eyes begin to well up and as I walk slowly toward the door, standing at the front entrance, I embrace him, not wanting to go. Unable to get my small arms to fit around his waist, I squeeze as tight as I can and breathe in the scent of him. He stiffens then relaxes, rubbing my back as I unwillingly release my grip. A single tear drips down my face and he crouches down, wiping it away with his large rough thumb. He kisses me on the forehead.

"You'll be just fine and you'll see me sooner than you know," he promises, standing up so he can, guide me out the door.

Adonis smiles. I take a few steps, hearing the creak of the door and the clunk as it shuts behind me. I linger for a while then I take a deep breath, feeling the fresh air of the morning fill my lungs. I feel the gravel beneath my feet and have the memories of last night filling my head. Had it just been a figment of my imagination to believe I am something that I'm not? I guess worrying about it won't bring me any answers, only time will tell and I'll take it from there. I begin walking up to the Halls of Ivy, pausing briefly to turn for a memorizing look at the cottage. Adonis is staring through the small front window. I raise my hand to wave, but before I can, he's gone and all I can see is darkness within the house. Creasing my eyebrows, I try not to think too much on it and continue walking.

I reach the Halls of Ivy and see Demetrius standing at the front waiting. His brows rise as I approach.

"Are you ready?"

I nod, still feeling the weight of the last twenty-four hours.

"Good, everyone is inside."

As I am about to pass him, he adds, "And Taura..." he pauses, his face betraying regret after the words left his mouth, "...never mind, I'll meet you inside."

I felt myself frowning at his odd behaviour, but instantly dismissed it. I needed to think on what was to happen today. As I walk in the classroom, the air is full of dust, disturbed by restless feet. I notice a large map of Nirvana drawn with chalk on the wooden boards of the floor. Whoever had drawn the emblem hadn't been a very good illustrator as it's barely circular. Isa, Dalton and Henrietta stand together in their usual small group. Kendall stands by a window, patiently waiting and still looking distant, as he had since the forest. Sunshine illuminates the dust in the air and Europa is analysing the terribly drawn chalk picture. Demetrius' footsteps stamp loudly from behind me, echoing through the preceding hall.

"Alright, everyone, gather 'round!"

Europa now notices me and runs over to stand by my side, grinning in excitement. She gives me a hello expression then draws her attention towards Demetrius who now stands in the middle of the badly drawn Nirvana map, right where the Doh should be located.

"Okay, everyone, I'm going to need you to stand within the Taurus Constellation."

The sector where our Taurus emblem is drawn is uncomfortably small. I don't know how all six of us will fit without bunching up tightly. Firstly, Isa steps on, then Henrietta and Dalton both scramble to stand beside her. It always appears their constant need for Isa's approval and direct attention is never about her but the thrill of being better than the other; it makes Isa feel important and so their relationship always feeds each other's egos. After Kendall steps on, I follow Europa, trying to stand as far away from Isa as possible.

Once we were huddled close, Demetrius says, "Good, now place your middle and index finger on the back of your necks where your purpose numbers are and repeat what I say."

I place my two fingers on the back of my neck and I outline the number ten with their tips, '*Who are you?*' my subconscious questions. The number begins to pulsate slowly with heat as though it recognizes my touch.

Demetrius goes on, "Close your eyes, chant with me and visualize the dormitory from yesterday and whatever you do, don't open your eyes until I say so." His voice is stern, and he shuts his eyes and begins, "Unum, Unum, Unum, Unum, Unum."

He appears to go into a trance. Kendall starts to chant next and then we are all chanting together with our eyes shut.

"Unum, Unum, Unum, Unum, Unum."

I suddenly cannot tell up from down, and it seems as though I'm floating. My purpose number now feels very hot, not enough to hurt me but enough to know its distinct presence. Then a warm sensation slowly crawls over my body and in an unexplained way, I feel I am here but I am not, until I am gone.

CHAPTER FIVE

THE THEORY BEHIND NUMBER TEN

When pursuit ignites, adventure takes flight.

My feet are now planted firmly upon a hard smooth surface but my hands are shaking; my eyes are still securely shut and I wonder if I'll ever get used to the teleportation disorientation.

"Alright, you can open your eyes now," Demetrius' deep toned voice commands. But I still don't open them until I feel an object skim past my nose at an unearthly rate. Reflexes immediately make my eyes spring open as my heart begins to pound through my chest. My whole body goes stiff, bracing to fight or flee until I see what lays before me.

"A library," I whisper under my breath; my body relaxes and I become entranced. But the library books appear to be alive - one tall old book floats in front of me; it has large eyes but no mouth. It looks down referring to its title, *Language of the Purpose Numbers*. Its eyes nearly squeeze shut as though it were smiling at me, then it darts away amongst the other books that whiz around, up near the tall ceilings, as zodiacs walk around on the floor. The huge and magnificent chamber is filled with floors upon floors, staircases upon staircases of books. At most of the multitude of tables, zodiacs are sitting reading or studying. Others are chasing their desired book around the room, like the book is freely teasing them.

I watch a particular Gemini as he moved along a case of books, trying to catch a large book that hovers at the other end. He begins to split, I guess it is to try and outsmart the book. As he rips himself apart directly down the middle, I wince at the method as body parts crack, pop, rip, and tear. Mucus drops on to the ground once the two sides are separate, the liquid looking much like residue from a placenta. Even in pictures, this process looks painful. A young Gemini can really struggle to control both his yin and yang once split. This Gemini appears to have great control over both; he must have had considerable practice. I watch as his yang goes down one aisle and yin goes down the other, attempting to flank the book. The book glances to each side, then pushes its back against the wall, sliding up with a taunting expression. The yin and yang agilely tiptoe and spring from around each corner and simultaneously the book flies up. The book looks down and bounces with amusement. The Gemini, now entangled between its yin and yang, slowly morphs back into one entity with both sides having a frustrated expression; it curses the book that levitates above.

I turn, hearing Demetrius talking to himself. "This wasn't supposed to be the destination, how did this happen?"

The others had also been looking around and were now slowly breaking away from the huddle.

Demetrius says, "Hey! Don't go wandering off. I have to go check when you're needed in the dining room. Don't get lost. Stay together until I return."

We all nod as he stomps across the room. To leave, he has to pull open two large, heavy doors with beautiful golden handles. I can see they have been designed to look like an open book's pages. The doors groan open as his back muscles contract and ripple, demonstrating his sheer masculine strength. He leaves the doors wide open and they begin to close by themselves, coming together with a deep toned thud. We all glance over for a moment, but no one else looks up from what they were doing.

Europa moves next to me. "Is he ever in a good mood?"

I shrug as she follows up with, "Seriously, have you ever seen that guy crack a smile. Probably doesn't find jokes funny either."

I laugh. "To be honest, they'd probably go straight over his head."

She laughs too and nods in agreement. "How amazing is this place! Who ever thought books could come alive? Just your kind of pastime."

She winks at me but before I reply, I notice the book that had brushed past me when I arrived, idly floating not too far away from me.

I grab Europa. "C'mon, I want to get that book."

She unexpectedly holds back, then tentatively follows.

"Wait, we're not supposed to leave the group!" she yells out after me.

I don't take my eyes off the book as it now darts away, yelling back, "Since when have you cared about not supposed to?"

I hear her suddenly pick up her pace to catch up to me. *That's what I thought.*

As we need to keep our eyes on the book while on the chase, we knock into other zodiacs who become annoyed with our recklessness and seeming lack of respect.

One Sagittarian yells, "Watch it, you heavy footed cows!"

Europa, who now runs beside me, turns back and pokes her tongue out. The book glancing back, now realizing how close we are to catching it, darts down a narrow passage between two shelves. Appearing to have the book trapped, we both stand side by side, trying to block any spaces with our arms held wide. It dances about appearing uncertain about where to go next and just as we come into arm's length, it bounces up and over our heads.

"Damn it!" I remark.

Then out of nowhere, a strange creature pounces on it from above, flattening the book to the ground. It was only half the size of the book, with wings as small as its head, and a long thin beak. Even though the book kept bouncing around at floor level, the small creature kept a tight grip, with its dangly arms, until the book gave up and completely stopped.

When the creature stood from a crouch, it revealed a skinny hairless body, gangly legs as well as hands and feet with long, narrow digits.

Europa and I look at one another in a 'what the heck' expression and begin to approach. The creature carefully opens the book and slides its fingers delicately over each page, transferring bugs to its beak, or causing moths to fly out. These are quickly gobbled up, and savoured for a brief moment, then the creature goes back to its urgent work. We stand staring at it.

Europa whispers to me, "That's one ugly...imp?" without taking her eyes away. The creature, so far undisturbed by our presence, turns its back on us and makes a high-pitch grunting noise.

Unexpectedly, a confident voice tells us, "He's a Liber Emundans, which means 'Book Purifier,' but we just call him Emun. He cleans all the books in this library. He lives on the bugs and moths from the books he cleans. Full-time job, but he takes it very seriously. Oh, and I'll warn you now, he doesn't like being called imp. He believes it is a vast misconception and massive insult."

I look up to see an elderly female Gemini, wearing large glasses that are broken at the bridge and fixed up with an unnecessary amount of tape as though she got too excited in the process. The glasses do not fit her but they emphasize the malevolent white and innocent black eyes that reside side by side. The white side of her hair is now grey and the black is now a dark blackish grey, and on both sides it is incredibly long, almost touching the ground. It seems she does not care for her appearance as it is an unbrushed, tangled mess. Her thin lips give her a harried look. However, her glasses, although well overdue for replacement, exaggerate the size of her eyes and give her a knowledgeable appearance. She quickly notices me watching her, as a Gemini does not miss a thing, and I quickly take my attention away from her untidy appearance.

Europa asks, "Who are you?"

The old Gemini lady, her white side turned more our way, smiles enthusiastically, seeming to be excited about what she's is about to say. "Well, I'm the one who runs this place! I'm Bibliotheca, but everyone calls me Bib. I'm the Librarian. I noticed you both recklessly running after this particular book, so I was going to tell you off. Or at least get the book for you before you knock one of the shelves over. But I can see Emun has already helped you out." She moved, and her malevolent side faced us, "When you first walked in, you should have seen the sign that says no running. But I've learnt the new-bloods need a little guidance at first." She sounded impatient and annoyed. She looked around the large library, probably searching for our overseer.

Bib turns around again. "I've read every book in this place and I'm now over half way through reading it all again for the five hundred and twenty-six thousandth time. Need something to keep this old mind sharp, you know what I'm saying?"

She winks tapping the white side of her head and adds, "I love a good challenging question! So, if you need any help, I'm your lady."

She smiles warmly and smile lines crease her white face. I've never seen a zodiac as old as her; she must have been here since the dawn of time.

Europa puts her hand out to shake. "Well, I do apologize. I'm Europa and this is my best friend Taura. She was adamant about getting that book."

Bib puts her old wrinkled and knuckled hand out and shakes Europa's at an unbelievable rate, making her arm jiggle with incredible speed.

"Well, I wouldn't expect any less from a Taurean, always up for the challenge. But next time let's do it without galloping around, okay?" she advised.

Europa smiles, slightly ashamed, and I notice Emun has finished cleaning the last page and is closing the book ever so gently. But before the book has a chance to fly off again, Bib splits her yin and yang so fast down the middle as though it's a natural process during her everyday activities, when it is normally quite challenging to a Gemini. The yin black stays beside us, closely watching us with a highly disapproving expression, as yang white enthusiastically grabs the book and returns to merge back into one entity again. While still holding the book, she takes her glasses and presses them back together – into the mess of tape at the centre. She puts them back on the high bridge of her nose, but with the tape, they don't fit very well. Both eyes read the title: *Language of the Purpose Numbers.*

The white eye, of her black side, enlarged by the glasses, looks at me from above the brim of the book. "That's interesting, you would have learnt about the purpose numbers in the Halls of Ivy..." she pauses for a moment, eyeing me sceptically. "You must realize this book has a much wider range of information." She turns slightly so it seems the other personality adds, "Very good, it will probably answer the purpose you seek then."

She hands the book to me and smiles, wrinkles ever so deep up close. A part of me wants to ask her age, but I don't dare. "Thank you," I say quietly, barely raising my voice.

She places her hands behind her back, standing up as tall as she can and says, "My pleasure, now remember, if you have any questions, please don't hesitate to ask."

Then she turns to walk away and I notice a large scar down her back as though electricity had struck her. I don't dare ask, but Europa blurts it out. Obviously unable to contain herself, "Miss Bib...what happened to your back?"

My eyes widen and I look at Europa in shock. Bib glances back, both sides of her face expressionless, and says, "That is for another time...when your attitude is less parochial, and your minds less hidebound." She walks away.

I abruptly look at Europa. "You shouldn't have asked such a personal question."

Europa shrugs, "She didn't seem to be bothered. Besides, you wanted to know just as much as I did."

I don't argue because she was right. Instead, I examined the book. It looked ordinary now, the eyes I had seen no longer apparent. "C'mon, I want to read this before Demetrius gets back."

Europa replies, "Okay, but if I knew a book could make you run so fast, I would have thrown one into training long ago."

I suddenly realized, I had been running faster than Europa, which has never happened before. I'd always believed I was so weak and ineffectual. The words from the night before, spoken by that strange creature enter my mind, *"You have a secret power."*

We find a table amongst hundreds dedicated to studying. *Does this place ever end*, I wonder.

As Europa sits next to me, she asks, "Why is this book so important anyway?"

I realize I hadn't told her any of the events that happened from the night before, but I'm not sure if it was even real. But why was that creature so familiar? I go quiet for some time, staring at the book, then I look at her intensely.

"What's wrong?" Europa prompts.

I begin to explain what happened when I got home. I didn't look at her, as I told her about the incident, but summed up with, "So when I saw this book, I thought it might have some answers. The purpose number '10' might give me some insight to why I am the way I am. Just seemed too ironic that it was the first book to float in front of my face. It was as though it knew I was wanting to know. When I saw it I had a feeling it might give me answers."

When I look up, her face is unreadable but she must be as confused as I was.

"The creature didn't tell you what the power was?"

It warmed me that she was not even doubting my story. I shake my head.

She looks at the book coming to some sort of conclusion, "Surely Adonis would know, did you ask him?"

"No, the creature said I should not speak of this to anyone, especially my father."

Her eyebrows raised. "And you believed him?"

Hearing her say it, made me think. "I don't know. Adonis was acting weird last night. I couldn't bring myself to ask him. I can't explain it."

Europa nods slowly. "Okay then. Well, let's take a look at this book, surely there'll be some answers," she remarks brightly. I always feel comforted by her optimistic vibe.

Opening the book, I realize how old and decayed it is. The heavy front-page lands hard on the table, but it's immaculately clean from Emun. As I start flipping through the pages, I notice they are all blank. Europa and I stare at each other, completely disconcerted. I return to the first page, sighing.

"Not even a table of contents? Prologue? Nothing?" I remark defeated. Instantly, just after those words slip from my mouth, words begin to appear on the page. As if typing itself out for the very first time.

Table of Contents
Purpose Numbers:
Purpose Number One
Purpose Number Two
Purpose Number Three
Purpose Number Four
Purpose Number Five
Purpose Number Six
Purpose Number Seven
Purpose Number Eight
Purpose Number Nine

Master Numbers
Master number '11'
Master number '22'
Master number '33'

The Theory Behind Purpose Number '10', Chapter 13

My eyes widen, planting my index finger on '*The Theory Behind Purpose Number '10.'*

Europa grins. "Quickly! Flick to page 180."

I begin flicking through, 110, 150, 165, 179...191. I flick back, looking closer I realize the pages between 180 and 190 have been ripped out, obviously in a hurry. I remorsefully touch the jagged pieces left behind. Whoever did this, clearly wanted no one to ever know about this strange number, just as no one wanted to talk about it either. Either way, pointedly ignoring the fact that I had that number planted distinctly on the back of my neck. Europa been silent since seeing the torn pages, probably finding no comforting words. We both sit back and sigh.

"There you are! I told you to stay in a group!" Demetrius's, loud annoyed voice startled us. "Come on, we're already late." He turns and walks away, expecting us to follow, while everyone nearby stares at us. Europa starts to follow but I don't want to leave the book behind. I consider my pack. There is a pouch at the front, with just enough room to fit the book. Whilst no one is looking, I shove it into my bag and catch up to Europa.

Demetrius leads our group through the big doors to the dining room. Everyone from the other Constellations, as well as the Elders are already seated. Only our table is vacant. Those at nearby tables, blatantly project impatient stares our way. Demetrius bows respectfully in the direction of Theophilus, who stands at the head of the Elders' table.

"Apologies, Patriarch and Matriarch, we were unfortunately teleported to the library. I am unable to explain why but I understand that is no excuse."

Theophilus remains silent and expressionless. For a moment, I am sure he glances my way. He gestures for us to take a seat.

Once again, an abundance of food awaits us. Even though we are all famished, we are hesitant to begin as no one else is. Theophilus, still standing, looks around, almost torturing us for being disrespectfully late. Then he nods, taking his seat and everyone digs into breakfast. The room becomes lively with conversation and other Constellations begin to converse amongst themselves. Taureans are not ones to chat when there is food around as we are more preoccupied with filling our stomachs.

Europa whispers at me with a mouth full of food. "I wonder who would go out of their way to tear those specific pages out."

I shrug, wondering the same thing. "I'm not sure, but now I'm starting to regret not asking my father."

I chew some more on my food. "Although I'm not sure he would even tell me...if it's as evil as that creature says it is. Knowing Adonis, he'd probably try to save me from the heartache, and address the situation, himself, without my knowing."

"Thwack!"

Audible over the buzz of conversation and chewing, the sound drew our attention to where Kendal was raising his head and looking around. A glob of porridge like food is plastered against the back of his head. We all turn to see where the food came from and I'm instantly captivated by the colours red and scarlet from the Aries Constellation as they laugh amongst one another, punching one particular Aries playfully. That one has bright red hair that's cropped short topping a young face with a chiselled jawline. He's a typical Aries, ardently strong. Even though none of them look their actual age, each of them being a child of the zodiac also explains their mischievousness.

Isa enraged, stands abruptly and almost topples her seat. "Well, aren't you going to do something about that, Kendall? I mean he just disrespected us. You must put him in his place!"

Kendall, who still hasn't spoken since the Uncharted Forest, wipes his hand on his trousers and shrugs. He didn't attempt to wipe off the remnants still left on the back of his head, just went back to eating.

Moving to stand over him, Isa goads, "Stop being so pathetic, Kendall. We have all lost loved ones. Grow a backbone for crying out loud."

It sounds as though she is speaking from experience. But I didn't know she had lost anyone; both her parents are still alive and she only hangs out with Henrietta and Dalton. I wonder who she speaks of.

Without warning, Kendall launched himself at her, holding her by the throat and slowly squeezing her airway, all the while looking intently into her eyes.

"Just because you've turned your sadness into resentment, doesn't mean we all have to do the same. You have no backbone and you thrive through hurting others. That's not strength, that's sheer weakness. Now leave me be!"

Angry tears well in his eyes. He gives her a push as he releases her, slumps back down, and places his elbow on the bench covering his face and pretends to eat. But I've noticed little of the food heaped on his plate has been touched, only played with as he slowly chews the tiniest of pieces. Isa slinks back to sit at her seat, stubbornly silent, red faced and scowling. I know Kendall only spoke the truth, she does like hurting others, but this is the first time someone has accused her to her face, in public. Her demeanour isn't a good sign, she'll sit there and stews upon her embarrassment. The rest of us say nothing and try to continue eating as though nothing happened.

I look up at the Elders, who don't appear to have noticed anything, too preoccupied within their own conversation, no doubt. But as I look, Theophilus turns his head in my direction, making eye contact. I look away quickly, feeling incredibly inferior to he who is at the top of the Doh's hierarchy.

I glance over at Isa. Her expression hasn't eased, she is livid with anger and ignoring the food on her plate. Europa whispers to me, "If she refuses to eat, I know we're in for a whole lot more trouble."

I agree but say nothing, not wanting to be the focal point of Isa's outburst. It looks as if she's going to explode any minute. At the next table, the Aries are celebrating, butting heads and mucking about. I am surprised that no one tells them to sit quietly.

After our bellies are full, Theophilus stands again.

"I hope you enjoyed that delicious meal. You should take advantage of every meal to stay fit and strong during your trials. You won't just be learning theory, you'll be tested physically too. In fact, today you'll get to experience the fighting arena, up in the Orbis Bellum. In time you'll get to fight one another there to enhance your abilities, power, and skill in combat. But that'll be later on once you've learnt the basics of one another's strengths and weaknesses. Since today is your orientation, you'll be meeting your Capricorn mentor and they'll take you through a short class to brief you on your studies. They teach a little differently from what you're used to, unless you're from the same Capricorn region but they are the best mentors. So make sure to embrace the opportunity. It is to the benefit of all to understand one another, and the other lands, and especially to understand who you truly are. This all makes a strong unity, because without purpose and awareness of each other, we are doomed to the Infernum and that snake you know of as... Apophis. Now your SNC overseer will be taking you through this today. So, I wish you all the best. And let strength run beside you."

He brings his hands together and bows, showing off the magnificent wings that sit tightly behind his back, and I'm surprised they don't throw him off balance as he bends over. In fact, I wonder how old he is considering the magnitude of his wings. Virgos' wings grow in size with age and I have not seen any depictions in any books of a Virgo with the same wing dimensions as Theophilus, not even their ancestral zodiac.

Everyone stands, and Demetrius leads us out of the dining room. My thoughts drift towards the twirling stairs that curl around the Doh, praying the classes and Orbis Bellum aren't too far up. As we stand waiting for further instruction, I notice the same fiery redhead Aries approaching us, weaving agilely amongst the crowd of new-bloods. He has a large scar, which I did not notice before, across his left cheek. It must have been from a deep wound. A large fire tattoo climbs up from the base of his neck, the fire tips continuing up across the borderline of his face. He carries a bow around his body, but without any arrows. It must be some sort of statement. It's obviously too tight as it places an immense amount of pressure on his chest, skin bulging out either side of the thin bowline.

I elbowed Europa to look as he confidently wove his way towards Isa, and gave her a forceful shove. She stumbled to the side, nearly losing her footing. We could almost see the steam coming out of her nostrils. Now was not the time to anger her further.

"Aww aye, wit make ye hink ye dinnae huv tae stick tae the rules?" he says, slowly making eye contact with each of us in turn. "Hink yer better'n the rest o us?" he insinuates.

Surprised by the accent of the Aries, I was perplexed by what he said. It sounded like a challenge, but I didn't understand all of it. I didn't know they had such a strong twisted way of speaking.

He is joined by the other Aries new-bloods, all typical Aries, never afraid of confrontation, always up for a good fight. I know this is not personal. They're probably just bored and wanting to cause a bit of mischief. I notice Europa tensing up, as are Henrietta and Dalton, but Kendall just watches idly, unmoved by the situation. The red-headed Aries smirks, then he and the other eight Aries tense, readying themselves. All wanting this outlet for physical action.

Then with added arrogance the red head says, as though taunting us, "Ba th' wey, th' name's Manley Luther." He winks, probably knowing us Taureans have thin skin when it comes to those who challenge us, especially on a personal level. Or maybe their arrogance is just irritating in general when they're on a rampage of self-satisfaction.

Isa was barely holding herself in check and she probably didn't want to hear the sound of his voice any longer. Manly never saw her coming. While he and the others were still strutting with self-importance, she launched herself and gave him an upper-cut to the chin. And as if in slow motion, Manley flew up, his head leading and his body following. Moments later, he came smashing down into the ground.

The other Aries surged forward, heads lowered, enraged. Dalton, Henrietta and Europa charge up beside Isa and a fight begins. Feeling obligated to defend the honour of our Constellation, I feel my foot push forward, almost out of my control. But Adonis's voice seeps into my head as one foot steps in front of the other. *"You must still be aware of your limitations due to your illness, just always remember that. It's very important, your life is very precious and delicate."*

But I've made a commitment now, so I make my steps confident, as I stare at the long strawberry-blonde hair of one particular Aries. His face is riddled with obnoxious piercings – eyelids, ears and lips, and the tattoos on his arms and torso seem to move as his muscles bulge. He is scraping his hooves on the floor, taunting me, as if he is about to charge one who he must think is easy meat. Surely he can smell my fear from a mile away. While he watches me, waiting for my charge, my confidence completely diminishes. But my feet don't stop, for the embarrassment of running away would be unimaginable. Then by the grace of Unum, I am forcibly stopped by an immensely strong force that wraps itself around my waist, below my pack, and pulls me aside, out of fighting range, and into the surrounding crowd.

"We got to stop running into each other like this. And what's with this giganteas backpack? Talk about making things hard, you do like a challenge, don't you?" a familiar voice says. I wriggle around and my bag is nearly shoved off my shoulders. Pulling on the straps, I manage to turn and I'm not surprised to see the bright golden eyes of Leon Sol. He releases me. I don't choose to discuss my backpack.

"What are you doing?" I demand, imperiously.

"Ah...saving your life? Much like last time. You really have a knack for throwing your life around aimlessly." My lips purse together and he adds, "Oh come on, you and I, and the rest of the crowd know you couldn't have taken on that monstrous Aries, especially with that mound of junk on your back. Have you looked in a mirror lately?"

I cross my arms and glare at him. *It is not junk! Stupid cat.* I keep those thoughts to myself,

"Cute," he says with a wicked smile.

Deep down I agree with him, although I'd never admit it due to his egotistical appreciation of himself. It makes me more determined to fight. I feel steam coming out of my nostrils and a blind rage. I try to re-join the others, but he restrains me as though I am placed in a straitjacket, with him holding me a little off the floor with little effort.

"Put me down! Put. Me. Down... or I will curse you to the sin of Venus!" I insist. To my annoyance, he just chuckles. This damn Leo makes me so mad. I go limp as my angry energy dissipates. The crowd starts moving away and I notice through the thinning crowd that the fight is over. It appears to have been broken up by a calm and beautiful Libran who stands directly centre of the confrontation. Leon places me down and I watch Demetrius, who had pushed his way through to his suddenly still new-blood charges. I see him smacking the back of Isa's head in disapproval.

The SNC Aries overseer moves his group aside. I hear him yell, "Why are you young new-bloods so defiantly difficult to manage? Get a grip! Is this the way you want to represent our Constellation? Acting as brainless as a simple goat just looking to butt heads with others! Also, tighten your tongues. We use the Doh's dialect here, we're not at home any longer."

Maybe I am the only one who notices, but both the Aries and Taureans who were fighting look dazed as though they've been bewitched. Both sides are pretty banged up from the clash.

The Libran is clad in a long sleeved gown in Libra's Constellation colour blue, which has two white stripes strapped over each shoulder and draping either side to the floor were the gown ends. She has a very dark complexion with platinum blonde hair and white eyes contradicting their usual blue. She looks around the room, with her hands held gently together. As we all admire her exotic beauty, the aura in the room becomes warm and relaxing. I feel happy.

"My name is Harmonia Ishta and I am one of the few Libran Diplomats who reside within the Doh, to deal with quarrels within Constellations and outside, like the one you just witnessed. I encourage you to not condone this type of behaviour as only one warning is given. And this is that warning. If I have to settle another matter such as this one again, everyone involved will suffer the consequences. This is for the safety of you and everyone living within the Doh. This is a communal place and we can't have such behaviour breaking the unity that has taken so long to achieve."

Although she is straight to the point and unyielding in what she says, she speaks it in a very pleasing manner, soft and alluring to the ear. Her white eyes grow incredibly bright then diminish to their natural blue. The strong happy emotion fades but I now feel calmer within myself. Harmonia raises her right hand to the sky. A powerful flapping sound is heard and a fierce gust of wind presses our hair and clothes down. The cause is a large black bird, of a type I have never seen or read about before, It glides down the last distance, and I put my hand up to cover my face, protecting it from the strong wind it is still pushing at us. One of its large clawed feet grabs her hand and she is lifted into the air as the bird flaps to gain height. They fly high into the fading vision of the Doh's infinite twisting walls, until they are out of sight.

Everyone stands in complete awe or shock at what they had just experienced. It had been quite a noticeable phenomenon.

I murmur out loud, "Why were her eyes that glowing white?"

Leon leans towards me and whispers, "Surely you've read about their ability to control our minds?"

My eyebrows crease together. "Of course I have!" I realized now that I had previously read about the Libran's ability, but never had the chance to experience it in reality.

Leon smiles, "Well, Libran Diplomats are PNC authorized. They're not as strong as an SNC Libran, but they do have great influence over our emotional state. When their eyes glow that penetrating white, you know they are using it. That's why you feel so calm and happy right now."

I nod and ask, "How do you know so much?" I wondered if he reads as much as I do.

Everyone now starts to move along, guided by the overseers. As we move with the crowd. Leon says, "Let's just say I have a little bit of experience with this place." He winks at me again and I roll my eyes.

Abruptly, Demetrius turns, spotting me walking with the Leo who he has made clear he dislikes. He shoves his way through the crowd and they either get out the way or they're thrown to the side. The way he moves depicts the image of a raging bull. As he stands in front of us, panting heavily with anger, he says,

"What are you doing with her?"

Leon puts his hands up in the air patronizingly and says, "It's okay, I was just stopping her from committing arbitrary suicide."

Demetrius looks at me then looks at Leon, "Well, next time..." he pauses, appearing to be lost within words of anger, "don't." He grabs my arm to pull me away and I see Leon's expression become impatient as he jerks his head to the side in irritation and says, though the words fall unintentionally from his brain to his mouth, "Well, I didn't see you around."

The zodiacs in earshot gasp. No one ever talks back to an SNC overseer. We are taught to have respect for those who have dedicated their lives to mastering their skill in order to protect us. Especially overseers, they need to be strong to take care of multitude of unpredictable new-bloods who can't control their power or ability as yet.

Demetrius stops in his tracks, uses my arm to push me behind him, and walks purposely toward Leon with a livid countenance. He looks him straight in the eye. "I know exactly what you're up to, child. I warn you. Stay away from her."

Leon's eyes slightly crease but he does not look away from Demetrius' dominating presence. Although Demetrius may appear to have a much bigger frame, and tower over the Leo, I can't judge the comparison, because Leon is not in his large animalistic form. He could possibly be bigger than Demetrius after his transformation but the fact the Leon maintains his composure, makes a point in itself.

Demetrius takes my arm and drags me back to the group. He lets go and I didn't realize how hard he was holding me until the blood rushes back and my skin burns slightly from his hard grip. He crouches down to my height and looks me in the eye.

"Promise me you'll stay away from him," he insists.

I never normally question his authority but curiosity gets the better of me.

"Demetrius, I don't deliberately seek him out, it's as though he's following me...but, may I ask why I should avoid him?" His eyes rumple together in disappointment at this suggestion that

I do not have full confidence in him.

"I know...but his father is..." he looks around seeming to be somewhat nervous, an expression I've never seen him portray and continues, "not to be trusted...nor his son." His dire need to explain is underlined by a sense of fear which I cannot explain. So, I nod as he adds, "A cub never strays far from the loins of its Patar..." It suggests that there is a long story behind a history of events involving Leon.

After we finish climbing numerous flights of steps, that seems to take hours upon my now exhausted legs, as I am still carrying the heavy bag filled with my precious medicine, we finally reach our destination. 'Orbis Bellum,' is written above large doors that appear to be rotting and have patches of moss and tiny flowers growing from its weathered exterior. At a closer glance, it appears to be quite moist as though a leak may be the cause.

The Cancerians stand first in line, nearest the entrance.

"There appears to be no handle?" one of the group comments and I realize she's right.

Their male overseer steps forward and says, "Well, why don't you take a look for yourself?" He steps to the side and a new-blooded female Cancerian steps forward. From behind she has short black hair and a tiny frame.

Standing in front of the strange entrance, she cautiously extends her bone arm-blade from beneath her forearm, each serrated edge looking sharper than a newly made sword from the blacksmith. She pokes it with the sharp tip, creating narrow deep cuts. She then manoeuvres to slice it and bits cut easily from it, falling to the floor in front of her. Now with more confidence, she withdraws her spear back into her forearm and determinedly lifts bits of grass and overgrown weeds in search of some kind of knob or handle. Now suspicious, the Cancerian girl looks at her SNC overseer for guidance and he looks back encouragingly to continue. She places both hands on the decaying door and pressing her head against it, tries to listen through it.

In that moment, the flora comes alive, wrapping vines and roots around her wrists and ankles, then her waist, gently drawing her into itself. She panics and immediately extends bone blades from both forearms and attempts to cut herself free, but the bindings stop her, flattening the blades against the surface of the door.

Everyone is open-mouthed by what they're witnessing. Her Cancerian companions lunge towards the door, extending their arm-blades and attempting to cut the flora away from her, but their overseer abruptly says, "Leave her!"

With clear hesitation and dismay, they step back and do as commanded. The girl sinking into the door is rigid with terror, her pitch black eyes staring helplessly back at us. I become apprehensive watching as roots grow and twist hard around her mouth. More greenery continues to engulf her until she is gone, swallowed by the decaying door which quickly returns to its original state. All the Cancerians have backed up against the next group of zodiacs, some with their hands covering their mouths in astonishment and one with tears in her eyes. That one steps forward.

"What just happened?! Where is Naida!? Where is my sister? Is she okay? Tell me she is okay?" she says between broken sobs.

The Cancerian overseer steps forward with reassurance. "It's okay, Naida is fine. She is now within the safety of Orbis Bellum. The entrance you see before you is known as the Bainbridge Plant. It only accepts zodiacs who are harmonious and without bad intent. It protects the arena from bad creatures or entities such as the Infernum. The Bainbridge plant will resist those who attempt to cut through it, as you just saw. It has the ability to distinguish between good and bad energy by the vibration you exude. So, even though Naida apparently became hostile, it was aware her intentions were good. So, I suggest you to allow it to take you in, and don't let yourself be fearful.

"Technically, once absorbed and taken inside the arena, you cannot die or be harmed. You will still feel the pain of a harmful blow, but it's only simulated by your mind from what it's observing. In this way, you can practice your skills and abilities to the fullest extent, in safety."

Everyone looks at him in disbelief, still stunned by what they just witnessed. So he puts both hands up in forfeit and says, "I'll demonstrate. I'll attack it first, allowing it to put its guard up and then I'll back off and allow the negative energy to dissipate."

Both his bone swords extend aggressively from his forearms, making a humming noise, within our proximity. His back is facing us but he glances behind and says, "Step back." A pulsating aura begins to make a pronounced circle around him as dust and dirt circulates and pulsates away. Then a large oval blue shield is produced around his hard, lean, athletic frame.

A few of other new-bloods gasp, one commenting, "Cool!" in awe.

The Cancerian overseer now begins slashing and stabbing the wall. Leaves, wood, bark, flowers, and moss fly everywhere until we can no longer see where he stands. Then it all comes to a standstill and we can hear him breathing slightly faster as the mess settles. The moist, fragile wall appears to have been untouched with not a leaf fallen. His shield instantaneously disappears and he withdraws his spears back within his arms. Turning around he says, "Now watch as I allow myself to be taken without resistance."

He gracefully jumps back into the wall and he is held ever so gently by the flora as it pulls him in without hard restraints like Naida. Now all the Cancerians, one by one, allow themselves to be taken by the wall and as each one is consumed, those that follow become more relaxed and confident. We're up next; Europa bounds forward for the sheer thrill and eagerly allows herself to be taken, a big smile planted across her face as she yells, "Woohoo!!! This is cra—" and she is gone.

I'm next. Stepping forward I can now see more detail on the wall and I notice it breathes, exhaling with a wheezing, whistling noise. Trickling water falls within its cracks and collects in little pockets. Taking my right hand, I press it firmly against the wall, the soft rotten wood feels cold beneath my palm. Then stems of flowers begin curling around my wrist, sprouting as it twirls around my forearm. I nearly panic until I remember Naida's petrified face wrapped within the wreath of vines that were pulling hard against her mouth. I take a big breath telling myself to stay calm. I shut my eyes as I feel it subsume me gently, pulling me into the bounds of its diversity.

CHAPTER SIX

ORBIS BELLUM

Beware ignorance, it lays unconsciously beside one's ego.

I slide out the other side of the very strange Bainbridge plant and down into a puddle of slime. I peeled my arms from my sides and flicked a clump of the stuff onto the saturated ground, then used one hand to wipe the residue from my face. I peer at what I have on my hands. It doesn't seem to smell but the texture is clammy, clear, and thick. I turn around to look back at where I entered and see that this side of the Bainbridge plant appears to be in a state of decay as well. It climbs the walls, sprawling out from a dense area where I slid out. That part moves up and down as though it were a heart, pumping blood to the crawling stems that grow sporadically and cling to the wall, a depiction of a poorly built spider's web.

The Cancer new-bloods are mostly in a huddle with their overseer, but I see Europa standing, and talking peacefully, to a now relaxed Naida, the Cancer who entered first. I stand up, wiping off as much slime as possible and notice the place we now stand on is a large platform with the start of two wide sets of stairs, one beginning on each side, with a drop behind us. Europa notices me and waves me to come over. I try to move but find my feet are securely stuck within the heavy slime.

"You have to pull hard!" Naida calls. I try harder, but only manage to overbalance and fall flat on my face, making a pathetic splat. Europa runs over and helps me up.

"You alright?"

I nod and she lifts me out and slides me onto a non-sticky spot, where I can now walk easily. I follow her over to Naida and she introduces us.

"Naida Odette, this is my best friend Taura Andreas."

Naida, now with a friendlier demeanour, nods her head in acknowledgement and ignores the new layer of slime I had collected. "Nice to meet you," she says in a polite conservative way.

Her short black hair is now pulled back from her face, held there by the remains of the slime. She has beautiful porcelain skin; her mouth is small as though she naturally purses it all the time, and she has a tiny nose that surely isn't functional for breathing. An almost pixie appearance, overall. But it is her large black eyes that capture me. They go on forever, you could become lost within their darkness.

I notice Europa and Naida seem dry apart from their hair. Looking down, I see the slime still dripping off me in clumps. I look at Europa.

"How did you..." I begin to ask, but she points to the ground. A large slug-like creature was at the back of my heel trying to attach itself to me. I jump out of the way.

"What is that thing?" I yelp. It had a long and slimy body with big lips and large eyes attached to long muscular tubes that were extending endlessly up from its body.

"It's okay! It just sucks the slime off you," Naida explains.

The strange creature was sliding over towards me, its eyes analysing me from head to toe, twitching its big lips as if anticipating a delicious meal. I watched as it lifted its large lips and latched on to my heel, and felt the slime being sucked from my skin and clothes. The stuff is quickly dragged down, leaving me feeling dry. The now bloated creature burped and turned to slither back to the large pool of slime I had fallen into.

"What is that?" I ask.

Europa shrugs. "Who cares, I'm just glad it did its job." She looked at herself to make sure there was no residue.

Naida chuckles, seeming to be comfortable with us.

"It's just a Potator. They're harmless; they live off all different kinds of slime, mould, and bacteria. They are very important for the eco-system. Here, they must use them to clean the slime from that Bainbridge Plant. They love that kind of stuff!"

Her enthusiastic explanation drew our attention back to the plant as Isa clumsily slid down the slime trail. She stood and strode out of the slime puddle, having none of the trouble I had experienced.

I ask, "How do you know that?"

Naida explains, "We have a few colonies of them that live within Vadosus, our large village, and around the outskirts of our huge rock pool. They're essentially our little cleaners, keeping our inhabitants clean of any nasty and unwanted diseases – handy little guys."

The Cancer new-bloods were watching Isa with what I decide is amusement. I wondered what my expression had betrayed when I had first seen the Potator. Isa wasn't impressed, but she didn't jump back as I had. She kicked the nearest one, sending it flying straight at the wall. Then, after a look down at her state, shook herself vigorously, sending slime in all directions.

I noticed that the Potador, apart from going completely flat, had simply begun sliding back down to the platform. Its soft boneless body must allow it to squeeze into small places and change shape easily. It comes out completely unscathed from a hard kick, unlike myself. For a moment, I daydream, how handy it would be to have that ability.

Then Naida's soft voice captures my attention. "I don't mean to sound rude, but aren't you a Taurean? Shouldn't you harbor sheer strength?"

I look up at her and she adds, "I just don't understand why you couldn't pull yourself effortlessly from that slime, like the others of your kind?"

I felt myself grow tense. I knew I was weak for a Taurean, though for a while, I had forgotten.

Before the situation became awkward, Europa spoke up, "She was born with a condition that prevents her from harnessing her inner strength."

I am grateful for her simple explanation, but Naida's face still betrays interest, as if expecting a longer reply. I wish her curiosity would be satisfied.

"Oh, I'm terribly sorry, that must be incredibly hard for you. But I'm just interested, how did the Elders – well, you know…"

We both look at her, hoping she won't ask the question, but she continues hesitantly, "How come they let you…live? We were taught your village in Herba killed those born with any kind of weakness, which I always thought was very sad as I believe each child has some kind of great purpose. But I respect your way of living as you wouldn't be the great warriors we know of today if it wasn't for certain sacrifices."

As those last words fall out of her mouth, she instantly purses her lips in contrition. My mouth feels as though my lips are sewn shut and I feel myself becoming angry. I had never been asked that question before, as everyone within the Herba community was already aware of me and my condition. And they hate me for it. I've never had to explain it before, it was just accepted and resented at the same time, and I could deal with that as I never had to justify myself to anyone. But now knowing I'll have to explain my existence time and time again within this place, makes me wish I could just go live with my father and never return.

Then Naida's says, "Oh my, I do apologize, I didn't mean to make you upset."

Was my facial expression that obvious? I had assumed my thoughts were purely internal.

She adds, "I was just curious as I thought you must have some secret power or something."

The world around me becomes still for a split second as the words from the strange hairy creature that entered my room just one night ago leaks into my mind: *You have a secret power you do not know of yet.*

Then Naida's words bring me back into reality, "It was just a thought. But I shouldn't have presumed. Your situation must be very hard for you already, without me or others prodding into your business."

The anger subsides and I smile slightly at Naida in

acknowledgment and feel gratified in experiencing a Cancers true, kind nature.

"Thank you," I say sincerely.

Then Europa cuts in, "Naida, do you happen to know anything about the purpose number '10'?"

I become slightly irritated that Europa is now involving another in that mystery. But Naida seems to be trustworthy and I know Cancerians are very faithful friends and intuitive. It makes sense, considering how well she had read my body language. But Europa must have had the same thought as myself when Naida mentioned a secret power.

Before Naida answers, she thinks for a moment. "I'm sorry, I thought there were only '9' purpose numbers and the master numbers. I have never heard of a number '10'. But I know who you could ask."

We look at her eagerly as she says, "The Gemini, Bibliotheca, she's the Librarian of the Doh. I am yet to meet her but I know everyone calls her Bib. She has read every book in this place over one hundred times! So I'd imagine she's your best bet. My mother always says, 'Once you're settled in the Doh and you begin your lessons, if you need any assistance with your studies, ask the Gemini Bibliotheca, you'll find her in the library.'"

My mouth slightly drops open. *Why didn't I think of that when she was standing in front of us?*

Europa comments, "I've heard she's up to reading through the books for the five hundred and twenty-six thousandth time."

Europa winks at me and I shake my head as though that wasn't necessary.

Naida replies, "Well, I doubt that, you'd have to be a ghost in limbo to be able to have that kind of time... Anyway, I should be getting back to my sister, since I nearly gave her a heart attack before. I know it's not much but I hope that helps!" She smiles and moves away.

Europa and I look at one another. She says, "Maybe Bib was over-exaggerating when she said that. Because that would take an awful lot of time!"

"Never mind that. We should try to get back there as soon as possible and ask her."

Europa nods in agreement.

By now everyone has fallen through the slimy Bainbridge Plant and the platform is getting overly crowded. I feel a large hand grab my shoulder. "Come on, you two. Stay close to our group."

It's Demetrius and he stays by our side as all the other zodiacs groups start to move towards one or other of the of the staircases.

Europa nudges me, then leans towards my ear and whispers, "What's with all the bloody stairs in this place? This is madness."

I smirk with amusement and nod, until I hear an aggressive grunt. A Sagittarian looks at us judgmentally and I'm uneasy as to what he is about to say as Sagittarians don't shy away from the brutal truth.

"That's because those in your Constellation are only interested in feeding their stomachs instead of fuelling their brains. They're blinded by an over-indulgent, savage way of life that inhibits you from appreciating the beautiful diversity of this magical building," he says without remorse, probably not even realizing how insulting that was. Europa and I look at one another, astounded by his claim and without knowing what to reply, we say nothing.

Then we hear a familiar voice. "I wouldn't call stairs beautifully diverse, when the only diversity they contain is the change in direction," Kendall says unexpectedly. It was his first sign of awareness since this morning's confrontation with Isa.

The Sagittarian returns Kendall's stare without conviction, as though showing some kind of respect for the intelligence he obviously doubted within our race, and probably thinking we're imprudent brutes. Having decided, the Sagittarius nods in deference to Kendall, who responded to the validation with a flick of his tail, and clops on. Kendall has always been serious and wise beyond his years, but staying humble in the presence of others. It made sense as his purpose number is '9': worldly, giving, altruistic, self-aware, intuitive, and wise.

Demetrius's, who had made no comment during the exchange with the Sagittarian, now betrays by his body language, his awareness of the Leos who are slightly in front of us. He slows us down to see which staircase they'll take. When they move to the right, he immediately signals us to go down the left stairway. My eyes linger on the beautiful Leo girls, who are mesmerizing with their long golden hair, golden eyes, athletic bodies and tanned skin. Their promiscuous aura, probably drawn from their Lion ancestor, adds to their exquisiteness. The trouble is that they know it, making their arrogance amplify their own admiration for themselves. But I remind myself they are ruled by the Sun – indicator and interpreter of everything revolved around self and energy.

Europa jolts me back to the present when she pulls me to her side to walk down the stairs. I become instantly mesmerized by the magnitude of the Orbis Bellum Arena. As I go down each step, holding the handrail, I hear the roar from the crowd of thousands who are filling the tiers of seats around the arena.

Two figures, looking small from our high position, stand either side of the arena, appearing to be waiting to start. One paces back and forth while the other waits patiently as though a statue. Then I notice a message being relayed up from lower down the stairs. The whispered message arrives quickly. I hear Demetrius being informed of its import by a Pisces SNC overseer and for the first time I see Demetrius express some kind of excitement. It is the first overt expression of emotion that I have ever witnessed from him. He gestures for us to listen and instantly changes back to his stiff and rigid demeanor, but I know he is holding back his excitement, trying to keep the usual authority in place.

"We've arrived just in time to watch a battle to involve the renowned and legendary Sagittarian, Ahearn Orion, who has served the longest time in the SNC army within his Constellation. You may remember that part of the Sagittarian SNC criteria is to go off on their own to explore the Uncharted Forest outside of the Constellations. During these journeys, new geographical areas have been discovered, as well as strange creatures and monsters that even the Doh has no record of.

"Ahearn has discovered more new lands than any other, places where there is only endless sand, where rivers widen into marshy bogs, and forests have grown up over ancient structures. He has fought not only the Infernum, but some of the toughest, fiercest seldom or never seen creatures in the Uncharted Forest and beyond and continues to come back to add this knowledge to what we know of our world. His bravery and courage is something to be admired."

Europa lurches forward out of excitement and interrupts Demetrius, "Who'd be that fierce to challenge such a relic! Tell us, who's his opponent?"

Demetrius, disgruntled by Europa lack of respect expresses a scornful expression. This quickly diminishes as he explains, with a slither of enthusiasm spread across his face for the anticipation of the fight.

"His opponent is an up-and-coming Scorpio, Imelda Kore. Both her parents died when she was very young, no one knows how or why but it made her the relentless warrior she is today, the first SNC Scorpio woman to ever show up and humiliate the men within her Constellation. Her determination and focus outdo those considered to have natural talent. Imelda never had a natural ability; she worked hard to prove herself to those who never thought she'd ever amount to anything other than a NC. Most considered her only suited to breed offspring, but nothing more. She is one of the fiercest women and a true Scorpio at heart, although she is much younger and less experienced than Ahearn and still very new to being an SNC. So the odds are in his favour. He hasn't taken up a battle in decades as he hasn't needed to prove himself, but the rumours of his old age must have gotten to him. There has been a lot of controversy about these two. So, all who witness today are watching history in the making. I'm surprised I wasn't informed earlier. Now we must keep moving, they won't start until everyone is seated."

Now I could tell the stiff dark figure was Imelda the Scorpio, and the one pacing back and forth was Ahearn the Sagittarian, obviously impatient to start and we're the cause of the delay.

The seats are made of hard wood and far from the front, barely in eye view of either figure, who are, in any case, so small, you can hardly tell what's going on.

Demetrius claps to get our attention and points down beside his chair. "There are Oculi under your seats. They look like two round crystal balls plastered together. Place them on your eyes and they'll latch on, enabling you to see the arena up close as though you are sitting at the front." He sits down and places some of these unusual looking crystals on his face. They instantly stick there and he glances at us to demonstrate but quickly looks away rubbing the side of his head. It looks as though he has large bug eyes and on Demetrius, who is such a serious zodiac, it is comical. Europa giggles once he's looking away.

"I'm actually impressed he is able to maintain his usual stern stature with those things," she says chuckling in between the words.

"He's got to maintain appearances, Europa," I reply with a smile. We both laugh take our Oculi out from under our seats and they do latch on to our faces with little discomfort. Straight away I can see the Orbis Bellum Arena in front of me as though we have front row seats. I hear Europa's voice beside me.

"Wow, these things are handy! Who needs front row seats when you have these?"

I hear Henrietta exclaim from a few seats down, "Oh wow! Ouch! Owe ou! Where am I?"

There is a slap as Isa replies, "Look at the arena, you idiot, you're going to give yourself even more brain damage by doing that."

Europa chuckles and I turn to look at the commotion, and I'm instantly met with immense amount of pain in my eyes and head as everything enlarges immensely, obviously too much for my eyes to handle.

"OU!" I yelp, quickly looking back at the Orbis Bellum Arena as everything goes back to normal size.

"Oh not you too," Europa laughs.

"I'm guessing that's what Henrietta did." I now understand why Demetrius only glanced our way. These things are deadly up close. Europa rubs my arm in sympathy.

"Don't worry, your secret's safe with me," she says sardonically.

I look down at Ahearn who steps hard and deliberate back and forth, not once taking his eyes off Imelda. He is large bodied and strong with incredibly lean muscles, striking facial features, long, wavy brown hair half of it tied up and the rest falling behind his back. As I look closely, you can tell the man has been through a lot of rough fights. He has large and small scars over his whole body. His dark eyes watch his opponent intently, while a slight leer is plain in his expression. His horse body ripples with muscles as he moves. His tail has been cropped short, probably to keep it from getting tangled or used against him within these types of scenarios. He holds a bow by his side in his right hand and arrows tightly secured to his back. A short sword in a worn brown leather scabbard hangs at his left hip from a belt around his waist.

I scan across to take a closer look at Imelda, realizing the arena is a desert environment and sand is blowing around, even though there is no wind where we are seated. Imelda's stillness is a complete contrast. It is as though nothing is important but this crucial moment; her focus is clear and profound. She is a powerful looking woman with long black hair, braided along her scalp and then into a ponytail. Her pronounced cheek bones and defined jawline highlight her strong features. The independence of a woman like Imelda makes her incredibly unattainable and exceedingly attractive. She wears nothing but a small violet leather crop, matching a barely noticeable skirt, the Scorpion constellation colour contrasts nicely against her hardened black exterior. She stands with a dagger in each hand, the blades facing towards her elbows and her tail high above her head at ready. Ahearn needs to be wary of that stinger.

Suddenly, a horn blares a deep echoing sound that vibrates through the arena. Looking around, I notice a large old shell sitting above Imelda's position.

It must be the signal to begin as Ahearn now gallops hard against the sand, clearly working harder than normal as he pulls his hooves in with every step. Imelda leans elegantly towards the ground as though crouching into a scorpion-like imitation, making her tail extend high into the air. She waits patiently as he approaches; her arms are spread out either side, the daggers at ready. Ahearn begins circling her, drawing back his bow, aiming carefully and shooting. But the shots seem to be off target, some landing in the ground beside her. Imelda slashes against the arrows with her stinger, the end of her tail obviously impervious to damage. The flying arrows are invisible, even to our Oculi enhanced sight, and are only apparent when sparks fly from impacts with the end of the stinger. Then they make a sharp crisp sound that carries to our ears. Ahearn fires another arrow and another, while continuously circling her, never getting close enough to be in range of her long stinger, which reacts every time he shoots an arrow.

Imelda never allows her back to be turned towards him. The distance he keeps allows her to move in time with him, giving her the upper hand as her defence appears to be impenetrable. But he doesn't allow her the range she needs in order to attack. Both stay within their comfort zones, trying to figure each other's strengths and weaknesses from a safe distance. Ahearn comes to a standstill as his arrows are becoming scarce. His muscles swell as blood pumps hard through his veins, easy to see as there is little fat on his lean body. Imelda is not letting her guard down.

"I guess you shouldn't have been so tactless to think your own self-image couldn't be beaten within any environment now, Ahearn," Imelda says patronizingly.

Ahearn begins pacing back and forth, hooking his bow on a carrier on his right side and pulling out the sword. This he makes a show of cleaning against his coarse horse-haired body.

"Maybe one so assured as yourself should heed such prophetic words, Imelda. The battle hasn't even begun," he says, smirking.

I realize the Orbis Bellum must be able to simulate any given environment. Ahearn obviously wanted the battle to take place within an environment similar to the Scorpio's Solitudiem Desert, where they reside within their Constellation. Most likely he wanted to prove his capabilities beyond any doubt, after being compared to one much younger and less experienced than himself. But maybe his own heroic image has gotten the better of him, and he is believing in his own legend. I've heard it happening before and Imelda appears to be unassailable and fearless at this point. It could be seen as he underestimates her. Imelda smiles and says no more, crouching down slightly lower, preparing herself for the next attack.

The exchange of provocative insults was inciting the blood lust of the crowd, adding drama to the contest. The cheers were getting louder as each spectator began to urge on their favourite, wanting the battle to resume.

Two magical holograms flicked into existence, the images focused on the faces of the contestants as they manoeuvred for position. The crowd roared louder, watching for signs of fear on their favourite's opponent.

Ahearn casually placed the short sword back in its scabbard, effortlessly reversing away from Imelda as if trying to heighten the tension. He pulls three of his remaining five arrows from the quiver with one hand, while retrieving his bow with the other. He positions the arrows against his bow and prepares to shoot.

The abrupt silence in the stadium could be broken by a pin drop. Imelda does not move an inch but is carefully watching Ahearn's every movement. He begins to gallop, gracefully this time as though the sand no longer impedes his movement. Imelda moves to watch him as he circles, this time steadily coming into range; she smirks as though she's got him. But as the large intimidating stinger lurches at him, he fires all three of his arrows. The highly reactive stinger responds rapidly, first lurching at the primary arrow then at the following two. Imelda's supporters cheered. Ahearn's supporters groaned as it seemed that the arrows had been off target, aimed at the ground behind her. But Ahearn was now riding hard in the opposite direction, circling around her and had his bow ready to shoot his last two arrows. Their trajectory was invisible, the only indication of their target was when Imelda's stinger fell to the ground with a thud and lay as if paralysed. Now the arrows could be seen, clearly lodged in a tiny area at the base of the stinger, that was only vulnerable when the stinger was at attack attitude.

Imelda's face registers shock and before she could react, Ahearn has galloped close with his sword in a downward position, aiming for her spine. She attempts to twist and run, but it's already too late, the stinger's dead weight slows her. The sword pierces deep, going through her body and into the ground beneath until only the hilt is visible from above. Ahearn holds it with both hands, signalling his victory over her. No scream or sound escapes through her mouth, only a gasp followed by the curdling sound of blood as it erupts and falls from between her lips. Her eyes are wide open in shock from the thrust she never saw coming. They cloud over into a clammy grey colour as though she were now blind. Then her body slumps as though her life had finally escaped her.

Ahearn's supporters were cheering wildly, but none of the new-bloods around me say a word. I grasp the side of my seat, recalling being told that you couldn't die within the Orbis Bellum? I take the Oculi from my face, dropping it clumsily on to my lap as I cover my mouth with my hands, staring stunned towards the arena. I have only been told stories of murder but never have I witnessed it. This is what we've been preparing for, but it never made us ready for the actual reality of death. Then I hear Demetrius's voice above the others around us that are making a commotion.

"Calm down! The slime you were covered with from the Bainbridge Plant protects you. The slugs only remove the unnecessary bulk, so you can function. She is not dead! Put your Oculies back on and watch!" he orders with a lack of empathy for our feelings of shock. I place my Oculi back on and focus on Ahearn who has already moved back from Imelda and is now cleaning his sword with an already dirty cloth.

I look at Imelda who still appears quite dead. Then the same sort of slime as that at the entrance begins to pour out of the wound in her back, continuing to flow until her body is completely covered by it. It pulls her into a tight ball and turns white like a pearl until we cannot see any part of her. When Ahearn has finished cleaning his sword, he walks over to the now white ball and pokes it with the tip. It bursts as though it were as delicate as a bubble and slime gushes everywhere. Imelda slides out on to all fours, gasping for air, dropping her head as though she had been reborn. Ahearn offers her a hand; she glances at it and turns away. Getting to her knees, she pushes up on to one leg, using her hands to help her, then gets up onto both feet, and reels as if tired.

"Still so defiant, Imelda. Why can't you just admit defeat? It wouldn't belittle the great warrior you clearly are."

She squeezes slime out of her braids and flicks them behind her. "Not until you or anyone else officially...kills me. There is no point admitting to something that is not yet true."

Ahearn smiles respectfully; even though she may have taken the defeat badly, depending on how you look at it, her continued belief in herself could be seen as admirable in the face of defeat.

I remove the Oculi and place it back under the chair, then rub my eyes as they readjust to their usual vision. I look over to see Europa on her chair, twisting with excitement. "Wasn't she amazing? I hope I'm as strong and fierce as Imelda by the time I finish the Olympus Trials. She kicks butt."

I glance back at the arena and watch as Ahearn and Imelda disappear through gates at opposite ends. To Europa, I say, "She definitely is something else."

Europa grabs my shoulders and rattles me. "To even take on a zodiac of that calibre says so much in itself. She was defiant even in the face of defeat...she was the definition of the underdog."

I grin and nod in admiration for Imelda. Her supporters are

beginning to chant her name and the feeling of profound respect grows with every additional voice.

Demetrius calls out, "Alright, we'll be heading to your classroom where you'll meet your first mentor and have an introductory session. Now follow me and don't get lost amongst the crowd."

We stay close together, pushing past other zodiacs. Some grunt, judge, analyse, stare, and others apologize. The dynamic of each region is so animatedly varied.

Once we step down to ground level, walking behind the walls of the arena, we come upon a wide dark hallway. The wooden walls look old and decaying. Vents are installed at intervals on either side and on the roof. The ground angles up on either side of a flat central path made up of a drain with a metal grating on top for us to walk upon. Rust seems to have riddled the metal of the vents, leaving orange tinged streaks leading down towards the drain.

Demetrius turns to us, as the other overseers do to their groups, announcing, "We're all going to walk through this together as a group. And this tunnel is going to rid you of the residual slime you still have on your skin." Everyone looks at the eerie tunnel with unpleasant thoughts.

Dalton burst out with, "But I like knowing I'm invincible. Wouldn't something like this help us fight the Infernum? Besides, that tunnel does not look inviting."

Demetrius asks, "Do you understand the term rejuvenation?" Dalton nods unconvincingly as his expression says otherwise. Demetrius adds, "Well, that's what the slime does, rejuvenates you, in other words, restore. When you die, a chemical reaction occurs. When cells start to die, the slime encapsulates you and revives every dying cell. It may look like you're dead but you're not. It's okay to have it on for a few days, maybe even a couple of weeks, but then you start noticing certain side-effects. Imagine if you had such a substance on at all times. In the natural process of things, cells die but the substance will continue to rejuvenate them, making your skin unable to shed, your hair unable to fall out and so many more natural processes subside within your body. Your skin will become thick, overcome with skin cells, making you bleed and crack, and only produce even more skin cells. You'll begin to grow an immense amount of hair all over your body as you are unable to shed through the usual natural process. There are so many other problematic side-effects. But yes, you will never die. But the pain that accompanies it is immense. You will wish intensely for death to find you."

Dalton's mouth dropped open. "Well, what are we waiting for? I ain't turning into some behemoth! No siree."

He begins striding determinedly for the creepy dark hallway and we wordlessly follow behind, the other zodiacs follow in a drawn out queue.

The tunnel is cold and damp. The humidity increases dramatically with each successive step and you begin to feel as though you could suffocate within its density. The darkness is absolute and we are basically walking blind. The overseers are constantly repeating themselves, "Continue walking straight and do not walk up the angled concrete, stay on the flat grated platform."

Europa places my hands on the back of her shoulders. "Hold on to me and don't let go," she says, whispering. Soon the humidity begins to increase even further and I hang my head down between my heavy arms. I am only staying upright by my grip on Europa. Sweat starts to drench my whole body, dripping down every segment of skin. I hear everyone around me beginning to pant hard and I too begin to breathe deep and heavy, feeling as though every breath is harder than the last. Now no murmurs are heard from the crowd as that would take further energy. The oxygen continues to deplete, the temperature continues to rise and it's as though we have walked into an oven. Anxiety now takes over, my eyes dilate, and my breaths become short and fast. My heart beats hard into the surface of my chest, and I know I'm about to go into a full-blown panic attack. But just as I feel I'm going to pass out, the air pressure changes. A hard, cold wind pushes against us. My hair stands high on end from the severe atmosphere change. I now shiver, squinting through closed eyelids at a light shining in front of us.

Everyone else's footsteps pick up pace, turning into a trot, but Europa stays walking, so I could keep up.

When we emerged, some of the others were leaning down onto their knees, others were leaning against Doh's wall, trying to catch their breath. I simply dropped to hands and knees, carried down by my heavy backpack, all energy drained from me.

Europa chose to sit next to me.

The overseers walk out as though they had just gone for a gentle stroll, their breathing appears to be normal and their stature is calm and relaxed.

We all look at them in disbelief. The Pisces overseer steps forward with an amused but compassionate smile; he speaks softly but is easily understood.

"Don't worry, new-bloods, you'll become used to it after a while. It's necessary to place the body under threatening conditions. It's the fastest and most efficient way to rid the body of the slime before it becomes toxic. The body reacts to survive under the massive temperature alteration, killing any foreign microorganisms. For some reason, the slime cannot survive these types of conditions either. No other technique has been found to completely destroy it – believe me, we've tried. So, unless you want to experience the terrible effects I described to you, and to turn into a Bwbachod, you will endure the cleansing tunnel."

We all glance at each other in question to see if any of us knows of Bwbachods.

Then a Pisces girl asks her overseer, "Apologies, Meredith… but what's a Bwbachod?"

Everyone nods in agreement, whispering to one another, wanting to hear about this unheard of creature. The fins on the side of Meredith's face sprawl out in anticipation. Pisces love telling stories, it complements their imaginative minds to elaborate on things they know. He glances at the rest of the other overseers and they nod in agreement.

"Well, before I tell you the story, I advise you not to judge your ancestors harshly. This is simply an unfortunate bit of history known within the Nirvana land which everyone learns of eventually. Plus, it'll stop you from ever avoiding the tunnel."

He rubs his hands together in preparation and uses them animatedly as he tells the story, "In the beginning when Apophis had started possessing zodiacs and the Infernum had taken over our forest and the twelve Constellations were just beginning to work together, we had to figure out a way to replicate a battle field scenario, where zodiacs could practice fighting against one another. But egos and differences got in the way and we ended up injuring each other more in preparation than in battle. After a while, large numbers of zodiacs were unable to fight due to bad injuries or on rare occasions, death. Because of the conflicting diversity between Constellations, we found it hard to get along in the beginning, especially Constellations that had a reputation for clashing

"Then, a now well-known Pisces alchemist known as Bainbridge Blaine, who had been studying the Potator for many years, came across an amazing discovery. In their native environment, wounded slugs healed rapidly and they could not be fatally injured. In good conditions, the population of the slugs stayed constant. They did not mate like higher creatures or increase in any other noticeable way.

"After studying their food substances, which he discovered to be toxic slimes and bacteria, Bainbridge found that when the bad slimes and bacteria accumulated – like when the surrounding natural environment was polluted, the slug population increased. Not only had that, any that were injured, appeared to rejuvenate within the trail of slime left behind by another Potator.

"When there was a high concentration of food for the Potators, some element in the residual slime that each exuded, caused the slugs to reproduce by dividing into two. Once the food concentration reduced, some of the slugs died off.

"After studying these slimes and bacteria, he created his own slime. Then he had to find a plant that could tolerate it, and he altered the plants genetic makeup in order for it to produce the slime on its own. This resulted in a soft mouldy-looking plant, the one you now know of as the Bainbridge plant.

"To keep reproducing this slime and to remain healthy, it requires particular minerals. As zodiacs pass through it, it absorbs those minerals from your skin. It leaves, as a by-product, some of this rejuvenation slime, which is also referred to as Bainbridge slime.

"Bainbridge's creation was taken up with great enthusiasm, with little thought to the long term consequences."

Meredith gave a theatrical sigh of regret, consistent with the delivery of the whole story. "The strongest and most powerful zodiacs, now known as the SNC, were tested time and time again. They began getting stronger. Everyone thought this was great and a major breakthrough to destroy the Infernum and take down Apophis. But not long after, these SNC started turning into monsters, unable to listen, short-tempered, and irritated most of the time due to the body's inability to shed everyday cells. It made them go...insane. Most died, but some inexplicably survived and flourished, their sanity was unaffected by disturbing physical side-effects, although they suffered from a low IQ, were unable to follow orders and became chaotic at times and unreliable. Over time, they started to breed, their cells genetically enhancing over generations. They were never tested against the Infernum, because until everything was known about them, no one knew if they were susceptible to the enchanting lullaby or wanted Apophis to have control over such a creature. They developed an ability to morph into anyone just by consuming a small portion of their blood. They'd transform into a perfect physical replication, able to use the donor zodiacs' special abilities and power. This was thought to be incredibly dangerous, so the creatures were eradicated. One still remains, but he is enslaved to Theophilus and securely controlled by him, no one knows why he was spared. It is told that he's kept as a safety resort because if anything were to happen within Orbis Bellum and the genetically enhanced slime adapted, becoming unaffected by the tunnel, his blood could hold the answer... Anyway, that's the end of today's history lesson. We better get you to class."

Everyone has now recovered from the tunnel's effect and ready to follow our overseers.

CHAPTER SEVEN

NATURE ELEMENTS AND QUALITY SIGNS

It's those of our enemies that unbind us.

We've now split off from the other new-blooded zodiacs and no one has spoken for a while as the long passages and stairways have led through unfamiliar areas of the Doh. Europa is just in front of me, but I need the handrail to pull myself up each step. My heavy backpack adds to my struggle and causes me to fall further behind. I stop for a moment to peer over the rail. Down the centre of the spiral staircase, there is only darkness, and I'd hate to think how far you'd have to drop before you come face to face with the surface. I'm sure your body would end as an unrecognizable, a pile of mush. Then I hear Henrietta yell over the ledge, "Echo!" and I glance up at her. Dalton is beside her, both have identical expressions of fascination at hearing the effect of the shout. I look over the ledge again and hear her one voiced word travelling down the deep stairwell, repeatedly echoing back as it diminishes into its depth.

Not to be outdone, Dalton yells down, "Taurus Rule!" Those words continuously travel down the stairwell, vibrating into one another. It's a terrible dissonance to listen too.

Europa places both her hands over her ears in irritation, stepping up each step with deliberation to express her annoyance, probably wondering why Demetrius hasn't put a stop to it. I wonder the same thing as I continue to hear the repeating words. Then, unexpectedly, I hear a different sound, a loud rustling coming from below, rushing up to where we are climbing the twisting staircase. It sounds as though many papers flail in the wind at high speed. Everyone stops to peer down into the Doh's deep, infinite centre, except Demetrius. The rustling now has squeaking sounds as though a stampede of something travels up towards us. Before I even see anything, I'm clipped in the face by a white furry, feathery thing and I stumble back to the wall and watch a blur of hundreds of white creatures flying up the Doh's centre. But I can't get a good look as they travel incredibly fast.

"Everyone, gather 'round!" Demetrius announces from higher up the stairs. Europa looks at me and gestures to follow. She runs up, I try to increase my own pace, to where Demetrius stands. The strange white-feathered animals continue to fly up the Doh's centre by the dozens now, still not slowing down. I see Demetrius holding one in his hand; we gather around.

"This is a Nuntius. They are as swift as a falcon. They deliver messages from the zodiacs who live within the Doh's premises to loved ones within their Constellations or to other zodiacs in different parts of the Doh. You've probably seen them on the odd occasion, handing letters out. But you won't get one of these until you have proven yourself worthy."

The strange white-feathered creature that he holds by the scruff of its neck, has a similar body to a large mouse. However, the long, thin tail curls securely around a rolled letter and a bunch of feathers grows from the end. It has big black eyes and tips of black at the ends of its paws and wings. It twitches around, frantically attempting to escape, but Demetrius has too firm a grip. Europa approaches the Nuntius, gazing at it affectionately.

"Aw, it's so cute. Can I pat it?" she asks, already reaching out before Demetrius has given his approval. Just before she touches its soft head, it twists rapidly and nips her on the end of the finger.

"OUCH!" she cries.

Isa snuffs. "That'll teach you!" she spits.

Europa now flicks her hand back and forth, rolls her eyes at Isa as Demetrius says, "I would have warned you not to approach a Nuntius when it has a letter to deliver."

Curious, I ask, "We've all seen them handing letters out, but why haven't we seen them coming in and out of our region?"

Europa stares at me and nods in agreeance to my query, then slowly turns her head to Demetrius.

Demetrius lets the Nuntius go and it immediately joins the Nuntius that trail at the end of the large group. Everyone moves over to the edge to peer up, watching them disappear into the distance. Demetrius answers whilst standing behind us, "You've probably had one brush past you but most likely mistook it for a gust of wind or a mouse. You're just unable to see them whilst they are on direct route to their patron. Their speed makes them pretty much invisible. However, enough on the creatures, we had best keep moving otherwise you won't get to your orientation session."

We eventually come to a small corridor with the Taurean emblem engraved into the concrete structure. It glows green and white as we approach. There are some markings on the floor, but I don't get a chance to look at them for Demetrius goes quickly towards a tall wooden door and gestures for us to hurry through. My mind gets caught on wondering why this door is so plain compared to the rest of the doors I have seen on the Doh's premises.

The classroom is bland, with small glazed windows opened slightly, and single person wooden tables and chairs clumped lifelessly in the centre of the room. Large dust-covered stone bricks make up the floor area and there is nothing stimulating about the atmosphere, only dust that drifts the air and clogs my lungs, probably produced from the large black board at the front of the room that is covered in chalk residue or from the dusty cobwebs up near the ceiling. Had I been alone, I might have ventured onto the raised platform to investigate the untidy pile of books and papers on a table at the back of it.

Once we have all entered, Demetrius announces, "Well, I'll be leaving you now. I'll be back later to escort you to dinner before taking you to your dorms for the night." He shuts the door and leaves us to amuse ourselves while waiting for our mentor. I notice individual names carved into small planks placed at the end of each small working table. Mine is centred at the front of a raised platform, with Europa on my right, bringing a smile to my face until I see Isa's name to my left. Before I sit down, Europa helps me take my heavy bag off, so I can place it between my legs under the table. I smile in gratitude. "Thanks, Euro."

She slumps down in her chair next to me. "That's okay...but what the hell is in that thing!? Didn't you bring enough the first time? Never thought you were high maintenance."

I smirk. "Yeah, neither did I," I answer convincingly. I didn't want to give anything away in front of the others and tried to cover my medicines as my father insisted so emphatically.

Once we are all seated, Isa blurts out ignorantly, "What a dump!" She scraped dust from her table and blew it off her finger. "My bovine Oma would keep her grave in better condition."

Dalton replies in confusion from the table behind, "But Isa... your Oma's dead."

Isa rolls her eyes not even bothering to turn around to insult him about his idiocy, which is standard. Then Henrietta punches Dalton on the arm. "Exactly...stupid." Dalton doesn't retaliate as he is too intent on the joke he did not comprehend.

"Don't hurt yourself," Kendall says unfeelingly.

Dalton glares at him with sudden fury. But Kendall just draws in the dust on his desk, not taking any notice of him.

The pronounced clearing of a throat, followed by a cough, jerks our attention from our preoccupation. We turn around to see a Capricorn standing in front of us on the platform that sits higher than the rest of the room. I recognize him from the dining room, it's the Capricorn elder, Aldous Darcy. His features are memorable. Big elongated horns that bend slightly back to the shape of his head, following his hairline downward. The long dark brown hair is tied back neatly into a pony tail at the back of his head and two thick locks drape down either side of his pointy ears and reach his chest. His goat tail sits upright from behind. He appears composed and has a wise and noble demeanour. His orange-tinged skin glimmers under the tiny bits of light that pierce through the dust-covered windows and his large eyes blink slowly in contemplation

"Good afternoon. You may call me Mr. Darcy," he says politely and we all follow suit, "Good afternoon, Mr. Darcy." He smiles.

"I'll be your general mentor for this year. I'll be teaching you about our world and life itself, all the things you won't have learnt in the confines of your Constellation. Capricorns are the general mentors and teachers within the Doh. But anything that is specific will be taught by specialists. Sorcery for example, is taught by the PNC sorcerer Pisces and healing spells and procedures would be taught by Aquarius PNC healers and so on. You'll never master any of those skills but it's good to have basic knowledge and ability within all areas. Plus, it lets you have a broader understanding of all your brother and sister zodiacs."

He took a moment to look at each of us in turn. "I don't normally take on first years but I felt I needed to extend myself this year and young zodiacs are quite unpredictable and genuinely more challenging. You seem to react with raw emotion which directly relates to traits your Constellation has instilled in you. But that is what you are here for, to grow, condition, and broaden your horizon of our world."

Aldous turns around to the blackboard and sighs at the mess that has been left there. As he proceeds to clean it competently, he says, "I'm not used to the first years' classrooms, there's always such a mess and disorder. I'm sure you've noticed. Although, the internal design is quite unremarkable."

He turns back, glancing at Isa, who looks away from his intent stare. "Unfortunately, there is a reason for it. Being that you're so easily stimulated, we believed you needed an environment that was literally bland and boring so you could concentrate more easily on your present studies. Don't worry, this won't be forever, only for the time being. Everyone has to start somewhere. And you can start by taking the rags out of your desks and removing the dust from them."

After he finishes cleaning the board, he writes with white chalk, 'Questions?'. Turning around, he says, "Now before I dive into what I was planning on talking about today, I want you to think about anything within the Doh you do not understand and I'll try my best to explain in simple terms, so you feel more comfortable and confident within your environment."

He stands patiently as Henrietta yells out, "Yeah, why are there so many blood...I mean stairs, why are there so many stairs? How are you supposed to get to places within this maze of a place if you are in a hurry? I mean what if there's an emergency?"

Aldous smiles, "Good question. Don't worry, you will only ever need to travel to every area once within the Doh. Remember how you teleported back home? That was because you had come from there and you could teleport back to the Doh because once you had arrived here you could visualize exactly what it looked like. Now that you've been to this classroom, you'll be able to teleport here every time you have class, and come straight from your dorm. It is only possible to teleport after you have your purpose numbers, so unfortunately everyone must venture through the Uncharted Forest to get here."

He waits for the next question, and it is Dalton who asks abruptly, "But why stairs? And why is everything so far away from, well, everything else!"

Aldous smirks in amusement and adds, "Well, anything that is good is never easy, is it? Imagine if we had everything close you'd take everything for granted. The layout teaches you discipline and respect for everything you obtain within the Doh. Besides, you haven't seen more than a fraction of this place. The zodiacs who live within its walls, such as most of the PNCs, haven't even seen a quarter. It has more to do with the fact that most don't want to travel the distance in order to see everything. The more you want to see, the further you must travel. It would probably take a zodiac a lifetime, and have it their dedicated purpose, to uncover all its secrets. Next question."

Kendall raises his hand respectfully and you can tell Aldous is impressed with his manner. "Yes, Kendall, what is your question?" he asks, reading the nametag from his desk.

Kendall gently places his hand in his lap and asks, "From the times we teleported, we chanted Unum. I was wondering, why that is? Considering the obvious?"

Dalton utters under his breath, "What's obvious?"

Aldous smiles again. "What a great question."

He glances at Dalton who is ignorant of the dim-witted expression he has on his face. He takes a breath, maybe feeling as though it was a mistake to take on first years, but goes on to explain, "The obvious being because he no longer speaks or converses with us in present times. You feel as though he abandoned us? So why would we acknowledge his name in a chant for teleportation?"

Kendall nods. Aldous draws a big circle on the black board and turns back around.

"First off, he does still speak to us. The only problem is, no one in these times can speak or understand his language. Only through death will the Wisdom Tree guide our essence back to Unum. It is unfortunate, that Apophis never taught anyone Unum's language. But without Unum, we would cease to exist. He connects us to everything and everyone. He completes us like this circle here. We call his name as he is the one who gives us the power of teleportation and every other power we hold within this world. He is our connection to all things. Our purpose numbers give us a direct connection to him. Every time we teleport, it's reassurance that he still exists within Nirvana. Because if he were dead or ceased to be, we would not be able to teleport. In fact, we wouldn't be able to do anything, we'd most likely turn into the instinctual animals like our ancestors, without a conscious mind. Our whole world, as we know it, would collapse into oblivion."

He swiftly crosses a line through the circle he drew on the blackboard and continues, "That is why we chant his name and that is why we still acknowledge and praise his existence till this very day. We may not know the reason why he chose Apophis to comprehend his dialect, but I'm sure it was for good reason. We cannot judge something we do not understand nor know the reason to. We can presume and make assumptions, but that is all it is. A presumption is not truth. You should remember that when you hear rumours murmured within these walls about anyone."

Aldous speaks with conviction and passion as though personally affected by the very repercussions of rumours spoken about Unum, who he still feels to have a deep connection with.

He cleans the board again, implying the end to questions by writing there, 'Nature element'.

"Now, I'm presuming you know your own nature element, unless you didn't pay any attention within your Halls of Ivy classes." He glances at Dalton.

We all nod murmuring the word, 'Earth.' He nods in confirmation and goes on, "Good, and I presume you know the other earth zodiacs."

He writes Capricorn, Taurus, and Virgo. We all nod once again. "Now, I'm going to explain to you what defines us as Earth signs, as well as what defines Fire, Air, and Water zodiacs."

He places the chalk down and stands in front of the class. "Now, take out your writing books which are within your desks as you'll need to know the definitions of each element."

Lifting the top of the table, we find the books and pencils to write with. Once we are ready, Aldous becomes animated with his hands as he speaks about the elements, clearly competent and confident of his knowledge.

"Earth signs are practical, grounded, and dependable. We generally don't like to take big risks and we much prefer a sure thing. In contrast, we believe in what we can see, hear, touch, taste, and smell. We know we can't live on just inspiration alone and have to put in the grounded footwork in order to obtain what we want. We are down-to-earth signs and like to take care of the finer details of living. Taureans, you are impossible to stop once you have your mind set on something. Virgos like to stay busy, paying very close attention to the smallest of the details. Their work is always seen as flawless by the eyes of others. They themselves, forever see way for greater improvement. Capricorns can organize many diverse details into a whole easy-to-follow structured project, planning and knowing how to get to the top of our field."

He exemplifies his clear understanding of the subject, not having to look at a textbook as he explains in detail. He then adds the words, 'Fire element' to the board.

"Now who can tell me the Fire zodiac signs?"

Europa puts up her hand and Aldous gestures towards her. "Uh is it Aries, Leo, and um...Sagittarius?" she answers hesitantly, unsure of her answer.

Aldous gives an assertive nod. "Absolutely correct. Aries, Leo, and Sagittarius are your three fire signs." He writes those on the board.

"Those graced by Fire are enthusiastic and genuinely larger than life. Being incredibly fiery, if left unattended, can burn out of control like any fire within a forest. So, they must be aware to mind those embers." Aldous winks at us acknowledging his witty joke. None of us laughs or even cracks a smile but since he is in his element of mentoring, he doesn't appear to be bothered. He continues, "Although they are magnetic, like any fire, they have the reputation for being hot-headed and very much into themselves. They find it incredibly hard to see things from another's point of view but are actually one of the softest signs deep down. They have giant hearts and want only the best for those they care for. Fire signs like to tackle obstacles head on, so you must be wary and have patience with them. They are the most adventurous signs of the zodiacs and have a strong sense of self. Aries tend to initiate things immediately and directly. Leos are creative and enjoy putting their heart into their craft. Sagittarians are investigative, free, and able to use their mind very well intellectually." He waits patiently as we quickly try to keep up with his enthusiastic fast-paced lecture.

Turning around and writing 'Air', he says, "Now, who can tell me the Air zodiacs?"

Kendall puts his hand up and speaks confidently, "Gemini, Libra, and Aquarius."

Aldous flicks the chalk in his hand with an affirmative nod.

"Absolutely, Kendall," murmuring the words Gemini, Libra, and Aquarius as he writes them next to Air.

He slaps his hands together after placing the chalk down, and begins the explanation, "Now, zodiacs of the Air elements are the maker of the intellect, smart thinkers and handle abstract reasoning very well. They love to analyse and can work out most dilemmas. That's why they enjoy indulging in relationships, communication, sociability, and intellect. Although humans are only known as a legend within our lands, the Air elements have been described as having the most human-like traits of any zodiac. Even though they find it difficult to understand emotion at times, they always have the need to discuss things to get a greater insight and understanding of all forms of life. Gemini rely on communication and a constant flow of information as they are easily bored. Librans gravitate towards partnerships, justice, and more beautiful forms of communication, which is why many are considered to be flirts. Aquarians love to exceed the boundaries in any area. They thrive on seeing themselves as vastly different from everyone else and gravitate towards close friendships."

Aldous looks at the time and goes straight on to the next element, writing 'Water', followed by the zodiacs, calling out their names as he writes. "Now, the last element, Water, which I'm sure you can all tell me include Cancer, Scorpio, and Pisces." He turns around clasping his hands together and continuing, "Water signs are intuitive and sensitive; they feel their emotions more intensely than any other zodiac. They are emotional and nurturing and like a river they run deep. Water elements are guided by their emotions in whatever they decide to pursue. They have strong emotional bonds and much empathy towards others, falling into the 'artistic' realm of the zodiac as they have intense and vast imaginations. They are incredibly selfless towards those they care deeply for, as they'll happily sacrifice their own happiness in order to see the fulfilment in others. Though, their emotions can get them into a lot of trouble as they have the tendency to take advantage of others, like water manipulating the earth's surface. The water elements are great craftsmen when manipulating any situations in their favour, frequently without many realizing. When dealing with high levels of stress, don't be surprised if they disappear for a while as they like to seclude themselves when dealing with hardships. Cancerian zodiacs often want what they can't have and hold on to anything that has value. Their passion drives them to succeed in any area that fills them with great purpose. Scorpios are natural-born detectives, great at understanding the logic behind others' way of thinking and reasoning. They come with intense emotion but contain it within a strong barrier. Pisces have more compassion than any other sign and are incredibly intuitive, reading clear emotion within any given situation, where most may remain ignorant. This makes them susceptible to taking on others emotions, making them drained." Aldous dot points important parts about every sign and turns around. "That's why they like to keep things cool and neutral. Now that's all the nature elements, time to move on to our quality signs."

Aldous gives everyone a moment to write the information down then cleans the board. I begin to wonder if I should have asked about my purpose number at the beginning of class. Aldous seems incredibly knowledgeable. But I don't want to bring more unwanted attention to myself. Especially from Isa, whose fire continues to be fuelled without my support; her anger grows with every passing year towards me. And I don't want others making accusations either. I have too many unanswered assumptions as it is. I guess I'll just see Bib first and see if she can explain anything.

Aldous appears to be looking for more chalk, gesturing to give him a second. I glance over at Isa who angrily carves something into her desk with her pencil, ruining its ability to write.

I ruminate about the time when we were briefly friends. The time when children have no judgment of one another and aren't aware of the world's dynamics and social differences. It would have been around the time I started at the Halls of Ivy, which was when my father deemed me well enough and I could leave the house without his shadow. I remember how Isa and I used to play in the grass fields just in eye view of our houses, laying in the grass where the poppy flowers bloom as they have the perfect amount of shade and sun. They used to make me sneeze but I still enjoyed the tranquillity; we could sit in silence with one another for hours or talk about nothing and everything. She used to have a kind smile and loving nature. She even brought extra food from home for me, telling me I was too skinny and needed to build some much-needed muscle. Then one day, she stopped coming outside.

Days, then weeks went by, and I eventually got the courage up to knock on her front door which was answered by her mother. Petra Edlyn, was a stocky, unattractive woman whose facial skin was blotchy, her nose riddled with broken capillaries and cheeks reddened as though she drank too much. Her horns had decayed and only a few strands of hair remained at the end of her tail that dragged dejectedly on the ground.

Like a curse, it has aged her far beyond her actual years. She may have been an attractive Taurean once, but that time had long passed. She gave me an intolerant glare and told me with spit spraying from her mouth that Isa couldn't come out of the house to play with me anymore as it was unhealthy to play with a sick child such as myself, one that didn't even resemble a proper Taurean; it could teach her bad habits. And from now on, I should leave her be.

Her mother was an angry woman, giving off the same resentful feelings as Isa shares towards me these days, as though there is a curse that had been passed down generations within the Edlyn family. I remember Petra's spiteful words as I walked away. "Your father is a wretched being. And there's a proof in the offspring."

I never went back after that and I stopped playing outside. Instead, I read every book I could get my hands on within the small Herba library. And there were not many, considering our race is defined by brawn not brains. But brain was the only ally I had. There were only the necessary books for schooling, which I memorized over time.

Those hateful words grew into a deep resentment inside me. Adonis said to me one day as he noticed how my angry and isolated behaviour had worsened over time, *"My dear, be careful whose words you decide to harness as you might be drinking their very own poison."* I soon realized the same curse had entered my heart and was consuming me. And those words had been a blessing, because I now harness power within knowledge, something no one could take away from me.

I stopped cowering inside away from everyone's sight and began reading books outside in the sunshine, amongst the poppy flowers I enjoyed the company of. Months later, reading in the fields, I heard a door slam. Poking my head up from beneath the grass, I saw Isa walking up the dirt footpath from her house with a small backpack. Without the intolerable shadow of her mother, I had thought it safe to approach her. She saw me running and her expression turned into the same hateful look her mother had given me when I had seen her.

"What do you want?" she snapped.

I stared at her blankly, astonished that I was looking at the same Taurean I once knew well. She was covered in horrible bruises but she had muscled up an immense amount and cropped her hair. I noticed one eye was severely bloodshot.

"Well?" she spat.

"Isa, I was just excited to see you. I missed you. I thought since your mother wasn't around, you might like to hang out?"

She snorted at me and continued walking, I grabbed her backpack from behind and tugged on it, "What's wrong, Isa?" She did not answer and I continued tugging. "What have I done? What lies did she feed you?"

Without warning, Isa spun around and punched me in the rib cage. I flew about five feet backwards, feeling a sharp intense pain in my chest. Skidding and tumbling on the hard ground, I ripped my already ragged pants and began bleeding from all sort of places. It felt like my sternum was broken, and I could barely breathe, let alone stand. With short distorted breaths, I looked up at her resentfully, tears in my eyes. The friend I once knew was no longer standing in front of me. This was somebody else, someone I did not know.

No remorse had stricken her, all she said was, "It's all your fault. All of this is your fault, Taura. You'll clearly never understand the pain I've been through. You just pretend it never happened. You're not my friend. We can never be friends and we obviously never were. It was you who fed me a lie."

She pulled the backpack over her right shoulder, glanced back at her home and continued on the path. I reached my hand out not for help but in remorse. Because although I did not understand, I could see she was in pain. I whispered between gasped breaths, "I'm sorry. Please don't leave."

My book had split in two from taking the majority of the impact as I had been holding the book over my chest where Isa had hit. That had probably saved my life. Glancing at her home, I started sobbing. I saw someone in the small crooked window. The curtains are yanked across, and I assume it was Petra.

Their house isn't there anymore. They moved away and the place collapsed into a pile of rotting wood. But, back on that day, I dragged myself into the side of the road where the tall grass grew, where no one would see my tears and hear my sobs. Fearful of my father being punished because I displayed such weakness, I painfully brought my knees up to my chest, curled my arms around them, keeping my sobs muffled until I fell asleep from pain and exhaustion. I woke up within the arms of my father as he carried me and saw the stars in the blackish blue sky and the fields had been lit up by the planet Venus herself. Night had fallen and as I watched a shooting star sprint effortlessly through the night's stars, I shut my eyes and did not wake for a long time. After that, it was a very long time before I stopped keeping everyone at a far distance. It was safe, it was protection against my now scarred heart. So much time went by reinforcing this strong emotional barrier, which I never expected to let it down. Then I met Europa and she forced her way in.

Europa has a way of doing that to others; she gives you no choice. She is the one who decides who will be her friends and who won't. That is why I love and adore her. But to this day, I still don't understand the words Isa said to me on that day when she broke my first bone. Now, there are many to match the caged vertebrae that still protect my beating scarred heart. But for some reason, I carry around some essence of guilt, which I cannot explain. What had been my fault? What had she been told that I had done that so wronged her? But maybe I'm not meant to understand the pain carried around by another.

I have not taken my eyes off Isa since I started daydreaming about our past life and was taken off guard when she looked at me and demanded, "What are you looking at?"

She is leaning towards me and pushing the carved bits of wood on to the floor. Then Aldous brings everyone's attention back to him as he raises his hand up with a box of new chalk.

"Perfect! Thought I'd never find one. I should really reorganize this chaos. Okay then, quality sign. Who can tell me your sign along with the residing zodiacs? I'll give you a clue. Us Caps aren't related to you in this one and I want to hear from someone who is yet to speak."

Europa and Kendall both slowly place their hands down and I feel everyone's eyes on me and Isa. I stare intently at the ground, then Aldous says, "Alright then if neither of you are going to decide, I'll decide for you. Isa, can you tell me your quality sign along with the residing zodiacs who you are related to you within this element?"

My head is pointed towards the front of the room but I glance to the side to see Isa's fist bunched up in frustration. Refusing to make eye contact with Aldous, she says nothing. Aldous turns towards me with impatience. I know no Capricorn likes a dilly-dallier.

"I'll take that as a no then. Taura, can you inform us of your quality sign?"

Still looking at the floor, I feel the blood rushing to my face. I nod and say with soft words, "*Fixed.* Taurus, Leo, Scorpio, and Aquarius."

Aldous claps his hands together, "Very good, Taura! Now, I'm going to test you even further. Can you give me a small definition of a fixed sign? I'm aware you probably haven't learnt of this yet. But maybe you can give me an idea of what you think, just to expand your minds. Make you think for yourselves."

I feel Isa's fuming glare burning into the side of my skull as though she is telling me 'don't you dare' as it'll make her look incompetent. But I say it any way, "Purpose of a *fixed* sign is to maintain, uphold, and defend possessions, responsibilities, goals, or desires in everyday life. They are not easily distracted when a goal is in place, although this can get them stuck in a rut." I recite it exactly as it was written in a textbook I have read numerous times.

Aldous mouth drops open. "My girl! How did you know that? I'm very impressed, you're the first new blood to ever recite the exact definition written within the text! You must be quite the bookworm. I'll be keeping my eye on you. I like the unassuming ones." He turns around and begins writing dot points on the board, and I hear the pencil break between Isa's hands, making my reflexes abruptly turn in her direction. We make eye contact, and she mouths the words with a slight whisper, "You're dead."

Then Aldous turns around and continues, completely oblivious to Isa's concentrated death glare. Or maybe it isn't his place to interfere as we are not from his Constellation. But I make a point of turning around and forcing myself to listen, taking my mind off Isa's unbroken intense stare.

Aldous continues, "Now, I'm going to add on to that if you don't mind, Taura." I look down at my desk and shake my head. "Great, because what you also need to know is there are twelve houses making up each of these qualities. Each one is made up of four of the twelve. *Fixed* is made up of Second house: *Possession*, which includes emotions, self, ability, needs, and wants. Fifth house: *Pleasure*, which includes creative acts, self-satisfaction, procreation, and children. Eighth house: *Sex*, which includes relationships, and 11th house: *Friends*, which includes clubs, organizations, and groups. Now I'll explain the last two qualities along with their four houses. Make sure to write all this down."

He went on to give the information about the other quality signs, *Cardinal* and *Mutual*, pacing his speech so we could keep up. I already know it, but I hide the fact by writing it in my book recalling the information came from a book titled *The Twelve Houses*.

Isa doesn't write down a single word. At that moment, her attention is fixated upon my existence. Now I'm thankful for not asking about my unknown purpose number ten.

Then Aldous looks at the time; brings his hands together and announces, "And that brings about an end to this time together. I hope you enjoyed it as much as I did. Make sure to study those notes as you'll be tested on them. Now, if you exit through the door you came in, I'm sure you'll find Demetrius waiting for you outside to take you back to the hall for dinner."

We all stand and pick up our books. I make sure not to forget my backpack and carefully place it on my back so the vials don't clink together as they could have moved amongst the hay. Isa gives me a patronizing smirk, suggesting she has me now.

Then I hear Aldous's voice, "Taura, may I speak to you for just a moment?"

A big wave of relief falls over my body and I nod attentively, heading up in his direction; even if it's just for a moment, it allows me to think. He waits for everyone to leave then looks at me directly with his large eyes and says with kindness, "Thought you might appreciate a saviour." So he had noticed Isa's angry behaviour towards me.

"You noticed?"

"Let's be honest, it's not hard to miss. But I'm sure within your Herba community, a blind eye is given or even encouraged by most."

He looks me up and down and I nod.

"I'm used to it, I just try to stay out of her way."

He grimaces, "Unfortunately, that approach won't work with you being in such close proximity to each other within your new everyday environment. Especially so since no one can be around to protect you every hour of the day or night. If, or should I say when, she snaps, your death won't be seen as any loss in your Constellation. I'm sure no one thought you'd last this long."

The blunt words chill me to the bone and I feel the blood drain from my face. I'd never taken that into account.

He continues, "I apologize for being so harsh but someone needs to warn you before it's too late. The hatred in that girl's eyes isn't of any small quarrel. It's a deep darkness and it's eating her alive. It grows with pure hatred and you appear to be the catalyst. Do you know why?"

I shake my head.

"That's a shame. If we knew, we might be able to find a solution. If it were within another Constellation, it'd be different. Unless you were Scorpio. Although I've seen them, on many occasions, to have sympathy towards one as helpless as yourself. Their austerity appears to be related to actioned failure, not an uncontrolled one. I've always believed their water element helps compliment their harshness. But regrettably when one from your Constellation sees red, there is no stopping them. They become ignorant of anyone's feelings. And unfortunately, you were born and brought up within that harsh Constellation. It wasn't always like that. One such as yourself gives them the appearance of weakness, a lack of determination to make only perfect warriors. This has, unfortunately, made them blind to other possibilities and given them a relentless tunnel vision to accomplish the obvious goal. That's why babies such as yourself are killed at birth. So, Isa would get a slap on the wrist, if that. This is because when victim and murderer are from the same Constellation the matter is dealt by the relevant Elders and I know Iden Terran is a religious believer in the Taurean law. Even if Constance Terran disagreed, he would have the last word.

"It is different when it involves more than one Constellation. Then such matters are dealt with by the Doh's regulations (as the opportunity for that to happen would be within the Doh) and the murderer would be sentenced to death by the Scorpio death serum, as it divides the unity they've built between residing zodiacs. "

I nod, his words must be to prepare me for my inevitable fate, my ending by Isa Edlyn's hands. Then he uses his index finger to lift my chin. He peers at me, and seems slightly annoyed.

"Are you just going to lay down that easy?"

Confused by the gesture, I shrug. He continues, "I have said these words to warn you, to make you aware of what may appear inevitable. But also to prepare you. You do not have to lay down like a submissive animal."

His words have spirit and angry passion behind them.

"I've always barracked for the underdog, and I believe you can stop this if you grow a pair of strong mental horns. You clearly have been beaten down so many times that you no longer hold belief in yourself. It does not have to be that way. Anyone can do anything, so long as they truly want it with all their heart. So, Taura Andreas, do you want your life and to live it your way, with all your heart?"

His words throw my thoughts into conflict. I've been told my whole life to take it easy, my staying alive depended on it. I look up at him and explain the illness I've had since I was born.

"Rubbish," he retorts, and I'm instantly taken aback, "You're going to let some supposed illness which no one can explain, define you? When there is no actual proof of it killing you? I'm surprised your father didn't encourage you to become strong in order to help your immune system, considering your Constellation and their regard for beating the undefinable."

I stare at him and say, "I'd never thought of it that way." I considered of the medicine in my backpack and the idea that maybe some training would have been beneficial for my condition.

Aldous throws his hands in the air as though it were obvious. "Well, of course you haven't! Your reality and world were created within the walls of your Constellation. Like every other new-blooded zodiac who comes through here each and every year. Thinking they know everything! Naive to the outside world, presuming their Constellation has taught them everything they need to know, no regard for question. Maybe now you can see how our world fell into turmoil when Apophis created 'The Infernum' and we were unable to reunite. No one could see past their own star. Now, do you see why we must all learn each other's way of living to get a broader understanding?"

My eyes grow wide as Aldous's direct and assertive passion about our world takes my understanding to a whole new level. He is a true Capricorn, but I do think he needed to let off some steam.

"I'm sorry for being so abrupt, my ambition for a restored world gets the better of me. And so many answers seem obvious to me, too," he says this whilst leisurely walking over to the small dusty window, as if fixated on something through its obscurity. Then he unexpectedly pulls open a tiny draw in a small wooden desk pushed against the wall before him. Taking something out, he fingers at it for a moment and curls it up in his hand. Staring at that engrossed point on the window again, he turns around and the light makes his orange-tinged skin gleam, identifying his true beauty.

"Here, take this." He opens my hand and places a cold circular object on my palm. It's a small, old, rusty ring. I look up at him, not understanding.

"I know it may not look like much, but that ring will give you unimaginable strength. Once you put it on, you'll be able to defend yourself, but you must also believe in yourself. Believe that this will enable you to enhance capabilities that you didn't even know existed in you."

The ring is so tiny, it only fits on my pinkie. For the first time, my small frame pays off. I twist my hand back and forth, looking at the ring at all angles to see if it has some sort of magical gleam, but it looks completely ordinary. But maybe that's the whole point to keep its power hidden.

"How does it work?"

"That is the part you must figure out on your own as it's harnessed differently by every zodiac. And don't be deceived by its exterior; misjudgement is probably its most powerful enchantment... Alright then, you better get a move on, I'm sure Demetrius won't appreciate being held up." He smiles encouragingly.

I pull my backpack securely on to my shoulders and head for the door. As I pull the door open, I'm stopped again by Aldous, "Oh, and just remember, Taura, you hold the strength within you. Use it when the time is right."

I nod confidently and say, "Thank you, Aldous," as I head out the door.

Demetrius is waiting and stands with the others upon engraved markings I had noticed in passing on the way in. Now, from the parts I can see, it looks like the circular alignment of Constellations from the teleporter, perfectly and beautifully sculptured into the floor, a vast contrast to Demetrius's poorly drawn chalk illustration back at our Halls of Ivy. My guess is confirmed right away.

"Taura, I was just explaining to the others that these engraved markings are specifically made all around the Doh. So you or anyone else can teleport at any time. They're generally found outside specific destinations, such as classrooms, chambers, the library, and so on. No one should have to look far. Now come stand with us so we can teleport back to the dorms. Now remember, when standing on the platform, you must shut your eyes, visualize your destination, and chant Unum's name."

CHAPTER EIGHT

THE DREAM

*Be wary the stones you choose to carry, time will make the load
heavy and your temper ready.*

After indulging in another hearty supper, during which we
were distracted from the day's events, Demetrius accompanied
us back to our dormitory. He informed us that he will teach us
to teleport on our own in the morning; also stating that when
the lights begin to dim it's a sign for bed. His expression implied
that if we were caught out of our dorm after that time, there
would dire consequences.

The door clicked shut, and I looked over at Isa, readying
myself for another confrontation, but she is already in bed with
her back to me. Beyond her, Henrietta is flipping through a book
from class, apparently uninterested in its contents. Dalton is
lying on the lower bunk, staring resentfully at the bunk above,
either still mad with Henrietta for grabbing his preferred bed
or maybe in confusion about class subjects. This puts me on
edge as it's unlike Isa to let something like me showing her up
go unpunished. Kendall is on his bed, reading, and Europa is
putting photos of her family around her bed.

I slip my bag from my shoulders and it lands harder than I
intended. Glancing around, no one seems to have heard the tiny
tinkle of glass knocking together. I roll my shoulders back and
feel liberated from the heavy weight that has left my shirt damp
with sweat. Pushing the bag into a gap under my bed, I
casually attempt to manoeuvre the sheet to cover it; *not aware
never there*. I drop my backside down on my bed with relief and
roll my head back, closing my eyes momentarily. When I open
them again it is to see the little yellow totem orbs fluttering

around the large upside-down tree.

The tree keeps dropping the occasional leaf, and these somehow bring into the dorm the smell of grass fields, trees, and the fresh air that is reminiscent of our Constellation. The leaves drift down, delicately swaying from side to side only to be quickly salvaged by one of the yellow orbs. When the orb floats back up to the tree, it uses the leaf to secure a nest.

My mattress dips beside me. I lift my head to see Europa sitting there, head slightly bowed down, our thighs close together. She is staring at a photo she has in her hand. She extends her hand out to me and gestures for me to take a look. I sit up properly and take the photo and notice it's been badly worn as though she has held it on many occasions. It's of me and her on the first day we met. Her arm is thrown affectionately around my shoulders and she has a big smile sprawled over her face as the sun shines through trees and over her long blonde hair. Her small horns are shiny as though she had just oiled them and her Taurus tail sticks up behind her. Perfect skin, beautiful features, and magnetic aura, she hasn't changed since that day.

I finally realize I had been gazing at her for so long, without noticing my thumb covering my tinier child self within the photo. There, my head hangs slightly in embarrassment, and my hair, appearing darker than normal, casts a shadow on my face and I clutch a large book desperately against my chest as though it were some sort of comfort. The porcelain skin on my arms looks translucent.

I always hated photos; I guess that's why Adonis has no recent ones of me at home as I always refused to be in any. When I was a baby, I had no choice, but Europa always seems to encourage me to do things I wouldn't normally do.

I sense Europa watching me as I analyse the photo, then she rests her head against my shoulder as we stare at it together.

"When I first saw you, I was captured by your beauty. Did I ever tell you that?"

I move to stare at her. *Is she delusional?* She lifts her head from my shoulder and smiles at me with a chuckle.

"It's true! You were unlike anything I'd ever seen! Kind of reminded me of the ancient creatures, Bibere Sanguinem."

I raise an eyebrow. "The blood drinkers?"

Europa laughs. "Without the blood drinking, of course. Just their beauty."

I shake my head. "You should really go see an Aquarian for treatment."

She tilts her head as if trying to work out if I'm being sarcastic. "What for?" she asks curiously.

I press my thumb below her eye and index finger against her eyebrow. Opening her eye and peering in, I say, "Because I think your vision is impaired." She smacks my hand away and rolls her eyes, defensive like every Taurean.

"Do you remember that day?" she asks.

I shake my head. "Not really. Only that you forced me to be your friend."

She grins, looking at the picture. "You don't remember how it came about?"

"Should I?" I try to recall details that no longer inhabit my memory. She glances at the green and white bed linen and begins rubbing the soft linen with her fingertips. She looks around the dorm at the others who all appear to be in their own little worlds, then lowers her voice to a tiny whisper and leans in. "Ever since you told me about that strange creature and this secret power you presumably have, it triggered memories that I'm surprised I'd forgotten. Because it was so bizarre at the time and still is. It was on that particular day when I first met you, I'd seen it."

I grab her hand. "My power?" I say with anticipation.

She nods slowly, staring at me as though it's too bizarre to say out loud. I wonder how she had forgotten and why I don't remember.

"At least I think so, there is no other explanation. You know how Adonis always kept you locked up inside and you rarely came out to play with anyone when you were very young? You only came out later, when you were allowed to attend school?"

I nod my head and murmur, "Because of my illness?"

She nods. "Well, there was a day I found you playing alone near your house and I remember, distinctly now, because I had just been allowed out again with my brothers and sisters. I'd been punished for wandering off on my own. Anyway, I remember noticing Adonis wasn't with you for once and I couldn't help myself. I had always been curious about you, because you were so different to everyone else. But I'd never dared go near you. Your father was and still is so feared within the Herba community. He made it damn clear to everyone that you were a very sick child and no one was to go near you. I understood why he was so over-protective as you were the only precious being left in his life. That fear fell away when I saw you talking to a large tree beside your home."

"That's not anything special, all children talk to wildlife."

Europa begins playing with the bed sheet again, still nervously. "I know, Taura, it wasn't that. I know this sounds crazy but the...the tree, it was responding to you. As though it were a conscious being. It wrapped its branches around you as though it were hugging you; it responded with nods and shakes when you spoke to it. It drew in the dirt and you drew beside it as though you were both communicating. Being the child I was, at the time I didn't realize how odd it was. You know children are ignorant to the conventional reality of the world, but a Taurean talking to a tree, that's not normal. Only the Sagittarians are able to do that and that's only after going through a tremendous journey through the woods when they're young and spending years learning tree language and so many don't come back. But you were a small child, a Taurean child. And no tree comes alive for a Sag, they're only able to read it and understand the story it can tell and how it has lived by the way it grows and moves. Don't you remember, Taur?"

I shake my head. It's as though my brain has blocked out important details of my life. I might remember events but not the detailed elements of the memories. I recall meeting Europa now, but that memory was only evoked as she told me. It seems that I create memories from the words others bestow upon me. I look up at her and she continues trying to trigger my memory.

"Once I saw this, I had to speak to you. I wanted to know how you were talking to the tree and I wanted you to teach me. I wandered up to you from within the fields where I was playing with my brothers and sisters. We were taking prints of insects with the Memoriae device. No one took any notice of me leaving, but as soon as I got near, the tree froze. I might have been imagining the whole thing. Then you noticed me, and stared at me, stiff with fear. You looked around for Adonis, but I told you it was okay and that I was a friend. You glanced at the Memoriae in my hand and asked, 'What's that?' in your tiny voice, and I explained it was a device that captured special moments in time. I got you to stand next to me so I could show you. You hesitated, then picked up the ginormous book you had next to you. I thought maybe you were going to use it to defend yourself." She laughed. "And this print is from that special moment." She points to the worn picture within my hand and I can see the branches of the tree falling beside me as the light hits her from the outskirts, but I still don't recall the memory. "Afterwards, I asked you how you were speaking to the tree and you looked at me with confusion and said, 'Can't everyone do that?'. That was when your father came roaring out of nowhere and asked what I was doing. He told me to leave, and took you up into his arms. I ran as fast as I could back home; I was terrified of your father. I kept this photo though, pulling down all the random pictures I had from our Constellation and placed us right in the middle of my wall so I could look at it. I knew we'd be best friends." She squeezes my hand. We both fall back on to the bed and look at one another.

"The annoying thing is, Euro, I still can't remember. And it just makes more unanswered questions. How could talking to trees be seen as a secret evil power?"

Europa ponders on it for a moment and says, "I know it doesn't make much sense. Maybe we need to sleep on it. And will go ask Biblio...Bibo...whatever her name is, tomorrow."

I smile looking at the picture. "Maybe you should stick to calling her Bib when we see her, she might take offence to you saying 'whatever your name is'."

Europa chuckles. "Yeah you're probably right, I'll make sure to do that."

The lights slowly became dimmer, reminding us of Demetrius's strict words about that specific sign meaning bed time. Europa kisses me on the forehead, smiles and hops over to her bed. I pull the warm quilt over my shoulder and lay my head on the soft pillow. Only a short time after we're all in bed, the lights automatically go out and the room is illuminated by the small yellow totem orbs that leisurely hover above us. They sway in and out of the tree, relaxing me into sleep.

I find myself staring into the big blue eyes of the woman who holds me tight within her grasp. And I watch the same singular tear fall from her eye and I wish every time that I could save her. "*Te amo,*" she says softly. I stare intently at her face but it is hard to see her face properly because it is dappled by shadows. The moonlight is the only illumination at that time.

"Who are you?" my older self wants to ask, but I can only stare as she lovingly holds me. And for a moment, I hope the dream's time might stand still. But once again I find myself falling and I feel the air stolen from my lungs from the impact of the ground.

I am woken by some sort of felt-like fabric smothering my face. I try to move my hand up to move it off. I can't. *What is happening?* Sweat is forming on my face, and the rest of me is shivering as if cold. My mouth is dry, and there is a tightness in my chest where my heart is pounding rapidly. I begin to panic, not knowing what's going on as I can't see anything. I find myself panting hard, unable to fully fill my lungs with air. Then I realise that several hands and arms are restraining me on my bed. A sense of self-preservation makes me try to fight them off. When I try to scream, my mouth is immediately muffled by a large sturdy hand. Harsh words are whispered close to my ear and I have no doubt of the speaker.

"If you make another sound, I'll slit your throat from ear to ear. You got it?" Isa's hissed voice has overtones of immense rage. I nod slowly and she carefully takes her hand away and I'm given a little relief to breathe within the thick fabric. Someone lifts me up, throws me on a shoulder and begins to walk. I assume I am being taken out of the room. I feel for the ring that Aldous had given me. *Was it only that afternoon?* I can feel its rusty texture still secured around my pinkie, which gives me some hope because I know Isa Edlyn intends to kill me.

I soon lose track of where we are, my body bouncing to the rhythm of my abductor's gait. Then I hear the squeaky sound of a door opening. The one who is holding me, takes one hand off me to punch another.

"Careful, stupid. Open it slowly." I recognize Henrietta's voice and I know Dalton would be opening the door.

I am placed on a hard chair that feels old because it rocks dangerously as soon as my body weight is placed upon it. The cloth is ripped from my head. Isa, Henrietta, and Dalton all stand before me. I choose to say nothing and wait, before adding fuel to their fire.

Isa begins, "So, you think it's wise to humiliate me in class, do you? What makes you so special that you think your life, and your opinions, are held above all others?" She spits and then grabs my face with one hand. I don't dare pull away from it as I know she is about to boil over and there is no one here to cause her to mitigate her force.

I look down from her face, thinking carefully before I speak. "Isa, I never asked for any of this. I understand the way you and others feel about me and it's completely justified. Why should I live when others who are stronger than me are still deemed unworthy? I get it. But it isn't my fault."

She doesn't immediately answer, and I look at her. Deep down, I know mere words aren't going to be my saviour today but I try to prolong the delay before the beating, in the hope I can figure out how to use this ring to save my life.

Isa glances at Dalton who immediately obeys some implied command. He smirks as he walks with deliberation to a position behind me. He grabs the side of my chair and shakes it with a chuckle. I grab the seat so I don't fall off. Next thing I know, he has taken my hair in a fierce grip, and pulled my head back into position against him in such a way that I cannot free it. His other arm traps my arms so that I cannot try to fight back, even if I had the strength.

My only warning of the imminent beating is when Isa's fingers squeeze into her palms, creating a strong and hard fist. Like a striking snake, her fist smacks hard into my right cheek, causing intense pain. I feel the bone breaking beneath my skin. Blood begins leaking from my nose, even as drool begins falling from my mouth, both mixing to saturating my pants.

Isa laughs hysterically, moving to stare at me as she says, "That's right, it isn't your fault, is it? Because you're just a victim, never taking responsibility for your own life and the repercussions it has caused. It's all Daddy's fault, isn't it? Well, sure your dad has played a massive part but you should have done us all a favour, Taura Andreas. You should have taken your own life if you feel so regretful about the other lives taken. But once again, someone else has to take out the dirty laundry and I guess today that person is me."

She looks at me, wanting me to argue with her, but the pulsating pain in my cheek has shocked me into silence. "Now your father, the feared Adonis, can feel the same pain he has relentlessly bestowed upon others in thinking he has the right to override the rules of our Constellation. They should have taken more than just your mother. They should have taken you too! But no, we must be reminded every day of your existence and what horrors it has brought upon our land and my family!"

Her words pain my heart. I couldn't bear to burden my father with any more agony than he's already endured. At that thought, anger begins to pulse in my veins. I won't allow her to hurt him. I twist the ring round and round my finger, praying for the ring to work. The throbbing pain of my upper cheek seems to prove it isn't.

Isa becomes angrier because of my non-responsiveness and begins punching me harder than she ever has before, and everywhere she can. The manic expression on her face is an indication that she is little more than a rage-stricken monster, fuelled by blood lust and red hot anger and blinded by her own self-conceited tunnel vision. Her harsh breathing causes foam bubbles to spray from her mouth as my blood spatters onto her face with every blow. I feel and hear bones breaking, one after another, face and body. The colour of blood fills my vision and then all sight becomes impaired from the intense facial trauma.

Then unexpectedly she stops. Any sort of anger I had, has now been obliterated. My head lolls sideways as Dalton releases it. My body is limp, and I now realize my back is broken, and I am losing the complete feeling and function of my body. All I can feel is the blood oozing profusely from my mouth and face and dripping off it as my head hangs heavily. I strain my eyes to look through the narrow slit in my swollen eyelids and see the repulsed expressions of Henrietta and Dalton who now each hold one of Isa's hefty, muscled arms.

Isa rips away from their grasps, panting, and says, "What are you two doing! You knew the plan was to kill her."

They say nothing. Both glance at each another expressionless, then Henrietta says, "Because you just continue to beat a dead battered body. She was dead after the first few blows. Her neck's clearly broken."

Isa snuffs, "Too bad it wasn't prolonged. Hell, dying quickly is more than she deserves. Her and her wretched father." She wipes her bloodstained hands on her clothes.

Dalton pointlessly adds his unneeded opinion, "Well, she definitely looks dead."

I feel incredibly tired, beyond any fatigue I have felt before. My body is yearning for sleep, but it is slumber I will not wake from. I fight to stay aware, but it's a battle I am inexorably losing.

I am picturing my pulverised insides, settling inside me, making me heavier... No, this will not be my end. My mind grabs the thought. *How strange?* I am no longer feeling the life drain from me with the last of my energy, I seem to be getting stronger. I want to live, with all my heart, I internalize forcefully. I don't want to be known as the girl who got beaten to death by the bully. I no longer want to be just the girl that should have died at birth.

"Alright, let's get rid of the body," says Isa.

"Wait, I think I saw her move," says Dalton.

I hear Isa whack him on the side of the head. "Don't be stupid, have you seen the bloody broken mess in front of you. She's unrecognizable... In fact, I think she looks better that way!"

Dalton shrugs, walks over, and throws me over his shoulder as I continue to bleed. He takes me on a short journey to the spiralling stairs in the centre of the Doh. I know because of the way their voices echo there.

"Alright, get rid of it," Isa directs.

Dalton peers off the edge and asks, "You want me throw her down the stairwell?"

I can imagine Isa giving him an angry glare as Henrietta says, "But they'll find the body."

Isa smacks her forehead with her palm, a gesture I had often seen and heard her do. "That's the point, idiots. Make it look like a suicide. No one will care about her life. Anyway she was worthless to our Constellation. Even if they did notice the battered bits, they won't think to question it. They'll think it's for the best. Everyone knows her life was insignificant."

With my neck and back being broken, I am just like a rag doll. I'm only able to know that in spite of somehow feeling stronger, my life is still about to end. With a pulverized jaw, swollen tongue and a crushed voice box, I can't even muster a scream. Dalton takes one more look over the edge and with oddly contradictory care, he gently slides me off his shoulder.

I fall head first. The air resistance makes my hands sprawl out. An unexpected gust of air causes my body to float level and then to rotate upwards and for a moment, I have a glimpse of three heads peering over the railing, before they disappear up in the darkness. *Is this really my fate?* I feel the air pressing hard against my back like it is a strong wind, but still I am aware of the inevitability that I am going land splat on the ground and my whole body will be an unrecognizable broken mess.

"I'm sorry," I say inside my head, thinking of Adonis. I squeeze my eyes shut and as I do I see the image of the lady's big blue eyes from my dream. If only I knew who you truly were, other than the loving woman in my dream.

"*Te amo*," she says again.

"I'm sorry," I say repeatedly inside myself. Tears leak from my swollen eyes, drifting away from my body and I seem to see them float right in front of my eyes, following me down to the end of my journey. The feeling is too overwhelming and I can't stop crying, "I don't want to die!" The sound comes curdled from the broken trachea as blood leaks down my throat and spits out of my mouth. Then, as if my desperation has forced it through, I hear myself clearly, "Please! I don't want to die!"

At that very moment, I feel the number '10' on the back of my neck begin to burn like it does when I teleport. My neck jerks as my whole body comes to an abrupt halt in mid-air. My mind wants me to look both ways and I find I can. Beside me, I can see the beginning of the spiral stair case and then I notice the floor beneath me. I've stopped just before I've hit the ground. *How was I doing that?*

Pain is making itself felt throughout my body. *Is it possible that somehow, my broken neck has healed?* Then the pain intensifies as my broken bones begin to snap, crack, and pop relentlessly into place. My skin begins to burn and my body jerks sporadically with uncontrolled movement. I continue to scream incoherently, becoming louder as my vocal chords realign. I wish someone would hear me, but no other life form comes to my aid and I don't have the energy to help myself. The pain is so overwhelming. *Why hadn't I just hit the hard floor?* The agony continues to increase, becoming so unbearable that I black out.

I awake with a slight headache. My cheek and body lay touching a stone-cold floor and my left arm has gone numb as though I'd been lying on it for a long time. *How long had I been out?*

I sit up and suddenly realize my body is fine. Maybe even better than before. I look over my hands, arms, and the rest of my extremities, lastly feeling my neck and face which are both completely intact.

"How could this be?" I murmur aloud. I take note of the ring, my gaze lingering on it. It seems Aldous had given me a marvellous gift after all. I think to look around at my surroundings and realize I am not in the foyer of the Doh where I had expected to land. I am concealed by darkness within a tiny corridor. *How did I get here?*

I don't know where thus passage leads from, for in one direction it is totally dark. However, a few feet the other way, the passage opens up onto a large well-lit hall. From my vantage point, the hall looks incredibly grand, and I stand up to get a better look. My shoulder knocked something that was hanging on the wall. It rattled loudly enough that I felt for it to still its noise, before walking to where the light just fell into the passage. There was no one moving within the part of the hall I could see. I risked a peek either way.

The hallway looked to be three or more times as wide as the classroom I'd been in and had a red velvet carpet lying along the centre of it, extending in each direction. Dark wooden walls, reached up high, towering over me. The trees whose lives had been taken to make them must have been majestic, and probably hundreds of years old. The light came from large glowing white globes, mounted on the wall at intervals. They were not as bright as sunlight, although that was starting to come in through the long slabs or glass in the high ceiling that alternated with sections of dark wood.

I ventured out further, and the globe nearest me brightened, sensing my movement. The light coming in from above reminded me of dawn, and I wondered if the globes were dim when the sun was fully bright. That was only a minor mystery. I really wanted to know where this place was, and where all the doors and other wider passages led to. Some of the doors were of ornately designed wood, like I had seen in other places in the Doh, others looked to be made of steel – all were much wider than the passage I was in.

How busy this area became, during the day, I had no way of knowing. Now though, I felt watched, but the only sign of life, if you could call it that, were the large old paintings like the one on the wall beside me. It showed legendary zodiacs caught in a moment of war stricken time. This one was titled *Fighting the Infernum*. It showed zodiacs fighting other zodiacs, the only telling of the possessed ones are their brightly painted purple eyes.

Other large paintings were spaced along the far wall and they seemed, from a distance, to be immaculately drawn, so much so that the zodiacs within might be watching me. Between the paintings were tall ornamented vases, or large carved curios on pedestals. I didn't dare go for a closer look, but I had never seen anything like them.

The silence that I had begun to take for granted was disturbed by the sound of voices coming from somewhere out of sight. I moved quickly, hoping the dark narrow passage I was in was too insignificant to be noticed. The voices became clearer, two different tones, one deep and masculine, the other high and feminine. Taking a careful peek out, I see the very tall figures of two PNC Aquarians, healers I assumed, who had just turned out of a passage and were carrying with ease a large casket by handles at each end. In shape, it looked like the wooden caskets we use back in the Taurus Constellation for carrying the remains of the dead. This though, was made of steel, with rounded corners. In length, an Aquarian could have been lying in it. Had one of them died?

As the two PNCs drew closer, the nearest globes brightened a bit and I hoped the one near me had dimmed again. The voices were clear now.

"She isn't exactly big, I don't know why we have to carry

her around in this oversized casket. Plus, it mustn't be very comfortable in there. I feel sorry for her," says the female.

"I know, but unfortunately Theophilus doesn't want to chance any one seeing her. You know it would cause an uproar. She's meant to be a mythical legend. We're nearly there anyway, and then she can stretch her legs, have something to eat and we can go get a bite before we begin testing. I'm starving!"

The woman laughs. "You are always hungry, where does it go anyway?"

The man glances over his shoulder with a sarcastic expression. "My arse!"

They both laugh as they place the casket down in front of a large steel door. With their hands free, they pull out some sort of device to scan the back of their necks. Their purpose numbers light up and the door clicks open. They pocket the devices and pick up the casket once more, the male PNC moving his end around so they were lined up with the door to go in.

Unexpectedly, something hits my shoulder, making me spin around and grab the cause of my fright. It's the stick handle of a broom. Glancing back and seeing the door slowly closing, I impulsively keep hold of the broomstick and race over to the door with the handle extended out in front of me, stopping the door before it closes.

I don't know what made me do it. The talk between the healers had made me curious. What sort of monster were they carrying that was meant to be a legend and Theophilus wanted no one to see? Feeling watched, I glanced back along the hall but saw no one, then slipped through the door, taking the broom handle with me. I didn't want anyone to think there was a prowler. I was out of my dorm, although it was no longer night, but I was certainly not meant to be where I was. Later, I would have to find one of the transporter places and go back to the dorm, but for now, I didn't want to be found.

A short dark hallway leads to another secure door with a high dusty window that gleams with a bright light. I move quietly to the door and stand on the tips of my toes, and wipe away some of the dust with my fingers. I peer through the bottom part of the window to see an immensely clean white room with infirmary equipment everywhere

Against the far wall, small and large liquid filled capsules with strange mutated creatures floating within caused me to focus my attention there. They looked as if they should be small babies of some unfamiliar species. In fact, they are deformed and look to be dead. Some have two merged heads, bulging eyes and their insides hanging out of their body and some don't have a single limb just a barely formed head. I press my head against the window so I can see around a bit further. My eyes just see the lid of the oversized coffin which has been opened and is now presumably empty.

The two Aquarians stand over something on a table, it must be whatever was held captive inside the coffin. The male holds up a syringe, and expels some air from it, before injecting the creature on the table. Then he opens a small compartment, takes out a variety of jars, and pours some from each into a bowl before returning the jars to the compartment. The bowl, which I guess to contain some kind of sustenance is placed on a tray next to the creature. The Aquarian woman seems to be talking to the creature, like a mother might talk to a sick child, patting it and encouraging it to eat. Then she gestures to the male to get a move on. He packs some things away in another compartment, then looks down at the female as he rubs his belly with enthusiasm. She gathers her things and they leave through another door. Their soft voices are probably reassuring the creature that they won't be long.

I wanted to see what was on the table and I jump up for a quick look. A soft, creamy pink creature lays on a table with no physical protection but its own bare skin, and that looks delicate. Its back is turned towards me as it lays on its side. Long mousy brown hair grows on the top of its head and falls delicately off the table. It has no scales, horns, tail, claws, or a hard shielded exterior. This is the first species I've seen that looks weaker than me. Unexpectedly, it sits up, it's back still facing me. It looks down at the food on the tray rummaging through the bowl, picking up bits and pieces to look at, but decides against eating. Its ribs stick out prominently on both sides of its bony spine. Its fragile exterior rouses my pity; it clearly needs to eat something because it appears to be starving to death. Its spindly arms struggle to lift it enough to slip off the table, and when it places one foot down after the other, it needs the support of the table to hold its weak frame up. *What is it?* I ponder. It begins to turn towards me and my eyes widen with curiosity. My mouth drops wide open. *It cannot be!* But it is the woman from my dream.

I know it's her from the shape of her eyes and an overwhelming feeling deep inside me that I can't quite explain. I just know.

Before I have a chance to see the colour of her eyes, she turns away again, now seeming to stare at the capsules of deformed babies. She pushes away from the table and moves unsteadily to place one hand against a tall tube and then press her head against it. *Are they her babies?* I wonder why are they deformed and dead in a tube, their skin wrinkled and grey as if in a state of decay; they should be laid to rest with the Wisdom Tree.

I place my hand on the glass and tears begin flooding uncontrollably from my own eyes. I want to know if she's okay; why she isn't eating and why they are preforming tests on her. I begin banging on the glass lightly at first with one fist but the glass proves to be immensely thick. So, I start using both fists hitting it as hard as I can to get her attention.

She suddenly glances my way, not noticing where the noise is coming from at first. Although she looks different, with her cheeks sunken in and a grey pigmentation tinging her skin, I know it's her by the big blue eyes. The same single tear falls from the same eye as in my dream. Then we make eye contact and I instantly know the dream was not a dream but a memory.

At first, she turns whiter than before as though she has seen the dead come back to life. And I continue to bang on the window as she stands, disbelieving what her eyes are seeing, clearly unconvinced of her own sanity. Then she runs over with tears flowing from both her eyes, staring at me with wonderment. We stand looking at one another through the tiny window, and I notice we look incredibly similar, apart from the colour of our eyes, plus my horns, tail, and slightly more athletic frame. She places her hand against the glass and I place mine against hers.

"You're alive," she manages to say with a voice which I can barely hear through the thick glass. I nod, although I don't understand why she'd presume otherwise. Maybe she thought I was abandoned in the forest on that particular night, the one I see in my nightmares. It is the only memory of her that still clings to my subconscious, reminding me of her existence.

"Who are you?" I ask. She looks at me confused as though I should know the answer. Her big blue eyes stare lovingly deep into mine, piercing my heart just like that very night. And I feel the answer already lays within me, but it couldn't be.

"Your mother ... my sweet girl, what have they done to you?" she says with tears still falling down her sunken face.

My world begins to spin. My mother? But my mother is dead? And this lady looks nothing like the face of my mother in the picture beside my bed at home. I don't even know what species this woman is. So many unanswered questions begin to demand attention in my already muddled mind.

"Penelope?" I ask. She shakes her head in confusion,

"Penelope? What lies have they been feeding you!" she spits with unexpected fury. "You know who I am. I'm..."

The two Aquarians come barging in. Their mouths drop open in unison, as they realise that their creature is talking to someone through the window. They stare straight at me.

The frail creature turns into uncontrollable rage and her voice rises, loud enough to be heard clearly through the window. "You told me she was dead! You told me they left her in the forest! I thought the world was doomed! What did you do with what's inside of her?"

The male approaches her cautiously, with his arms sprawled out as though trying to calm a wild beast.

"Please, you must come with me. I don't want to have to give you the injection," he says with sincere concern. She picks up a small sharp object on a nearby steel table and starts flailing it about.

"If you lay one finger on her, I swear, I'll kill every last one of you!"

I'm instantly taken back by her hostility; she reacted so instinctively and so intensely to her emotions, unlike any adult zodiac I've ever seen. The Aquarian soon restrains her and she turns towards me still trying to struggle free. "Run!" It sounded like a heartfelt plea.

I stare at her big blues eyes. The eyes I thought I'd never come to know. I don't want to leave her here. Then I notice the other Aquarian female trotting toward the door. I turn and run back to the other door but it's locked. I realize I don't have a way to open it without the two Aquarians' purpose numbers and whatever they scanned them with. I press against the corner of the wall and she comes through, approaching me calmly. She kneels down to my height and holds her large single hand out to gently take mine. "It's okay, I won't hurt you. Come on, you'll have to come with me. This is no place for someone like you."

CHAPTER NINE

THE BWBACHOD

Ugliness is the most misunderstood of beauties.

Now being led down hallway after hallway, I have no idea where I am or where I'm being taken. Each new passageway looks the same as the one before. A red carpet to walk along and portraits on the walls. I have no idea who most the zodiacs are or why their likeness was there, though I recognize some elders, and a particularly famous Taurean. I wonder how I did get near that infirmary. I hadn't been anywhere like these passages before.

I'm being escorted by the Aquarian female who caught me outside the chamber of the creature who said she was my real mother. If she really was, it would explain why I am weaker and more petite compared to other Taurus females, even if I do have horns and a tail. It makes me question the story I have been told all these years. Who am I really? And what am I if my mother is that strange, weak, and fragile creature?

I manage to get the courage up to ask, "May I ask where we are going?"

The Aquarian glances behind her. "You don't have to linger so far behind, I won't use my heavy hand on you. I promise." She smiles kindly. I manage to produce some sort of comforting expression, recalling what I've read about the Aquarians, appreciating their kind, and magnetic mannerisms. I can see why they make friends so easily and why animals love them. Their aura is powerful yet neutral and inviting. Even though she found me in an area that is completely off-limits to someone of my status, she still manages to keep a warm but detached demeanour as she probably takes me somewhere that is probably not going to be all that kind, but I will feel comfortable getting there. I walk slightly faster, trying to keep up with her larger steps and as soon as I'm walking beside her, she says, "May I ask how you managed to not only get close to that restricted infirmary but find it in the first place?"

I can't really answer because I don't know myself. I peer at the ground and say, "It's a long story."

She smiles. "I bet. Well, you will get to explain your long story shortly."

We eventually come across two large wooden doors, made out of a warm dark timber with beautiful artwork crafted upon it – a large snake, I presume to be Apophis, stands upright; the giant Wisdom Tree with all its animals and creatures surrounding its trunk, basking in all its glory, and the twelve zodiac emblems, in a circle around the other carvings. My eyes slowly scan each element, even the tiny animals, and marvel at the immense detail that's gone into them. As my eyes focus on a small rabbit, I notice the two humans standing above it. I didn't notice them at first amongst the busy scene but I recognize them as they are always mentioned in our historic studies, drawn in the exact same way as here: the legendary Adam and Eve. I look closely at Adam's face, I recognize the detail there from all the books about him and then I turn to Eve who is also like the figure in the books until I peer closely at her eyes. They are the big eyes of the woman from the infirmary.

I turn to the Aquarian woman. "That creature in the infirmary, that...that was Eve!" I don't even ask for confirmation that she was Eve, the female human. I already knew it.

The Aquarian doesn't look at me; in fact, she maintains her composure and says nothing, not even to agree or disagree with my theory. Then I realize I had been so taken by the artwork, I hadn't realized that we had been standing at the door for quite some time. She could have hurried me in before I had noticed, but she didn't. Did she want me to know? Am I half human? And what did Eve mean by 'what did they do with what's inside of me?' Is she implying my supposed secret evil power?

The grand doors begin to open revealing an even larger room with even taller ceilings and ostentatious artwork than any other room I have seen before. A fire burns brightly in a massive marble open fireplace, creating the warmth that gently caresses my face as I walk in. Opposite the doors, beyond the open fire, is an immense window that allows a panoramic view over the Nirvana valley. Magic must be involved, for such a view is impossible from anywhere within the Doh. Particularly as the view is slowly changing. From here, we can peer at the world as if we were the gods ourselves.

A long table stands at the end of the room in the exact centre of the glass wall. It has a stuffed trophy animal sitting beside it on the right-hand side. The preserved creature which looks to weigh about the same as a Taurean cow, has high front shoulders and a sloping back. It is half again my height, positioned to appear snarling with its mouth open and lips curled, showing off its large sharp teeth. It was obviously a ferocious and powerfully built carnivore and I hope to never bump into one. I wonder what Constellation it's from. We approach the table but are not really close to it when the Aquarian places her arm in front of me as though there were some kind of danger.

A deep fierce growl starts to intensify, coming from the animal whose life I'd thought had been extinguished long ago. My heart began to pound so hard, that all I can hear is the thunder of my pulse reverberating in my ears. *Thump, thump, thump.* Now profusely sweating, my body prepares itself to fight or run, but before my reflexes find the courage they need to react, the Aquarian gently holds my arm and says, "Don't make any sudden movements. It's not a dangerous animal, unless you provoke it. It may come across as cold and detached but that's only because it's an independent creature. Slow to show emotion unless they deem you trustworthy. It just doesn't trust you as yet. It's actually very humble and loyal soul. It's only doing what it's told as it's an incredibly faithful and protective friend."

I don't take in much of what she says as I am fixated on those sharp teeth, dripping with saliva, clearly hungry for its next meal. Unable to calm myself, I try to hide by slowly shifting my rigid body behind the Aquarian as she still maintains her calm and comforting aura. In spite of this, the animal doesn't take its eyes off me. In fact, I don't think it has even taken notice of the Aquarian. How could it define me as the threat in comparison to a large Aquarian who could be mistaken for a close relative of a giant? Then I hear a familiar voice within the room.

"If you don't calm yourself, he'll be able to follow that wretched fear scent anywhere you go, no matter how far or quick you can run. He won't harm you unless I say otherwise. His name is Kerit, he is my most dearest and trusted friend."

A large, screeching bird is thrown from behind Kerit. His head twists rapidly, catching it instinctively with his mouth without even seeing it approaching him. The bird squawks loudly until a loud crunching sound of bones breaking between Kerit's teeth, silences it. It is apparent how easily he'd devour me after chewing me within those large jaws. I wince, listening to the bones being pulverized, and blood dripping from his jowls to the floor. I try to breathe deeply to calm myself as I can see he is attracted to my fear scent. I momentarily glance away from Kerit's gory countenance and intense stare, knowing who ever resides within this room and from whom I await a reprimand, stands behind this creature who would so willingly devour me in any moment. In that moment of panic, I glance down and notice single white feathers scattered all over the floor, and being most numerous around Kerit. I start to hear a pronounced scraping noise, and two large white wings appear from around the creature. The lower wing edges drag on the ground, leaving a trail of feathers behind. And now I place the voice and the overgrown wings – Theophilus. He turns towards us and for the first time I'm able to see his facial features close up, piercing green eyes slanted downward, thin lips and high cheekbones. He is clean shaven with shoulder length white hair, sleekly pulled back and not one hair out of place. He is wearing the same long robe that he had worn when I had seen him in the common room, in the Virgo colours of green, white, and yellow. For a long ruling zodiac, who must be quite old, his face looks incredibly young, but his demeanour and prodigious wings say otherwise. In such close proximity, he makes me feel as insignificant as a mouse. His large wings face me when he looks out the large window. "He needs to eat whilst his food is still alive so he obtains the most efficient nutrients. Once a creature is dead, most of what is good dies with them," he says blandly as though lives were nothing but to be objectified, to be used at will.

After a pause, he remarks, "So, I hear you have been prying around restricted areas?"

His voice, which had been welcoming when the new-bloods had first entered the Doh, has changed. His now stern and direct manner is a complete contrast.

He glances my way, waiting for a response, and I stand completely stiff not knowing what to say but the truth. "Uh... yes. It is true, Patriarch," I say in a quiet tone. I don't see the point in justifying it as I myself don't understand how I came about it.

"So, tell me how you knew about it, as it's incredibly far away from any area you've travelled to? It would have taken you weeks on foot, unless you had already been there before, in which case teleportation could have been an option."

I twist the ring around on my finger, thinking of Aldous and wanting to explain without involving him as this might be a ring that's forbidden to someone like me. I look up as he still stands turned away from me.

"To be completely honest, Patriarch, I'm not entirely sure how I found that particular infirmary." I tell the story of how I was kidnapped during the night, beaten so brutally my spine was broken, paralysing me from the neck down. Then how I was thrown down the centre of the Doh's spiral stairs. I mentioned my recurring dream and that the woman's eyes had been one of the last images I had in my mind when I had stopped just above the stone ground floor. I described the brutal pain that followed, caused by what I believed was my bones rejuvenating, and how I had passed out and then woken right next to the infirmary. I added about the ring I had supposedly come across in the library and had noticed it had some sort of power prior to being taken during the night past, trying to divert the story away from Aldous. I take the ring off and go to place it on the table but Kerit insists on growling heavily.

"It's okay, Kerit, leave her be."

The creature obediently stops, but his ears are pressed hard against his head and his stance is threatening. Turning around without meeting my gaze, Theophilus picks up the ring and looks at it carefully. He holds it up high and brings it back down. Turning towards the table, he holds his hand out flat with the ring sitting delicately in the centre of his palm.

"So, you presume this rusted, worthless junk teleported you there?"

I nod cautiously.

He crushes the ring effortlessly within his fist then allows the broken pieces to fall from his fist to the table as though it were fine gravel. My mouth drops open and my eyes widen as he stares at me in a coldly emotionless manner. "Wherever you found it or...should I say, whoever gave you that ring, told you a lie. It was just an old, rusty, worthless piece of trash. And I want you to remember there are eyes everywhere within this place. So be careful the lies you decide to feed me next."

The blood drained from my face and I nod, pressing my chin against my chest. Kerit's heckles are now standing high and he hasn't taken his eyes off me.

Theophilus turns back around and asks, "Now that we have that established, do you know what the creature in the infirmary was?"

My eyes glance at Theophilus whose wings now face me again and I quickly shift my eyes back to the floor. "The female human...Eve?" I hesitantly answer.

His head turns towards me, but only so I see his face in profile. "Indeed, you are correct. And I presume she told you, you were her daughter?"

I nod again, my bewilderment must be clear in my expression. I wonder how he knows all this information.

"Before I explain why that is a preposterous concept, let me explain the story behind Adam and Eve. They were created to be a part of our world, but to be honest, I never understood their purpose or why Unum had created them in the first place. They are weak and unable to defend themselves as you have seen. Plus, they are too emotionally chaotic and as you also saw, unpredictable. Many of us could see they would slowly kill one another due to their own greed, gluttony, laziness, wrath, lust, pride, and envy. And we knew, due to these over-encumbered emotions, they would destroy anything that got in their way. So when Unum left, Adam disappeared, and Eve went crazy as she had lost her first daughter and developed many emotional problems due to Adam's abandonment of her. Now you may presume that it could be you, but that would be impossible as that happened centuries before your time. You may look alike but that's only because you embody certain traits similar to those of her long-lost daughter, in particular your physical qualities. She has done this before, reached out. We believe she has a strong telepathic power and you probably do to, that is probably how she connected to you. And that is why we keep her hidden and only known as a legendary tale. Because unpredictability is not something that can be controlled, only contained."

Suddenly, the door slams shut behind us. I turn around and to my disbelief, I recognize the creature that came in as the one who had been standing in my bedroom the night before last. We make eye contact and his expression becomes instantly tense, probably not noticeable by others who aren't aware of our first encounter. His eyes quickly dart away, pretending not to recognize me, as he hurriedly walks past me with a pan and brush.

Kerit starts to foam uncontrollably at the mouth, then emits small broken rumbles. A mighty roar, makes the creature jump in fear and clean even faster. Theophilus watches, being amused by the torment Kerit induces upon the poor creature, as expressed by its facial expression. Then Theophilus slowly holds up his hand and says, "Calm yourself, Kerit, there is no need to do that every time the Bwbachod enters the room. I understand his presence is irritating but we have to allow him to do his menial jobs. After all, everyone must have a purpose."

He smiles patronizingly and doesn't even acknowledge the creature as he sweeps the broken pieces of the ring from the table, and goes on to sweep up the moulted feathers from the floor, without coming close to the pile of feathers near Kerit.

My mind was thinking, *He's the Bwbachod?* I hadn't known what they looked like. So, it didn't occur to me when the Pisces SNC overseer was informing us that Theophilus had the last one enslaved, that I had seen one. The Bwbachod quickly cleaned up the remaining mess and left as fast as he entered, deliberately avoiding my intent curious stare.

"Now as I was saying, before I was rudely interrupted... Taura Andreas, you appear to have some sort of gift that you were unaware of until now. It also appears you don't want to recognize it in yourself, as you seek other superficial objects, such as that pathetic ring, to give it justification. You must learn to harness your gift, but don't reveal it to anyone. Many within this place don't like anyone who is different to normal.

"We generally like to be certain of what to expect, otherwise zodiacs like you might end up like the Bwbachod race. You might find yourself enduring the same experience as you did last night over and over again. I don't know if this strange power of yours will save you every time, since you yourself don't know how to control it. So instead, I encourage you to try to understand. Bring forth its true identity in your own time. I understand, however, you won't have much time between your studies for such things. So, I'm going to allocate someone to help you, and who will also report on your progress. But this, too, must remain a secret.

"And last of all, you must not inform anyone about Eve, otherwise I will have you eliminated. I'm willing to help you but I'm not willing to help one who causes unnecessary rumours which could be detrimental to the Constellations' unity. Something of this nature could cause some to lose faith in the system and

I am willing to eradicate anyone who disrupts the balance and peace that has taken years to build. Do you understand?"

I nod repeatedly to assure him. "Yes, Patriarch, and thank you. I promise not to tell anyone."

He turns towards me and forces himself to look at me; it's as though he tries to hide some kind of disgust.

"Good. Now go on with your day as if nothing had happened and I shall call for you again."

The Aquarian female escorts me to a side door that resembles others I have seen within the Doh. As we go through, I see the room is a planetary site for teleportation. And I ask as we enter, "May I ask what that Kerit creature was?"

She glances down, closing the door carefully behind her and not making eye contact with me. "He was once a bear. But now..." she shuts her eyes for a moment, searching for the right words, "now he is more like a distant relative." She gestures with her hand, introducing me to the room, not wanting to add anything more to her previous statement. There is another of the constructions of golden planets in a planetary orbit, representing our ruling gods, spinning around in a controlled trajectory. It looks identical in features to the one outside our dorm, just more elaborate, like everything else within this sector of the Doh. The golden planets slow their trajectory as we approach so I can step on the platform. The Aquarian female grabs my hand gently and unexpectedly. She glances around as though there could be someone listening and releases a small frustrated sigh. Looking at me intently, she says, "Be careful."

Not understanding the reason for the comment, I nod.

"What is your name?" I ask.

She lets go of my hand and steps away from the orbiting golden planets and says, "Cordelia Dion."

I smile slightly as the planets now begin to pick up pace.

"Thank you, Cordelia," I acknowledge that she had been kind to me even though I'd placed her in a difficult situation. Shutting my eyes, I begin to chant our creator's name Unum, visualizing our dorm.

CHAPTER TEN

INHABITANTS OF LIVING

Belief lies within the stories of our upbringing.

Having brought me back to familiar ground, the rapidly rotating planets slow to a halt so I can step out. Pausing momentarily to catch my thoughts, I have the infirmary and Eve's big blue eyes and fragile body on my mind. Do they have other incredible powers such as the telepathic abilities Theophilus spoke of? Is their fragile state a ploy to be underestimated and to be overly protected in that infirmary? And who's going to teach me to connect and control my supposed power?

Arriving at our dorm, I glance up at our Constellation's poem. Before entering, I murmur the last two lines: *Beware colour red, fixed arrow makes his bed.*

Isa comes to mind. Theophilus didn't give me advice on how to deal with her. Now she'll be well aware something is just not right as she saw me fall to my death. I wonder what she'll do in response; the thought brings me fear and dread.

"Well, hurry up and recite the rest of the poem. I haven't got all day." The voice gives me a start.

I frantically glance around the hall, but it appears to be empty.

"Up here, genius."

I look up and notice the impatient and irritated expression of the Taurus doorknocker, its eyes peering down at me, beneath his large golden eyebrows.

"Oh sorry, I haven't entered on my own before."

It rolls his eyes. "Memory of a gold fish you have."

I quickly read the rest of the poem aloud and he sighs.

"Don't breed them like they used to," it remarks disappointed.

The emblem above the door glows bright and the door begins

to open.

To my relief, no one is there; class must have already started. The little yellow totems dance around me as I enter. Gently pushing them out of the way, I grab my books, then as I turn to leave, the other backpack catches my eye. I had nearly forgotten to take my medicine. Thinking of my father, and that I am already late for class, I grab a vial and shove it in my pocket.

Once I am back out through the door, I turn around and say to the doorknocker, "Maybe you shouldn't be so quick to judge... I mean, you're the one who knocks on doors for a living."

The knocker rolls its eyes as though it's been alive for too long and has lost all patience. It now looks at me as though seeing me for the first time; staring for so long, it becomes almost uncomfortable.

"You know...I've seen those eyes before." Its eyes drift away and his expression becomes hard as though trying to recollect a lost memory. "You can read a lot from someone's eyes. I see the same ignorant eyes coming through this door each and every year. But those eyes, they were different from the rest." It pauses, thinking on it for a moment.

I curiously answer, "Was her name Penelope...May?" I suggest my mother's maiden name as she would not have been married to my father when starting the Olympus Trials. His large eyebrows raise in recollection.

"Penelope May. Yes, that could have been it," it says musingly. "She represented the old Taurus ways of life... Not like now, all brawn, no brains. You should be grateful to have such eyes. They have a history that tells no lies."

Before I can ask more about her, the knocker shuts its eyes and transforms back into the lifeless doorknocker he deceivingly portrays.

Movement from the abstract glass art between my dorm and that of the Geminis' draws my attention. I had only ever glimpsed the Taurus symbol hovering within when being hurried to or from the transporter. Now I realise that there is also a Gemini symbol in the sphere, as the two transition into a merged symbol for a time, rotate slowly, then separate again, coming to rest facing the relevant dorms once more. While they rotated, I noticed that the symbol at the back could be seen as a reflection in a glass panel attached to the dark wood of the wall.

As I started to move towards the transporter, my own movement was reflected in that glass. There was more of me to be seen than I could see in the mirror I had at home. It made me wonder, who I really was, if not Penelope's daughter, and what was embodied in the depth of my eyes. No answer came, so I took a deep breath and headed for the transporter.

With a quick glance at the other side of the dorm doorway, I made a note to myself to look at the other abstract glass art around this hall, when I had a chance. Right now, I just hoped I was not too late for class.

Standing hesitantly before the classroom door, I feel for the vial in my pocket. I take it out, popping the lid and shoot it down, wishing I had some water with me to wash the horrid taste out of my mouth. I delay several long moments before I enter, taking a few deep breaths. I glance at our Taurus emblem above the door and enter the classroom. As I push the door open, I hear Aldous's voice. He's has only just started.

"Alright, today's lesson is all about the Constellations' inhabitants and living." He stops as I enter. "Well, look here. Taura! I thought you had gone astray," saying the last word with a trace of spite as he glances at Isa. "No one knew where you were. I hope you're okay?" he gestures for me to go to my seat.

I nod, feeling the discomfort of everyone's eyes staring at me. They seem to be waiting for my explanation and I manage to croak out, "I wasn't feeling well. So, I went to the Aquarian healers in the early hours of this morning."

He smiles warmly. "Well, we're all glad you're feeling better. Please take your seat."

Europa is beaming at me with excitement, clearly relieved of some previous concerns. I notice Isa's expression through my peripheral vision, but I don't dare acknowledge her. She stares at me as though she has seen a ghost, which seems to be a recurring expression of late. Dalton and Henrietta just stare blankly. Aldous looks at all three of them.

"Did you three want to make a memoriae? Or did you have something to share with the class?" he asks suggestively.

Isa quickly readjusts herself. "No, Mr. Darcy," she says, finding her voice. She continues to glance at me periodically as though I might disappear.

"Okay then... Now as I was saying, Constellations and inhabitants of living. Unfortunately, this lesson won't be a very interactive one. You'll need to read from an old text and take notes of the important content as you aren't allowed to take the books with you. I've placed a copy of the book inside each of your desks. And be careful, they're very old."

I open my desk and take out the neatly placed book. It is old and tattered, has a fading dark green coloured cover and golden border. Written in bold writing is the title, *The Deeper Understanding of the Twelve Constellations*. Aldous begins writing on the board with some new chalk he had found since the last class and I suddenly notice he has tidied up the whole classroom. No more cobwebs hang from the corners of the room, there is not a speck of dust in sight, and the air is no longer dusty. I see the windows have all been cleaned and are open to air out the room. Even his desk is neatly organized.

'Page number 55' is written on the board and underlined. Aldous continues to write more underneath as he speaks, "Alright, turn to page 55 and get started. You will need to know the names of the areas that each Constellation inhabits, certain Constellation specific rituals, how the different zodiacs go about everyday life, why they do things the way they do and how it has shaped them into the particular zodiacs we have come to know today. And the allocation of duties of each Constellation's NCs, PNCs, and SNCs. I'll be doing some marking at my desk, so if you have any questions, please put your hand up. This is learning time, so no talking."

I see Europa beaming at me and I smile, reassuring her.

Aldous clears his throat, a reminder of where our attention should be, and I turn my book to page number 55.

I looked down at the page, the information about the Scorpio Constellation. My mind skipped immediately to Imelda Kore, and how Europa had said she wanted to be fierce and strong like her. Well, my friend had a better chance of managing that than I did. From what Demetrius had told us about Imelda, I was in a similar position to what she had been when young. What was it about the Scorpio Constellation that helped make her what she was?

The Scorpio Constellation

Scorpios love the warm sand and hot sun and live within a desert called Solitudiem, inhabiting houses made from sun-dried mud bricks, which in turn are constructed from the plentiful dry, sandy dirt mixed with a mucus all Scorpios excrete. These houses are given a smoother finish using stucco made from the same substance, smoothed over the brick and allowed to dry in the sun to a very dense solid.

The mucus, called 'Mundet', is a non-toxic excretion that keeps the tube within the Scorpios' stingers clear, and flushes them after being used to eject 'Venenum' the deadly poison, or 'Somnum' the toxin that causes sleep or paralysis. When the Mundet builds up, it is ejected and stored out of the sun. The substance is collected regularly and used for the benefit of the community for brick making and sealing roads and paths.

All Scorpios, once they are past puberty, can consciously produce and eject both Venenum and Somnum. The potency of each is affected by emotion, and to a lesser degree by diet and seasonal based food choices. The males' Venenum increases as a hormonal reaction to protect their mates and young. Hunters may use either compound to kill or capture animals used for food. Neither Venenum nor Somnum affects the Scorpios when consumed, only when injected.

Scorpios are possessive of what's dear to them, keeping their families well protected, not interacting with each other all that often unless they have profound respect for the other. They do not waste time on those who they deem unworthy; even their children must interact and marry those who are respected amongst the community.

Although they may seem hard, Scorpios, being a water sign feel an immense amount on the inside. These zodiacs are taught to fight from the moment they are born due to their harsh living conditions. To be the highest sought-after male and female within their Constellation, they must defeat every Scorpio of their sex at the age of 20 in a combat field known as Mortem Arena. This displays ambition and bravery, striving to be the best and depending on what young Scorpios exemplify will depend on how sought-after they are within Solitudiem. The bravest of the brave marry one another, to breed stronger, fiercer offspring thus obtaining the highest respect within their community, something Scorpios hold most important. After Mortem combat, the weakest Scorpios commit a ritual called Secundum, by which they stab themselves in their intestines, using their own stinger, and pull it up towards their sternum. If they accomplish this ritual, they will keep their dignity and respect within their family. However, if unable to perform the Secundum ritual, they will be banished from the community, as it is believed they will only breed weakness within the tribe. Living on the outskirts of Solitudiem is incredibly dangerous as terrifying monsters live within the desert, and without the protection of the community, these Scorpios generally die not long after they've been banished.

NC Scorpio

NC Scorpios stay within Solitudiem, working within the community and every month a proportion of the NC Scorpios are taken to have their Venenum and Somnum glands drained, as these compounds are needed throughout the Nirvana land for both medical and punitive reasons (Venenum is used to put those who have done great wrong by Nirvana to death and Somnum is used for healing and surgical purposes, mostly used and prescribed by PNC Aquarian healers).

As the active compounds are constantly being produced, and replenish quickly, the zodiacs still have plenty. The stronger ones, those zodiacs who have not just donated Venenum and Somnum are able to protect their tribe from the monsters that challenge their existence.

PNC Scorpio

These Scorpios are mostly seen as guards within the Doh. They work alongside a few other zodiacs like Cancerians and Sagittarians enforcing the law.

SNC Scorpio

The Scorpios of this class are great fighters, as their bravery and focus has no bounds. Their skill to fight is bred into them from the day they are born.

Having to reread this section of the book was in no way a disagreeable task even though I recall most of it from reading it before. It reminds me of my gratitude to Constance who used to secretly bring me books like these from the Doh, when I was younger, as I was unable to participate in most activities. I only make notes of elements I had forgotten in detail, wanting to get out of class as quickly as possible.

The others don't seem to be reading as fast, and they need to make notes too, which further slows them. Time seems to be dragging on.

Still thinking about Imelda, I thought that she must have been immensely focussed on proving herself. She had lost both of her parents when young, I'd only lost one – but no one had expected her to be anything more than just a breeder of babies. She hadn't wanted to be considered weak. Instead, she had become a relentless warrior.

Well, most Taureans considered me weak and useless, and would prefer me dead, but surely there was something I could be good at? None of the books I recalled reading had suggested anything, but that was before I learnt of my secret power.

I re-read the note at the end of the chapter. It echoed my earlier thought when it mentioned unlocking our true potential. But how was I to do that? Was that what Aldous was referring to when he gave me the ring?

Please Note:

In every Constellation, SNC is an incredibly hard classification to achieve, in some more than others. If more could be trained, there would be a greater potential to be able to conquer Apophis and the Infernum, but unfortunately, there are very few SNCs.

It wouldn't be difficult for the Infernum to take over our land as they have the same abilities as we do, only they are more powerful because they are not in control of their power.

Apophis is the only one who has the ability to release the true authentic power of any individual. This is why testing at the Doh is so gruelling. The trigger for each zodiac to release their true power must be found, as it is the mind that dictates the level of power we can achieve.

Each zodiac must conquer their own mind to unlock their true and endless potential. Sending zodiacs in to fight against a force like the Infernum, who are controlled by a powerful and ancient evil such as Apophis, without proper preparation would be suicide and the end of life as we know it.

I begin to feel the effects of my lack of sleep last night, as my adrenalin boost has worn off. Aldous walks around the room checking our work. He stops beside my desk and picks my notebook up, he then glances at me with a suggestive smirk, knowing I must have read this book too. Aldous places my notebook down, before moving to the front of the class.

"Alright, that'll do for today. Put the books back in the desk and make sure to go over those notes and memorize them," he says sternly. After a pause he adds, "You'll have class tomorrow with the Aquarian Elder, Cassidy Dion to learn about your totem animals. Demetrius will guide you there and I'll see you later in the week."

As we get up, Europa becomes eager, quickly collecting her books and moving to stand beside me in anticipation. But before she opens her mouth, Aldous speaks again, "And Taura. Mind if we have a word? Won't take a moment."

Europa's expression becomes annoyed, she rolls her eyes subtly.

"I'll wait for you outside," she whispers. I nod. Turning around, I catch Isa staring at me as she walks out of class. I being her usual focal point of attention.

Aldous waits as everyone leaves the room and I stand facing him, feeling for the ring that was once sitting around my pinkie.

"So, I see the ring gave you the strength and courage you needed?" he says, looking down at my hand, his expression betraying curiosity. "Although I'll admit I didn't expect it to work so fast." He gestured towards my naked pinkie.

I shrug, "Mr. Darcy...what was the ring actually designed to do?"

His expression betrays his amusement, as if he knows something I don't.

"What do you think it was designed to do?"

I shrug. "I'm not entirely sure...to give me courage and strength?"

He smiles. "Precisely, and it's done exactly that, hasn't it?"

I feel as though we are on two separate pages of a book. So, keeping Theophilus's words in mind, I ask without trying to give too much away, "Well...by courage do you mean finding places unknown to you? And by strength do you mean...the strength to heal one's self?"

For the first time, Aldous appears to be without words, thinking on it for a moment.

"Well, not entirely, unless those sorts of things were already hidden within you."

I want to growl with frustration. "What are you trying to say?"

He meets my eyes. "The ring was nothing but an ordinary ring, it held no power. But by telling someone otherwise, that it holds and gives great power, it gives them the inner strength and courage they wouldn't have had otherwise. Essentially, it makes you believe in yourself. Now would you have believed in yourself if I had just told you to?"

I shake my head.

"Exactly, some may see it as deception but really that's an ignorant way of thinking. It's a gift of encouragement to lift a blindfold for someone that otherwise would have been lost within darkness. Sometimes, we have to find belief in something as ordinary as we see ourselves in order to see the magic we chose to ignore."

Aldous's wise words of wisdom cease to astound me, now I understand. I nod with enthusiasm, not knowing what else to say as he adds, "Well, I'm glad you found your feet. And whatever did happen last night, it appears Isa won't be bothering you anymore. Just don't let your head get the better of you, keep an eye on those inner thoughts. Now you better get a move on. I'll see you soon."

He turns around and returns back to what he was doing during class.

"Thank you," I say quietly as I walk out of the classroom, knowing he refers to my negative mind that cripples my reality.

Only Europa is standing outside the door, the others must have transported away already. She turns around quickly on hearing me come out. She gestures for me to look at something behind her. I peer around her to see Leon. My mouth drops open as he shoves a piece of paper into Demetrius's large chest and suddenly my hearing comes back to the present moment.

"You have no jurisdiction here, I've been asked by Theophilus himself," Leon says officiously. Demetrius rips the paper from Leon's grasp and begins reading it fastidiously. When he finished, he let it drop from his hand to the floor, finally stepping on it and twisting it under his boot.

"Well, it doesn't make sense for a zodiac of your calibre to teach her how to fight, especially from another Constellation, she should be learning from someone of her own region."

Leon shrugs. "Well, isn't it obvious? Clearly, no one in her

Constellation took the time to teach her. Seeing as you all saw her as worthless. They must think highly of me if someone of my calibre has been assigned to help her harness her natural-born skills. Something in which she should have been taught in the first place."

Leon's pent-up anger towards Demetrius begins to show as his muscles begin to ripple and his rage begins to take over, but he contains the incipient transformation by closing his eyes momentarily and taking a deep breath.

Demetrius smirks at him. "Clearly...because you have so much control over yours... Didn't realize how much influence Daddy had."

Europa pushes me back against the wall as Leon's bone structure begins to change, bones break and expand as his muscles ripple and grow from the increased blood supply and a layer of skin rips from his body. Then he transforms into the more animalistic version of himself: the natural born killer I've read so much about. In that form, he isn't really much taller than Demetrius, I was interested to note. Then, he releases a giant lion roar that echoes within the hall and covers Demetrius's face with saliva.

Demetrius stands completely still and without fear. He casually wipes the drool from his face with his hand and flings it to the floor. Then, with a patronizing expression, he spits on the ground beside Leon as though he has just proven his point.

Turning around he sees me and says, "You've seen what he's capable of, Taura. He's reckless, not to be trusted. I'll be keeping a close eye out, don't worry."

Still glaring at Leon, he pushed Europa into the circle of the transporter and began the chant.

CHAPTER ELEVEN

THE CARE TAKER

Careful the thoughts you nourish
– you'll unknowingly grow a forest.

Leon Sol is hereby the caretaker of Taura Andreas, holding complete responsibility in teaching Taura on how to reach her full potential within her region. He is given full access to Taura, after class hours to teach her how to harness her inner powers. Anyone who interferes with this process will have to answer to Theophilus Malis.

Signed
Theophilus Malis

I fold the crumpled piece of paper, holding it in my hand as I follow him up another of the numerous flights of stairs. As he lets me get my breath back on one of the landings, he reaches out and gently takes my hand, removing the paper to place it back in his pocket, but holding on to my hand a little longer than comfortable.

"Thanks," he smiles charmingly, "and I just want to apologize about before. That genuinely isn't like me, but your overseer definitely knows how to get under my skin. He's a very serious kind of fella, wouldn't you say?"

I'm taken aback by his charismatic way of talking as I had thought him rather arrogant when I first met him. He's kind of appealing. I'm not used to one expressing so much, but he makes me feel comfortable. Taureans don't talk a lot, they just learn to get on with things.

"Yeah, he's always been like that," I say.

"I guess I'll have to get used to it," he chuckles. "So, are you okay with this?" he asks kindly, staring at me but I look away from his penetrating golden eyes.

"Why wouldn't I? Theophilus did assign you to me."

He laughs again. "You Taureans, it's all yes sir, no sir. You never think twice about anything, do you?"

I shrug. "I'm aware you're going to help me find my inner power and I'm going to do the best I can. What else is there to think about?"

He smiles. "This is true. My purpose number probably doesn't help me. I have to consider every detail."

I glance at the back of his neck, noticing the number '4', the same as Isa which makes me cringe momentarily, but I quickly remind myself it's their purpose, not personality.

"Maybe," I say as we come to an average-looking door and Leon pulls out a small crooked key.

"Here we are. You'll have to unlock it so it works properly." He hands me the small ugly key and I look at him, not fully understanding what he meant. But he gestures for me to continue and without question I insert the key and turn it. A glimmer of green and white light shimmers across the door as I open it. Walking in, I'm taken back by the ordinary room. It's not much bigger than my old room at home. Greying wooden floorboards with matching wooden panels that make up the walls and ceiling. Two tiny cracked windows, set in opposite walls, only show darkness outside and no sign of star or sky.

When the door shuts, the temperature drops significantly and the energy in the room makes me feel lonely and sad. Leon becomes incredibly amused by my facial expression, as he circles in beside me, kneeling on his hands and knees, remarking, "Wow, you don't even need to talk. Anyone could read your face like an open book. So that's how you guys express yourselves, can't hide your face, can you?...relax, this is only a reflection of how you perceive yourself currently, which helps me out a lot since you're not a talker."

His seeming insensitivity annoys me. I look away, the muscles of my face rigid and he instantly knows he's hurt me.

"I'm glad you find this all so amusing," I proclaim between

my teeth.

He puts up his hands in submission and says, "I apologize, I can see why you might think I'm mocking you. I promise that is the last thing I want or intend. Let me explain. I know this isn't a true reflection of you, it's only an illusion. A story you have heard or told yourself so many times you now believe it to be so, but I know that isn't the true story. And that's why I'm here to tell you the new story, the one you have buried beneath years of negative thought."

I become stiff all over, my eyes beginning to fill with tears. I look down, piercing the ground with my eyes. I've felt invisible for so long, I don't know what existing really feels like. A single tear begins to fall from my face and I curse it as it escapes. I don't even know this zodiac and he has broken me down in a single sentence. *Am I that predictable?* The room begins to shrink and he gently grabs my hand.

"It's okay, this room isn't a reflection of who you really are, just as it seems now. There is so much more to discover, don't you worry. Come on, look over here." He walks to the middle of the room and points up. I find my hand becoming clammy within his, so I pull it away moving it to hold my elbow. Looking up to where he points, I notice a tiny little white ball that moves in and out on itself with tiny bolts of lightning.

"A cloud?"

He nods. "The cloud is a perception of your inner power, what you currently harness. And this room demonstrates how you feel about yourself. It was designed to reveal what a zodiac feels and the power they hold at any current moment in time. It won't betray the make-up or mind of an individual. I don't think anything could replicate the unique imperfections of one's soul."

I stare at the tiny cloud that stays secure in the centre of the room and ask, "What is this place called?"

He glances at me then at my tiny cloud. "Well, it's a little too obvious really. It's called the 'Reflection Room.'"

I nod in agreement and ask, without facing him, "What does your reflection room look like?"

He smirks, "I'm flattered by your curiosity, but right now I don't think that's a good idea to think on or see, as you'll only compare. How about when you achieve everything you came here to overcome, I'll show you. But until then, we have a lot of work to do." He waved a hand so he pointed all around the room. "By the way, Theophilus explained that your power isn't the usual strength endowed ability from the Taurus region. What does he mean by that?"

I shrug. "No one really knows. But I have a feeling it has something to do with my purpose number."

I turn around lifting my hair and he gently touches my neck which makes my hair stand on end. I pull away and turn around. "Have you seen a '10' before?"

He shakes his head. "Never. What have you experienced, power wise?"

I become hesitant to tell him as to say it out loud would make it sound preposterous. But I remind myself that's the purpose of these lessons. "I've self-healed?"

He shrugs unimpressed, "Pisces and Aquarians can self-heal with their knowledge."

His dismissive comment angers me. "I've healed a severed spine that caused paralysis from the neck down. And I've teleported to places that I've never seen before," I state.

He grins. "Now, that's impressive. You're going to have to use more words when you're around me." He winks. His ego begins to irritate me again.

"Why is a new-blood like yourself teaching me how to harness my power anyway?" I ask.

His facial expression changes to a more sincere one. "I thought you guys didn't second-guess authorized decisions?"

I cross my arms, angered by his stereotypical assumption. "Well, I am asking. I thought you said everyone is uniquely imperfect, which means I'm not that predictable! I'm not like everyone else! And I don't know why!" My voice deepened to a powerful dark tone and as my rage simmered, my words become unrecognizable.

Droplets of rain begin to fall and his expression turned serious. "You need to calm yourself, Taura."

He points to my cloud. Tears begin to flood from my eyes and rain falls even harder down onto the floor. The room quickly begins to fill with water and the walls crack and shake. Leon presses up against the wall.

"Taura, you need to breathe. Everything is okay, you're safe. This is a safe place. Breathe!" I look up to see my cloud has turned into a dark storm, engulfing the whole ceiling with lightning sporadically shooting from unpredictable directions.

"What is happening to me?" I whisper, collapsing into the flooded water that is now as high as my shins. Drawing my knees up to my chest, I rock back and forth. Squeezing my eyes shut, I'm suddenly overcome by what feels to be a lost memory.

Penelope's face appears. *My mother?* She holds me up high within her grip and spins me around; the spinning makes me laugh as I become more and more dizzy. Then she drops me down into her grasp and holds me tight. She looks so beautiful as I stare into the eyes that are now mine. She begins walking, looking at an object in front of her and I just stare at her exquisiteness. Turning me around, she faces me to the tree that Europa spoke about on the day she had met me, the one that hangs over my cottage. But it's currently riddled with some kind of dark disease, spreading from its roots all the way up into its branches. She stands beside it and places my tiny hand against its rotting bark and I can feel its pain. It's in so much pain, it brings tears to my eyes. She gestures for me to do something. I shut my eyes and I feel a deep warm sensation build up inside of me. Opening my eyes, I notice my whole body is glowing a vibrant blue. I gently place my tiny hand on the tree. At first, nothing happens, but suddenly the disease begins to subside, drawing away from the tree's extremities and coming into the palm of my hand. Leaves sprout and flowers blossom instantaneously as the disease dissipates, merging into a dark black stone that I now hold in my fist. Unexpectedly, I'm shaken roughly. Someone had grabbed Penelope from behind. It was my father Adonis and he is yelling at Penelope. But I cannot hear their conversation, it is as though all sound has gone silent. He throws his hands up in the air, gesturing to the field beside us. Penelope yells something back bringing me to her chest as she storms back inside the cottage. Adonis follows with a dark expression of fear and despair.

"Taura, Taura!" I'm shaken awake, "Taura!"

I see Leon's face worriedly staring at me.

"Thank Unum, you're okay. You passed out."

I press my palms against the floor, looking for the water that had filled the room. But the room and the cloud are as they were before I lost all control.

"What happened?" I ask.

He looks at me in disbelief. "Well, your power grew at an immense rate and then you passed out. I've never seen anything like it. This room takes down any mental walls, spells, or potions that hold control over you. It's so you can harness and connect to your powers without fault. Although I didn't expect that to happen so fast, but anger is your current trigger and anger is unpredictable and can't be controlled. So, it can be incredibly dangerous as you just experienced."

I touch the cold wooden floor. "How do you know so much about this room?"

He brings his legs into a crossed position and sits upright. Looking away with a slight glimmer of shame, he quickly turns it around, making deep eye contact with me as he begins to share his story.

"Well, partially what Demetrius said was correct. I guess that's why I lost it. My father, Cedric Sol."

I glance down at his forearm, remembering the memorial tattoo of that name displayed in bold writing, clearly expressing the pride for his father. "He's the Head Commander of the SNC army. So he has a lot of influence within this place and was able to bring me to the Doh from a young age. He introduced me to the 'Reflection Room' and taught me how to harness my deepest inner powers earlier than any other Leo. On record, I'm the strongest animalistic Leo hunter for my age. I've even gotten the upper hand on a few SNC Leos before. But I still have a lot to learn and have to go through protocol like everyone else. I guess that's why so many don't really like me as they have this perception about my identity, until they get to know me of course."

He winks again and I roll my eyes. He grabs my hand and shakes it. "I'm kidding. Just don't do what you did before. I promise I'll behave."

I instantly smile without meaning to.

"See, I knew I'd make you smile."

I punch him, succeeding in hurting my hand and I thrust it under my arm pit to ease discomfort. He puts his hands up in capitulation. "Alright, I think that's enough for today, you're probably going to feel really tired after releasing such power like that."

I nod in agreement and shake my hand to ease the pain, and he can't hide his amusement.

As we go to leave, the sound of glass hitting the wooden floor echoes. I turn around to see my tiny green vial, innocently rolling around in a circle. Adonis's voice instantly penetrates my mind, *"You must never, and I mean never, inform any other of this medicine."*

Leon's voice gives me a sudden fright as I feel for the missing vial in my pocket even though it stares blatantly at me from the floor. He walks over and picks it up, analysing it as he stands.

"This yours?"

I'm good at keeping a secret but outwardly lying is another story. But what would be the harm in telling him either, it's only medicine, and he is helping me, like the medicine. Using it to sabotage me wouldn't make sense.

"Taura?" he asks again as I've gone deep into thought. "Words, remember, I need words. I can only read so much from your face. And right now you look like a constipated bull, can't do much with that."

My eyes glance up at him. "Right, sorry, I was just deep in thought. It's nothing really." I go to take it from him but he pulls it away.

"Well, if it's nothing, why can't you tell me?"

I look away then. He's right, why can't I tell him? It would only make sense. But there is a part of me that's holding back, from loyalty to the promise I made my father.

"It's, just uh, my medicine. You know, to keep me healthy."

He looks at me inquisitively. "No, I don't know. Why would you need medicine?"

I realized then that I hadn't told him about my condition. So, I tell him the usual story from when I was born and that's why I look the way I do. "It's just for my immune system is all."

He hands it back to me. "I see, I thought you were just the runt."

I scowl at him, and he raises his hands again. "I mean it in a positive way. Don't take this the wrong way but I've never found the Taurus women to be exactly, well...attainable."

I raise an eyebrow.

"Can you blame me? They are masculine, hard, tough and independent. How can I win a female of that calibre? How can I ever be of service? I need to feel important; it gives me purpose, to help the ones I love. I am a Leo, you know?" he says sarcastically.

I smile. "So what are you trying to say? That I make you feel needed?"

He smiles. "Not exactly."

I tilt my head to the side and he throws his hands up in the air.

"You're attractive alright... Beautiful. Besides, you're much less intimidating than your fellow female Taureans. I guess that's why Libran females are seen as the beauties within Nirvana. Until they lose the plot, good thing they got that give-away eye colour alteration," he says humorously.

"I'm glad you find humour in objectifying females of any race."

He looks at me with confusion. "Well, I wouldn't want to make you angry, that's for sure."

I feel myself losing control again, so I storm out of the room instead,

"Oh, come on, I was just kidding!" he yells, then hurries out after me.

I lock the door with the crooked key and I turn to hand it to Leon.

"You know what I like about you, Taura," Leon says as he takes the key.

"That I'm attainable, unlike every other Taurus female."

He laughs. "Not quite...you're different."

I look at him questioningly. "Now you're the one who needs to elaborate."

He smiles. "Well, I call you beautiful and you tell me off for objectifying females."

I glance away. "Oh, yeah. I guess I don't take compliments all that well."

He laughs. "I'll keep that in mind. Insults only?"

I smile and nod. "Yeah, I can work with insults." He draws up the same rough teleportation circle as Demetrius does.

"How did you memorize that symbol, it's so complicated," I say. He looks up at me and stands clapping the chalk from his hands.

"I told you, I've been coming here since I was a young cub. Now stand in the circle." He's drawn the circle smaller than normal, which makes me have to stand closer than I feel comfortable.

"Go back to your dorm and I'll be seeing you soon." I glance up at him and nod.

"Where are you going?" I ask.

He smiles. "To objectify some females," he says sarcastically and I shake my head in amusement. Visualizing the dorm, I chant the name Unum and open my eyes to the usual fast spinning planets that come to a slow.

Other zodiacs come and go as they please, in and out of their dorms, some stopping to watch me for a moment before continuing with their own business. It must be almost time to go to supper. I step out from the transporter to be unexpectedly confronted by Demetrius who I hadn't seen amongst the crowd.

"What did he make you do?" he demands.

I instantly recollect Theophilus's words, *"I'll allocate someone to help you, who will report your progress. But this too must remain a secret."*

I glance around the room knowing he sees all and I don't want to reap the repercussions he warned me of.

"Taura!" Demetrius says impatiently.

I instantly stiffen and look directly at Demetrius. "Nothing, he didn't make me do anything." I go to walk past him towards my dorm and he aggressively grabs my arm.

"Don't ever walk away from me like that again!" he says with an undertone so no one overhears. He stares intently, penetrating my eyes with his sheer anger. I feel the pressure of his grip harden.

"Demetrius, you're hurting me, let go!" I begin to make a scene, pulling at his reinforced arm, securely attached to mine. Not moving an inch as I plummet my body back and forth to release his grip. He suddenly lets go and I fall back on to my arse, my books scatter and everyone has stopped to watch the commotion. But I am now filled with anger.

"What is your problem? He is just trying to help me! Something you never took the time to do!"

Demetrius's expression softened to a remorseful grimace, but before he answers, I abruptly pick up my books and storm off to the Taurean dorm, entering as Kendall emerged, and slamming the door behind me.

I lean against the door and slide down, allowing my books to slide out before me and I bring my hands up to my face, feeling I just wanted to hide. I was glad the dorm seemed empty. Unexpectedly, I feel little warm sensations brushing against my skin and I notice the yellow orbs nudging me and settling down against my shoulders as if offering comfort.

"Taur! Finally!" Europa comes rushing out of the bathroom. "I heard the door slam. I see they've warmed up to you too. Cool, aren't they?"

I nod holding one within the palm of my hand and she effortlessly starts playing with another yellow orb with hers. Then she gives me a considering look.

"So...what has happened to you this past two days? I knew something was up when Isa and her duo kept making sarcastic jokes about your disappearance. And now they're looking at you as though you're a ghost and then you're taken away by Leon!? What in Unum's name is going on?"

I take a moment and linger at the yellow totem orb that nuzzles into my palm, wondering where to start and what to say, still wanting to keep my promise but wanting to tell my best friend everything at the same time.

"I'll tell you but you must understand I can't tell you everything... right now."

She nods with a concerned expression from the tone of my voice. "Isa, Dalton, and Henrietta kidnapped me last night. And Isa beat me so bad she broke my spin, paralysing me from the neck down."

Europa's mouth drops open in disbelief as she looks me up and down.

"They threw me off the Doh's centre stairs...but before I hit the ground, I stopped, levitating a few inches off the floor. My bones began to rejuvenate, forcing themselves back into place and healing, but the pain was so excruciating, I passed out. That is all I can tell you right now. But what I want is to go to see Bibliotheca as soon as possible to find out if she knows about this number."

Europa's eyes have nearly dropped out of her head. "Wait, she did what? And you did what!? That good for nothing...piece of..." She mumbles curse words under her breath then pauses momentarily, "Well, at least it makes sense why they were all staring at you, the way they were. Definitely thought they'd seen a ghost."

I nod. "And that's why I must try to avoid that scenario again as I don't know how to control it, kinda happened spontaneously. I'm not sure if I could do it a second time."

Europa's mouth still hangs wide open. "Wow, I'll never complain about a bad day again. Well, I don't think you have anything to worry about. When Isa saw you, she looked positively petrified and Isa doesn't easily scare as you know." She instantly stops, realizing something. "Wait, why can't I ask about Leon? Where did he take you? And what was that piece of paper, the jurisdiction thing? Helping you out with your power? But he is only a new blood himself?"

I smile at her eagerness to know what's going on. "Like I told you, I can't tell you everything right now. Let's just say he's helping me."

She rolls her eyes. "Oh alright, but you'll have to tell me eventually. Because I swear that lion has a thing for you and I don't trust him."

I laugh. "Don't be ridiculous, have you seen the female Leos; they're absolutely stunning: lean, athletic, long golden hair with tanned skin but not overwhelmingly intimidating. They draw you in with their warmth of the sun." " I realize I repeat the same words which Leon had said not too long ago as I too now objectify my own sex. Europa shrugs, unimpressed.

"I could kick their arses, that's all that matters."

She appears to be slightly put out by my comparison to female Leo's and is staring at the ground.

I nudge her. "And I don't doubt you. You'll be just like Imelda Kore."

She peers up and sees me smile, her usual enthusiasm rekindled, and nods assertively. "Alright, let's go find Bibo, biblilo, bibly... whatever her name is."

I laugh and nod. Putting my books away, I notice *Language of the Purpose Numbers* corner edge sticking out of my other backpack. Knowing I need to return it, I take the backpack with me, with it concealed inside. As we leave, Europa suddenly blurts out, "Oh bonkers, it's 3:30. We have to be back in our dorms by five and be ready for supper in the common room by six. We were told that when you had your secret flirting lesson with Leon."

I roll my eyes.

"Oh, shut up. Okay, we will have to be quick about it."

CHAPTER TWELVE

THE PHOTOGRAPH

Memories harness the power of invincibility.

We come to a stop in front of the library's immensely huge wooden doors.

"How are we going to get these open? I mean Demetrius struggled on the day he messed up the teleportation and we arrived in the library. Maybe we should wait until someone comes out?" I suggest.

Europa smacks my shoulder. "Argh, we don't have time for that. C'mon." She walks up to the doors and lingers at the golden open-paged handles that appear to be pristine and never touched. As she touches one side of the golden book handle, the book begins to flip through its thin glimmering golden pages at an unearthly rate and the doors begin to open as the pages turn, loudly whooshing as they swing wide. The smell of old books, carried on warm air, is drawn into my nostrils. It is one of my favourite smells but with a library this big the scent is all the more enticing and the warm air comforting.

Europa looks at me with an eyebrow raised in suspicion. "So, our humble SNC overseer was just showing off his big muscles after all."

I chuckle. "Maybe it's different when you have to open it from the inside."

Europa snuffs, "Yeah right, you just think his dingleberries don't stink," and she walks into the library.

"His what?" I retort.

Books fly past us, glancing behind them as zodiacs inconspicuously try to follow them without starting a full-blown chase and other zodiacs nearly bump into us as they read whilst walking to their study area. I begin to admire a beautiful Libran female, recalling Leon's spoken thoughts. Although I was aware intellectually, I had not taken notice of their profound beauty before. Or am I only admiring now because he mentioned it? Lost in thought, I unintentionally bump into a Pisces and his books are knocked out of his hand and his thick glasses become twisted around his face; he stares off into the distance as though he hadn't realized what had hit him.

"Oh, I'm so sorry! Let me get those for you," I insist.

He suddenly looks down, only noticing me after I had spoken, readjusting glasses that are already broken and held together with thick tape in the middle. I realise that those particular glasses look incredibly familiar. Now his already large eyes become even larger through the lenses.

"That's quite alright, you just caught me in a train of thought is all." He now focusses his attention on me. "Mind me asking what creature you might be? You appear to be that of a Taurus but you seem to be a cross breed. Too petite to be compared to the brute of a bull," he remarks as I pick up his heavy book. I struggle to pass it back to him.

"You could say I'm the runt of the bunch," I say with minimum sarcasm, noticing I use another of Leon's quotations. What's wrong with me, I don't even sound like me.

The Pisces laughs. "I like it. You could say I'm the blind of the bunch. These glasses aren't exactly flattering, but they belonged to someone who I dearly cared for. Besides, they have character and I do believe they bring out my deep blues." He pushes his face into mine, blinking frantically, trying to act flatteringly beautiful in an amusing way.

I chuckle at his awkward quirkiness but I love his confidence in his imperfect sense of humour. The idea someone can be completely comfortable in who they are is intoxicatingly magnetic. Now standing up straight, he pushes his webbed hand out towards me.

"My name's Manfred Harwood. What might yours be, mighty runt?" I grab his cold hand that's wet and damp, remembering they must always stay hydrated.

"The mighty runt's name is Taura Andreas," I say, trying to keep my deceptive confidence that somewhat resembles the Leo I am unreasonably drawn to. He shakes my hand energetically, making my whole body quiver along with it. "It's a pleasure to make your acquaintance."

I nod and smile in agreement, thinking it's nice to be in a place where no one really knows who you are.

"Taura! Taura! Taur!" I hear Europa calling. Manfred turns around, fiddling with his glasses as he peers at the figure now heading our way like a charging bull. Europa's blonde hair is floating behind her as she strides towards us, roughly nudging other zodiacs out of her way.

"There you are! What are you doing? You know we don't have much time? And I can't find whatever her name is anywhere!" She now stands in front of me but before I can answer, Manfred has already stuck his hand out into her personal space.

"Hello, I'm Manfred Harwood. I ran into your friend just now, my mistake. And she insisted on picking up my book when I clumsily knocked into her." He winks at me as if trying to save my arse, knowing too well it was I who knocked into him.

"It's okay, Manfred, she's my best friend, Europa Castellanos," I say reassuringly. Manfred's expression becomes confused as if to wonder why someone's best friend would be yelling at them in such a domineering way; clearly he hasn't spent too much time around Taureans.

"Oh, well, in that case. It's a pleasure to meet Europa Castellanos, the best friend of mighty runt." He forcefully shakes Europa's hand but she rips it away in anger.

"What did you just call her? Mighty runt?"

Manfred becomes flushed and confused at the same time. "I do apologize, I thought it was an inside joke?"

Europa spits back, "You think calling someone a mighty runt is a joke? What's wrong with you! Clearly you are not like any Pisces I've read about," she says with ignorance towards his feelings and it's instantly obvious to me that she's hurt them.

"No, no Europa, you've got it all wrong. I told him I was a mighty runt." She stares at me.

"Why would you call yourself that?" she asks astounded. She must be wondering what I have changed into, like I was questioning myself not too long ago.

"I was kidding. Look, it doesn't matter, he was actually being very friendly and nice."

Europa takes a big breath to calm herself down. "Sorry... Manfro," she says bluntly, fixated on the ground as it's hard for Taureans of either gender to admit when they're wrong, that's why our most common known trait is our stubbornness. Manfred smiles, probably knowing our traits as Pisces love their broad knowledge,

"It's Manfred, but that's quite alright, easy mistake. It's nice to see someone who has a deep love for a friend." His tone is suggestive, as if he sees Europa in a way no one else does. She suddenly goes bright red and I'm now confused. I know Pisces are incredibly intuitive, understanding someone's personal agenda just by interpreting an individual's body language. That's why they make great subtle manipulators, but their motives can be hard to interpret. Right now, I can't think what he was meaning.

"Now, who is this 'whatever' her name is? You are looking for?" he asks curiously. Europa, who has gone as stiff as a plank, says nothing. So I answer, "Bibliotheca the Librarian. Europa struggles to say her name is all."

He nods his head, knowing whom we speak of and his expression forms into an admiration. "Oh yes Bib, well, you may find it a little harder than you presumably thought. I'm sure others have spoken about her but I'm sure they too are unaware of a certain inconvenience to her existence, most are."

Europa now loosens back to her normal and pushy demeanour. "What do you mean?"

Manfred gives an awkward expression, "Well...she's dead... but not gone."

Our jaws drop open in disbelief. "She can't be dead unless it's been recent, we only just met her a few days ago!" Europa adds.

Manfred takes a moment, letting the information sink in. "She's been dead for decades. You would have met her ghost; she has never left this place since her passing. Many don't think she ever will. So, unfortunately, to find her is more difficult than originally thought. Most zodiacs like yourselves stumble across her. But when wanting to find her again, can't seem to do so. Some say it's when you're not looking for her that she will appear."

We both look at one another, knowing we're in dire need of finding her. "Who's the living librarian?" I ask. Thinking Bib's wisdom and knowledge must have been passed down to another. Manfred's expression once again doesn't look too promising.

"That's the other mishap, there isn't one. Bib is the current and still remaining librarian. She still does all the same duties as she did before her death. Just no one sees her doing them, so the Elders thought instead of upsetting her unresting ghost, they'd let her continue doing the job she always loved and maybe that might help her pass over, thinking maybe there was something she'd left unfinished. But decades have gone by and she still remains. What is it that you needed from her?"

Europa looks at me, knowing she doesn't want to answer such a question for me.

"Oh, it was to do with the purpose numbers."

I pull out the *Language of the Purpose Numbers* residing tightly within my backpack. But as I lift it out, its eyes open, becoming alive again within the library's walls. It sporadically wiggles hard, back and forth to win its freedom.

"Hold on to it tight! Must be an older tucker!" Manfred says, helping me hold on to it and Europa now jumps in too. And I struggle to speak as I try to keep a grip on the book.

"It has...a page inside, that's ripped out...the theory behind... number ten," I manage to say.

"Man, this thing is strong!" Europa adds.

Manfred tensely says, "I need you both to keep a hold of it. I'm going to let go, ready! 3, 2, 1. Hold on!" As he releases the book, it begins to get the better of me and Europa but Manfred acts quickly, gently gliding his middle and index finger down the spine of the book. This seems to calm it and it shuts its eyes and appears to fall asleep. We both relax and he quickly takes it from us.

"We must be fast, it'll wake soon." As he flips through the book, looking up the index and gliding through to the page I spoke about, he runs his finger down where the pages had been torn. "Hmmm," he says as the book now sprouts awake, slams shut and spurts away, weaving about the other thousands of books that soar through the library's high-ceiling walls.

"What the hell is that book's problem?" asks Europa.

Manfred answers as he still watches the book that is above where he stands. "The oldest books within the library have the strength to fight against you and will only allow you to read them if they deem you worthy. The new-bloods like yourselves are seen chasing them around the library as they hold the most ancient information from the beginning of time. Very useful in end-of-year exams, but they never catch them. They're usually the ones who are looking for a quick fix as they didn't take the time to study all year." He smiles as though amused by an old memory. He adds, staring appreciatively at his hands, "And that book is the most ancient book I have ever held. It must have wanted you to see something. Probably to do with those torn pages. Whoever did that traitorous act, if caught would be sentenced to death by the Scorpio's death serum, Venenum. Old books like that are very precious to our history." He still watches the flying books.

"How do you know so much about the library?" I ask.

He smiles, reminiscing. "Bib told me. When I was a new-blood, she used to visit me all the time as I lived in the library. Bit of a loner I was...well, still am actually, which I know is a strange trait for a Pisces but I still love a good chat, maybe I chew too many ears." He laughs. "And I too was unaware she was a ghost until much later on. But she no longer visits me as I now yearn for her and her company. But back then I was too preoccupied with my studies and found her more of a nuisance. She would just appear when no one was around and share random factual information with me about the library and other things. I miss her dearly, she was my first and closest friend," he says as his eyes well up, recalling the time he spent with her. His glasses begin to fog up and he wipes the tears from his large eyes. Taking off his glasses, he cleans them, carefully avoiding upsetting the messy tape that keeps them from breaking in two.

Then I realize. "Those glasses...they're Bib's, aren't they?" He places them back on the bridge of his nose as they too do not fit his frame, constantly falling down his face.

"Indeed they are. She left me the original ones from her time in this realm on the last day I saw her. Now I can't bear to part with them," he says, readjusting the frames so they sit comfortably.

"How did she die?" I ask.

He blinks a couple of times now, getting the position right.

"To be honest, that was one story she unfortunately did not share with me."

"I wonder if anyone else has read all the books in the library," Europa says, hoping someone else holds the valuable information we seek and changing to topic as we are short of time. Manfred shakes his head and the glasses slide down, and he needed to push them back up onto bridge of his nose.

"Unfortunately not, it would take several lifetimes," pausing and thinking on that remark. "Actually probably more, for someone to read all the books within the library and not only that, all the ancient books would need to deem you worthy, so life experience is a necessity. Only Bib would have such profound respect from those books as she takes the utmost care of them," he pauses for a moment, looking at me inquiringly. "I wonder why it would want to show you the theory behind number ten?" asking in a way that suggests that he knows I already know, but not insisting on an answer. I turn around and lift my mousy brown hair from the back of my neck, displaying the unbeknown number ten. He holds the side of his glasses so they don't fall down as he bends over to get a closer look. He squints, peering at the strange number.

"I see, that makes an awful lot of sense now," he says as I turn around.

"Do you know of such a purpose number?"

He shakes his head, "Unfortunately not, but I understand why the book came to you. Obviously wanted you to know something, but someone else clearly didn't. And they've gone unbelievably out of their way to make sure you wouldn't...because to risk such a crime is, is insane."

Then, unexpectedly, Manfred becomes stiff and rigid in his appearance, his eyes now glaze with a contrast of moving white and grey, as though he is seeing something we cannot. Grabbing my shoulder, he presses against me, glancing around as though someone could be listening and whispers in a strange voice that is not his own. Europa leans in.

"Taura Andreas, you must heed this warning... There is something greater here than you could ever imagine. There are powers at work, greater than I've ever felt before... Taura, I have a feeling you are in great danger and I believe you must find out the truth in order to save yourself. But there is much conflict and turmoil within such a journey. Things aren't as they appear."

He stands back and stands up straight again, readjusting himself, and his eyes slowly return to normal. I feel the hair on the back of my neck stand on end and Europa becomes overwhelmingly emotional.

"What do you mean save herself? What's going to happen? How do you know?"

His eyes blink hard as though trying to readapt them to the present moment, readjusting his glasses again.

"Blimey, darn it... I apologize for that. I've been studying within the Olympus Trials for many a year now to become an SNC sorcerer as I've proven my strong capabilities within my psyche. But my intuition can be quite strong at times and comes on quite spontaneously without premeditation. I'm still learning to control it, but it seems to be taking longer than most, and they won't deem me worthy until I have full control of my powers. I came to the belief Bib could help me as she is so knowledgeable and it was on that very day I sought her out; she disappeared from my reality and I still subconsciously search for her, that's why I can no longer see her. But what I felt after you showed me that number was the strongest message I've ever received, you must not ignore it," he says with urgency.

I stare at him. "Okay, but none of it makes any sense. How am I supposed to discover the truth and be careful of such powers when I don't know the purpose of the power?"

He tries to look reassuring, but his emotions are clearly visible on his face. "Unfortunately, I can't answer that for you, only you can discover that truth. All I can tell you is when you search for something that is of great importance to your essence, Unum has a funny way of helping you. I believe it has something to do with seeking out clarity within purpose, but that is only a feeling I have. But I must get back to my studies...and please, Taura..." he places his webbed cold hand on my shoulder, squeezing it tight, "be careful, I know nothing makes sense right now. But soon all will be revealed in due time. And remember to keep your mind open and clear."

Not knowing what to say, I say nothing, only nod in acknowledgement. He smiles at Europa and says, "Take care of her, I know you will. And both of you. Be careful." And just as abruptly as he came, he disappears into the crowd.

"Well, that only adds more questions. I wish someone would tell us what the Sacci is going on," Europa says impatiently with an edge of acidity.

I then realize that the only other creature that seems to know any more than we do is the last remaining Bwbachod. But I don't know how we will find him.

Europa looks at the big clock displayed high above the big entrance doors. "Oh dingleberries, it's almost five. We have to get back to our dorm! Will have to figure that our later, C'mon."

I passively follow Europa's aggressive movement through the crowd, towards the doors. As we approach, I notice a tall, slender Virgo staring directly at me with piercing bright green eyes and by his expression, appearing to know me. I look behind, thinking he must be looking at someone else, but his stare does not alter. He has light brown hair that's parted in the middle and like every other Virgo, there's not a hair out of place. As the large doors surge open, another zodiac enters, Europa yells, "Hurry! Before it closes!"

She grabs my hand and begins to pick up her pace, dragging me behind her. And as we pass, the Virgo who still continues to hold my gaze, deliberately bashes into me, making me lose Europa's grip. I fall to the ground with his dropped book beside me. I look up to see him slowly disappear into the crowd, he glances back and continues on.

"Wait!" I yell, picking up his book, standing frantically to my feet. "You dropped your..." But he's already gone as if he were only a ghost, which does make me question, as nothing is out of the ordinary within this place.

"What are you doing?" Europa is now in my face and grabbing my hand again. She swiftly pulls me through the big doors that nearly squash our tails within its heavy clutches as it closes behind us. Holding the book the Virgo dropped under my arm. Europa and I teleport back to the dorm.

As we return, all the SNC overseers are standing out front of their residing regions. The Constellations' stones glow above the doors which means the zodiacs can come and go without reciting the poem every time they enter. Demetrius stands outside of ours. I quickly hide the book within my bag before anyone notices it. As we approach, Demetrius locks eyes with me, still looking regretful about the argument between us earlier in the afternoon.

"Are you two okay? Where have you been?" he asks genuinely without his usual assertive approach.

Europa smiles. "Just to the library, had to catch up on some study," she says charmingly and I say nothing, continuing to follow Europa into our dorm. Demetrius grabs my arm to stop me then quickly releases it, trying to control his strength.

"Taura..." he glances around as the other SNC overseers watch and for the first time I see Demetrius's demeanour become somewhat edgy.

"Yes?" I question as Europa also intently stares too.

Appearing to be tongue-tied and not knowing what to say, he answers, "Never mind. Make sure everyone is organized before six for supper." He seems to regret the words that instinctively fell out of his mouth. I stare at him for a moment, giving him a second chance but he does not budge. He holds the door open, I enter and he shuts it behind us.

"What was that all about?" Europa asks.

"Don't worry, just something trivial," I remark.

"Oh good, because I'm not sure if I can live up to your level of drama these days," she sarcastically chirps.

"Yeah, me neither," and we both laugh, finding humour in a mysterious situation.

Isa lies on her bed staring at the yellow totem orbs that hover leisurely around the room. Dalton and Henrietta quarrel over some contraption and Kendall lies on his bed reading. Isa glances over as we walk in laughing, becoming instantly irritated by our presence but also inquisitive as she watches me from the corner of her eye. Dalton and Henrietta stop quarrelling and begin to whisper, sitting on the bottom bunk side by side. Ignoring their stares, I sit beside my bed, facing away from them and Europa stares at Isa challengingly until she slowly looks away, sitting beside her bed on the opposite side facing me.

She leans over and whispers, "We will have to talk about our next step when these vultures aren't around."

I nod in agreement.

Pulling out the book from my bag and to my surprise it's a common book found in any Constellation library. It reads: *Zodiacs Appearance, Abilities & Power*, the exact same book I keep beside my bed at home and the one I read just before I ventured through the uncharted forest for the first time.

Europa asks, "Why'd you take that from the library?"

I look at the book from front to back.

"I didn't mean too. A Virgo dropped it beside me when I fell before we left the library."

Europa becomes disinterested and I begin flipping through the pages and as soon as I do, a photograph falls out, landing face down.

"What's that?" she asks curiously. Picking it up, I notice in small writing, 'Vaughn and Benedict.' Turning it around, I see the same Virgo I saw in the library standing next to what appears to be his twin, very similar at first glance but both uniquely different the longer you stare. The one from the library is happier and attractive in stature with a big smile spread across his face making his eyes squinted whilst the other stands rigid with a solemn expression, with a slight smirk but obviously not wanting to be in the photo. Both have their arms wrapped around one another and you can feel the unconditional love between them. Their wings pushed up against each other as feathers are captured falling down within the photo.

I hand it over to Europa and she observes both sides.

"Who are they?"

I shrug as she hands it back. "I don't know. I recognize the Virgo called Vaughn to the left, he was the one who bumped into me in the library. He's the one who dropped this book. And I think it was deliberate. He was staring right at me before he bashed into me, dropping the book next to me."

Europa stares at the photo. "But why?" she says rolling her eyes up to the ceiling and frustratingly sprawls her legs out in front of her as if she's had enough of unanswered questions. Then there is a knock on the door.

"Dinner's up, time to go," Demetrius says as he pokes his head through. I slide the book under my bed and put the photo in my pocket.

When we enter the dining room, all the elders are already seated and all the new-blooded zodiacs are entering together. But the room is on a much larger scale than we had originally been exposed and monumental in its presence. It's as though they had reconstructed the whole premises within a day. We're seated at our usual tables, but they are much longer than I recall. Already seated at the tables are the other zodiacs who live within the Doh studying the Olympus Trials, but clearly in years ahead of us. In them, the arrogance and volatility attributed to new-bloods, eradicated by knowledge and training. We, as some of the newest arrivals, instantly know our place. Our same seats are at the end of the table, furthest from the Elders and closest to the door.

Once everyone is seated, Theophilus stands, elegantly brushing his already sleeked hair back with both hands, tiny white hairs curl perfectly around his ears, poking out from underneath. Then, clasping both hands together, he begins to speak. "As you all can see, a few things have changed within our dining room. The new-bloods will now be dining with the rest of us, we who have been within the Doh's premises for more than a year. Their potential will determine where their journey leads and how much time they'll need to spend within the Olympus Trials to obtain their classification."

Theophilus glances around, seeming to look at every recently arrived new-blood. "Some of you may only need to spend a year here, whilst others may need to spend five, ten or more. At first, we like you to feel comfortable, so we don't introduce you to the older zodiacs until later. And for you, that time is now. I suggest you try picking their brains if they allow. You may find they have valuable information you'll be needing later on in your studies. Now, let's all enjoy the company over a well-earned meal. Please begin."

When he is again sitting regally upright in his chair, food begins to appear on all the tables as if it had already been waiting, invisible to the naked eye. Steam lingers off the food and I didn't realize how hungry I was until the many different aromas reach my nose.

I don't waste time getting started eating my food, and keep going while I admire the reputable Taureans that sit at the table with us. They still enjoy their food just as much as we normally do and do not talk while they eat. Europa is gobbling her food so fast, that I am not surprised when she pushes her plates away and leans back in her chair with a full belly.

"Ahh, that was good. I needed that," she says rubbing her now prominent food baby. Isa is still gorging herself senseless as she stares at me beneath her thick eyebrows. Henrietta and Dalton are just playing with their food now, flinging it at one another, while Kendall continues to eat in a deliberately and relaxed manner.

I place my hand in my pocket, feeling the photograph that had fallen from the book not long ago. A flash of Vaughn's face projects into my mind, a memory of the intent stare he pressed upon me. I have a feeling he wanted me to have this photo; why else would he deliberately bash into me, dropping the book? I continue picking at my food, glancing at Europa, who now lies in a food coma, knowing she won't be much help. I attempt to look over at the Virgos, but it becomes apparent that it's too hard to see past the Gemini, Cancerian, and Leo Constellation tables. I accidently catch a glimpse of Leon. My heart begins to skip a beat as I notice another female persistently flirting with him, obvious by her body language. She is incredibly beautiful, more so than I. My face grows hot and I begin to shake, I recognize that my blood now pumps with jealousy, and I find myself losing what little appetite I had left. My possessive streak is taking over. How can I have feelings for another zodiac I barely know? My father would be furious.

Unable to help myself, I glance over again and see them both flirting. My fury increases, I try taking a few deep breaths to calm myself, but when I close my eyes I feel the pressure of tears behind them. How could I be so stupid? He's just doing a job. The tears well up uncontrollably; I squeeze my eyes tight, but I know I won't be able to hold them back for long. I feel a hand grab my shoulder.

"Taur, you okay?" Europa asks. I shake my head, stand abruptly as the tears break free and I begin to run for the door.

Europa grabs my hand to stop me and I turn around to face her as tears flow profusely down my face.

"Taur, what's wrong? You can't leave; it's forbidden to leave the dining room when eating has commenced. C'mon it's okay."

But I'm glued to the place I now stand, as firm as a tree and unable to move. No other table has noticed me yet but I know they soon will. Unexpectedly, a reputable Taurus male stands and approaches with a compassionate and calming aura.

He walks over to me with an unreadable expression and says, "The food's spicy, ain't it? Gotta be careful of that grass curry, hits you right in the you-know-what. Don't worry, I've been seen running out of here crying from it too. Wretched stuff, don't know why they still serve it." He smiles at me and hands me a napkin and guides me back to my seat and he casually goes back to his. I blow my nose and everyone continues eating as if his excuse was sufficient and reasonable explanation.

Europa leans in and whispers, "It wasn't really the curry, was it?"

I smile, thinking how stupid I could have made myself out to be and become immensely grateful for that Taurus, I should thank him. I shake my head.

"I knew it, are you okay?"

I nod, and she looks at me understandingly. She knows I've been through a lot recently, so she decides not to press the question, and I'm happy to allow her to assume it's related to recent sequence of events.

The chattering in the room begins to rise and the older, reputable zodiacs begin to leave their tables to converse with other zodiacs. While most of the new-bloods stick to their Constellation's tables, clutching to familiarity, it seems we are allowed to do the same if we wished.

"We should casually walk past the Virgo table. I want to see if I can find that Virgo I ran into, he might be connected to all this," I suggest to Europa.

"Do we have to? I really couldn't be bothered carrying this food baby around." I look at her, unimpressed with the laziness she conveys. But this trait is renowned within our Constellation; when we work, we work hard and fast like a charging bull, but when we're lazy, it's as though you're trying to move a five hundred ton sleeping bull, especially after a well-earned meal.

"Are you serious?" I ask, trying to guilt trip her.

She sighs and slowly pushes to her feet, "Alright, alright, let's go."

We walk past the charismatic Gemini who banter continuously, and I watch a few who attempt to split and miserably fail whilst others tease them. None of them are offended by the mockery as they throw it back and forth. They move at such high speed, your eyes are unable to keep up with their flickering changeability as though in a constant fast-forwarded state. When we are approaching the Cancerians and I hear our names being called

"Europa, Taura! Over here!" I turn to see a familiar face, Naida the Cancerian, we met at our introduction to Orbis Bellum.

Europa grabs my hand and insists on going over.

"We won't be long," she says. I find I'm becoming reserved as all the Cancerians watch us carefully with their mysterious black eyes; they don't trust strangers. But Naida continues to smile as we approach. I stand just behind Europa.

"Where are you guys headed? Far from your own territory for new-bloods," she comments, squinting with a perky smile. And I find this Naida different from the last encounter, probably feeling more comfortable within her own region. Europa unexpectedly pulls the photograph from my pocket.

"Actually, we're looking for one of these Virgos."

She points to Vaughn, determinedly wanting to get this over with. Europa continues, "He accidently bumped into Taur in the library, dropping his book with this inside. We thought he might like it back." She was trying to sound more subtle. I look at Europa in surprise and she shrugs at me to suggest we haven't gotten anywhere so far on our own and I know she's right. Naida looks at the picture for quite some time then shrugs.

"I'm sorry, I don't recognize either of them, but I'm only a new-blood myself."

As she goes to pass it back, the Cancerian sitting next to her grabs her arm, taking the picture from her hand and says, "Yeah

I know one of them, not the one who you ran into though," says the Cancerian inexplicably. Naida jumps up and faces the speaker.

"How do you know, Artemis? You're only a new-blood too!"

Artemis smiles. "You know I don't tell you everything."

"Don't be stupid, of course you do," Naida smacks her playfully and turns to us, "Europa, Taura, this is my know-it-all sister, Artemis Odette," she says teasingly. Artemis has long black hair that's braided all the way down her back but it's obvious she's the more contained sister, having prominent features and harder facial features than perky Naida who's more delicate to the eye. But you can see the similarities once it becomes apparent that they are sisters.

"Nice to meet you," Europa says warmly, and I nod with a welcoming but less eager demeanour.

"Might I ask how you know the other Virgo, Benedict?" I ask, getting straight back to the point.

"You don't mess around, do you?" Naida says light-heartedly.

I smile and shrug, and look straight back at Artemis who still stares at the photo, handing it back to me and says, "It's no secret. He's Theophilus's boy."

Europa and I look at one another in surprise and Artemis looks uninterested, as the information is useless to her.

Naida turns around to her sister and asks, "If it's a not big secret, how come you didn't tell me?"

Artemis glances back with obvious annoyance, like siblings who spend too much time together.

"Because if you didn't spend your whole time talking, you might actually hear something other than your own voice." Naida pokes her tongue out at her sister and smirks.

Turning to face us, "It's true, I do love a good chat," she says, not being obviously offended by her sister's harsh words. But I guess having such large families, you become exceedingly comfortable in who you are, as they'll always pull you up, not afraid of offending you.

Artemis adds, "It's no big deal, he was pointed out to me by our older brother, Derk, who's a reputable zodiac," she says with pride towards her brother who she clearly looks up too.

Europa then asks in astonishment, "How many siblings do you guys have?"

Naida laughs. "To be honest, I've lost count! But I wouldn't recommend it. I mean look at what I have to put up with!"

Artemis chuckles but with a crude expression, "It's you who everyone else has to put up with," and they both laugh looking at each other affectionately.

I tug at Europa's arm and she nods. "Alright, best be getting this picture back, great seeing you again Naida, and nice meeting you, Artemis."

We both continue walking down the aisle between the Cancerian and Gemini tables, and Naida yells, "Don't be strangers!"

We wave, turning the corner of their short width table, rapidly approaching the Leos. Their gold, orange, and yellow become profound compared to the sea green and silver Constellation colours of the Cancerians' table, standing side by side. Not establishing where Leon is, I keep my eyes fixed to the Virgo's green, white, and yellow.

Europa then says, "Your boyfriend's spotted you."

I become tense. "You know he's not that," I muttered, disappointed that what I said was the truth.

Europa's expression suggested more than irritation, but distracted my own feelings, I didn't ask why. Instead, I was trying hard not to look at Leon, but to my dismay I find my eyes going to his and staring into them, even though he is far down the table. That detail gives me hope that he won't call out to me, making our association known to everyone in his vocal path.

The same Leo female I had noticed before sits near him, lingering in his company. I feel a renewal of the jealousy I had felt earlier. Then she curiously follows his gaze. She spots me and I quickly look away but just as quickly I find myself staring back.

And just like their close relationship with fire, the Leo female's eyes light up with flamed fury. She stands abruptly, sweeps the golden cup that was beside her onto the floor, and turns on Leon. From my distant position, the enraged confrontation sounds like a growling roar. When she finishes, she storms off, moving from the far end of their table, further from me. She glances back to see if Leon is following. If she had given him an ultimatum, he was ignoring it. He was unmoved by her tantrum.

She suddenly shoots me a livid glare, and I feel the hairs on my neck standing on end, and a cold sweat breaking out on my back.

Leon's eyes have not yet broken away from mine, and I am warmed to see his faint smile, and the subtle gesture of a small wave of acknowledgment my way. I realize that he too would have been told to keep our association a secret. I smile awkwardly and quickly turn away, my face flushed but I am relieved at the same time, even as my heart flutters.

The table with the magnetic, warm, vibrant Leos is a contrast to the upright and practical composures at the Virgo table. No one's ego is being dominated by another and they all socialize appropriately with superb manners. Some are still eating modestly, slowly consuming their meal, probably making sure they chew their food properly. A few sitting at the end of the table look up, as we try to observe them inconspicuously. However, knowing the Virgos great attention to detail, it is not surprising that we are noticed.

"May we help you?" one asks.

Judging by Europa's shuffling feet, and lack of quick reply, she is intimidated by the penetrating green eyes that seem to see right into you.

The faces looking our way were all quite different, but the zodiacs themselves all moved in the same way, demonstrating their instilled moral value of no one being no better than another.

"Uh, we were just looking for someone within your region known as Benedict?" I ask apprehensively. Without acknowledging our inquiry, the speaker calmly places his knife and fork down and ever so slightly leans over, looking down the long table, holding his robes against his chest, making a point of not getting them dirty. His eyes swiftly shift back to us and I can't help but stare, his eyes are so intensely beautiful.

"He's down the other end of the table," he says, not seeming interested as to why we ask for him. Picking up his knife and fork once again, he continues eating, thoroughly chewing his food slowly. I notice he had separated the colours of the food on his plate into a pie-like assembly.

"Oh, uh...thank you," I say.

"You're welcome," he replies plainly.

Europa seems surprised, expecting him to question us since every other zodiac we have met seems curious as to who we are. No one does. I guess being so preoccupied in the details of your own life, the idea of asking about another would make things too complicated and not asking would seem logical to a Virgo as it would drive attention away from their own inner complex thoughts. Or he's just being modest and keeping to himself, either seems likely.

I nudge Europa to walk down the aisle between the Virgos and the Librans with their calming blue and jade green colours. As we look for Benedict, I find myself considering the contrast between the Constellations of Libra and Virgo. The Librans touch each other affectionately with ease as the expression of love and romance comes naturally. Their pleasing manner is warming as some gestures a welcoming hello as we pass by and you can't help but be captured by their flirtatious self-expression. Others gesture for us to sit with them we politely decline.

Europa whispers in my ear, "The women are incredibly beautiful."

I nod in agreement and add, "Yeah, the men too, they are as pretty as the females."

You'd almost think they'd stolen their beauty from the elves, but the Librans are more enticing to the eye. Elves, when seen in a visual depiction, are more subdued as they blend in with the natural colours of the forest. Even so, their eerie beauty is profound.

Approaching the end of the table, I look carefully at each individual Virgo, comparing them to the picture I pulled out of my pocket to make sure I don't mistake someone else for Benedict and not wanting to offend anyone. I finally spot him at the very end of the table, playing around with his food. He appears to be uninterested in his companions, deep in thought. I nudge Europa and gesture over to him and she sighs with relief and we hastily approach. He has separated all his food into the appropriate colours like others around him, but unexpectedly proceeds in crushing them into an unrecognizable mess. The Virgo sitting across from him notices us and stops eating, but we eagerly stare at Benedict who doesn't seem to notice our presence or just ignores us.

"Uh, excuse me, are you Benedict Malis?" Europa asks. He stops playing with his food momentarily, glancing up at us but immediately returns to playing with his food.

The Virgo sitting across from him intervenes. "Yes, that is Benedict Malis. Excuse his manners...he's not like the rest of us," he says without emotion. Still, the implication is clear, the speaker is disappointed by how Benedict portrays himself, and represents his Constellation.

We nod acknowledgment, looking back at Benedict who now stares at the other Virgo with empty eyes, unaffected by the words that set him apart from the others.

He returns his attention to mashing his food, more deliberately now than before and gathering other bits of vibrant colours that lay on the table to mix into the mess he's created. Not once did he place anything in his mouth in spite of being noticeably thinner than the rest of the Virgos. He has so little flesh on his face that his cheekbones are clearly defined, his hair is untidy, even his wings hang limply and look like those of a bird in the midst of moulting. Even so, with the slight dimple in his chin and long eyelashes with prominent eyebrows, he'd be an attractive male if he'd just put some meat on his bones. The other Virgo intervenes again, "It'd be best if you just ask him what you are here for as he's in a particularly bad mood today.

He's not going to acknowledge you, he barely acknowledges us."

We nod again in gratitude and the speaker returns to thoroughly chewing his perfectly nourishing meal, appearing to be uninterested as to why we were there even if happy to give us some handy advice. I look at the picture then glance at Europa and she nods, clearly feeling uncomfortable as I am.

I place the picture down in front of Benedict and say, "Your brother Vaughn, he uh...bumped into me in the library and dropped this picture of you two. I thought you'd like it back. Seems to be a priceless one to lose."

Benedict instantly stopped playing with his food, becoming stiff as he saw the picture. His eyes lingered at it momentarily and for a moment I thought I saw a tear build up in his near eye. He quickly composes himself again.

"That's impossible," he says with an uninterested monotone that's stern to the ear. Europa and I look at one another, waiting for him to explain, but he doesn't.

So, Europa determined to get some answers, asks, "Why is that impossible? We went out of our way to find its rightful owner and this is the thanks you give us."

I nudge Europa for her to stop and she does, but scrunches her face up. Benedict doesn't react to her probing. Instead he focuses on a delicate green leaf, placing it carefully next to bluish mushroom that blends together perfectly. Moments later, he slowly squishes them together with deliberate intent. Europa gestures for us to leave and as we turn, he says, "He's dead."

We both become stiff, glancing back to see he now holds the picture in his hand and as we turn back to ask another question, Theophilus's powerful voice echoes through the extensive dining room.

"Alright, it's time for everyone to go back to their seats. You must get an early night as I'm sure you all have a big day of study tomorrow. I hope you enjoyed your meal and I shall see you all tomorrow for breakfast. And always remember, allow strength to run beside you."

Everyone quickly begins moving back to their table and we

know we won't be given leniency by the reputable zodiacs who immediately obey Theophilus's commands. But as we attempt to hurry back to our table, I'm unexpectedly grabbed and I turn around to see my arm grasped by Benedict's skinny hand which have large veins that pulse from under thin skin. My arm, caught by his large knuckled fingers, holds me there as he stares at the ground.

"Where did you see him?" he asks plainly but with clear motivation behind it.

"The library," I quickly answer and he lets go without acknowledgment of my response, which makes me question if he even heard me. I wait a moment but he seems deep in thought again and I know that is all I am going to get from him.

I'm back at the Taurean table in time for the zodiac Constellations to begin moving out of the dining area; first the reputable zodiacs, starting with the Capricorns, then their new-bloods. We follow after the Aries whose red and scarlet colours beam bright, representing the differentiated colours of blood reminding me of the near-death experience I had. It gives me a feeling of some unknown danger that constantly follows behind me.

Walking out of the dining hall together, Europa turns to me. "Well, that was a waste of time... Are you sure it was Vaughn who ran into you in the library?"

I nod affirmatively, remembering those exact eyes that penetrated me.

"I'm sure...the only other explanation is he could have been a ghost like Bib?"

Europa nods in agreement. "Yes, that would make sense. But then why did he leave you that picture? And more importantly, why you?"

I shrug. "I don't know. Nothing makes sense at the moment. It could be connected to Manfred's message."

Europa sighs. "Maybe. Still doesn't help. The more information we find, the more confused we seem to become."

As we wait for our turn to teleport up to our dorm, I

notice Benedict walking down a narrow corridor with a Leo I am not familiar with. One who is large and more muscular than any other Leo I have ever laid eyes upon and covered in thick armoured plates with giant peridots further decorating his already extravagant attire. His Constellation colours, gold, orange, and yellow colour the armour where there is a symbolic emblem of Leo engraved prominently on either side of his shoulder plates. I nudge Europa and gesture to the two older zodiacs as they go into a room. After a rapid look around, she says, "Quick, while no one is looking."

We follow agilely down the corridor. As we come to the door where they entered, we can hear voices growing louder as we approach. Europa turns to me, placing her index finger over her sealed lips and we hear a voice.

"I can assure you that is not true," says a deep powerful voice that is more robust than Theophilus's stern and assertive tone, this one more intimidating to the ear as roughness coats the undertone.

Then Benedict's voice is heard. "Dad told me he was dead! How is it possible then? No one knows he even existed, do you think they know it was..." he says without finishing his sentence as though he can't bear to say the words.

The deeper voice replies, "Your brother? No, definitely not. How would they? You know he is dead, you saw what happened with your own two eyes, no one could survive that. She must have been making it all up and a ghost would be very unlikely."

Then a loud bang is heard. Me and Europa both jump, ready to make a run for it but it's soon followed with Benedict's now upset voice, "Why would she make it up!? And if he is a ghost, why haven't I been able to see him!? He was my brother!"

There is a brief silence followed by sobs.

"Vaughn did not die during the fracture of time, so a ghost is impossible. Only those whose passing got caught within the broken transition of that war-torn day stayed within limbo. You know that, that's why the librarian will never leave that library; she is forever caught within a loop and you should be grateful your brother isn't. Because that is what I'd call hell," the deep robust voice says sternly.

Europa and I look at one another in shock then edge in closer.

"And you know if it were known that one of the Malis boys was nearly taken by the Infernum, it would portray weakness within your bloodline and Theophilus's Patriarch status will be re-evaluated by the rest of the Elders. And if that were to happen, everything he has been working towards will fail, years of effort wasted."

Benedict suddenly stops sobbing and says patronizingly, "Yeah...because killing him seemed like the more logical decision to save his own arse."

Suddenly, an exasperating curdle is heard, and Europa and I glance around the corner to see the huge Leo holding Benedict up with one hand, his fist curled effortlessly around the Virgo's scrawny neck. Benedict's wings sporadically expand and contract in distress, and more of his limp feathers fall down to the floor. Then the Leo throws him into some shelves, making them collapse on themselves.

"Your father has given you everything! You spoiled little brat! You know it killed him to make that decision. To see your own blood nearly taken by the Infernum, anyone would prefer death than to see their own son turned into one of those mind-controlled creatures. He would have done the same for you, if he hadn't taken your place... Or is that what you wanted for your brother? Just how you selfishly wished he were in limbo so you could see his ghost. Vaughn was ten times the Virgo you ever were and he should have taken the throne. It should have been you that day but he decided to give his life to save yours and that was the stupidest decision he ever made. And how do you repay him? By continuously humiliating not only your loyal father but your Constellation. Now get yourself together. You can see yourself out."

Benedict immediately replies solemnly, "I wish it had been me too..."

The Leo snuffs in disgust, murmuring, "Pathetic," and begins to leave as Europa and I make a quick, quiet run for it, regaining our position back with our Constellation group just before we become next in line to teleport back to the dorm.

CHAPTER THIRTEEN

GARDEN OF EDEN

Consciousness confronts the cross road of death and rebirth.

Europa and I spent a few hours lying restless on our beds waiting for everyone in our dorm to fall asleep. Only then did we cautiously hop out of bed and sit looking at each other in bewilderment.

In a low voice, Europa said, "What did he mean he didn't die on that war-torn day? So he couldn't be a ghost and if that's the case, who did you see?" She sighed and added, "And Bib's in limbo, what does that mean? That doesn't sound good."

I shake my head, unable to explain it. "I have no idea, but I definitely saw the Virgo in that photo. I can't believe Theophilus was involved in having his own son killed. No wonder Benedict is the way he is."

Europa nods, saying, "Yeah, depressed beyond reach, they must have been incredibly close. I wonder how long ago that happened."

I shrug, answering, "I'm not sure, but they were both quite young in the photo, at least 12."

Someone began snoring which was followed by a toss and turn. I gesture to go to the bathroom just in case we wake someone without realizing, as we could be crucified for discussing such information.

Quietly shutting the door, Europa lets out a big sigh of relief. "This is so frustrating! It's as if we are only finding tiny bits from a much larger puzzle. None of it makes sense!" Europa says in defeat.

I nod and I think of Eve, whom I'm forbidden to talk about. But I can no longer keep it to myself, telling Europa seems like the logical thing to do at the moment and might help us solve this baffling puzzle. So, I tell Europa the whole story of what happened after Isa had nearly beaten me to death. Europa's eyes nearly fall out of her head, not blinking once during the whole saga.

"Adam and Eve are real, not mythical? I can't believe it! And she's kept within these walls told as a legend! And Adam's in the uncharted forest? Surely he's dead now or enchanted by Apophis's Infernum army. Why didn't you tell me this sooner!?"

"I couldn't. Theophilus has literally threatened to execute me if I spoke about such secrets. So you can't let this go any further than this room."

Europa nods asking, "Of course not. But tell me, what was Eve like?"

"We didn't speak much; she just told me she was my mother, which at first thought made sense, since we both have very similar feeble physiques and she's the lady who's been reoccurring in that same dream most nights. But Theophilus informed me that it was impossible, considering the time frame when I was born... Basically told me she's insane, due to her being a human and all. It's common in their species as they are quite chaotic when it comes to their emotions and I'll admit she did reflect that."

Europa hangs on to every word, thinking on it for a moment. "It does seem strange though. I mean you've been dreaming about her your whole life. I wonder if you're connected in some other way because let's be honest...you're not exactly good with handling your own emotions at times."

She half grins, not wanting me to get angry. At first I did become hot and angered by her comment, but thinking on my irrational emotions around Leon, I do see her point, especially after my display in the dining room this evening. "Yeah, I guess I see your point," I say, speaking through my teeth. Being a Taurus and admitting that you're something you perceive as weak can be hard to do.

Europa adds, "Don't take what I said the wrong way.

Obviously there is something special about you, otherwise you wouldn't have that purpose number everyone keeps warning you about. But the emotions could have something to do with it... Look, let's find that Bwbachod, he is the only one who appears to know anything. And he was the first one to warn you of this secret power before you were even aware of it. Because I doubt we'd be able to find Eve again. We must always look to our roots, you know. What is today, grows from the past."

Suddenly, I realize something. "Wait, if the Bwbachod already knew of my power, do you think Theophilus knew? Do you think that's why he warned me? He is enslaved to him and might have heard something?" I question.

Europa shrugs, saying, "Who knows? Anyway, before we make any more accusations, we first need to find out the truth. Just like Manfro told us...then we can save you. Whatever that's supposed to mean."

I smirk, "You mean Manfred?"

Europa rolls her eyes. "Does that really matter right now? Anyway, we better get to bed before someone notices us missing and decide on a course of action tomorrow."

We were woken early to be taken to a new destination to meet with Cassidy Dion, who was to teach us about our totems. That meant there was going to be another long journey throughout the Doh. I made sure to take my medicine before we left. I found a large dirty fingerprint on the vial, which brought the comfort of my father's presence to add to that of his picture that sits on my bedside table. It evokes memories of when I was young, and I would rush to him when he came back from a long day of hunting in the uncharted forest, gathering our food for the following week. On numerous occasions, he'd be dirty from digging up edible plants, or killing the occasional rabbit, but would pick me up effortlessly, getting my clothes as dirty as his. Winter was always a hard time as animals went into hibernation and nutritious vegetables and fruits would wither in the colder months. I was always curious what he'd seen but he'd never discuss those ventures with me, he told me visions of those dark places should not tarnish that of a small child. Although not much time has passed, I miss his shadowing presence. There is a particular patch on my clothes, still holding an obscure stain. I remember it from when I was a young calf. It happens to be part of the garment I wore then, that has remained relatively unworn. My father would cut the best sections from garments discarded by other Taureans, to make bigger ones for me, and use pieces of my old ones to patch places that grew tattered from wear, as with the clothes I use now. I rub the stain with my finger, remembering that it was from a time when Europa and I were playing near my home, and we hugged the big tree that I had supposedly cured.

The memory of my father returns, and I now wish I could ask him the many questions that are lingering in my mind. I particularly regret not telling him about the Bwbachod that had entered my room that night.

We've been walking up more stairs than ever before, passing through various doors and down several long corridors, all decorated differently to the ones before. Demetrius approaches me as I'm now walking on my own, having grown tired, and Europa is a few feet in front of me.

"How are you travelling?" he asks.

"Can't complain," I say as he looks ahead with clearly something on his mind.

"How are your lessons going with...the...Leo?"

"His name is Leon," I say and he nods, conflicted.

"Yes, I'm sorry...Leon. How is it all going?"

I look up at him curiously as I can see he's really trying to be civil about him. I look around to see if anyone is listening. "I was told I'm not allowed to discuss my sessions with anyone."

He glances at me with slight irritation but takes a big breath, and continues. "Well...he did show me the jurisdiction letter. So technically, I am already aware he is attempting to teach you to harness your inner power. "

I think on it for a moment, knowing it would be nice to discuss with someone who is a classed, reputable zodiac. Although I do trust Leon, but I've known Demetrius my whole life.

"Yeah, it's going okay. I've only had one session but I was able to conjure up some power. But I don't know how to control it. It's only when I'm angry that it comes about, and then it's uncontrollable."

He nods, carefully listening and I wait for him to ask me about the power, but he doesn't.

"I'm presuming you're training within the Reflection Room?"

I nod. "But I presume you haven't been able to conjure up the same power by your own free will outside of that room?"

I contemplate on it for a moment, thinking about the time I healed myself but I hadn't done it by my own will. So, I shake my head, knowing that telling another would make things more complicated than they already are. He nods affirmatively with confirmation.

"Do you know something I don't?" I ask.

His expression becomes transfixed and he ignores the question, then asks with deliberation, "Have you told Leon about the medicine you take?"

I become puzzled and anxious, feeling guilty about going against my father's word and now I feel as though something may be very wrong. I answer with insinuation, "What if I had?"

Demetrius's expression becomes rigid and cold with concern, "Did you give him the medicine or not?"

His look is now urgent and I become completely confused. "No, why would I do that? Why would he want the medicine?"

He thinks on it for a moment, once again ignoring my question. "Taura, you must listen to me. You must promise me not to give him a sample. It's very important, as I'm sure he will ask you for a vial. Probably say along the lines of being able to improve it somehow...as he thinks its impairing you from your true potential. He'll probably also ask if you've been able to use your powers outside of the reflection room and that's how he'll go about obtaining it. But you must refuse, no matter how charming he may seem; it's very important. Do you understand me?"

Bewildered, I stare at him, annoyed that he is hiding something from me. "Why? Tell me why? What are you hiding from me?"

He sighs with frustration, looking away in despair. "I'd tell you, Taur, if I could. But I can't, it'll only place you and others in great danger and then I won't have time to save anyone. You just need to trust me on this." His stare is sincere, and I nod in agreement.

"Okay, I promise. But you must promise to tell me what you're talking about, eventually."

He now nods with assertion. "In due time. But right now, it's too dangerous."

He looks ahead and I follow his gaze to see a dead-end at the end of the passage. Then unexpectedly Demetrius places one of his large hands on my shoulder and says, "Thank you, Taur," before pacing ahead to get in front of our whole group.

Isa is standing in front of the blank, high-ceilinged wall, and staring up. "Dead end!" she says annoyed, rolling her eyes and turning around, presuming Demetrius has led us down the wrong path. Ignoring her ignorance, he walks up to the wall, placing his right hand gently on its surface and says, "For the power beseeched in me, I promise to do no harm. Or I am only the primitive animal known as the bull."

Suddenly, several tiny green lights appear and at an incredible speed begin to work together to draw up a giant door with decorative plants and animals. As they finish the perfect picturesque image, the animals and flora begin to move and the picture takes a life of its own. Then the door begins to open.

A large beautiful garden with fresh air full of the fragrance of blossoming flowers, greets us. Tall trees sway, animals that I recognize and strange creatures I've only ever read about wander within. I stare at a particular tree that moves in a peculiar way. Its green leaves move independently until they all fly off, and I realize they were actually strange birds that camouflage themselves as leaves. The tree is now leafless but then I notice it's not really a tree but a strange creature that looks like a dead tree and gets around by using its roots as legs. Its face droops down into its bark-like skin and its eyes are disguised there. As it slowly moves along, a small footpath is revealed.

Demetrius turns to us, "If you took notice of the words I spoke before summoning the door, you'll be aware if you harm anything within this realm, you'll be turned into your ancestral bull and forever live out your days as an animal. So, if you want to get back out of here in one piece: Don't. Touch. Anything."

Europa and I look at one another in wonder and turn back to admire the flawless beauty within this weird place as we all follow closely behind Demetrius, trying not to step on anything.

He explains, "This place is known as Eden, some refer it to as The Garden of Eden. It's where all the animals and flora from all regions live together as one. It is believed that if something disastrous happens – say a disease or illness drives a species into extinction or if the balance of nature goes out of whack, like if we interfere too much – we can use the species within Eden to restore their existence, although this is a rare occurrence and it's not confirmed if this is the purpose for this place."

Kendall asks, "What about the life that has ceased in the Uncharted Forest? Surely, there used to be creatures living there."

We all slow, considering the unexpected question. Kendall had an excellent point. Once again he was displaying his inherent wisdom.

Demetrius drops his head, seeming to be studying the path. When he turned to answer, he quickly erased the frown from his face.

"No creature that lived in the Uncharted Forest before the Infernum, resides here. It is only creatures who currently live in one of the twelve regions, who are represented."

That wasn't enough for Europa. "Why's that?" she asked quickly.

And we all wait for Demetrius to answer, and it's clear he does not wish to continue the conversation; he glanced around, as if cautious about anyone who could be in ear shot.

"I do not know. It probably has something to do with the fact that the Doh was built after the extinction of those creatures. Now, that's enough questions. Follow me in a single file."

We needed to be in a single file behind Demetrius as the pathway has become quite narrow and the garden denser. Then we emerge at the edge of a large lake, the water seeming to be pitch black.

Dalton proceeds to ask, "What's with the black lake? Is it poisoned or something?"

Before Demetrius answers, Kendall stops beside the lake and gives Dalton an expression of needing to explain something simple to an idiot. He crouches down and gently touches the surface of the water and a rainbow-like glow follows his touch as he draws a picture of a book within the water.

"Do you read?" says Kendall patronizingly. Dalton snuffs through his nostrils, angrily. Kendall adds whilst playing amongst the water, "It's called a Fingunt Lake, there is one like this within the Sagittarius forest, Maga. It's black because the fish and insects that live within it are albino in appearance and are incredibly sensitive to light. When their eggs inhabit any kind of water, this beautiful occurrence happens, as their faeces destroy the translucent effect in the water, causing it to go black but leaving a by-product fungi causing this rainbow effect when touched. But it is incredibly nutritious to particular animals that inhabit the area, killing off bad bacteria that might cause certain diseases, although only some will drink it as it is poisonous to others but it keeps a sort of balance in the area."

Then unexpectedly, Demetrius begins clapping hard and deliberate, "Yes, that is correct, Kendall, feel free to enlighten everyone else when ignorant questions are asked." He glances at Dalton, who is now looking furious. Kendall's expression stays neutral as he continues drawing with the rainbow fungi.

Demetrius continues as everyone but Dalton now pokes at

the lake, creating the strange but remarkable rainbow effect. "Adding on to that, in reference to the balance, there is one specific animal called the Albous Aqua which thrives off eating the albino creatures within a Fingunt inhabitant lake. They keep them from spreading to every other bit of water in the area, which would throw out the balance and kill off other specific animals who don't thrive from their existence." He stares at the lake then gestures us to follow, "Anyway, best be moving on, Cassidy will be waiting our arrival."

After skirting the lake, we emerge from the dense growth into sizable clearing where a large old tree grows directly in the centre, its old gnarled branches twist up high into the sky where multi-coloured leaves grow and some fall delicately to the ground.

Lush green grass covers the ground, thriving within this amazing indoor garden. It is moving on its own accord, seeming to have a consciousness of its own since no wind blows here. As we start to cross it, small creatures scatter back into the thick foliage of the garden, past the smaller, droopy trees growing around the outskirts of the clearing. These trees have slender flexible branches, with glowing white lights at the ends which light up at different times to make a brilliant show as though they were welcoming our arrival.

Now, around the large central tree and hovering amongst the colourful leaves, are a plenitude of the multi-coloured totem orbs like those we saw at our first meal at the Doh. Then, unexpectedly, the tree groans, revealing a large mouth that yawns. Dark yellow eyes appear, formed from the twisted trunk that grows from the earth. It does not say anything, only observes us.

Then Cassidy Dion, the Aquarian Elder, appears from behind the tree and it watches him as he walks out in front. His long blue hair, still confined in tightly plaited multiple braids, drapes down in front of him. The flowers caught within the braids look to have just bloomed. He is wearing a comfortable white robe, rather than the more elaborate one he wore at dinner the other day and his large belly hangs noticeably over the belt he wears around his waist. The eyes looking down at us are kind and over shadowed by bushy eyebrows, while his cheeks are slightly pinkish. The long beard, unrestrained by braids, must surely make his face itch.

All respect to the Elders aside, what captures my attention most is the fat little otter that sits on his shoulder cleaning itself.

Demetrius bows and glares at us in a highly suggestive manner, reminding us to show respect, and we mimic what he does.

"Good morning, everyone! I hope the beautiful scenery made up for the long journey." Cassidy smiles warmly and we all nod in agreement.

Then Demetrius steps forward. "I do apologize for the inconvenience and short notice, Cassidy, but I must attend to some...important business that cannot be left unattended. Do you mind if I collect them after class has ended?"

Cassidy nods unconcerned. "Of course, I'm sure they won't cause me much trouble." He winks at us, but our faces stay expressionless. He chuckles, "I forgot how serious and rigid you Taureans can be. That's okay, this lesson will loosen you up; we just need to wait for the others to arrive, which I'm sure will be in any moment. I shall see you after, Demetrius, carry on your... important duties."

Demetrius bowed again to express his thanks, then looks intensely into my eyes before leaving and disappearing back into the thickness of the garden from where we came.

Europa whispers to me, "Others?" and at that exact moment, all the other new blooded zodiacs appear at intervals around the clearing, coming in between the trees with the waving light tipped branches.

Then Cassidy bellows so everyone can hear, "Come! Come! Everyone, take a seat around here and we shall begin."

All the other zodiacs look around as we did when we first entered, and the few little creatures that had stayed within the grass now scatter to the outskirts of the garden. Cassidy continues to gesture towards the other zodiacs who are guided by their overseers.

"Come sit around on the luscious green grass where the Taureans are lying; you'll notice it's incredibly soft to the touch, like a newly knitted blanket. Babies could fall asleep in this stuff."

As everyone gets comfortable, sounds of gasping comfort are heard as some sit down into the grass. Europa plays with a few strands, gently scraping it along her skin. Once everyone is seated, the overseers stand in the back behind everyone and Cassidy delicately places his little fat otter friend on the ground next to him and gives him a tiny dried-out fish from a little pouch on his side pocket.

"Alright, let us begin! Now your totems have been mentioned as you know. They live within your dorms, but I'm sure you still don't really know what they are. They are the little coloured orbs that hover around your beds while you sleep."

Everyone nods in agreement, though some are still distracted by the environment.

Cassidy's expression now becomes excited. "Yes. Well! I bet you didn't notice that for every one of you there is one of them in your dorm."

Now I immediately remember there being six little yellow orbs in our dorm. He now points to his fat friend who rolls around on his large tummy kicking the dried fish with his back feet. I hear from behind me a few 'aww' noises as some zodiacs adore the small animal, likely coming from the Libras that sit close by. The little otter soon tires himself out and falls asleep, and the fish falls to his side. "This is my totem, Obog the otter, and he is a complete reflection of me. As you can see, I love my food and sleep. I don't believe I tire myself that easily but he seems to prove otherwise! Maybe it's something I need to work on and maybe a little more exercise." Cassidy laughs in amusement of himself, holding up his big belly within his large sturdy hands, jiggling it.

He continues, "They are your guides; they teach us many

things about ourselves and show us what we are turning into metaphysically. Each Constellation has their own animal representation, but each distinct animal is a complete representation of you. Obviously, otters are the Aquarians' totem as you can see from my friend. And in actual fact this isn't his mature metaphysical form, in truth he looks nothing like an otter outside of this garden - within Eden he has transformed back into his original state. But I'll explain more as we go along."

He raises one hand high and a silver-grey orb comes floating down into the palm of his large hand. "For instance, Aquarians would see these little silver-grey coloured orbs in their dorms, where a river flows upside down on their ceiling, leaking down the walls. This is where the first stage of a totem otter's life begins, and it is similar for all zodiac totems." He gently pushes the orb back up into the large multi-coloured tree where other orbs inhabit and the tree watches it with its big yellow eyes. Cassidy lingers at it momentarily then clasps his hand together with enthusiasm. "Over time you'll become more connected to your totems, but at the moment they are just getting to know you and still in the foetus stage of development. Once you obtained your purpose numbers, your totem was born into the tree you see behind me and they awaited your arrival within the other tree you first saw in the dining hall. You'll soon learn which specific one is yours as it will continue to approach you. They all look the same at the moment. But you'll start to notice distinguishable differences between them, especially over time, as it will transform into its physical form; one can't say when that will happen, it'll be determined by the individual and how quickly they grow within themselves over time."

A Scorpio puts his hand up in question and Cassidy gestures to him. He asks, "Why don't we see our superiors or anyone else with their totems around the Doh? Or in our Constellations?"

Cassidy raises his eyebrows. "Great question! You probably have seen others with totems, but didn't realize they were their totems. Your overseers don't like to keep their totems around when they're on duty as you can't control your totem. In a way it is because they have their own identity and feed from your emotion, and as a result, it becomes impossible to cover up how you are truly feeling. Right now, I'm a bit tired as I had one of those sleepless nights, so Obog here...demonstrates my fatigue... In regards to your Constellations, totems aren't allowed to be kept within Constellations as they react on how you feel and can be too unpredictable. They can't really be controlled by any normal NC zodiac. So, without a Libra diplomat around at all times, it would cause too much chaos between residing zodiacs. So, NC zodiacs' totems lie dormant within their orb forms and live within this beautiful Garden of Eden."

The little otter now snores with large amounts of drool seeping from its mouth and Cassidy shakes his head in an amused but disproving expression, "As you can see, it can be quite embarrassing to have them around when you're not feeling your best." He chuckles, but I now notice the dark bags under his eyes from lack of sleep, which I wouldn't have noticed if it wasn't pointed out by Obog.

Now an Aries puts his hand up and Cassidy gestures to him. He asks, "What do you mean they represent us metaphysically?"

Cassidy raises his eyebrows again and smiles warmly.

"What I mean by that is, physically you may have the same animal as your other Aries friends and family, but they'll never look the same as each other. For example, if you contain a kind essence, your totem will be incredibly innocent looking and welcoming to everyone who comes into its presence as they feed from your essence. However, if someone say ... holds a deep dark resentment in their heart, their totem will appear to be monstrous or scary or both, and sometimes they can be very dangerous, some have been known to kill others. But those totems are locked away and the zodiac will have to be treated to clear any darkness within them. Even if two individuals had the same natures, neither totem would look the same, as everyone expresses themselves differently, they are a complete representation of who you are at that current moment in time. Now don't take Obog's current form for truth, because, outside of the Garden of Eden, he is far from cute in reality. Now before we have any more questions, I'm going to go through each zodiac's totem and explain their traits as every animal chosen is in fact an actual animal representation of each zodiac. So, everyone should keep your ears open as you may learn something you didn't know about your neighbouring zodiac."

Cassidy clears his throat, places his hand out again and this time a blue orb glide's down into the palm of his hand, and he gently brings it out in front of him. Whispering a few soft words which no one can hear, the blue orb turns into a giant black bird. "Libras, I'm sure you recognize the colour of the orb. This is your totem animal, the raven. Friendly, social, and greatly enjoys being part of a group. Despite their talkativeness, Libras and ravens are very discreet and are therefore great at keeping secrets. The ability to keep an objective mindset allows them to see all sides of an issue, making them great mediators and diplomats. It is this ability, however, that can cause hesitancy in decision making as they strive to be fair at all times. While genuinely cheerful and upbeat sorts, an atmosphere of distortion and confusion may send them spiralling into moodiness or become unbalanced, which is soon known by the contrast in eye colour. So as long as you are clear in expressing your point, you will find them an exciting friend or partner." Then the raven flies off and turns back into the blue orb and returns to the multi-coloured tree.

Cassidy does the same gesture again but this time a violet orb floats down. He looks towards the Scorpios this time and the orb turns into a slithering snake.

"Scorpio! Your totem is the snake! Scorpios and this reptile embody intensity and transformation. With a love of secrets and a penchant for uncovering the mystery of the universe, those of this totem are able to entrance those around them. Even those who are daunted by their intense nature will feel drawn to his or her mysterious psyche. Just as a snake periodically sheds its skin, Scorpios of the snake totem will undergo occasional life transformations, sometimes leaving others in the wake. While the feeling of new situations and experiences enthrals snakes, it is important they do not completely alienate their old companions in the process, or they will find themselves unable to sustain life-long relationships." The snake now begins to grow longer and thicker, curling itself around Cassidy and he calmly smiles, opening up his hands and allows it to then slither back up the tree. Soon after it returns to its violet orb.

The next orb is gold, and transforms into a large bird with large eyes and it appears to turn its head nearly three hundred and sixty degrees which astonishes everyone. "Sagittarians, your totem is the owl! The guardians of the underworld. Sagittarius and owls are good at embracing their personal darkness, spotting deception, and keeping secrets. Intuitive and perceptive, owls love the acquisition of knowledge and bringing the mysterious out of the dark. They place a high value on integrity and ingenuity. While genuinely easy-going and friendly, they can also be bold and reckless. It is important for them to remember the art of tact while dealing with others, as they can be accused of lacking compassion. Characterized by a constant need for freedom, whether real or perceived, they have trouble with the sensation of feeling tied down. They are very adaptable and thrive on change, and while this is advantageous in many ways, it can lend itself to trouble where solid commitments are required." The owl expands its wide wings and flies up into the tree turning back into the golden orb.

The next orb is pristine white and it turns into a large fat bird with a black neck and head with a white body. It honks loudly and Cassidy follows up with, "Capricorns, your totem animal is the goose! Capricorns and geese are powerfully insightful, focused, and determined. Resourceful and imaginative, they're more likely to reach his or her big lofty goals than most. While their perfectionism allows them to perform tasks with the highest integrity and care, it is important for them to not be overly critical of themselves. Though much of their energy is focused on their life's many goals, they make extremely dependable partners and friends. As practical sorts, they tend to dislike insincerity and tend to be more tolerant of it in others and able to spot it better than anyone else. While never insincere, it is common for them to adopt a masked persona, hiding their feelings from others. While sometimes a hard nut to crack, those with the goose totem are wonderful zodiacs to get to know and well worth the effort." The goose walks up to Obog who's still fast asleep and honks loudly in his ear making him jump out of his skin and running up behind Cassidy, making everyone laugh and the goose turns back into a white orb.

Obog climbs up Cassidy's shoulder and he scratches him on the head as he proceeds to get comfortable. "Well, Aquarians, it's time for our own totem. As you know it's the otter. And what we have in common with these tiny animals are friendliness, adaptability, sociability, inventiveness, and creativity. These original thinkers often times use their creativity to produce unconventional ideas which may seem wild at first but brilliant upon second glance. Born during 'cleansing time,' we enjoy reformation efforts and helping others succeed. True humanitarians, we possess the amiability and intellect necessary to succeed ourselves. We can be more spontaneous than others are comfortable with. And our dislike for conventional ways can cause friction with others who we work closely with. We should learn to hone our creative ability to produce unique ideas, while respecting others' needs for rules."

The next orb is bluish green in colour and turns into a large dog which immediately releases a penetrating howl. "Pisces, your totem is the wolf! Pisces and wolves are highly intuitive and empathetic sorts. This intuition allows them to see what others may not, allowing them to act instinctively. Sensitive, romantic, and protective. Both make loyal companions. They need love, which at times come in conflict with their need for independence. Though their intuitions are usually correct, sometimes they may neglect 'thinking' or 'feeling.' Their deep capacity for empathetic feeling may cause them to absorb others' negative emotions. It is important for them to spend some time alone so they may return to their normal compassionate state." The wolf prowls around, sniffing after the scent of the otter who teases the wolf from the safety of Cassidy's tall and broad shoulders. And just as it prepares to jump up to where the otter sits, it turns back into the bluish green orb and the otter sighs with relief.

The next orb is yellowish green in colour which turns into a medium-sized bird with a yellow beak.

"Aries, your totem is the falcon! Aries and falcon are energetic to the core, leading exciting lives, full of whirlwind activity. They are thrilling to be around due to their exuberant and self-assured nature, even despite the touch of arrogance many exhibit. A natural leader, others are often infected by its enthusiastic and enterprising spirit. Although they should refrain from making hasty decisions as their impulsiveness and exuberance can cloud reason. It is also important for them to learn to follow through even when a project or relationship loses its zest of novelty. While they love being on the go, they benefit from taking a step back and relaxing." The falcon takes off, soaring around the tree and turns back into its orb once it zooms up through its tall branches.

The following orb is yellow and I immediately recognize the colour from our dorm. Cassidy places it on the ground and it turns into a fat hairy creature with large front teeth, and I soon see why he didn't proceed in holding it. "Taurus, your totem animal is the beaver! Those represented by the beaver are hardworking, dependable, and industrious. If you want a job done right, ask these guys. Their attention to detail, mental acuity, and persistent effort makes them excellent workers. They work best when the seas are smooth and work hard to transform their home into a secure, comfortable retreat. Interior décor is often times important to them due to their fondness of beautiful items. Their love of stability makes them excellent long-term friends and partners; however, their tendency towards continual improvement in themselves and others may come off as controlling if left unchecked. If they learn to be more flexible, they can become a modelled worker and a loyal friend." The beaver now begins gnawing on the tree, which immediately moves its roots out of the way and flings the fat animal off and it goes flying, turning back into its yellow orb and returning to the tree.

The next orb is orange and turns into a large animal that stands on all fours and has large antlers.

"Gemini, your totem is the deer! The Gemini and deer are engaging conversationalists, tending to be broad and knowledgeable on a large range of topics, exhibiting a charming enthusiasm for life. Popular and well liked, their finer qualities often times make up for their tendency towards moodiness and narcissism. They can just about make any one laugh, and entrance listeners with their animated stories. These zodiacs thrive on life's challenges and love variety; however, this adaptability often times leads towards flight behaviour. They should learn to slow down once and a while and to temper their moods when needed." The deer proceeds at nibbling the grass then turns back into its orb.

The next orb is rose in colour and turns into a tiny little blue bird with a thin beak. "Cancer, your totem animal is the woodpecker! You are both warm, emotional, and deeply sensitive, empathetic and great listeners. They are the ones who we come to at times of need. These great nurturers make great parents and invest considerable amounts of efforts into their homes, desiring a beautiful haven that is both comfortable and beautiful. They are considerate friends and loyal workers. They're generally ruled by their heart instead of their head. But it's important for them to remember to not always sacrifice their own needs for the sake of others." The woodpecker now begins violently drilling into the tree at an unimaginable rate. He turns into a blur as he moves back and forth. The tree pulls him off with a small root, curling around his tiny body and he quickly turns back into the rose-coloured orb and the tree trunk quickly heals over.

The next orb is red in colour and turns into a pink fish that stands on its back fins on the other side of Cassidy's shoulder. "Leos, your totem is the salmon! Leo and salmon are warm, exhibit enthusiasm and exude energy that is contagious. Just as the salmon do, Leos like to swim against the current, confident that their way is the correct way. In most cases, it is. It's this determination that makes them great leaders, easily getting others to join in on their ambitious ventures. They are emotional beings, choosing to invest a lot into their relationships. Because they give so much, they also expect a lot back. They are easily hurt if not shown adequate approval and affection. While appearing confident or even arrogant on the outside, they require the positive attention of those around them to thrive." Obog tries to catch the fish by sneakily trying to jump over to Cassidy's other shoulder where the salmon stands but the fish glides out of the way, now using its bottom fins as wings and Obog falls straight down to the ground but Cassidy quickly catches him within his large hands, laughing at the attempt.

The next and last orb is brown in colour and turns into a large, thick hairy beast that positions itself on its hind legs and stands at about seven foot tall. "Virgo, your totem is the bear! Virgos and bears are independent, work best in routines, and are often resistant to change. Practical, with an eye for detail, those born under this animal make great workers, though they are humble almost to a fault. Their hard work and good ideas may go unnoticed if they do not learn to praise themselves occasionally. Virgos born under the bear are fond of familiarity which makes them great partners and friends, though they may come across as cold and aloof to some. This is because their independence makes them slow to show their emotions, not because of a lack of feelings. A true diamond in the rough, once you get past their humble exterior and reserved nature, you will uncover invaluable work ethic and lifelong friends." The bear gives a powerful roar and I instantly recognize it. Fear trembles through me, remembering what the Aquarian Cordelia Dion had told me when I asked what Theophilus's creature Kerit was: *"He was once a bear. But now...now, he is more like a distant relative."*

Cassidy now asks as the bear turns back into its original brown orb. "Now, are there any more questions?"

I look around but no one appears to have any. So, I hesitantly put my hand up and Cassidy eagerly points to me and says, "Ah yes, the small Taurus girl."

Europa looks at me curiously as I've never had the courage to speak in front of more than a couple of zodiacs. I swallow hard and pray I don't trip over my words. "What if your totem...was incredibly dangerous and scary...but, uh, did as you commanded? I mean...in regards to you saying they act on our emotion...what if you really disliked someone, or were afraid of someone, and it would have reacted to protect you, but it didn't because you knew it was wrong... And, well it stopped, against all primitive instincts?"

Faint murmuring from some of the other zodiac groups suddenly ceases. The crack of a stick snapping makes me swivel to look at the source. Isa is holding two halves of a stick, and staring at the ground. Sweat is beading the part of her face and neck that I can see. Maybe she thinks I'm investigating a way to protect myself further against her.

Cassidy hums in regards to the question, bringing my attention back to him. He stares at the tree, which plainly stares back, then turns back to look at me strangely as he caresses his beard, contemplating. I feel the eyes of every zodiac focused on me, knowing it's a very specific question.

"Do you mean hypothetically, because I've never heard of such power over a totem? I mean you can have influence which relates to you controlling your own emotion, but do you refer to complete dictated control?"

I nod, then begin to wonder if anyone has seen Theophilus's totem. Thinking on Cassidy's information, I now begin to doubt it. Zodiacs are most likely to keep their totems hidden, especially when they have something to hide.

"Well, hypothetically, to have such a power over an emotionally controlled entity, I'd say the zodiac would have to be incredibly powerful. They'd need to have great willpower over their strong dark emotions and that would clearly be embodied within their totem too. But to control it would take power beyond that gained in one lifetime, I'd imagine. And to increase a zodiac's lifespan, well, I don't want to even speak of such evil that would entail."

I become increasingly curious by the last statement. "A zodiac can increase their lifespan?"

Cassidy's expression becomes hesitant, probably wondering why I would want to know such information. Then he smiles warmly. "My gosh, you are a curious one, aren't you. Well, yes, but to speak of such treachery is forbidden as it's punishable by death, injection by the Scorpio's death serum, Venenum ... but we are going off topic now. Are there any other questions regarding your totems?"

I take that as my cue to sit down and as I do, Europa looks at me questioningly.

"What was that all about?" she whispers.

I don't dare want to speak of Theophilus amongst such close proximity to others. "I'll tell you later."

A few more questions are answered but I become too deep in thought to pay attention. After they've been addressed, I notice Demetrius is now back. Everyone disperses back from where they came and Demetrius guides us back through the Garden of Eden.

CHAPTER FOURTEEN

SAMPLE

Truth seekers are courageous but they walk alongside loneliness.

Walking up to our dorm after teleportation, I see Leon leaning against the wall beside our door, with one leg bent against the wall and the other stiffly planted to hold him up. He has his arms crossed leisurely; he turns towards me and smiles flirtatiously.

Europa whispers, "He doesn't leave much to the imagination, does he?"

I smile. "No, he does not."

Then Demetrius is determinedly by my side and I look at him, his expression impatient but forcefully contained, "Remember what we spoke about. You promised."

I glance at Leon and sternly look at Demetrius, whispering so no one else can hear, "I promise, just so long as you tell me what is going on."

He nods firmly. "I will. A day has already been set."

I stare at him in question. "What day?" But we can no longer continue as the group comes to a halt.

The others recite the poem and walk into our dorm as the doorknocker sighs with irritation on hearing that same old poem, each word spoken once again, and seeming to be torturous to hear. Each Taurean stares at Leon with untrusting eyes as they enter. Isa especially, she is keeping me in her peripheral vision. Glancing my way, she gives me a strange expression of doubt and caution. She slows momentarily and snorts with judgment before following the others.

Europa stays by my side as I stay to speak with Leon. Demetrius too stands firmly beside me, and Leon looks up at him, two prides just as proud as each other.

"You take care of her, you hear," says Demetrius.

"Of course, I'm already doing a better job," says Leon challengingly.

Demetrius sniffs at him, "Yeah, we'll see about that." He abruptly turns his back and storms off, saying out loud, "Enjoy it while it lasts. The blindfold will soon be lifted...Leon Sol."

Leon watches him as he disappears into the crowd of new-bloods who now come and go within their dorms.

"He sure hates you," says Europa with conviction.

Leon looks at her, clearly holding back the fire that now burns within him. "That he does." He stands up from the wall and gestures to me. "Shall we get going then, Taur?" he says warmly.

Europa's energy becomes possessive. "Since when did you start calling her Taur?"

He glances back at her, brushing her comment off as if it was unimportant.

"Since now."

Her eyebrows draw together and she looks like she is going to explode; she turns away and says between her teeth, "Your ego stands up to its reputation!"

She looks at me, warning me to be cautious, and storms into the dorm, slamming the door behind her.

"Oh, that'd be bloody right, no consideration for the guy who lives on the door!" the door knocker yells. Everyone in the premises stops to look at us momentarily.

Leon glances at the door and remarks, "I guess she hates me too?"

I shrug. "She just doesn't trust you is all."

He smiles. "Well, that's something new...let's get going, shall we?"

We teleport to the Reflection Room, and as we enter, I notice it hasn't grown in size but it's more inviting in appearance. The small windows on either side no longer have sporadic cracks and the wooden interior is now more welcoming as opposed to feeling cold and lifeless.

Leon glances around the room as he comes in. "Well, it looks better in here. I can see you're becoming more confident within yourself." He looks up to the tiny cloud with small bits of sparking electricity that sporadically lights up. "Hmmm, although your power still remains the same, which I find surprising."

I walk over and linger at the cloud. "Why's that?"

He looks at me. "Well, since you have become aware of your unbeknown power, it's curious to me to see your cloud remain the same. Generally, when awareness occurs, it gives it general growth. Just from knowing about it even if you haven't used it."

He walks closer to me and I become rigid. "It's kinda like negative attention; it's still attention. But ignoring something altogether makes anything wither. Ignorance made your power weaken without you even knowing it."

I watch him carefully, wondering if he is going to bring up my medicine, just as Demetrius foretold. But before the conversation heads down that path, I ask, "Who was that girl in the dining room? She seemed awfully mad at you."

Leon smiles with intoxicating warmth. "That's a random question and quite off topic? Why? Were you jealous?"

I become angered by the arrogant comment, wanting to dismiss him. "Why would I be jealous? There is nothing to be jealous about," I say with spite.

He smiles again, appearing to be amused by me. "Well, she was jealous of you..."

I feel the blood drain rapidly from my face, this conversation is much worse. He watches me carefully and I know I can't hide the now obvious, no matter how hard I stare at the ground.

"She's just a Leo who has been wanting to court me since I was a young cub but I've never been interested in her."

I feel myself becoming calm again. "Why?"

"Because she isn't interesting... Although I probably lead her on every now and then when I'm bored, which I should probably stop doing. But I'm not going to lie: it's flattering to the ego."

I roll my eyes. "Yeah, you should probably stop."

He chuckles, "Probably? Now you tell me. Why did you ask that strange question to Cassidy Dion in the totems' class? It seemed awfully specific."

I forgot he would have been in that class for new-bloods. And I realize he might know some information about the Bwbachod, considering his father is Theophilus's right-hand man and he's ordered by Theophilus to conduct these sessions.

"If I tell you, do you promise not to report it back to Theophilus?"

He stares at me carefully but out of curiosity he nods. "I promise."

I linger back and forth from the ground to his gazing stare and explain when I first met Theophilus I had also met his totem called Kerit. Explaining he was able to control it even though it looked monstrously deformed and he was able to command it even though it clearly wanted to rip apart his enslaved Bwbachod and myself.

Leon listened carefully, thinking for a moment and reminding me of my father's expression when he selectively chooses the right words. "Yeah, I've met Kerit. Not many have. I'm actually surprised he allowed you to see him as those who do generally take him the wrong way, especially knowing the information we were taught in that class."

"What do you mean?"

He explains, "It is believed that Kerit was manifested that way from all the turmoil Theophilus has been through, which creates the drive to fight the Infernum, to keep us alive. The stress of creating a systematic structure, for us all to work together, has proved to be more difficult than originally thought and that task landed in his lap. Being a humble Virgo enables him to control his emotions so rigidly that he is able to control Kerit. Since our totems change due to our growth, I also think going into such a powerful position has also enabled him to grow these particular elements. But many wouldn't realize this so, he tries to keep Kerit hidden. Most would presume he has turned evil, but maybe he thought you were different and that's why you were allowed to see him."

I become guilt-ridden, feeling I had judged Theophilus too harshly.

"And I bet you feel bad now as many have before you. It's okay. It's completely understandable that you would presume that, knowing what you knew. But knowing what you now know makes you realize you shouldn't jump to conclusions. There's always more to the story than appears."

I nod guiltily. "Can I ask you another question?"

He stares back at my cloud. "Sure, but we should be getting on with the lesson soon."

I begin perspiring. "Do you know why...he kept that singular Bwbachod alive and enslaved?"

Leon's eyes raise and his face relaxes, thinking on it for a moment then his expression comes to some sort of epiphany.

"If I tell you...you must promise not to repeat it. Spreading such information could be considered traitorous. Do you promise me?" His big golden eyes stare deep into me and I nod assertively, my eyes widening. He turns away and starts pacing as he tells the story.

"Good, I'm only telling you this as I believe I can trust you... That Bwbachod...was once the son they never knew." I look at him in confusion and he continues, "You know how Bwbachods over generations obtained the ability to become anyone in personality, ability, and power? They would shed their skin and turn into whoever they wished, just so long as they drank some blood of the zodiac they wish to replicate as it has in it the relevant genetic DNA make-up." I nod again in understanding. "Well, that Bwbachod who is the remaining one was swapped at birth by its mother Bwbachod for the twin Vaughn Malis. She made her baby drink some of his blood and he turned into the baby Vaughn. She stole the real Vaughn and disappeared, never to be seen again. It's not commonly known information but Bwbachods are more powerful when they are young. This is a primitive power that increases their chance of making it to adulthood. But anyway, as time went on, the baby continued to grow, only knowing himself as Vaughn Malis, ignorant to his mother's actions. And once he turned thirteen, puberty set in and the only reality he had known started to become distorted as he started transforming into the Bwbachod he really was.

"He was probably confused and scared half to death but not wanting to be found out, he continually transformed back but it became harder with each transformation. It's believed puberty had changed his hormonal balance in regard to the Bwbachod gene or he just ran out of juice, but no one really knows. Anyway, Theophilus soon found out and banished him to the Uncharted Forest. Benedict was originally going to be told another story to protect the memory of his brother Vaughn. But unfortunately, life doesn't always go as planned and Benedict somehow saw his brother walking into those woods that day, as the brother he had known. He ran after him and was never able to remember what happened after he heard that magnetic lullaby for which we all pray to have a deaf ear. The Bwbachod, disguised as Vaughn, protected the only brother he knew, saving him and taking him away from the forest as quickly as possible, hoping it would be before he became completely cursed.

"Fortunately for Benedict, he snapped out of it and came to himself again. It is the only case I have ever heard of. But unfortunately, Benedict awoke to see his brother walking back into the Uncharted Forest, and thought he had been enchanted by the lullaby. He also saw his own father stab his brother in the heart from behind with his Virgo golden sword. He has been told, ever since then, that his brother had saved him from the Infernum by giving his own life, and that his father, Theophilus, couldn't bear to see his son taken by that kind of evil and wanted to kill him by his own hand. But as everyone knows, Bwbachods can't die, another reason why they're so dangerous. So, what Benedict saw wasn't his brother dying but it was actually the Bwbachod in the guise of Vaughn. Theophilus never wants Benedict to know that the brother he loved was a monster, a genetic mutation of a zodiac. He wants him to remember Vaughn as the Virgo he knew, and not have his memory tarnished.

"Once he had been taken away, the Bwbachod rejuvenated into his original form, never able to transform back into Vaughn again. Any other Bwbachods had already been eradicated at this point in time and Theophilus kept that Bwbachod alive, pretending he had kept him hidden this whole time, since long before Vaughn's disappearance. Explaining if anything were to ever go wrong in Orbis Bellum, his genetics could be used to help, so logically, it would be appropriate. Others believe he kept him for other purposes. But I believe it's because he is the only thing that links him to his real son. So, as much as he loved him once, he resents the creature for replacing the son he never knew and feeling like a failure as a father, because he could not recognize his real son from the fake. This is what has caused deep, conflicting turmoil. Probably another factor as to why his totem looks the way it does.

"Not many know of Vaughn's existence, which I think makes Benedict increasingly resentful towards his father, having to pretend his own brother, who he loved dearly, never lived. However, he is too naive and blinded by emotion to see the bigger picture of the responsibility his father must uphold within Nirvana."

Recalling the day I was in Theophilus's domain, I now feel deep sadness for the Bwbachod. How could somebody treat someone else so badly when they used to love them as their very own son? Why did the Bwbachod risk so much to warn me?

Leon brings me back to reality. "Love and hate. The most contradictory yet closely bonded emotions. Either one can be used unconditionally...and either one can be used against you," he says, lingering at the tiny window in my room that now begins to break again, as a reflection of the sadness I now feel.

I ask, "And the Bwbachod has never confronted Benedict...to tell him the truth?"

Leon shakes his head. "I used to play with the twin brothers when I was young, before any of this was known, as our fathers have worked closely together for many decades. From knowing the Bwbachod as Vaughn, who was conditioned to a Virgo way of life, I'd presume the Bwbachod doesn't want to tarnish the memories Benedict has of Vaughn either. He doesn't want

Benedict to be conflicted in the way his father is. He'd rather Benedict remembers him for what he was, not what he is. I guess that's why he stays so immensely loyal to the Malis family."

I think on that for a moment and question that loyalty in light of my first meeting with the Bwbachod as Leon adds, "May I ask why you wanted to know about the Bwbachod?"

I become flustered by the last question. Shrugging, "I was just curious really, I was told they were eradicated. And the remaining Bwbachod was enslaved to Theophilus... I guess I just wanted to understand why."

He looks at me with consideration, then drops his initial suspicion and nods his head in understanding. Then I ask, "Why didn't you tell me the story Theophilus has told everyone else? That it was for the purpose of the Orbis Bellum?"

Leon shrugs. "I guess it's nice to share the truth for once as opposed to constantly keeping secrets, to keep the ignorant guarded within faith. Sometimes, the more you know, the bigger the burden. So it's nice to share the load sometimes."

I nod in relation to the burden of my own secrets. "Yeah, I can understand that."

We both stand in silence for a short time then Leon says, "Alright, let's lighten up the energy. Let's try to harness some of those powers of yours without conjuring it up randomly with sporadic aggressive emotion. You told me you could self-heal?"

"Yes?" I answer, confused as Leon randomly starts jumping up and down on the spot, breathing deeply with strange grunting noises as if warming up to something. "What are you doing?" I ask.

"Well, genuinely if you can self-heal, you should technically be able to heal others too. So you're going to try it out on me."

I look at him puzzled. "But you're not hurt!"

"Precisely."

He continues jumping up and down on the spot, breathing in deeply and unexpectedly smashes himself into the wooden wall like a rag doll, over and over again. The room begins to tremor, until I hear a snap, crack, and pop, followed by an exasperated groan.

"You're going to seriously hurt yourself! Stop that! A small cut or something less extreme will suffice!"

I run over to him as he holds his shoulder and I notice it's dislocated and possibly broken.

"Are you crazy?"

He smiles, despite the obvious pain written over his face. "Only a little...now I need you to kneel down and I'm going to sit next to you. You'll take a big breath and imagine my arm back in its original condition. But you must believe you can heal me, that is the most important part." he says grimacing in pain.

We sit down and I place my hands over his muscular, lean shoulder, and I am aware of his physical warmth beneath on my skin. Instead of fixing his arm, I'm distracted by thinking this is the closest I've been to any male other than my father, and he would not be pleased by this image.

"Concentrate," Leon reminds me. "Now breathe in deep and slow. Imagine my arm in perfect condition. Feel yourself healing my arm." His tone is harmonious to the ear. I breathe in deep and I imagine the bone going back into its original state, I feel warmth going from my hands to his body. There is silence for a moment, until he groans again in immense pain, followed by sounds of rapture and deep inner popping. I open my eyes briefly to see the same blue aura I remember from when I ostensibly healed that tree and the same one from my dream when I reached out to Eve after she'd fallen to the ground. Then the aura begins to fade and Leon opens his eyes in panic.

"Don't stop now!"

I shut my eyes once again and continue imagining his shoulder in perfect condition. Leon now groans even louder, as the bone and muscle continue to reverse into their original condition. My whole body begins to heat up and I can see the light blue aura beneath my eyes.

Leon unexpectedly pulls away and collapses on to the floor, looking exhausted. He looks up at me, his mouth slightly opened in awe. I notice my whole body is now saturated in the blue aura and my hair is standing on end. The number ten on the back of my neck is pulsating. He looks toward the cloud as do I, but it no longer represents the contorted cloud with sporadic electricity, instead it appears calm and powerful, bounded within the same blue aura. Now it begins to leak the blue aura on to the floor as though it is turning into water. Splashing over the floors' surface, it is absorbed into the cracks of the decaying wood, filtering through. Tiny veins of lightning shoot up the walls, and the glow infuses my surroundings. I feel the number ten continue to pierce with burning heat and the pain becomes more intense. I become agitated, panicking, I fall to the floor, squeezing my eyes shut. I curl into a ball holding my knees to my chest, wanting it to stop but it's as though this force has a life of its own, living dormant inside of me and I cannot control it. The room goes dark and I feel a hand placed gently on my back.

"Taur, don't be afraid, that was amazing!"

I still lie there scared by the power I let loose, but Leon continues, "You did it. My arm's all better, in fact, I have something else to show you."

I open my eyes and get into a sitting position, noticing the room has returned to normal and so has my cloud, except the little sporadic electricity is a little fierier than normal. Leon pulls up his shirt up to reveal his incredible physique - not an ounce of fat on him, rippled with lean muscle. He was like that already, so what else had changed as I healed him?

"I used to have a giant scar at least 10 inches long from a battle I had with my father when I was quite young... Taur, it's completely gone!" He twists and turns, showing his incredibly torso, not realizing I can't take notice of the scar I'd never seen. "It had faded over the years but my skin appears to be brand new. Not even one of the hundreds of little nicks are left on my arms." He laughs with excitement. "I'm going to be underestimated now as our Constellation finds someone with many scars to be a great warrior and threat, clearly demonstrating the physical pain that they've experienced and endured."

He continues looking at himself and the shoulder he broke,

moving it up and down. I stand, feeling insecure and conflicted about what I'd been able to do and seen.

"Did you not see what happened to my cloud?" I question.

Leon continues to admire himself and takes a moment before realizing I've spoken. "Huh? Your cloud? Yeah, it's a little more powerful now. We're definitely on the right track!"

I instantly get a bad feeling. The memory of Penelope encouraging me to heal the tree and how my father seemed angry about it. Is the Bwbachod's warning true? Is this some sort of evil? Has my father just been trying to protect me?

Leon is now looking at me. "Taur, have you been able to do anything like this outside of this Reflection Room?"

Demetrius's words now find their way back into my presence. I now know what Leon is leading to and my body becomes rigid.

"Well, yes, when I was thrown from the stairs?"

I can tell he is now reading my body language so he approaches me carefully. "Yes, but that was out of extreme circumstances, your body probably acted on instinct for pure survival. What I mean is, have you ever been able to do this just as you did then, thought something and it happened?"

I nod again. "When I was very young I think, but I'm not sure if it's a memory or a dream. I healed a tree."

He nods calmly. "Yes, but it hasn't happened since you started taking that medicine, is that right?"

I become angry at him as I feel he is about to break the bond we have created with mistrust, why else would Demetrius warn me against him and predict this. But I still nod, curious to what he will ask next in hope it is all a misjudgement. He smiles warmly.

"I think you should give me a vial; we may be able to change it somehow as I think it's affecting your ability outside of this room. I could give it to one of our top Pisces alchemists or sorcerers, see if they can improve upon it?"

Fury fills me and his expression betrays concern as he glances over at my cloud.

"Taur...what's wrong...calm yourself, remember what

happens when you get angry in this room."

He stares at my cloud as it continues to grow. Sparks like lightning arc from my body and I know I'm about to lose control and I can feel my temperature rising and the number ten pulsating harder than ever and there is no sign of it ceasing. I squeeze my eyes shut, feeling the power that wants to take control of me and before all is lost, I run out of the Reflection Room as fast as I can.

Leon does not chase me and I eventually come to a stop when my legs can no longer continue the panicked flight. Without intending to, I've come to the library just as the giant doors open for a group of Scorpios to exit. They talk amongst one another until they notice me, covered in sweat and frizzy hair. They become silent and curiously analyse me with unreadable expressions. But without a care, I walk into the library and find a quiet and reclusive spot to sit to gather my thoughts. Sitting silently, watching the lively books fly above me, I catch site of Emun, the book purifier leaping from book to book as they fly about. He agilely cleans them as they go, sometimes falling but his tiny wings find the strength to carry his awkward, skinny, long body for a short time until he lands on another nearby book and vigilantly continuing his duties.

"Isn't it fascinating? The sight of purpose, it can overcome any obstacle."

I nearly jump out of my seat to find Bibliotheca standing beside me and I stare at her as the blood drains from my face; she kindly looks at me, adjusting her large glasses that remind me of Manfred, and I now notice the slight translucent tinge in her skin that I did not recognize before, reflecting the ghost-like image that stands before me.

"Bib..." I say, barely able to muster up the vocal chords in my throat.

"Yes? Are you okay, my dear? It looks as though you have seen a ghost."

Frozen in my current position, staring at her broken memorable glasses, I remember what Manfred had told me, *"It's when you're not looking for her will she appear."*

I slowly begin to relax but not wanting to take my eyes off her, just in case she disappears. She begins fluffing around the bookshelves.

"So, did you find what you were looking for with that ancient book you...borrowed?" she says, glancing behind her and looking at me as her glasses fall slightly down her nose. She uses her index finger to press them back up hard against the bridge of her nose, clearly the glasses were never made to fit a Gemini or Pisces' face. It occurred to me that the tape, where the bridge had snapped, was to make the frames wider and maybe once they had been too small. I wonder who they might have originated from.

"How...how did...you know?" I question.

She turns back around fluffing over the books again.

"When you've lived for as long as I have, you pick up a few things...especially in this realm." I get the distinct feeling she is aware that she is a ghost.

"Well, not exactly..."

I stand up and walk closely behind her just in case anyone is listening. "The information I was searching for was torn from that exact book."

She glances down toward me as I am at least a foot shorter than her, her glasses annoyingly fall down her face again.

"*The Language of the Purpose Numbers*? Was that the book?"

I nod. "The secret behind number ten section had been ripped out. That's the information I have been looking for quite some time... Do you know what had been written within those torn-out pages?"

She lingers at me, pushing her glasses back up to her face again and continues to tend to the books. "*Tu es via, veritas et vita. Nemo venit ad Patrem, nisi per te.*"

My whole world comes to a standstill and I feel sick as though I have spun around too fast. The exact words spoken within my dream from Eve, who presumably believes I am her daughter.

"That was the first language ever spoken. Although it has

been lost amongst this time. The Patriarch doesn't see it necessary for the new-blooded generations to learn. So, soon it shall die out amongst many other sacred things of our time… ludicrous, I think."

I grab Bib by the arm, ignoring what she had just said. "What does it mean? Those words?"

Bib blinks at me as though she thought I knew.

"You are the way, the truth and the life. No man cometh to the father except through you." I look at her expecting more, but she does not continue.

"Is that it? There was nothing else written in that section? What does that mean?"

She pats my head. "My dear, it cannot be explained by another, only you can find its meaning. And although you may not remember, this is what you wanted, so only you can embark upon this chosen journey. By walking the path you elected, you will learn everything you need to know in due time. After all, you are the number ten, you should tell me."

She smiles gently and my eyebrows crease together in frustration.

"I should tell you? How would I know? None of this makes sense to me!" My frustration escalates. She looks at me kindly, patting my head patronizingly again and she disintegrates into the sandy colour of dust. Sighing, find a pencil nearby and write the meaning down on a scrap of paper before I forget. Shoving it in my pocket, I notice on the large clock in the library above the entrance doors that it's nearly hit five o'clock. Redoing my hair, I gather myself together and quickly venture back to the dorms.

No one is walking around the hall, but all the overseer SNCs are standing by the doors of the dorms of their respective new-blooded zodiac charges as per normal, awaiting the time to take us to supper. Demetrius, standing by our door, notices my approach.

"Where have you been?" he says with urgency.

"Just the library, I needed some time alone."

His eyebrows crease together and he looks around and the

other SNC overseers, who seem to be angered by my tardy arrival, suddenly grabs my arm, appearing to be furious. I become frightened until he whispers, "Relax, this is just a ploy for them to think I'm angry at you because you didn't stick to curfew. Just to cover both our arses."

I relax for a moment then go back to being rigid, pretending I'm intimidated as he jerks me around and asks, "Did you give Leon a vial?" I shake my head and he sighs.

"Why? What's wrong?" I ask as I don't think he believes me.

He looks at me intensely. "Are you sure?"

"Yes, I'm sure, that's why I ran away to the library...because you were right. When are you going to explain all this?"

He glances away momentarily then intensely looks back at me again with feigned anger.

"Thank you for trusting me. Obviously I can't explain here. I just need you to go inside and make sure all your vials of medicine are still there."

I nod. "Okay, I'll be right back." He releases his grip and I quickly go inside. Europa is quick to stand from her bed where she had been playing with her yellow totem, which now floats by her shoulder.

"That was a long lesson? How did you go?"

Alarmed that someone may have taken my medicine, I unintentionally ignore her, quickly going to where I had stashed my bag, but I cannot find it. I look further under my bed and around my draw set but find only my necessities backpack. Thinking I know the culprit, I storm over to Isa who is leisurely playing with her yellow totem.

"Where is it, Isa?" I demand.

She looks at me with annoyance. "What did you say to me?" she demands in turn.

"You heard me, give it back."

A line becomes visible between her thick eyebrows; she turns away without answering, and continues playing with her totem.

Europa followed me and now whispers, "Is everything okay, Taur?"

Ignoring Europa again, I walk over to Isa and ruthlessly push her off her bed, which she did not expect so fell clumsily to the ground with a giant thud. Everyone is now staring at me in confusion. Dalton and Henrietta now stand side by side, but don't interfere as fear still lingers at my being a living ghost. Kendall sits up on his bed, placing the book he was reading beside him. Isa pushes herself up and flicks back her frizzy hair that had fallen on to her face. Abruptly standing, she walks around to me and stands over me in a full blown rage.

"I'm not afraid of you, you're still just the same old pathetic runt. You're just harder to kill than I had originally thought. I guess you tricked everyone though, huh... I can see why your father went to great lengths to keep you a secret. Even killing those who suspected him."

I push up against her. "Just give me my backpack back, Isa. And don't you dare say another thing about my father, you don't know anything!"

She shoves me and I stumble back.

"I don't have your stupid backpack, why would I want to touch anything of yours?"

I front up against her again. "Because you have been out to ruin my life since we were kids. All I ever wanted was to be your friend!"

Isa suddenly laughs, an exaggerated act as though she were some kind of wicked creature.

"Don't play coy with me. How could you think we'd continue being friends after what your father did; my mother blamed me you know!"

Suddenly confused, I step back.

"Oh, I guess you still don't remember, that's convenient... Even after my father died, I consoled you. But you forgot, just like now... What kind of friend does that! I needed you!"

I look around at everyone and I get the feeling everyone knows something I don't. "What do you think my father did?"

Isa rolls her eyes, throwing her hands up in the air in frustration, then Europa steps in and says, "Taur, don't you know why everyone is so terrified of your father?”

I shake my head. “No. I thought it was because he was a fierce warrior and because he was allowed to keep me when no one else is allowed to have a weak Taurus baby. To be honest I…I never really thought too much about it.”

Europa grabs my shoulders and looks at me in the eye. “Taur, you know Taureans respect and celebrate warriors, they wouldn’t be frightened by one. Our whole Constellation revolves around being a great warrior and they wouldn’t be afraid of someone who was allowed to keep someone such as yourself. Sure they think it’s unfair but that’s not the reason they’re frightened…”

I can see Europa struggling to tell me, and I look at her impatiently. She looks down and glances back at me.

“Taur…Adonis killed Darius Edlyn… That’s why they’re frightened of him, because he killed one of his own kind. Everyone knows that.”

I shake my head. “No, he couldn’t have… Why would he do that? He has no reason to. I don’t remember this?”

Isa smirks. “Do you know how many times I told you when we were kids? I’ve actually lost count. It was as though you had been brainwashed, forgetting another memory as every day went by. And you would pretend as though we were still best friends. That’s why I hit you that day… I’d had enough. I just wanted my friend to be there for me but you only seemed to remember when I was mean to you. So, I became your tormenter because at least you’d remember that. My mother beat me relentlessly you know, she blames me for his death because I was friends with you. Thinks I got too close.”

I shake my head again and again.

“Why would he kill Darius? Can you tell me that?”

Isa looks at me intensely, still simmering and I look at Europa.

“I’m not sure if any one really knows why, no one speaks of it since it happened,” says Europa.

Isa snuffs, “I can tell you why.” She pulls out a necklace that is hidden under her garments, a round black stone is attached to a thin old rope. The black stone is encapsulated within melted glass.

"Recognize it?" she asks and my mind begins to have flashback of the memory being held in Penelope's arms. That black stone had fallen into the palm of my hand after I'd cured the tree from a terrible illness. I walk up to Isa and she allows me to hold it. "From that expression I guess you've remembered a few things. Your father used this pebble to kill my father Darius. He pushed it down his throat and he became immensely ill, dying soon after."

I pass it back to her. "But why? Why would he do that?"

She puts it over her head again and says, "Because since the very first day my father saw Penelope, he unconditionally loved her, even though it ruined his relationship with my own mother. Petra hates you as you resemble the woman who took my father away from her in every way. My father knew Adonis was only using Penelope as he had never showed an interest in her until just before you came along. But he could never put his finger on what he was using her for. He never trusted him and always kept a close eye on him. Knowing Penelope had struggle conceiving, no one even knew she was pregnant. But one day, he did find out the truth and your father killed him for it, so he was never able to tell anyone the truth. As soon as he forced him to swallow this, he was bed-ridden and died by drowning on the black infectious tar that filled his lungs. This was the stone that came out of his mouth once he had passed."

Europa now stands in front of me, facing Isa.

"And how are we supposed to believe you, since you say he died before he was able to tell the truth. How do you know all of this?"

Isa snorts at Europa. "Because he did!"

Tears begin to well up in Isa's eyes. Spit flies from her mouth as her fury erupts. "On his death bed, he was able to force all this out despite enormous pain and before he was able to tell me the truth of why...he died. In front of my very eyes! I was only ten years old! Your father took my father away from me!

I tried to tell you! But you never remembered! And you played the victim! Where were you when I needed you?"

I become stiff and guilt-ridden, if this was the truth, then Isa's tremendous pain and hatred towards me was understandable, but how could I not remember? I look up and see the tears streaming down her face, but her expression still betrays her hatred and rage.

"Isa...I'm—"

The door suddenly opens and Demetrius's face peers in.

"Taura, you're going to have to come with me immediately." He looks at everyone who is now standing in a tense circle; glancing at Isa, his demeanour serious. "Is everything okay?"

Isa wipes the tears aggressively from her face.

"Everything is fine," she says bluntly. She looks at me and gestures me to go. Turning around, she hops back on her bed and rolls over. Demetrius, clearly not wanting to get involved, accepts Isa's word and signals for me to come.

I stare at Isa's back and genuinely want to stay and talk to her and tell her how sorry I am for not being there for her. My mind fills with questions about my father's actions. What was he trying to hide and why can't I remember anything?

Without saying any more, I follow Demetrius out the door as he says to the others, "The Gemini SNC overseer will accompany you to the dining hall with his Gemini new-bloods. I have some important business to attend." He shuts the door and guides me out of the dorm.

"Demetrius, what is going on?" He glances down at me, but seems edgy.

"Did you find your medicine?"

I shake my head. "No, I thought Isa had taken it. But I don't think so now."

Demetrius sighs. "No, she didn't. It's just as I thought. We've been discovered."

I look at him urgently. "What do you mean you've been discovered? Who's we? Demetrius, what's going on?" After Isa's revelation, dread was gnawing my insides.

Demetrius looked around and pulls me into a quiet secluded area. He kneels down to my height and places one of his large hands on my shoulder. "It's too dangerous to tell you within the Doh's walls, there are many ears. But just know, everything your father has done has been to protect you. Some of the things you may hear from here on out may be conflicting, but know deep down, Adonis truly wanted to protect you. You're very special, Taura, more special than you could ever imagine. And some way, somehow, we will resolve this."

He looks around again apprehensively, "Listen carefully, you must not release your true power. You hear me? It's very important. As soon as you do, we are all doomed." He looks around again. "Luckily, I was able to inform them of my suspicions before this happened. But know that they'll come for you and don't be frightened when they do; just know, you must go with them. That's all I can tell you."

He looks around again and sees another zodiac SNC approaching and he quickly stands whispering to me, "Now, you must not speak about anything we've discussed even though none of it makes sense right now. But it will, I promise. You must trust me on this, Taura. No more suspicious questions." He looks at me intensely and I nod, still unsure of anything and now I'm also frightened.

Then I see an SNC Cancerian approach. "Demetrius! What's taking so long? Theophilus is waiting." Demetrius nods and takes me to a teleportation area accompanied by the other SNC. I'm asked to envision Theophilus's chamber. Now I know where they're taking me and I know this can't be good. I chant the name Unum as we teleport to the Patriarch, knowing the last time we'd spoken he'd threatened to kill me.

CHAPTER FIFTEEN

FATHER

Loins of truth; conditioned, created identity.

As I again approach the ornate doors that will bring me face to face to Theophilus, I pause to study the same detailed carving. This time, my eyes are drawn to the figures of Adam and Eve, the ancient ones from the beginning of time, then to Apophis the snake who has declared war against our world and the Wisdom tree in all its unspoken glory, now kept hidden for reasons unknown. All the remarkable creations of Unum, drawn into this ostentatious piece of artwork, stand proudly upon these doors, creating an intimidating atmosphere before entering. I focus my gaze back on Eve's image and think of her as being the woman in my dream and hope she is okay.

The high wide doors begin to open and, for a moment the scene seems to come alive as if the doors were breathing in and out. It occurs to me, as Demetrius and I start to walk through, that the power of the knowledge withheld by that picture is tremendous indeed. If only they could speak and reveal the unspoken truth.

As the doors open further, the air pressure changes and I begin to feel increasingly nauseated by who and what we're about to confront. The first thing I see is Kerit, who lies leisurely by the fire lit in the large marble fireplace, sprawled out and peacefully asleep on an old rug. Except that his body rises and falls, he is well camouflaged as a dead stuffed animal. In his current state, I am seeing a truer resemblance of him than one reflecting anger or hate as he was in his conscious state.

Coming around the fire pit, I look around the room. All I can see through the panoramic glass window are grey clouds slowly going by as rain saturates the glass. The warmth from the fire would have created a comfortable atmosphere if we had come in more friendly circumstances. Looking away from the fire, I notice a large portrait of Theophilus that must have recently been hung. It only shows one side of his face, as his large wings curl around in front of him. Under his white hair, his penetrating green eyes glance over the top of his wing as though he is hiding something behind them.

"Good evening," says Theophilus in an unemotional voice. Startled, I turn to see those same wings turned towards us as he stares out into the cloud-covered sky.

Demetrius stands closely beside me and I feel his tension, like a vibration in the air. It is the first time I have sensed him like that and I don't dare look at him, lest I see obvious fear in his eyes. I am suddenly aware of a large presence behind us and then I smell the terrible stench of Kerit as his pungent breath brushes past the top of my head, pressing my hair down with each exhale.

"I'm very disappointed to find out that treachery is amongst us," says Theophilus as he slowly turns our way, his gaze unwaveringly focused beyond us. The blood drains from my face as my eyes widen. *How could he possibly know?* I only told Europa and she wouldn't have told a soul. Unless someone heard us? My heart begins to race at thought that I might implicate innocent people in this business. Like Europa, she knew nothing about my medicine, only Demetrius did. Leon did. Who had told him? All I could do was utterly implicate myself and admit my treason.

Kerit grabs Demetrius by the shoulder and he emits an intense drawn out groan of pain and I know his bite is hurting him intensely. Tears well up in my eyes.

"What are you doing? Let go of him!"

Without thought, I grab Kerit's large jaws and try to force them apart, but they're completely locked and I don't care that I look pathetic in the attempt. The large bear eye, that's nearly as big as my head, looks over at me and he snarls.

"Taura, we discussed this in our last conversation. You know what happens to those who try to implement treachery in what we've worked so hard to achieve as a unity, they must be eliminated. It disrupts the peace and causes chaos to a system that's taken many decades to create...it's a shame too. Demetrius had great potential and SNCs are few and far in between these days."

I ignore his statement and continue pulling on Kerit's jaws and Demetrius has now fallen to his knees. Blood is pouring profusely down his chest and on to the floor, growing from a small puddle to a large one.

Demetrius grabs me with his free arm, his usual strength is not there, and looks at me with an expression that is more resigned than reassuring. "Taura, it is okay. Please stop before you hurt yourself."

I fall to my knees by his side and begin sobbing.

"But he didn't do anything. Let him go! Can't you see you're killing him?" I shriek.

Theophilus now turns to show his usual side profile and still doesn't look directly at me. "Now, Taura, we both know that is not true... I know he told you not to give a sample vial to Leon, who was only trying to help you. I'd call that sabotage. No one was allowed to interfere with your sessions. So now I've had to intervene and have the whole lot confiscated, which has interrupted an already busy day. This could have all been avoided if Demetrius just worked with us."

Theophilus signals Kerit and he immediately picks Demetrius up as if he were some kind of toy. Demetrius groans as his heavy body dangles by his shoulder. His blood leaves a vivid trail as Kerit takes him out of sight via a passage that opens from the room. I scream, "Where are you taking him? He's losing too much blood! Can't you see he'll die?"

I collapse on the ground and continue to sob in my hands.

"I know you were fond of him. But sometimes we have to do things for the sake of a larger purpose. Besides, I didn't bring you here to witness that, you're here for a more important reason. That just had to be dealt with in the meantime."

My tears stop and I slowly look up at him, my eyes burning and an equally fiery anger begins to pulse through my veins, growing like an unremorseful cancer with every heartbeat. The number on the back of my neck begins to throb furiously. A small crack on the large window behind Theophilus starts to splinter and zig zag up the glass. His head glances towards the crack, watching it grow as he continues.

"The Infernum. We haven't had an attack in years but unfortunately today Apophis has decided to strike...within the Taurus Constellation."

My anger subsides momentarily and time begins to slow as I feel a fierce pain in my chest, followed by a nauseated, wrenching in my gut.

"And it comes with great regret that I need to inform you of this unfortunate news at an already hard time. But your father Adonis...has died in the process of protecting the village Herba."

The words slip into the air idly, lining up to penetrate my chest like a series of rapid knife stabs. My chest begins to restrict and I feel as though I can't breathe. I collapse to the ground unable to move. I press my hands over my aching heart, feeling the pit of my stomach fall beneath me and I stare into the abyss; the world around me becomes distant and all I want is to hold my father one last time. My heart keeps beating and I wish it would stop just so I can be with him in the moment of death.

"Love preys on those with an ignorant eye, hiding behind a beautiful mask, waiting to reveal the identity of one's worst nightmare.

"And that face is a representation of the hate that was blinded behind the ignorance of love. Realizing hate is unpreventable if you allow love to exist within the chambers of your heart. Love is dangerous, as it is forever fleeting in one moment until one day it is taken...unforgiving in its essence. Turning into the monster that rips us apart from the inside out."

Tears fall like burning rain down my face and I wonder why I haven't stopped breathing.

Theophilus continues, "Two such conflicting emotions yet one can't exist without the other..." he pauses for a brief moment, staring into the clouded stormy nothingness through the cracked window. "I know this is an inconvenient time, Taura, but you're going to have to be isolated from everyone else for a while as your unbeknown power has proven to be too unpredictable and we just can't have that around others. It's too dangerous, especially when it has been reported that it's currently controlled primarily by your emotional state. So, when you're going through a time like this, I believe you are too hazardous to have around others." The crack on the window starts to splinter into a large web as I stare intently at him from the floor, thinking what an inconsiderate monster he is. I become blinded by my anger as though I've fallen into the black hole where my heart once laid. A thick prominent crack forms, shooting straight up and down where Theophilus stands and now he deliberately turns to face me, staring unwaveringly straight into my eyes. His expression emotionless, he says, "Remember it was you who wanted this. Now you too will feel the emptiness."

The words ignite a large pulsating rush of energy that throbs from my chest to my head and a purple aura begins to emanate from my skin, another power takes over and the splinter in the glass sporadically crawls in random directions from the main crack behind him, creating a theatrical affect as lightning now forks from the stormy clouds. And just before the glass shatters, I feel something hit me in the back of the neck, a sharp pain and my body goes limp. As I fall to the ground, I see the Bwbachod's face standing above me.

"Vaughn," I mutter under my breath and I feel I too am falling into my own black hole and I pray it consumes me.

Unfortunately, I feel consciousness returning. Opening my eyes, I find my vision is quite blurred. I slowly sit up from what feels like a cold steel table. I have a splitting headache but for a brief moment from the unconscious to the conscious, I have forgotten the emotional pain. A brief moment of ignorance as disorientation cradles me with comfort, until the ache in my heart begins to pump through my veins and more tears flow profusely down the cracked, dried-up river on my cheeks. For what feels like a long time, I sit motionless at the end of the cold table, growing a small puddle beneath me in hope it'll grow large enough to drown myself in.

My father Adonis, he may not have been perfect but he was and always will be my father. I can still smell the bark and woodland smell from his itchy beard, which scraped against me as he kissed me goodnight, every night from since I can remember. I can still feel the calluses on his hands, representing the hardworking Taurean he'd always been. He always smelled of dirt even when he bathed, but that smell always brought comfort to me as it reminded me of home. I still remember when he picked me up when I fell, brushing me off and pushing me on. He'd listen to me speak of nothing and everything without a single interruption and looked at me as though I was the root of his existence. I'd follow him everywhere, sometimes in complete silence just because I wanted to be in his presence as he made me feel safe. He was my hero and now he is gone, and all I can think about is that solemn expression he had watching me as I left the cottage that day. What was he hiding and why couldn't he tell me?

Unexpectedly, I hear the whoosh of a door opening. I look up to finally see that I'm confined within a pristine white room, so white, in fact, you can't tell the floor from the wall as though each corner of the room goes on forever. A rectangular door shifts open and all I can see is darkness behind it. The Bwbachod steps in and I become angered by his presence.

"What are you doing here?" I ask bluntly. He glances up at me but says nothing, only coming over with some food and crushed herbs in a small cup. He glances around as though someone could be watching.

"I know it was you in the library. Why did you want me to know about Benedict and you? What is the purpose of all this secrecy! What is this stupid power?"

He presses his index finger to my mouth. "Shh," and looks around as I smack his hand and the tray falls abruptly to the ground.

I glare at him, impatiently waiting. "Tell me!" I yell.

In a low voice, he anxiously blurts out, "Remember the day you teleported to the library by accident with Demetrius and the other new-blooded Taureans?"

I am confused as he hurriedly continues, "That was you. You did that. You must have been thinking about something important that was related to finding out particular information that drew you to the library."

My memory flashes back to that day when *The Language of the Purpose Numbers* found me, and we met Bib, and I had been questioning my purpose number beforehand. He nods, realizing my expression confirms his guess. "And you know how you randomly teleported to the infirmary and met Eve. You must have been thinking something in relation to that. Anything you feel closely connected to, you can teleport to. You don't need the teleportation device or markings or the need to physically travel to a destination first in order to get there again like everyone else. You hold it within you. You are the one, Taura."

I stare intently at him, noticing his anxiety heightens and he becomes increasingly fidgety.

"What do you mean I'm the one? The one of what? That only adds another question, nothing is being answered! Tell me what is going on!" I insist in a much lower tone.

The Bwbachod takes a big breath and quickly whispers, "There isn't enough time to tell you the truth! I came here to help you! I warned you this would happen if you made your power known. I wanted nothing more than to keep you and others safe. I thought your father was in on it, but he wasn't. And now I feel terrible as I could have possibly saved him but there may still be time...to save him, but only you have the power."

My eyes widen. "What do you mean he wasn't in on it? You're not making sense! Theophilus already told me he was—"

He grabs my hand to make me pay attention. "He may still

be alive, there is still time. Your powers are significantly disabled within this room...but if we create a diversion, you can escape and do as you did those last couple of times when you teleported unknowingly...Taura, you must teleport back to your Constellation and find your father before he is murdered. But you must not delay as they'll be on your tail."

I look at him sincerely. "Why are you doing this? Why are you helping me?"

He sighs, "Because I know how it feels to lose everyone you love." The ache in my heart is triggered anew by those words and the story Leon had told me returns to my mind. I look at him not as the race of the mutated zodiacs but for the beautiful being he truly is. "I saw you in the library as Vaughn, I thought you couldn't transform into him anymore?"

He now looks at me curiously. "I don't know who you saw, but it was not me. It is true I no longer hold the power to resemble the image of the son they once loved. I now and always will remain the mutated zodiac who took their son...but you will not carry the load of a heavy burden as I do, otherwise this place will never be restored to its prior glory. You are the one, Taura."

He looks at me determinedly and as I go to comment on the last statement, he yells, "HELP! HELP! SHE'S ESCAPING!" He proceeds to throw himself into the wall incredibly hard, enough to leave a splattered blood mark. He draws out a small button, presses it, then crushes it within a clenched fist. "Go!" he whispers urgently as the door opens.

I jump off the table and run as hard as I can through the door and don't stop. My lungs begin to burn and I have no idea where I am, every corridor I turn down looks exactly the same as the one before and I'm completely disorientated. I pass room after room which looks identical to the last and I can hear the sound of footsteps gaining ground. I stop and remember what the Bwbachod had said, *"You don't need a teleportation device...you hold it within you."*

I breathe deep and hard, bending down on to my knees, trying to catch my breath. But every breath feels it's needed more than the last. The floor vibrates as the sound of footsteps becomes louder.

"Quick, she's over here!"

I hear the pursuers from a not so far distance and déjà vu hits me as I'm reminded of the dream with Eve when she is trying to escape with me in her clutches. I try to concentrate on what I had done before when I had teleported unconsciously but I don't know how and I'm rushing due to panic. I continuously think of home as I squeeze my eyes shut, time and time again thinking of my small cottage, the smells, the feelings but I continue to open my eyes to the same place and I know they'll be here any minute. I can't let the Bwbachod down, he's risking his life and this will be the only chance I have to save my father. Tears begin streaming down my face as I feel the over-encumbered sensation of defeat.

PNC soldiers have now turned down the hallway, spotting me, and I squeeze my eyes shut one more time thinking of home, opening my eyes I see them coming towards me, only meters away now and it ceases to work. I sigh and let go in the face of defeat and murmur, "I'm sorry, Dad." I think of his large hand scraping against my soft skin, caressing my face. And he would always tell me, *It's okay, my dear.*

I burst into tears, falling to my knees and one of the soldiers grabs me. With tears flowing down my face, I wait to be dragged away, but the next words spoken surprise me, "Thank the planetary gods, we got to you in time."

As I turn to look up at them, the sensation of the grabbing hand is gone and blinding light overwhelms my vision and I shut my eyes in reaction to its intensity. Suddenly I feel a cold wind caress my wet cheek and the gentle tickling of grass against my hand. I open my eyes to see the familiar field right outside my house, back within my Constellation.

I slowly stand, looking around, thinking I must be dreaming or they tranquilized me. I check myself over and everything seems to be in place, but I'm still not entirely sure how I did it or if I did it. I suddenly recall what Theophilus had said about an attack by the Infernum. As I now stand cautiously alert, carefully looking around the premises across fields to the woods between here and Herba, nothing appears to be trampled or damaged. It looks exactly the same as how I left it.

I hear an unexpected crashing noise coming from behind my cottage, and without thinking, I dash through the field and head for home. As I approach, I slow down, hesitant of what will be revealed behind my cottage as I look intently in the direction from where the noise came. Then a wind gust blows fiercely and the large tree that hangs over my cottage home rustles violently. It is vigorously shedding leaves onto the rotten roof, which in the past has helped build up resistance against the rain, keeping us dry. All feels eerily still and I wonder if everything I now remember and have been told is true about that old tree because now you would not believe it to be so, it is too normal in its stature. I recall the memory of Penelope encouraging me to heal the tree as a baby and think of that tiny black stone that fell from within. The stone that presumably went on to murder Darius Edlyn, Isa's father, dictated by my father's actions. But it makes me wonder about the balance of life taking its natural course as we cannot do as we please without repercussions of our actions...like saving a tree that was meant to pass. Did it induce a karma effect by taking another? Maybe Darius' death is really blood on my hands. Who am I to dictate who lives and dies?

Suddenly, another frightening crashing noise grabs my attention as I anxiously walk along the side of the cottage. I breathe in the smell of old damp pine, keeping my body close to the old raggedly aged wood. I hear a familiar voice that I cannot put my finger on, but it's not my father's.

"I always knew you were a traitor. I just never had any proof until now and Theophilus was blinded by who he thought you were."

I hear another crash followed by my father's voice, which brings me conflicted comfort as his life is still in danger. He sniffs, followed by, "You're all blind if you think what you're doing is for a great purpose. Don't you see the repercussions? Things weren't supposed to be this way. You're going against the natural process of life."

I take a big breath, slowly peering behind the corner of the cottage and I see the same Leo that was with Benedict and wonder who he is.

"You're just stuck in the old ways, Adonis. It's your typical Taurus trait, familiarity. Things aren't what they were, you need to embrace change. It's for the greater good. Your mind has just been poisoned by them... I cannot believe you used that potion to prevent her from developing the one true power. How stupid do you think we are? Of course we'd eventually find out."

The Leo angrily smashes a small wooden bucket against a post and it breaks into several pieces. Adonis walks over to the Leo whose back is now turned and I suddenly notice something uncanny about my father. It appears he's aged several decades in the short time since I last saw him; he looks ancient and even his voice is husky and worn out.

"Cedric, I would have done anything to keep her safe from what they think she's meant to be used for and I'd do it all again if I had to... Besides, Unum is our creator. Theophilus has become tarnished by jealousy and hatred. How can't you see that what he is doing and ultimately wanting to do is the most traitorous of any crime within Nirvana. It'll destroy any chance of returning things to the way they were and who knows what will become of him and our world."

Cedric abruptly swings around and backhands Adonis right in the jaw, making him stumble back. I nearly scream but quickly restrain myself. Cedric Sol? Leon's dad? Theophilus's right-hand man?

"Unum abandoned us, Adonis, along with that traitorous snake! He wanted to use us for the benefit of those under-developed creatures. Nobody wants things to return to the way they were! Can't you see Theophilus wants to embrace us and our own new world as opposed to being used as a pawn within another world?"

I can see my father becoming angry now and the supposed old age doesn't seem to inhibit his ability to take a hit. But he controls himself by taking a big breath and shutting his eyes, glancing away briefly.

"We would have lived our usual lives; it was only in death would that existence become our reality; he wasn't going to take anything away from us, it was just going to be part of the natural process. If you had been ignorant of that fact, you wouldn't have known any better."

Cedric smirks. "Well, it was his own mistake in telling us then, wasn't it? Why do you think Theophilus keeps so much hidden from the Constellations...to protect them! Otherwise everything would fall apart just like it had on that day and the Infernum would have consumed the whole of Nirvana by now."

They both stare at each other with the conviction of their own personal opinion and I can feel the tension building.

"You know the Infernum is a natural manifestation from what we've broken. And what about Nirvana? How do you know it will survive? Our world is currently made up of deceit and lies. What is Theophilus offering you to make you think this is for the greater good... or what is he holding over you?"

Adonis pauses momentarily, allowing what he said to sink in.

"Cedric, without the harbouring and consumption of essence, immortality isn't possible. And there is no proof of what he plans on doing with Taura will even work! It's a risk that could kill us all!"

Cedric's frame starts to ripple as anger poisons him from the inside; if he becomes any angrier, he'll turn into the animalistic version of himself and by looking at him, I don't think my father can take him on in his current state.

"You know nothing of my personal reasons. Your accusations are ironic, coming from the SNC who never questioned Theophilus's authority. You took the essence without question. And now look at you, growing a conscience, you've become weak and pathetic," Cedric sneers.

Adonis looks down upon the ground in regret then faces

Cedric with outward confidence.

"Yes, it is true, I was a part of the original murders to take control and prolong ever-lasting life, all for the cause of a better world. But Cedric, over time, I realized. It had nothing to do with liberation, we were just reacting out of fear of something we didn't understand. And through that action, we have created only pain for all those who live in Nirvana. This isn't going to free our world, this is going to destroy it!"

Adonis sighs,

"But I know you're not going to listen... at least in death I can be happy knowing I was no longer like the Taurean I once was, ignorant, stupid and afraid. I can die knowing, I tried to save our world not destroy it due to my own selfish greed."

Those last words sent Cedric into an uncontrollable fiery rage and my heart begins to race as his armour begins to break off piece by piece as his body begins to expand into a muscular lean killing machine. Adonis grabs the same old axe he has used for decades to chop wood; he is defiant even in the face of death but a glimmer of hope still sits within me. My father's demeanour still remains calm and collected, his breathing a controlled pattern. The top of Cedric's armour has now broken off and fallen to the ground revealing an incredibly muscular upper body with clearly prominent large veins pulsating hard. His facial features have become more animalistic in appearance, much like that of his lion ancestor. He breathes deep, which gives a rippling echo within his throat, his ears are pressed back hard against his head, and his eyes look intoxicated with incipient blood lust and he has my father in his sight. I stand stiff and rigid, my feet seeming to be stuck to the ground, still unnoticed.

Adonis stands ready and says, "So...this is how the story ends."

Surely he feels he can win, even against Cedric in his animalistic form. He was a great warrior before he needed to care for me. He's not acting like he feels old, like he fears death.

A tear drops unnoticed from my eye until I feel it land on to the top of my dirty foot. Cedric's feet shift deep into the ground, his large claws piercing the soft dirt as though he is about to pounce and my father still stands ready. Before I have a chance to blink, Cedric pushes hard off the ground, springing at my father who swings his axe but Cedric dodges one swing after another, darting from side to side, but Adonis never turns his back on him, switching the axe from hand to hand, dexterously so as to not leave an opening.

Old or not, Adonis was still focused, countering Cedric's moves, but then Cedric closes in, pressing to the ground, preparing for a giant leap and as he does, just like a feline pouncing on its prey, I release a frightening scream.

In that very moment, time slows as Adonis turns around and sees me and his axe arm instantly drops. He has never let me see him kill anything, except snakes, and doesn't want me to see him killing now. He has left himself defenceless. Tears stream down my face the axe drops from his hand and bounces on the ground. I immediately realize I have locked in my father's fate. Apprehension surges through me. Cedric leaps, claws sprawled and giant teeth ready to penetrate. I instinctively run as hard as I can and as I blink, I stand between my father and Cedric, who sees me abruptly in front of him and tries to withdraw his claws and enormous fangs.

As I accept my fate, coming to peace with saving the one zodiac who I truly love, something grabs me around the waist and I'm yanked away and held up high. Watching from above, I twist to look at what has me and see it is a branch of the same tree that I had once healed that holds me within its grasp. I scream on such a penetratingly high note, that I hear glass shatter in the windows of nearby houses. Cedric collides with my father, pinning him to the ground as his claws clench to hold him and he engages his large jaws around Father's neck. Blood begins to spurt and drain from his body, but ever since seeing me, my father has not ceased to look at me. His expression apologetic as though he has failed me. In this moment of his dying, his whole guard is down. He always had an aura of strength about him, now he looks old, vulnerable. His aging eyes, now so sincere and honest. It is as though I'm looking at him for the first time. His gaze lingers on me with unmistakable pride as his eyes slowly begin glaze over.

Once the huge lion that is Cedric Sol had stalked a short distance away, the tree placed me down gently beside Adonis. A quick glance showed me that Cedric is still imperiously vigilant and watching me closely, but not about to intrude on this dreadful private moment.

I turn to stare into my father's watering grey eyes as blood drains from his neck. He smiles at me, lifting his now heavy hand to gently touch my face.

"Taura...how did you?" he says, his voice coming hoarsely.

"Shh, shh, don't speak, Dad. I can heal you. I promise. Just hold on a second..." I say, sobbing as I try to stop the bleeding. I close my eyes, holding the edges of the wound together as I try to imagine him as he was. I attempt to harness my healing powers, but all I feel is blood seeping through my hands and it fails to work.

He coughs blood everywhere and forcing out the words, "Taura, you are...the one. The only one...who can save the zodiacs..." He coughs several more times and the deep red of his blood now warms my quivering body, saturating my clothes. "I told you. You...were special. I love you...so...so... mu—"

His hand slides off my face leaving a prominent bloody hand print as his last breath escapes him. I grab it so I can continue to hold it against my face, trying to feel, one last time, those same callused, hardworking hands that had always warmed my tiny face. But now the warmth and the familiar smell begins to fade and I try to gather his scent, firmly pressing his hand against my face. I squeeze my eyes shut and breath in deeply. Dirt and blood scrape and smear against my skin, his scent fading amongst the thick discharge of gore and waste. His body begins to shrivel up as though he had been dead for many decades and has become an unrecognizable empty rotten shell of the man I once knew. Unexpectedly, hundreds of blue orbs begin to escape from his body and I watch as they disappear over the large protective walls into the uncharted forest.

Still clutching my dad's decaying old hand within my grasp, I scream, "Daddy! Daddy! Wake up. No, no, you can't be dead! I'm sorry, why won't it work! Stupid, good-for-nothing power, why won't you work when I need you...Daddy!"

I relentlessly shake him and push down hard upon his now unrecognizable wound, but only succeeding in crushing his trachea into dust. I gather the bits and pieces together trying to make it heal, but I know his life is long gone. I can only stare at the empty, broken vessel that was my father. I sob uncontrollably, still in disbelief, but reality hits and another overwhelming sensation of pain consumes me. I cry harder than I ever have before, throwing my body into the pile of dust my father had rapidly degraded to, rolling in it, sobbing relentlessly; the thick residue sticks to my wet face as I inhale his remains - never wanting to let go.

THE END

APPENDICES

An excerpt from:

The Language of the Purpose Numbers

TABLE OF CONTENTS

MEANING OF A PURPOSE NUMBER
A purpose number is the sum of the numbers of the day you were born. They reveal the traits you will carry through life and foundations you will be drawn towards. Our purpose number gives us great insight into our desires and what give us satisfaction and purpose within this journey we call life. It gives us an element of understanding of why we came into this world and what we are here for.

FIND YOUR PURPOSE NUMBER
To establish your purpose number, you must add your whole birth date together.
For example: 15/05/1990 = 1+5+5+1+9+9 = 30.

You always round it up to a single digit 30 = 3 purpose number. If you had say, 31, as a total you'd add 3+1=4 purpose number.

MASTER NUMBERS ARE THE EXCEPTION TO THE RULE
The only numbers you don't round up to a single digit is the master numbers, so if your date of birth equates to either 11, 22, or 33, you do not add these two-digit numbers to a single as they would be your purpose number.

PURPOSE NUMBERS

PURPOSE NUMBER ONE
Leader
Hard-working
Determined
Self-Motivated
Ambitious
Independent
Innovative

Strengths
Great at beginning new projects
Fantastic multi-tasker
Focused and driven
Making decisions doesn't scare them
Embrace every opportunity
Huge goals and dreams

Weaknesses
Lack sensitivity and patience
Have a tendency to be selfish at times
Pride can get the better of them
Inclination to be a 'know it all'
Too concerned about vanity
Can come off as too aggressive at times

Ideal Career Paths
Self-employed or entrepreneur
Politics or Corporate leader
Anything that allows them to embrace their independency, as they don't like to take orders.

Life Challenges
Acknowledging that they're wrong and that's okay.
Understanding that the journey is as good as the destination.
Accepting and dealing with authority figures.
Feeling unrecognized for their talents and hard work
Implementing the big dreams and plans in their head.

Life Friends
Two and seven
Two for their sensitivity
Seven for their spiritual and introspective demeanour

PURPOSE NUMBER TWO
People person
Intuitive
Sensitive
Team player
Peacemaker
Caring
Spiritual

Strengths
Great team player
Considerate and thoughtful
Handles pressure incredibly well
Sincere and Honest
Tends to see the best in others

Weaknesses
Putting others needs before their own
Oversensitive
Evades confrontation
Reluctant to initiate
Can be quite shy

Ideal Career Paths
Teaching in any form (not just school system)
Humanitarian fields
Creative pursuits that allow them to express themselves
Being in service to others (medicine, nursing, counselling etc...)
Career in spirituality and personal growth

Life Challenges
Placing your needs before others
Voicing personal opinion
Not taking things so personally
Being indecisive and knowing what you want
Learning to be happy on your own

Life Friends
Two and four
Two for their ease and friendly nature
Four for their honesty and hard work

PURPOSE NUMBER THREE
Creative
Generous
Charismatic
Playful
Joyful
Optimistic
Witty

Strengths
Their incredibly creative and innovative
Communication comes easy to them
Others are drawn to their charming and magnetic personality
Their energy uplifts and your happiness radiates to those
around you

Weaknesses
Tend to hold grudges when hurt by those they trust
Tough time with money and managing finances
Lack of focus and procrastination
Need for praise and affirmation by peers

Ideal Career Paths
Career in entertainment (acting, writing, directing etc...)
Career that allows them to use their creativity and express themselves (artist, musician, performer)
Ventures that allow them to work with others and use their communication skills (marketing, public relations, project management)

Life Challenges
Have a tendency for escapism when things become hard
Frivolous and superficial
Tendency to be moody for no apparent reason

Life Friends
Two
Their intuitive and understanding nature helps ground you while feeding your need for self-expression.

PURPOSE NUMBER FOUR
Strong
Honest
Determined
Practical
Hardworking
Down-to-earth
Organized

Strengths
Their perseverance and organizational skills help them achieve large projects and huge goals.
Because their honest and have high integrity, others know they can trust them.
They are comfortable with growing a small project or business into a larger vision.

Weaknesses
Have an inclination to be bossy and a bit of a know-it-all
They can be rigid at times and quick to judge their co-workers or peers.
Overly cautious and careful nature, which can lead to missed opportunities

Ideal Career Paths
Anything that incorporates a methodical and disciplined approach, such as construction, law, engineering, finance, or science.
Teaching to pass on skills and talents is something they highly value
Careers that value their organizational skills and ability to see through large projects, such as project management, marketing or producing.

Life Challenges
Since others easily trust and depend on them, they will often find themselves shouldering the burdens of others; they need to learn to say no.
Have a tendency to become biased, judgmental, and stubborn when under stress, which can create unnecessary conflict. They must learn to see things from others points of view.

Life Friends
Seven
Their spiritual and genuine nature complements and inspires them.

PURPOSE NUMBER FIVE
Magnetic
Fun loving
Adventurous
Curious
Flexible
Restless free spirit

Strengths
Ability to adapt to any new situation
Unafraid of the unknown or uncertainty
Great at meeting new people
Captivating personality
Persuasive and have a way with words

Weaknesses
Have a dislike for routine and repetition
Easily distracted by adventure and change
Tend to lack focus and direction
Self-indulgent

Ideal Career Paths
Sales, marketing, and public relations
Careers that allow them to travel and explore
High-risk careers, like firefighting, stock broker, or stunt man
Project base careers so they don't get bored

Life Challenges
Balancing their need for freedom while staying focused on their dreams and goals
They have many talents but need to embrace discipline and perseverance
Learning to manage their self-indulgent side and avoiding extremes
Allowing and understanding others desire for security and stability

Life Friends
Seven
To keep them balanced and grounded

PURPOSE NUMBER SIX

Loving
Warm
Compassionate
Reliable
Understanding
Responsible
Sensitive

Strengths
Natural sensitivity on relating how others feel
Deep desire for responsibility and leadership
They understand on how to make others happy

Weaknesses
Their caring desire can turn into meddling
Jealousy
Perfectionistic tendencies

Ideal Career Paths
Careers that reward their responsibility, such as managerial or leadership roles
Humanitarian career paths
Teaching, philosophy or justice

Life Challenges
Learning to balance work, emotions, and responsibility
Accepting that their desire to be in control by finding a career that rewards that tendency Allowing themselves to release control when their on holiday or vacation.

Life Friends
One
For their drive and ambition, which you can relate too.

PURPOSE NUMBER SEVEN
Mystical
Intuition
Sensitive
Dreamer
Playful
Introspective
Perfectionist

Strengths
A natural connection to the spiritual world
Intellectual and analytical – able to turn date into knowledge
Independent and comfortable being alone
Incredibly intuitive nature that usually proves to be right

Weaknesses
They can have trouble connecting with others as they've be found to be aloof and mysterious
Perfectionistic tendencies which can inhibit them from starting anything at all
Can be found to alienate and isolate themselves

Ideal Career Paths
Anything that incorporates seeking truth and wisdom, such as a priest, teacher, or researcher.
Analytical, scientific or technical careers.

Life challenges
Learning to rely and trust others
Moving outside of their own reality and being social with others. Letting go of the belief that everything must be 'perfect.'

Life Friends
Four
Their hardworking and determined ways keep them grounded

PURPOSE NUMBER EIGHT
Ambitious
Visionary
Organized
Authoritative
Efficient
Tough
Materialistic

Strengths
Can take on big projects and complete them.
Natural manager and leader.
Unafraid of hard work.
Their ambition and organizational talent will get them far in life.

Weaknesses
Materialistic gains masked by greed can cloud their perspective
Self-recognition and statues may cause self-harm and pain
Can have a tendency to be self-righteous or dictatorial
Workaholic

Ideal Career Paths
Law
Business
Politics
Management of large organizations
Positions of influence and leadership

Life Challenges
Balancing material world with the spiritual world
Knowing their limits so they don't burn out
Knowing the importance of what they can't buy (friends, family, love, compassion)
Tendency to be detached

Life Friends
Four
They're grounded and practical just like them, but while they see the big picture, they see every detail.

PURPOSE NUMBER NINE
Worldly
Giving
Altruistic
Self-aware
Old school
Intuitive
Wise

Strengths
Since they are highly intuitive and wise beyond their years, others often come to them for help and advice.
Their inner strength and perseverance carry them through obstacles and challenges most cannot bear.
An intense and incredibly vivid imagination that allows them to create with ease and joy.

Weaknesses
Disappointment is often met when they work towards goals that have the intention of acquiring wealth and materialism.
Tendency to allow emotions to flare up and carry them away, which can lead to unnecessary conflict.
Their humanitarian side can get the best of them if they don't set boundaries and learn to say no.

Ideal Career Paths
Career that allows them to help others
Their strong creativity that allows them to express themselves (arts, literature, drama, travel or luxury services)
Natural born leaders as they are great at resolving conflict (project manager, teacher, judge, healer)
Can also be great in positions dealing with money and business but can be a bit more of a challenge.

Life Challenges
Leading towards a life that allows them to work towards a higher purpose, benefiting humanity and the world.
Finding an outlet that allows them to express their deep emotion and intense creativity.
Learning how to manage finances and overcoming negative emotion towards wealth and money.

Life Friends
Three.
Creativity and imagination that matches theirs.

MASTER NUMBERS

MASTER NUMBER 11
Intuitive
Visionary
Charismatic
Inventive
Dreamer
Deep
Thinker
Spiritual

Strengths
Great ability at picking up on others' emotions and intentions.
Because of their great energy and clear vision, others are inspired by them and drawn to their charm.
Their incredible intuition allows them to act as a bridge between higher and lower realms of thought – consciousness and subconsciousness, subtle and blatant.

Weaknesses
Perfectionistic tendencies that may inhibit them from finishing a project.
Because of their highly intuitive senses and intelligence, most things come easily to them, which may express impatience and frustration within others.
They are delightful when everything is going their way but once they have one or several setbacks it can place them into self-blame, depression and pessimism.

Ideal Career Paths
Anything to do with spirituality, mysticism, and personal growth.
Art, Literature, music or anything that allows them to express their creativity.
Academia teaching, science – careers filled with discovery, research, and revelation.

Life Friends
Seven
For their insight and spiritual nature.

MASTER NUMBER 22
Balanced
Determined
Materialistic
Powerful
Strong
Practical
Influential

Strengths
Have the ability to manifest their dreams and goals more easily than others (But only when disciplined and organized).
Have great influence and charisma, making them excellent leaders.

Weaknesses
Generally want total control and micromanage everything.
At times have a tendency to be materialistic, caring about status and personal achievements only.
Can become overbearing or dictatorial when their patience runs out.

Ideal Career Paths
Careers that have ascendance through promotion, job title or income as they'll genuinely rise to the top wherever they reside.
Careers that allow them to show the world how things should be run: politics, policy-making, leadership roles, teaching, or writing.

Life Friends
Seven
For thought-provoking conversations and their spiritual nature.

MASTER NUMBER 33
Intelligent
Philosophical
Wise
Inspiring
Loving
Nurturer
Compassionate

Strengths
They are master teachers
Many will come to them for guidance as they have great wise advice that resonates with many.
Born to lead as their compassionate and nurturing natures captivate those around them.
Their energy is incredibly uplifting and many will just want to be in the company of a 33.

Weaknesses
Compulsive lying in order to save others' feelings from being hurt.
Can manipulate the truth to project an image of themselves of being more superior or special than average.
Can have a tendency of dependency which can inhibit them and destroy self-confidence.

Ideal Career Paths
Careers that involves being in the service of others (helping those who are less fortunate).
Make great spiritual leaders, healers, humanitarians, and teachers.

Life Friends
Six
As they are an extension of the purpose number 6 they can relate to them on many levels.

An excerpt from:

Zodiacs Appearance, Ability and Power

On the traits and features of the different zodiacs

Aries:

Descendants from large mountain goats, they are incredibly loud, courageous, and adventurous although you do get the impression that they love to argue, as they generally have to be right all the time. They have large circular horns, athletic stature, and back legs of a goat, standing upright. They have the ability to run through anything once they pick up enough speed, so stand out of their way, as they'll break through anything. This ability is derived from mountain goats as they protect their territory and land by literally ramming with their heads. They are generally seen undertaking demolition tasks throughout the Nirvana, as they are great for clearing large areas for construction. They're genuinely good with small weapons as they are incredibly agile, and are quite nifty with a bow and arrow.

Gemini:

Descendants from yin and yang, they used to have two heads but now their good and evil co-exist in one body. They are incredibly charismatic, intelligent, and witty, but they lack consistency as they are always in two minds about everything which can make them quite anxious. Their appearance is split down the middle: one side has black hair with malevolent looking features and the other has white hair with innocent, delicate features. They can split into two separate zodiacs, yin and yang, as two beings, being able to move as fast as lightning, though this transition can end in destruction if not taught properly. They are generally used for big tasks within the Doh, such as geography, architecture, writing history and much more. Having two people in one can produce a large amount of work in a short period of time.

Cancer:

Loving, protective, and faithful zodiacs, but they are overemotional and pessimistic if failure occurs. They're descendants from crabs. They have black eyes and small sharp spears that protrude from the top of their forearm that expand into long sharp weapons. They have the ability to produce a shield of protection that inhibits anything from penetrating through. They are great soldiers to use for the frontline in many numbers for battle.

Leo:

Loyal, optimistic leaders who always speak the truth. However, their famous egos have the tendency to undo them. They can be quite dominating and impatient too. Descendants from lions, they are lean and athletic. The males are always bigger than the females, and they have lion tails and ears with golden eyes and thick golden hair. Small fangs protrude from their mouth and sharp nails that stick out from their hands. When in battle or threatened, they have the ability to transform into a bigger animalistic version of themselves with a more muscular frame. Their claws grow longer, sharper, and their small fangs become more prominent. Once this transformation occurs, they become resilient to pain, making them great animalistic fighters; they're generally great commanders within the Nirvana Army as they are great delegating leaders.

Virgo:

Intelligent perfectionists that pay great attention to detail. However, they are overcritical and judgmental as everything must be perfect. Virgos are tall and slender as they are the descendants of angels with large angel wings and piercing eyes. Their wings grow larger with age. They have the ability to fly and power to control elements of the wind to help guide them in the direction they wish to go. They are generally great in political roles within Nirvana.

Libra:
Romantic diplomats who use great tact when getting things done. Libras are the descendants of scales distracted by superficial beauty and can be prone to changing their minds as they struggle with making decisions. Libras are radiant and beautiful with an elf-like appearance; if unbalanced, their eye colour changes, one blue and the other green, if balanced both eyes stay blue. They have the ability to control the minds of others, but if not taught properly, they'll only carry an influence over others. They are generally used in quarrels relating to Constellation matters, as they are great diplomats.

Scorpio:
Brave, ambitious, faithful friends, who can read people very well. Do not cross them as they are incredibly resentful, jealous, and possessive creatures; they do not handle deceit well. Descendants of Scorpions, they have a long black tail that attaches from the base of the neck all the way down to their tailbone, which grows out from the body. Thorns protrude from their elbows, knees, ankles, shoulders, and head. They have strong features with black hair. Scorpios have the ability to store two separate poisons in their tail: one that can put you to sleep and one that can kill you. They are incredibly bad at controlling both poisons when they are young, so stay clear if you are another zodiac as they're immune to their own poisons. They are generally seen as guards within the lands of Nirvana, as they put to sleep those who disturb the peace, and their poison is used in death sentences on those who commit serious crimes. If the culprit is a Scorpio, then other approaches must be taken.

Sagittarius:
Vivacious, intelligent, and generous zodiacs who have a great sense of right and wrong. They are tactless when it comes to the brutal truth and at times take things for granted. As they perceive themselves to be perfect, they are often overconfident. Descendants of horses, their appearance is of a horse body

attached at the base to a human torso, sitting upright from the neck. They are magnificent creatures with large lean muscles and strong attractive features. They have the power to talk to the forest and have great ability in archery, rarely missing a target. They are generally seen as hunters and gatherers of food and resources.

Capricorn:

Practical, cautious, and most ambitious of the zodiacs. Born with great wisdom, never going against the odds. Stubborn, never changing their minds, they can be perceived shy as they only enjoy the company of close friends. Descendants of a goat and a fish; although a strange mix, they have an incredible aura of beauty about them. Having a light orange and golden-tinged skin, some with an elongated fish tail and others with a small goat's tail, they have horns that track from the front of their forehead, curling only slightly around to the back with slightly pointed ears poking through their thick hair. Their eyes are large and oval-shaped above a small flat nose. They have telekinetic power, the ability to manipulate objects with the mind, although without constant practice, this skill can diminish quickly. Generally, they are great teachers and mentors within Nirvana.

Aquarius:

The humanitarians of the zodiac. They are famous for the ability to make friends, and are intelligent and independent. In other ways, they can be inconsistent as they never follow a particular pattern, detached at times or stubborn, as they do everything to the extreme. Descendants of man with water. They are large zodiacs, approaching the size of giants with thick bluish hair. They have the power to talk to animals and other creatures depending on how skilled their tongues are. Being such radiant humanitarians, they make great doctors who care for the injured and sick zodiacs and animals throughout the land.

Pisces:

Kind, selfless, and compassionate zodiacs. They are incredibly intuitive, which they rely on when making decisions. Although famous for escapism when things become hard, they are over sensitive and pessimistic when things don't go their way, and idealistic situations can seem mediocre to them. Pisces are slender and delicate looking zodiacs. Their descent from fish is portrayed strongly by their appearance with thick, leathery bright blue skin having tinges of orange sporadically appearing on their illuminating physique. They have big oval eyes with small fins that grow from the outer corner. Two large fins grow from the bottom of the knee, sprawling out at the top of the ankle and two fins growing from the wrists expanding out at the end of the elbow. These fins enable them to swim swiftly through the water at high speeds. They also have thick leather-like rope hair and webbed feet and hands. They have the power to control water and must always have access to it, as it's a part of their life source; they make great sorcerers/alchemists.

Taurus:

Strong-headed, independently determined, generous, and patient at times, although Taureans are stubborn and ignorant of others' emotions when expressing their truth.

In the Taurus Constellation, as descendants of the bull, the males have large horns and the females have small stumpy horns, both have a bull tail, and are incredibly muscular and lean. The females being smaller in stature. Their power is that of incredible strength, making them natural great warriors. Their ability enables them to pick up any weapon and wield it with great accuracy, agility, and strength. Although this talent comes at a price with an upbringing of toughness and rigid routines. If a Taurus wants to make it to adulthood, they must be fastidious in their approach, otherwise they'll perish as the elders are incredibly regimented, constantly testing their physical capabilities. They're generally seen as great officers/second-in-command within the Nirvana Army as they are great at following orders, rarely failing to deliver.

An excerpt from:

The Deeper Understanding of the Twelve Constellations

Chapter on 'Constellation Inhabitants and Living', p55

THE SCORPIO CONSTELLATION

Scorpios love the warm sand and hot sun and live within a desert called Solitudiem, inhabiting houses made from sun-dried mud bricks, which in turn are constructed from the plentiful dry, sandy dirt mixed with a mucus all Scorpios excrete. These houses are given a smoother finish using stucco made from the same substance, smoothed over the brick and allowed to dry in the sun to a very dense solid.

The mucus, called 'Mundet', is a non-toxic excretion that keeps the tube within the Scorpios' stingers clear, and flushes them after being used to eject 'Venenum' the deadly poison, or 'Somnum' the toxin that causes sleep or paralysis. When the Mundet builds up, it is ejected and stored out of the sun. The substance is collected regularly and used for the benefit of the community for brick making and sealing roads and paths.

All Scorpios, once they are past puberty, can consciously produce and eject both Venenum and Somnum. The potency of each is affected by emotion, and to a lesser degree by diet and seasonal based food choices. The males' Venenum increases as a hormonal reaction to protect their mates and young. Hunters may use either compound to kill or capture animals used for food. Neither Venenum nor Somnum affects the Scorpios when consumed, only when injected.

Scorpios are possessive of what's dear to them, keeping their families well protected, not interacting with each other all that often, unless they have profound respect for the other. They do not waste time on those who they deem unworthy; even their children must interact and marry those who are respected amongst the community.

Although they may seem hard, Scorpios, being a water sign feel an immense amount on the inside. These zodiacs are taught to fight from the moment they are born due to their harsh living conditions. To be the highest sought-after male and female within their Constellation, they must defeat every Scorpio of their sex at the age of 20 in a combat field known as Mortem Arena. This displays ambition and bravery, striving to be the best. And depending on what young Scorpios exemplify will depend on how sought-after they are within Solitudiem. The bravest of the brave marry one another, to breed stronger, fiercer offspring thus obtaining the highest respect within their community, something Scorpios hold most important. After Mortem combat, the weakest Scorpios commit a ritual called Secundum, by which they stab themselves in their intestines and pull the blade up towards their sternum, if they accomplish this ritual, they will keep their dignity and respect within their family. But if unable to perform this Secundum ritual, they will be banished from the community, as they are believed to breed weakness within the tribe. Living on the outskirts of Solitudiem is incredibly dangerous as terrifying monsters live within the desert, and without the protection of the community, these Scorpios generally die not long after they've been banished.

NC Scorpio

NC Scorpios stay within Solitudiem, working within the community and every month a proportion of the NC Scorpios are taken to have their Venenum and Somnum glands drained, as these compounds are needed throughout the Nirvana land for both medical and punitive reasons (Venenum is used to put those who have done great wrong by Nirvana to death).

As the active compounds are constantly being produced, and replenish quickly, the zodiacs still have plenty. The stronger ones, those zodiacs who have not just donated Venenum and Somnum are able to protect their tribe from the monsters that challenge their existence.

PNC Scorpio

These Scorpios are mostly seen as guards within the Doh. They work alongside a few other zodiacs like Cancer and Sagittarius enforcing the law.

SNC Scorpio

The Scorpios of this class are great fighters, as their bravery and focus has no bounds. Their skill to fight is bred into them from the day they are born.

THE SAGITTARIUS CONSTELLATION

Sagittarians live within a forest called Maga. From the time they can fend for themselves, they are sent out in the wilderness with only a bow and arrow on their back. This ritual is known as Deambulo where they must learn how to become one with the forest Maga. During this time, they hunt and gather food from what Mother Nature has to offer but take no more than they need. This is how they develop the skill to talk to the forest and obtain an incredible skill in archery, rarely missing a target. Being in solitude for so long, they become finely tuned to how the forest speaks and once they become one with the forest, they are able to find their way back to the Sagittarian village called Philoponus to reunite with their family. Each return is followed by a month of celebration. The ones who do not find their way back, that disappear, never to be seen again, are believed to have become a part of the forest. These are thought to be the ones who whisper to the Sagittarians who have the ear to listen to Maga. The Sagittarians who are now one with Maga are worshipped as it is thought that without their silent whispers through Maga, the Sagittarians would cease to exist, never able to find their way back home to Philoponus.

NC Sagittarius

NC Sagittarius stay within their constellation, hunting and gathering for all who live within their village Philoponus. They breed and mentor each new generation.

PNC Sagittarius

These Sagittarius hunt and gather for the Doh's food supply. They're able to go deep into the forest, places that are hard to track even with a well-developed map, gathering and hunting for rare delicacies.

SNC Sagittarius

Sagittarius of this class venture far from the known and charted places, are certified and deemed capable to search for Infernum inhabitants and new geographical information which is given to the PNC Geminis, adding to Nirvana maps. But even they can go missing or be possessed by the Infernum when within uncharted forests. This is the reason why this is a highly skilled class; only a select few Sagittarius make SNC status .The ones with the greatest potential are also used within the Nirvana army, who take advantage of their great skill in archery. These SNC never miss a shot, no matter what the conditions.

THE CAPRICORN CONSTELLATION

Capricorns live on an island known as Lava-Lacus Asphar. It consists of a large volcano and a solidified lava flow surrounded by water. Their main village is called Aquaterra, which is located at the base of the volcano where there is flat land. It is centred between Deus (the volcano) and the surrounding water known as Motus, as Capricorns need constant access to both.

When a Capricorn is born, they are either physically endowed with a fish tail or goat's tail. This distinction determines where the child will reside for the next 11 years, before coming back to Aquaterra. If one is born with a fish tail, they will live in and beside the water Motus, learning all the water has to teach about life's erratic, unpredictable, passionate, and exhilarating emotions. It is believed this creates their deep philosophical wisdom and understanding the ways of life, these things being as unpredictable as water. One born with a goat's tail will live on the volcano, Deus. There they learn all about life's sturdiness, durability, resilience, and strength which they also believe is represented by the harsh, dry living conditions existing on Lava-Lacus Asphar. Understanding the landscape and how to survive is a serious business and not a time for idle play.   The fittest survive the harsh lessons, and it is believed this creates the Capricorns' highly ambitious traits.

Once the 11 years end, youngster in the two groups come together within Aquaterra. NC Capricorns guide these young ones as they mentor each other, exchanging the experience and knowledge they have learnt for the life skills and traits they still need to master. Those who were taught by Deus lack empathy, kindness, and emotion. Whereas those who come from Motus lack strength, sturdiness, and resilience. By the time they turn 21, they have become outstanding mentors, assimilating within themselves the strength of Deus and the emotion of Motus. Due to this intensive blending, Capricorns are perceived as hard and cold, showing no empathy. But this cold exterior is due to Deus's teachings, and covers the deep emotion they feel intensely inside, as taught by Motus. They never allow anyone to read or see their true state of mind emotionally, until that one has earned respect and trust. This mysteriousness gives them an elusive beauty.

NC Capricorn

Most spend their time with the children within Aquaterra, teaching them about philosophy and wisdom. Some reside in Motus or Deus, attending to those who spend those first precious 11 years learning to understand the unpredictability of water or the harsh merciless mountain.

PNC Capricorn

They are the mentors and teachers within the Doh as their higher understanding of life is highly sought after. SNCs still look up to their Capricorn mentors, as a PNC Capricorn is carefully selected from amongst the few greatest mentors.

SNC Capricorn

They are a small selection of Capricorns who have an incredibly strong connection to their telekinetic powers. If shown to have great potential, they are put through gruelling training to perfect this ability.

THE AQUARIUS CONSTELLATION

The Aquarians live within a secret village called Coelum and most rarely venture from there. The town is accessed through a high cave that is hidden behind a giant waterfall. Only the residing Aquarians and the animals of the forest know of its location. Healers only come out to speak to the animals who come by the waterfall when they're injured or in need of assistance. These creatures must make a specific noise in their own tongue to call to summon them.

When an Aquarian is born, they're taken out of Coelum and placed beside the waterfall, where a family of animals will be waiting to take the baby and make it a part of their own community. This is how Aquarians learn to talk to the animals and once this ability is acquired, the family of animals will guide them back to Coelum to be reunited with their Constellation relatives. But if an Aquarian does not come back, it is believed they have become one with the animals that fostered them, taking on their form and being a closer link between the animals and their former kin. The Aquarians are able to communicate more readily with the animals because of these links with their ancestral bloodlines.

NC Aquarians

NC Aquarians heal the animals of the forest who fall sick or become injured. Although they'll never interfere with the balance, for example, those who eat flesh must also survive.

If an animal was injured by an unpremeditated action, or a natural accident, but manages to come to the narrow safe zone around the waterfall lake, an Aquarian will come when summoned.

When a hunter has tracked a weak or young and silly creature, these being fair prey, the Aquarians will not interfere. However, if the hunted creature was injured, but clever enough to escape and had the stamina to reach the lake, then they would be deemed worthy of help. In that way, the strongest and smartest will breed more like themselves.

PNC Aquarians

These Aquarians are the Healers within the Doh, healing those who are sick or become injured in battles. The general Aquarian is fluent in a couple of animal languages, particularly that of the animals that brought them up.

SNC Aquarius

Aquarians of this class are fluent in a vast range of mystical animal and creature tongues. They are selected from the few who show great potential for learning and becoming fluent in new dialects and communicating with other animals and creatures beyond the ones who brought them up. Some of these other creatures and animals are powerful or have special abilities that make them particularly useful to the zodiacs, especially in battle. The rarer the animal or mystical creature, the more complicated the tongue, so this skill takes years to master as there are many dialects within the Nirvana land. Over time it has also been documented that a powerful Aquarian such as an SNC can persuade and control the minds of animals, becoming one with them.

THE PISCES CONSTELLATION

The Pisces live in a beautiful giant lake that extends for many miles, called Mollia. It is surrounded by many different types of wild and cultivated plants. They can walk amongst the land zodiacs but they need constant access to water or moisture, otherwise they'll die from dehydration. As a precaution, they all carry around Scindet, which is a substance that when mixed with water, expands into a film of figure hugging protection to cover their whole body. It lightly adheres, on a molecular level, to the surface of their scales, trapping water to keep them hydrated for up to a full day. The Scindet is confined in a tear shaped phial which fits easily into the palm of their hand.

Once a year for a 12-hour period, there will be a blood moon. This is the time when the Pisces will reproduce as the moon's light turns all of Mollia Lake red, allowing them to see the violet-lit pathway to a secret protected location. Portum, which is a vast pool in deep cave, is accessed via an underground river. It is protected from the lesser aquatic creatures and the treacherous environment of Mollia Lake by a rock barrier. The adult Pisces, have no trouble navigating over this when going to mate and lay eggs.

When the fish-like hatchling Pisces emerge from the eggs, they must use their innate intuition to find the food they need to grow and develop. This food, a fungi named Colstridium, only grows in the dark of Portum's pool, but the hatchlings' eyes are suited to the dark. If their intuition is weak, they will find insufficient food and will die from starvation, becoming a part of the lake.

As the baby fish grow, they begin to develop the attributes of their elders, but also lose the ability to see in the dark. At that time, they are drawn to the faint light that reflects in from the lake outside. Driven by hunger, their instinct is to flip over the rock barrier to enter the main lake, and their intuition will drive them towards the areas where their elders reside. The majority of Pisces offspring either never grow enough to leave Portum, or die on the way to their elders. The ones who have strong intuition survive and grow into the adult Pisces we see today. Since the survivors are incredibly intuitive, the most knowledgeable make great alchemists or sorcerers.

NC Pisces

NC Pisces stay within Mollia, living within their small community, helping one another out with everyday living and aquatic life. As a community, they use their intimate knowledge of their watery environment to help to improve it and allow all lifeforms to thrive. They can also control the water's temperature. Being selfless beings, they enjoy nurturing other Pisces, other zodiacs, and other creatures. They also study the herbs and methods of aquaculture within their environment.

PNC Pisces

These Pisces work within the Doh, making large scales of powerful potions. These Pisces are carefully selected as they have both a high level of intelligence and a passion for science. They are able to make potions that are incredibly complicated and dangerous. There are also the sorcerers: Pisces who are born with a strong psyche are capable of reading bones and casting spells.

SNC Pisces

Pisces of this class are born with a great connection to the water, as they are able to control it in remarkable ways. Creating water spouts and tsunami-like waves which can transport solid objects. But this type of Pisces is incredibly rare. On record, only one shows this kind of potential every decade.

THE ARIES CONSTELLATION

The Aries live on the largest mountain in Nirvana called Hircum Mountain. The majority of the population resides in Cornibus Village which is situated under the peak of the mountain. Some Aries do live in small huts scattered around Hircum. However, being half goat, they love to be up high.

Aries are renowned for their constant confrontational arguments. Being ruled by the planet Mars, the god of war, it is no wonder they'll never back down from a fight. On a battlefield, this is a great advantage as the Aries defeat many enemies simply because they never give up until their last breath.

Within Cornibus Village however, the frequent fights

between such focused combatants often caused damage to or destruction of homes and communal areas. Apart from the battles themselves, the need to undertake reconstruction of the damage took Aries away from their normal daily duties.

To minimize time lost from important tasks, the Aries Elders, Ardon and Athena ordered a fighting stadium to be created to provide a venue where combatants can satiate their urge to fight. They called it Compono Stadium. Now when two Aries clash verbally, (the first stage of a challenge between fighters) they have to settle it within Compono. Here they can smash into one another until one is knocked out or the other gives up (a rare occurrence). Each successful attack carries a point value and the opponent with the most points at the end of the twenty minute fight, wins. Records are kept of each individual's wins and losses within Compono. The Aries with the most wins is vastly sought after as many try to challenge him/her.

With such a magnetic charisma, the Aries definitely know how to celebrate a victory. Never holding a grudge against one another, they genuinely enjoy a good battle and how well they perform is how respect is earned within their region. This is often taken as arrogance by zodiacs from other Constellations who don't enjoy confrontations like the Aries.

NC Aries

NC Aries stay within Cornibus village, find a mate and breed many children. As they are the child of the zodiac, Aries are great with kids. They tell traditional stories of their courageous ancestors to not only their children but all youngsters of the Constellation. In this way they are teaching them the ways of the dynamic, fiery, adventurous Aries. NC Aries also create mining tunnels within Hircum Mountain, mining for gold and other prized stones and minerals.

PNC Aries

These Aries clear areas for construction within the Doh, create new pathways through the uncharted forest or clear areas within other Constellations for the erection of new edifices. On occasion when a Sagittarians is searching a deep part of the dangerous uncharted forest, they sometimes come across a blockage which inhibits them from venturing into a particular area. A PNC Aries will then be sent in to clear the blockage for the Sagittarius.

SNC Aries

A SNC Aries is a rare individual. They are gifted with an immense amount of strength. Like most Aries, they can destroy anything in an allocated area by charging through it.

These Aries are able to devastate a considerable area in one hit. Their smashing impact creates a domino effect. When the object they hit impacts another, a ripple effect is created resulting in great destruction. This skill is of great use when fighting a large army as they can kill a vast number of individuals at once.

THE TAURUS CONSTELLATION

The Taureans live within a village called Herba on a large, green, flat paddock. Although Taureans are known to be natural great warriors, this talent results from an upbringing of toughness and rigid routines. When a Taurean is born, they are inspected by the Elders, to determine if the baby is strong and suited to represent the land. If determined weak or feeble, the baby will be carried to the woods and left to die and become a part of the land. If determined strong, the baby will be brought up and taught how to fight from the day they can walk. This protocol is established for both male and female. If a Taurean wants to make it to adulthood, they must be fastidious in their approach otherwise they'll perish. The Elders are incredibly regimented, constantly testing them, placing them in situations where they must fight for their lives, whether it's proving themselves physically or mentally. They are psychologically challenged too, enduring camps which leave them feeling all elements without the comfort of clothes and they must hunt for their own food and water. It is these challenges that make the Taureans who they are today: grounded, independent, patient, stubborn, possessive and incredibly determined zodiacs, which can be displayed by a tunnel vision effect. Also, these teachings keep them humble as they appreciate the good things in life and see the beauty in all things. They are the type of zodiac who won't go down unless you put them down. Their greatest pride is to die on the field of battle. However, due to their harsh, brutal lifestyle, this Constellation must be monitored as it is the sector with the lowest population.

NC Taureans

NC Taureans have simple but important lives within Herba and love the routines for daily life. They also keep the foundations for the Taurean generations to come by implementing the ancient gruelling teachings of great past warriors. They love to farm and grow their own food, but some own their own small shops within the small community village.

PNC Taureans

These Taureans are personal bodyguards for zodiacs who need protection when going into different Constellations or venturing into the uncharted forest under the guidance of a Sagittarius. They also help soldiers within the Doh to learn a vast variety of skilled weaponry.

SNC Taureans

This class of Taureans aren't rare but aren't common either. As their upbringing is so harsh, they're taught to strive for the best, this is where their tunnel vision for a particular goal comes into play and their patience genuinely gets them to where they desire. An SNC Taurus is an incredibly skilled fighter, strong and hard to kill. All should be warned not to make one angry because once they see red there is no stopping them.

THE GEMINI CONSTELLATION

The Gemini live within a habitat that constantly alters, called the Labyrinth. It is a diverse and complicated environment, which reflects their yin and yang to extreme circumstances.

Non-Gemini zodiacs and even the periodic PNC visitors from other Constellations are reluctant to venture there as the walls and passages constantly change position. At times, travellers are confronted with creatures which must be defeated, or by fays who challenge them with riddles they must solve, in order to move forward.

In truth, although the paths within the Labyrinth may seem unpredictable and dangerously confusing, the various impressions and conceptions of the travellers must always have an opposite. So, in order to navigate through, one must almost never take the predictable route; as the opposite is always the obvious solution in order to go in the right direction. An easy idea to follow, but when encountering the various dangers and potential misfortunes, an incredibly difficult task to maintain.

The main village in the middle of this puzzling Labyrinth is called Simul Village. This is where all Geminis reside. It's a beautiful, dynamic place where the residents are constantly changing tasks and activities to overcome their tendency to get bored easily.

A Gemini can get around the Labyrinth effortlessly, without colliding with monsters or having to solve riddles because they know the right path. However, if they are unfortunate enough to take the wrong turn, a Gemini has no trouble solving riddles or defeating the Labyrinth's strange creatures. This is because, when they're children, one of their daily tasks is solving the Labyrinth; the adults believe this is a great way to stimulate and occupy their active minds. Some children do perish or become lost forever in this paradox of reality and time, and these are believed to develop psychoses and transform to become the monsters within the passages of the Labyrinth. That's how the Labyrinth constantly changes, never being the same at any point in time. The Geminis just become accustomed to reading the Labyrinth walls. They're able to guide zodiacs from other Constellations through to Simul, if permitted. But if a non-Gemini zodiac ventures in alone, they normally die or go insane.

This environment represents the Gemini's dynamic and forever changing and growing personalities. It teaches them to be dynamic, never to miss a thing, enthusiastic and versatile. It's what gives them their charismatic personalities. However, since it lacks consistency, this too is reflected within them along with boredom as they're accustomed to constant stimulation.

NC Gemini

NC Gemini stay within Simul, helping to maintain their vivacious community, this expresses their serious ambitious side to strive for constant growth and stronger community. This makes Simul a place where many would love to reside, as it's beautiful and animated. The Gemini frequently hold festivals and competitions/tournaments where Geminis have a good time and are challenged to grow – forever stimulated.

PNC Gemini

These Gemini put together geographical maps of areas discovered by Sagittarians or design beautiful pieces of architecture (example; The Doh). These Geminis are carefully selected amongst the few who are able to channel their highly strung energy into large in-depth projects, never missing any small detail.

SNC Gemini

A Gemini of this class is one of the rarest SNC zodiacs born within Nirvana. Being so ardently dynamic and mastering their ability to control their individual yin and yang, once split (an incredibly hard ability to master), Gemini can actually fight like a bird, dancing in flight as they hit with perfect precision, knowing where each other will be at the exact moment. This makes them highly sought-after.

Cancerians live in a large shallow rock pool within a village called Vadosus. Smaller rock pools are constructed on the outskirts of Vadosus as some Cancers like solitude with their family, only having to come to Vadosus when in need of supplies or a village communion. They enjoy the water from their crab antecedents but don't depend on it for their survival like the Pisces. Cancerians learn to become agile and quick due to their rocky environment, having to pounce from rock to rock in order to get to any place of importance. From falling on the rocks from a young age, their skin becomes tough and hard.

Since Cancerians are incredibly family orientated, they generally have large extended families. With an average Cancerian couple having up to six children, they effectively create a community of their own which makes them unbelievably protective. Within each family group, grandparents play a huge part. They pass down their wisdom and are shown great respect.

Creating such secure family structure, a Cancerian develops deep feelings and passion as they are brought up surrounded by unconditional love, this gives them the ability to believe in themselves, without unreasonable doubt just like those of their loved ones. This belief and passion can come off as unrealistic, to other zodiacs but not to a Cancerian.

Be warned. When their Planetary Moon is full in the sky, their strength triples, their emotions become chaotic and their behaviour irrational. It is highly stressed for all other zodiacs to avoid Cancers during this time, until the full moon has passed. This transition is called 'the Lupus period.'

NC Cancer

NC Cancers are set on having a large family of their own within Vadosus. All they want is to love and nurture, to bring up their own children and teach them the ways of the crab and traits of their own family. In doing this, they create an environment which they can call home and in which they watch their children grow up.

PNC Cancer

These Cancers have a passion for protecting, serving, and helping their world to become a better place. They can be seen as soldiers within the Doh alongside the Scorpios, or may be used in secret assignments within the Doh as they are light on their feet and can generally go into and out of places unseen.

SNC Cancer

They are highly sought after as they make great assassins; light on their feet, they move at unfathomable speed and are incredibly quick to react. These particular Cancerians are also able to produce a shield so powerful, it goes beyond their own body to cover a small army.

THE LEO CONSTELLATION

Leos live on a large rock called Superbia, which stands above a vast valley that contains many animals for them to hunt. It is very rare for an individual Leo to separate from their pride. They sleep together, eat together, train together, and hunt together. Learning all about team work, they take it in turns leading the pride into a hunt.

The main leader, who has control of all within the Constellation, is known as the Masculum-Rex, some referring to the leader as Rex. The Masculum-Rex has a special ability which is the mental power of persuasion over all the prides. If a Leo somehow manages to resist this and becomes rebellious, they are declared outlaw and exiled to live on the outskirts of valley where food supply and shelter is nearly non-existent.

To intentionally disobey a Masculum-Rex takes great difficulty as the whole pride is strongly connected to him. Those who are exiled, most likely die soon after as Leos can't live in isolation; they depend on others to give them purpose. Although a Masculum-Rex is not an Elder, the pride will always follow his instruction unless an Elder commands otherwise. The prides will not like it, but they will obey, unless the Masculum-Rex objects to the command and then they will stand by him until death.

Nevertheless, an Elder can challenge the Masculum-Rex to an Imperium: a battle to death to take leadership of the pride. In fact any Leo can request an Imperium, even those who are declared outcasts, as a last resort or because they believe their pride leader has become incompetent or too old to lead. However, they must prove themselves to the pride in order to take over control. An Elder cannot have both roles. When such a challenge has occurred in the past, it was so the Elder could pick a more suitable Masculum-Rex. The zodiac chosen must be a Leo who all the prides respect, otherwise they will not follow his leadership. Such a failure will lead to a breakdown of the pride and the whole Constellation, which in turn would disrupt the zodiac balance. Since Leos are able to transform into a more animalistic version of themselves, they make incredible hunters. There is nothing about their makeup that suggests weakness; they are natural born killers.

NC Leo

NC Leos are those who just wants to be a part of the pride and nothing more. Some may aspire to achieve Masculum-Rex status one day, but they genuinely enjoy everyday Constellation life.

PNC Leo

These Leo are generally the commanders within the Doh soldier community. Rarely seen amongst Doh soldiers, they keep order behind the scenes, organizing and scheduling a rock solid system. Their great leadership skills make others gravitate towards them. Rarely having a problem with others challenging their authority.

SNC Leo

Leo's of this class are the commanders or leaders within other regions of the Nirvana Army. They are never seen watching from a far, as they love to get in amongst the thick of battle, to be able to show off their animalistic killing ability and bask in their skill.

THE VIRGO CONSTELLATION

Virgos live on a vast floating island called Insula Island. It constantly moves around the sky within their Constellation. To find Insula from the ground is like trying to find a needle in a haystack as the sky is constantly occluded by dense cloud. Fortunately, there is one distinct indicator: a small area of continuously pouring rain. Above that area of cloud is where you'll find Insula Island.

The reason for this strange occurrence is existence of the large river called Iudicium. A dormant volcano captures water from the sky, most of which is evaporated from the ground below, and this collects within its crater. This is the source of the Iudicium River which supplies water for the Virgo population and is a vital part of Insula's landscape. Eventually, the river finds its way to one of the many cliff points, and cascades down to the surface. Due to this, flooding doesn't occur on Insula and with the movement of the island, the strange patch of never ceasing rain moves over the surface below.

The river is also known as 'the judgment river.' Soon after the baby Virgos start walking, they are placed in a flat bottomed, waterproofed basket which is placed in the river. By this time, their wings have grown big enough to support them in flight, and have been exercised from birth. The current takes the basket all the way to the cliff. As it falls, if the baby Virgo's natural instinct is strong enough, he or she will begin to fly. Then, the gathered family and friends, fly to join their fledged child and return home with them to celebrate and give the child their official name.

If a baby Virgo does not fly, they perish upon the hard surface below. When this sad event occurs, family and friends offer the spirit of their child to Unum. It is believed if the baby Virgo did not fly, it was simply too weak due to a birth defect. Virgos only want perfection within their Constellation.

When other zodiacs come across their small bodies, they are thought to be fallen angels. As such, the tiny bodies are buried with all care under the nearest tree, and placed in Unum's care.

When other zodiacs come across their small bodies, they are thought to be fallen angels. It is believed if the baby Virgo did not fly, it was simply too weak due to a birth defect. Virgos only want perfection within their Constellation.

On the island there is an ancient village made out of pristine stone. This is Lapis village where all Virgos reside. No other zodiacs are allowed to set foot on the island, as the Virgos believe they'll disturb the perfect serenity they've created over the generations.

Zodiacs in the Constellations neighbouring Virgo, or at the Doh, may see Virgos coming and going from Insula, but only from high points on their own land, and when the island is close to the relevant border. However, if a zodiac from another Constellation wants to talk to a specific Virgo, they must meet on the surface near where the rain falls ceaselessly.

NC Virgo

NC Virgo stay within Insula, keeping to the perfect order of their routine way of living. Most NC Virgos spend a lot of time within their organic farming estates as Virgos will not eat any plants they have not grown themselves, or animal products from beasts they have not provided quality feed for. Their diet is a plain one that provides them with the perfect nutritional balance to keep their bodies in optimal health and enables them to achieve perfection of mind, body, and soul.

In between farming duties, Virgos can regularly be seen meditating or partaking in disciplined rigorous training. The Virgos never complain nor boast about their achievements as they are humble zodiacs.

PNC Virgo

These Virgo are generally involved with the politics within the Doh, trying to find ways to create order and perfection throughout the land. One imperative task is to come up with new ways to make sure everyone has a purpose within each Constellation. These ideas and concepts are then passed on to the Patriarch and Matriarch.

SNC Virgo

Although all Virgos can control elements of the wind, an SNC can control the weather. They can create havoc, like hurricanes and tornados or the perfect day having sunshine and blue skies. Once they have mastered this ability, they are given long golden swords to shine bright in the sky, a signal to those on land that they are being watched upon by safe eyes. They may be seen flying above the land, scouting out particular areas, especially when the Nirvana army goes into battle.

THE LIBRA CONSTELLATION

The Libras live within a village called Arbor Domus that is concealed up high within the tallest trees of their Constellation. Within the village, the huts are beautifully constructed from the available natural resources. Bridges connect all the Libras homes together and these are made from local wood along with rope made from hanging vines. Within this tight knit community, a larger hut exists in the middle of the homes, and this is where the Libras gather for goods and services and socialising events. Libras live amongst the flora as nature gives them balance and harmony.

When a Libra becomes unbalanced, a state clearly betrayed by their eye colour, they are sent below, to the floor of the Pacem forest, until they find peace within themselves again. An unbalanced Libra is careless, erratic, over emotional and irrational, saying or doing particular things that are extremely out of character. Once placed on the forest floor, they frantically look for the way back to Arbor Domus, but the village will only appear when they stop looking and manage to find harmony within themselves again. Then the way back will be clear to them once again.

This situation is the same for any zodiac who visits within the Libra Constellation. They will first be stepping into Pacem. Anyone is welcome, but if the zodiac has turmoil within their essence, then they'll never find the way to the village. Every zodiac is warned of the dangers, because if their essence is corrupted, the forest will never allow them to leave. Unless such zodiacs find peace, they will become creatures of Pacem's shadows until the end of time. It is known that the turmoil within the corrupted minds causes those zodiacs to transform into a Wendigo creature, similar to a cannibal. The same goes for the fallen Libras who do not find themselves again.

NC Libra

NC Libra take care of the forest, helping it flourish and grow. Some spend more time with the animals, making sure not one baby is unattended or unfed. Some work on the trees and flowers, every Libra has a place. But once the sun goes down, they'll return back to their haven, Arbor Domus, as the Wendigo's live within the shadows and that is when they hunt.

PNC Libra

These Libra deal with quarrels within different Constellations, settling matters by offering solutions for they are natural born diplomats and have great influence over others. When this doesn't work long term, they'll use their power of telepathy to influence the zodiacs to help maintain peace. If this technique fails, the zodiacs involved must sit a trial.

SNC Libra

Although all Libras have influence over others and some telepathic abilities, SNC Libras have exceptionally strong telepathic power. Capable of hearing the minds of all who are near, and if their power is channelled, it can be used to search out particular zodiacs who have disappeared, if they are still alive. SNC Libras can also control others physically and speak to them through their minds. This type of Libra is not merely rare, but are in fact the rarest of the SNC zodiacs; this kind of power takes decades to master and requires a disciplined and gifted mind.

Please Note:

In every Constellation, SNC is an incredibly hard classification to achieve, in some more than others. If more could be trained, there would be a greater potential to be able to conquer Apophis and the Infernum, but unfortunately, there are very few SNCs.

It wouldn't be difficult for the Infernum to take over our land as they have the same abilities as we do, only they are more powerful because they are not in control of their power.

Apophis is the only one who has the ability to release the true authentic power of any individual. This is why testing here is so gruelling. We must find the trigger for each zodiac to release their true power as it is the mind that dictates the level of power we can achieve.

We must each conquer our own mind to unlock our true and endless potential. Sending zodiacs in to fight against a force like the Infernum, who are controlled by a powerful and ancient evil such as Apophis, without proper preparation would be suicide and the end of life as we know it.

An excerpt from:

The Twelve Houses

There are twelve houses making up these qualities. Each one is made up of four of the twelve.

The first quality sign is **Fixed.** Taurus, Leo, Scorpio, and Aquarius. The purpose of a fixed sign is to maintain, uphold, and defend possessions, responsibilities, goals, or desires in everyday life. They are not easily distracted when a goal is in place, although this can get them stuck in a rut.

The four houses making up **Fixed** are:
2nd house: *Possession*, which includes emotions, self, ability, needs, and wants.
5th house: *Pleasure*, which includes creative acts, self-satisfaction, procreation, and children.
8th house: *Sex*, which includes relationships,
11th house: *Friends*, which includes clubs, organizations, and groups.

The next quality sign is **Cardinal**. Aries, Cancer, Libra, and Capricorn. These signs are restless, active, self-motivated, ambitious, and they are often leaders in their community although they can be overly domineering.

The four houses making up **Cardinal** are:
1st house: *Self*, which includes life and body;
4th house: *Home*;
7th house: *Partnership*, which is away from self to another;
10th house: *Social Status*, the role they take within the community.

The last Quality sign is **Mutual**. Gemini, Virgo, Sagittarius, and Pisces. They are highly adaptable, flexible, and communicative, coming up with solutions faster than they can bat an eye, but they can get lost in detail.

The four houses making up **Mutual** are:
3rd house: *Communication*;
6th house: *Health*;
9th house: *Philosophy*;
12th house: *Unconsciousness*, trying to make sense of one's self.

Constellation Poems:

CAPRICORN

A goat fish we see
Oh, so ambitious is he,
Patience embedded,
Caution dreaded.
Practical thoughts
Wise as thy never sought.
Change of mind,
Don't react kind.
Stubborn creature,
Shy nature.
Don't be blind,
By this frontier state of mind.

AQUARIUS

A large man we see.
A humanitarian is he.
A friendly giant,
All or nothing defiant.
Interest range wide,
But an independent tide.
An ever loyal friend,
Nothing he can't mend.

Be careful one so large,
Unpredictability in charge.
Detachment is a trait,
Inconsistent runs late.
Aloof he may seem,
Deep thoughts dream.

Power to talk
With animals that walk.

PISCES

A fish we see,
Oh, so selfless is he.
Sensitive in nature,
Compassionate saviour.
Intuition so strong,
Never guided wrong.
Imagination runs wild,
Thoughts never mild.

Hard times are near,
Escapism is clear.
Idealism never found,
As pessimism bound.
If interest hazy,
Fish become lazy.
Emotions run wild,
Water controlled child.

ARIES

A ram we see,
Oh, so versatile is he.
Lively with passion,
Positive worn fashion.
Courage he bares,
Curling horns impair.

Impulse burns,
Stubbornness churns.
Arrogance, strong,
Thinks no wrong.
Stand for confrontation,
With this combination.

Fierce like fire,
Adventure inspire.

TAURUS

A bull we see.
Oh, so generous is he
Dependable and patient,
Loyalty nor absent.
One as independent,
Persistent profound intended.
Tunnel-like vision,
Move for revolution.

With good there is bad,
Possessive gone mad.
Stubbornness breeds,
Like self-indulgent needs.

Beware the colour red,
Fixed arrow makes his bed.

GEMINI

Two heads we see.
Intelligent is he.
Such wit and humour,
Enthusiasm glamour.
Soft-spoken words,
The adversity crossword.

With air comes misdirection,
Adds self-destruction.
In constant two minds,
Anxiety binds.
Superficial lacks detail,
Fall through the cracks and fail.

With one head,
Two shall break bread.

CANCER

A crab we see.
Oh, so creative is he.
Loving and faithful,
Shield of protection grateful.

Passion runs wild,
Drives the inner child.
Praise thy with love,
Comforting glove.
Emotion beware,
As suspicion lives there.
Drop of pessimism,
Raging alcoholism.

Illusionary shielded exterior,
Raw flooded interior.

LEO

A lion we see.
A leader is he.
Kind and caring,
Optimistic wearing.
Loyalty strong,
Beware thy wrong.

With arrogance,
A king advance.
With a strong head,
Patience falls dead.

Ego dominates,
As possession gravitates.

Beware this king,
Or watch his teeth sink in.

VIRGO

Angel wings we see.
Oh, so watchful is he.
Intelligent and practical,
Perfection unstable.
Eyes see from a far,
Analyse and alter.
Reliable we trust,
Perfection is a must.
Fastidious from within,
The building blocks begin.
Harsh spoken words,
Judgmental eyes stirred.
Overcritical kind,
Endures fussy mind.

Conservative exterior,
Fly above inferior.

LIBRA

Scales we see.
Oh, so charming is he.
Tactful in approach,
Diplomatic coach.
Romantic lover,
Balance thy mother.
Always fair,
Two sides take care.

Sociopath detach,
Superficial latch.
Decision nor made,
Unreliable behave.

Eyes beware,
The unbalance can declare.

SCORPIO

A scorpion we see.
Oh, so brave is he.
Focused ambition,
Strong intuition.
Faithful friends,
Beware the back end.

One strike,
Resentful bite.
Secrets build,
A jealousy field.

Manipulation mastermind,
Be careful pretence 'once mine'.

SAGITTARIUS

A horse we see,
Oh, so straight forward is he.
Generous heart,
Intellect not far apart.
These think as one,
Philosophical thoughts run.

Tactless without bounds
As self-perfection runs around.
Consistently difficult,
Impatience results.

Stern creature,
Iconic archer feature.

AFTERWORD

Brief background to the making of the series, The Olympus Trials (TOT).

I had many battles with bringing this series into fruition. It took many years of dedicated research into astrology and numerology.

I am not an astrologer nor am I a numerologist, but I hope, with my many thousands of notes and errors and corrections, I have done enough to bring a true essence of the world of astrology/numerology into the fictional tale known as The Olympus Trials (TOT). I hope too, that I've done enough for the astrologers and numerologists. I apologise for any errors which are of my own accord. There is so much ignorance around astrology and numerology. Even so, many are curious about what it is to be influenced by the stars, from the day they were born. Many only know of their sun sign, but there are depths which they are yet to discover. I know there are those who are aware, and I hope this met your expectation. There is so much history behind the stars yet there are no true stories that ring of true significance to that of the zodiacs, nothing I found iconic. So, this was my mission, my dedication to the universe beyond our own tiny world (Earth). I wanted to create a world where everyone had a place, a zodiac, a character, a number and purpose. I wanted to use the traits of the zodiacs and bring them to life through my characters. I wanted to create mysteries and surprises that all remain purposefully attached to the core of astrology/numerology. And I hope I have achieved exactly that and I hope you enjoy the journey of The Olympus Trials.

Let's walk amongst the stars.

ABOUT THE AUTHOR

Chauntelle Leeder was born (1990)
in Australia on the Mornington Peninsula.

She says she is married to her husband (Les Clarke) the way wild geese pair for life, not by paper but by the forces of nature. They have three children, Saxon, Rogan and Mia.

She has had a desire and even greater interest for uncovering truths about the unknown - believing, the stars and the universe are one of the places where a lot of our uncertainties await.